THE

HAMLET

WARNING

BOOKS BY LEONARD SANDERS

The Wooden Horseshoe
The Marshall of Stud Horse Flats
The Seed, pseudonym Dan Thomas

THE
HAMLET
WARNING

BY

LEONARD SANDERS

CHARLES SCRIBNER'S SONS / *NEW YORK*

3 5 7 9 11 13 15 17 19 H/C 20 18 16 14 12 10 8 6 4 2

Printed in the United States of America
Library of Congress Catalog Card Number 76–15814
ISBN 0–684–14651–7

For Florene

"Two revolutions ago, my son took a gun
and went into politics."
  —A Dominican Mother
  *Santo Domingo: A Country
  Without a Future*
  by Otto Schoenrich
  (New York: Macmillan, 1918)

"So far as we know, everybody in the world
who has tried to make a nuclear explosion
since 1945 has succeeded on the first try."
  —Theodore B. Taylor
  Nuclear Physicist, Designer
  of Hamlet
  The Curve of Binding Energy
  by John McPhee
  (New York: Farrar, Straus and Giroux, 1974)

PART ONE

Chapter 1

Loomis was awakened by distant gunfire. He lay motionless with the caution of long experience, listening, analyzing, the old familiar tightness rising in his groin. This might be the day. Traffic had ceased on Calle 30 de Marzo a block away, an ominous sign. At his bedside, Mozart was still playing softly on the tape deck, Geza Anda's recording of Concerto No. 21 in C with the Vienna Symphony Orchestra, a strange counterpoint to revolution. From two thousand yards away came a dozen more scattered rifle shots, the explosion of a grenade, a burst from an automatic weapon, then silence.

Loomis sat up. The taste of last night's rum was strong in his mouth. His head throbbed. Already he was sweating heavily from the heat. He was old and tired and not yet forty-eight. And he was thoroughly sick of war. But he long ago had lost all illusions. He knew what the sounds meant and what he had to do.

Tossing back the thin sheet, he swung his bare feet to the cool tiles. He paused on the edge of the bed until a momentary dizziness passed. Geza Anda was in the midst of an exquisite and intricate passage, one Loomis loved most of all. He waited until the movement ended before switching off the tape deck. He didn't bother searching for slippers but crossed barefoot to the veranda, pulling a robe around his nakedness as he walked out into the fierce morning sun, now ten o'clock high.

Santo Domingo, the oldest city in the western hemisphere, lay sweltering under a soft tropical breeze off the restless Caribbean. From his veranda, the city was a symphony of smells: of flowers and ocean spray, of fish and sugar cane, of fresh coffee, rich river silt, and, above all, of permeating poverty. Narrowing his eyes against the glare, Loomis looked out across Calle 30 de Marzo to the roofs of the Old Town, a remarkable contrast of modern, dazzling white stucco and crumbling, golden-baked masonry centuries old. The lush green of palm, mahogany, almond, and laurel filled spaces between buildings, a constant reminder that the city was not far removed from the jungle.

Nothing seemed amiss in the main business district. Loomis walked to the edge of the veranda and put a hand on the huge, bullet-scarred Doric column for support as he leaned over the railing for a better view. Below, at the *palacio's* wrought-iron east gate, framed in the brilliant red of carefully cultivated poinsettias, the six sentries were alert, peering to the southeast, where a dark plume of smoke was drifting up against the bright blue sky.

Always the unexpected. No matter how much planning, how much attention to detail, always the fucking unexpected. At Tarawa, the Higgins boats had grounded on the coral reefs three hundred yards from the beach. North of the Chosin, on the drive to the Yalu, the Chinese started a whole new ball game. At the Bay of Pigs, no bombers. In Vietnam, the real enemy had been nine thousand miles away. And Uganda. What the hell had happened in Uganda? He couldn't remember.

Behind him, the phone rang. He crossed to the bed and picked up the receiver.

"How is the head this morning?" Bedoya asked in English.

"I may live," Loomis said. "That's the only encouragement I can offer."

Bedoya laughed. "Four or five more *cocolocos,* and you might have been on the verge of getting drunk."

"That would be a terrible thing to contemplate," Loomis said.

"We've got a rumble." Bedoya was proud not only of his English, but also of his mastery of slang.

"You could have fooled me," Loomis said. "I would have sworn it was shooting. What's happening?"

"City Bank. A robbery."

"Well, get the jeep out. We'll take a run up there."

"O.K., Captain."

Loomis cradled the receiver, making a mental note to give Bedoya another lecture on titles. He'd never been a captain. He wasn't one now.

He went into his awkward, oversized bathroom and waited patiently for warm water. Living in a palace was no bed of roses. Trujillo's attempt to reproduce the glories of the Italian Renaissance in Portland cement had ignored certain conveniences and in all respects had only partially succeeded. Despite his size, six feet three and two hundred and twenty pounds, Loomis often felt dwarfed by the high ceilings and immense spaces of the *palacio*. His quarters, in the extreme northeast corner of the second floor, had been Trujillo's own offices. The corner room, now divided into the bath and bedroom, once served as Trujillo's outer office and waiting room. Trujillo's personal office, facing east, was now the main portion of Loomis's quarters. Loomis didn't consider the historic aspects worth the price. The rooms, heavily scarred during the bombings and shellings of the 1965 revolution, retained a heavy institutional aura despite the efforts of the decorators with their draperies, paintings, and Louis XIV trappings. But Loomis didn't especially mind the dehumanized atmosphere. He'd survived in far worse surroundings.

He washed away the night's accumulation of sweat. As he toweled his face, he studied his reflection in the full-length mirror, assessing the damages of decades of war, barrels of booze, and various emotional disappointments too numerous to mention. He scowled at the image. He would win no beauty prizes.

He dressed carefully—a fresh pair of slacks, boots, an old Corps blouse, and a Stetson. Unlocking the arms cabinet by his bedroom door, he hesitated.

The engraved .380 Belgian automatic was a gift from El Jefe. He usually wore it. But for certain, one-shot protection, he preferred a dependable revolver. He strapped on the .357 magnum Colt Single Action Army. He took down a 9 mm Schmeisser MP40 machine pistol, checked the load, locked the cabinet, and walked down the stairs to the huge corridors leading to the east portico. En route, he checked guard stations, making certain no one had left his post in the excitement. *Palacio* security was marginal, at best. The major problem was that the *palacio* was not designed as a residence, but as the seat of government—the congress and the presidency. El Jefe, a widower, had installed an apartment adjacent to his office shortly after his rise to power. Gradually, he had commandeered and sealed off most of the sprawling east wing into a virtual fortress.

Bedoya was waiting at the wheel of the open jeep, grinning widely at Loomis's obvious hangover. Bedoya was a twenty-eight-year-old Boca Chica native whose parents had been slain in one of the Trujillo regime's periodic housecleanings. They were buried in an unmarked grave—the pastures of Trujillo, in whimsical Dominican vernacular. A revolutionary from the time he was in knee-pants, Bedoya knew the background of every governmental official of importance and the political persuasions of each prominent Dominican. Loomis probably would have made him his second-in-command even if they hadn't established a quick, close rapport. Bedoya was tall and thin—almost frail—but Loomis knew that his wiry build masked a surprising toughness.

Behind Bedoya, a young soldier clung to the mount of an M1A6 air-cooled Browning machine gun, pointed skyward. Loomis swung into the empty front seat and winced at the pain shooting through his head as Bedoya gunned the jeep down the drive toward the east gate. They zoomed past the guardpost and roared up Calle Julio Verne toward the growing pall of smoke.

Loomis pointed a thumb at the soldier behind them, and spoke in English. "Does he know which end of that thing to point?"

"Sure," Bedoya said. "He has even fired it once. Think I would bring along an amateur?"

The street, normally crowded in the relative coolness of morning, was now deserted. Cars and trucks stood abandoned along the curbs. Curious faces peeked from shop windows and doorways.

As the jeep neared the tree-shaded Parque Independencia, Bedoya slowed. An army truck and a squad of troops blocked the street. Beyond, near El Conde Gate, an overturned, bullet-riddled 1965 Chevrolet was burning furiously in a bed of pink bougainvillea. Seven bodies lay sprawled in various positions around the car. One body also was burning. Two of the dead were wearing the drab-green uniforms of the Policía Nacional. Bedoya signaled to a sergeant, who approached the jeep.

"This is Señor Loomis, captain of security to El Jefe," Bedoya said rapidly in Spanish. "Where is the senior officer present?"

The sergeant pointed. A crowd of civilians was being corralled beneath the trees, apparently in a search for witnesses. A colonel stood nearby, bellowing orders. "Colonel Escortia," the sergeant said.

Bedoya drove the jeep up over the curb. As they passed the blazing car, the stench of cordite and burning flesh failed to improve Loomis's lingering hangover. He leaned close to Bedoya.

"I am *chief* of security to El Jefe, and a civilian, you simple moron," he said. "When you introduce me to the colonel, get it right."

Bedoya grinned. "O.K., Captain," he said.

Loomis recognized Colonel Escortia from the newspaper pictures. There was no mistaking that small, rotund, compact figure. Although Loomis had made a routine study of his file, they had never met. He remembered that Escortia had weathered several revolutions, always fortunate enough to be stationed at some remote garrison in the *cordilleras* and able to remain relatively clear of capital politics. This time he might not be so fortunate. The colonel had just been returned to the Distrito Nacional as a reward for his successful campaign against an elusive, especially barbaric band of guerrillas in the Cordillera Central.

The colonel turned and glanced briefly at the jeep, then studied Bedoya and Loomis as they stepped out and walked across the thick, lush carpet of grass toward him.

Bedoya, surprising in any language, spoke in flowing, for-

mal Spanish. "Colonel Escortia, permit me to have the honor
of presenting the Señor Clay Loomis, chief of security to El
Jefe."

Escortia saluted, then shook hands. His eyes lingered over
Loomis's Colt, boots, and hat. "Of course, the *norteamericano,*" he said. "Your reputation precedes you, Señor. Even in the remote regions where I have been stationed, we have heard of you. I understand that you speak
our language like a native and that you have taken the ills of
our poor country as your own."

The colonel spoke as casually as if they were meeting at
some embassy lawn party. Eloquent, Old World bullshit.
Loomis tended to like it. He attempted to match the colonel's aplomb.

"You are very kind," he said, falling naturally into the
formal address the colonel had chosen. "Clearly, the bandits
of our city are learning the lessons you have been teaching
the rural insurgents."

"Unfortunately, I also have much to learn," Escortia said.
He gestured toward the bodies. "These were the decoys. I
took the bait."

Rapidly, he explained. Ten men were involved in the robbery, sealing off all entrances to the bank. A clerk tripped a
silent alarm, alerting headquarters of the Policía Nacional.
When word came over the army radio, relayed by the police,
the colonel correctly assumed that if the bandits successfully
escaped from the bank, they probably would flee westward
on Calle El Conde and away from downtown congestion. He
promptly moved men to El Conde Gate in support of the
police routinely stationed there. As the car roared toward
them from out of heavy traffic, the bandits opened fire. In the
fierce fighting that followed, no one noticed until too late
that a second car braked, made a right turn onto Palo Hin-
cado, and presumably fled northward into the residential
section. Escortia assumed that car contained the other five
men and the money from the bank.

"Any description?" Loomis asked.

Escortia glanced at the roundup of witnesses. "Five men
in an old Pontiac," he said.

"How seriously was the bank hit?"

"Two dead. Three wounded."

"I meant, how much money?"

Escortia sighed and raised his eyebrows. "The first estimates are more than five hundred thousand pesos."

"Ramón El Rojo?"

"Who knows? The bodies have no identification. But it is probable. The weapons they used are of Polish and Czechoslovakian origin. I have the entire area cordoned. There is still hope."

Loomis looked back toward the *palacio*. All seemed peaceful there. If the bank robbery were a diversionary move, Ramón no doubt would have struck elsewhere by now. All tactics pointed to the bank, and to the bank alone. The five dead revolutionaries had been sacrificed for five men in a Pontiac and half a million dollars in pesos.

The soldiers were now separating the witnesses, checking ID's, herding the civilians like cattle, rifles and automatic weapons at ready. The people didn't protest. They were accustomed to it. They'd had plenty of practice. A flock of parakeets in the trees overhead seemed far more disturbed by the soldiers' actions.

Parque Independencia. The irony of the charade was not lost on Loomis. Here, on this spot, now painstakingly landscaped and rich with tropical flowers, the flag of independence once was raised over the Dominican Republic. But the true independence was brief, only a few short months between three hundred and fifty years of demeaning colonialism and one hundred and thirty years of the worst succession of dictatorships the world has ever known. Now, after almost five centuries, were these people ready to throw off their shackles?

The bank robbery might have been the first major step. Or, it might be the first decisive move toward another century of enslavement. Loomis did not know which. But he suspected the worst.

"The car," he said to Escortia. "Was it green over green, an old model, about 1964?"

Escortia looked at him with interest. "That is the description."

"May I borrow a squad of men?" Loomis asked. "I have often seen such a car. It might be worth checking."

Escortia didn't hesitate. He turned and called out orders. A sergeant ran toward a parked truck. A half-dozen soldiers lounging by the tailgate jumped in, and before Loomis and Bedoya reached the jeep, the truck was moving across the street to join them.

Bedoya started the jeep. "Where to?" he asked.

"Club Carioca."

Bedoya laughed aloud as he floorboarded the jeep. "Going to see the girls so early in the morning? What a tiger!"

Loomis ignored him. "There's usually a green Pontiac parked at the curb about two blocks this side of the club," he said.

They were moving fast up the 30 de Marzo, the army truck seemingly glued to their rear bumper. "I can't imagine anyone being so observant coming out of the Club Carioca," Bedoya said. "What devotion to duty."

Loomis didn't answer. He had noticed the Pontiac many times only because he once had owned a car of the same model.

Bedoya put the jeep into a tire-squealing turn to the right, and they sped up Teniente Amado Garcia toward the Duarte Bridge. The truck behind followed Bedoya's every move. Loomis's stomach began to churn. Another jog to the right, then a hard left turn, and they were heading northwest out Avenida Duarte. For one bad moment, Loomis thought he was going to be sick. He remembered an old remedy of the Corps.

"Stop just beyond the next intersection," he told Bedoya. "There, on the right."

The jeep skidded to a stop. The truck's brakes complained loudly, but the driver managed to bring it to a halt a scant six inches from the jeep. Loomis stepped out and went into the nearest bar.

"*Dos Criollas,*" he told the bartender.

He took the two opened bottles, left a peso on the bar, and hurried back out to the jeep. When the soldiers saw him, they broke into a cheer. Loomis grinned and waved the bottles aloft. Another story to be added to the Clay Loomis legend. He stepped back into the jeep. "O.K.," he told Bedoya.

The beer helped. And the straight street made the ride much easier. Loomis finished the first bottle, pushed it beneath the seat, and started on the second.

"I was hoping that one was for me," Bedoya said.

"I never permit my men to drink on duty," Loomis said. "It looks bad."

Bedoya laughed. "A half-million pesos," he mused in English. "I didn't know there was that much money left in the whole country. I thought El Jefe had sent it all to his banks in Switzerland."

"Don't joke like that," Loomis warned.

"I'm not joking," Bedoya said easily. "You ever hear of a poverty-stricken ex-dictator? Begging in the street? Ever since I was born, and even before that, we've had presidents sending money to Switzerland. All the Trujillos. The whole family. Then there were others. And what happens when they get themselves killed? I think Switzerland must be a very rich country. Maybe when I am an old man I can go over there and say, '*Amigos,* I am Alfredo Bedoya, who has served his country faithfully and well. If it isn't too much trouble, please put a million pesos or so into my account, for I have need of it in my old age.' Surely they wouldn't miss a million pesos."

"If you keep up that kind of talk, you're not going to have an old age to worry about," Loomis told him.

They turned off Duarte and headed toward the Barrio Obrero, passing long stretches of gaily colored homes. Through poverty and war, Dominicans managed to keep their wooden, jerry-built houses well painted. Any color would do—pink, blue, green, yellow—as long as it was bright. Many women were working in the gardens and hanging wash. The soldiers yelled compliments to those deserving. Loomis finished his beer and marveled at Bedoya's skill in avoiding collision with wandering chickens, goats, dogs, and naked children.

Bedoya slowed as they approached a collection of low, cinder-block business houses. Loomis searched the street. The green Pontiac was not parked in its usual place. He pointed with his empty bottle. "There," he said. "Stop just the other side of that big door."

Bedoya braked toward the curb, holding up one hand to warn the truck driver. Loomis stepped out onto the pavement and levered a round into the chamber of the Schmeisser. He heard the machine gun bolt work twice; at least the soldier knew how to load his weapon. Loomis scanned the windows along the street as he spoke to Bedoya. "Take old Deadeye here and go cover the back. Count the doorways. Don't make a mistake. Don't let anyone come out unless they're holding onto the top of their heads with both hands."

Bedoya nodded and sped away, the *soldado* clinging desperately to the machine gun mount as the jeep wheeled around the corner.

Loomis signaled to the soldiers to spread out along the street, which was now deserted. People in the *barrio* seemed to have an uncanny ability to sense impending trouble. The soldiers eyed the windows and roofs nervously as Loomis moved toward the big wooden door. Holding his Schmeisser in one hand, he hammered the brass knocker against the polished backplate. He waited a moment and was lifting the knocker again when the Browning opened up behind the building. Beneath the noise of the machine gun, Loomis could hear the chatter of several light automatic weapons.

He tried the door. It was locked. He drove his shoulder against it. A sergeant and two hefty soldiers joined him, but the door wouldn't budge. It seemed as solid as steel. A heavy bar in place behind it would be the only thing that could make a door that unyielding.

"Shit," Loomis said, wishing he had sent at least two or three more soldiers with Bedoya. He ran to the truck. He got it started, put it in gear, and drove toward the building, angling the right side of the heavy bumper at the door. The soldiers had just enough sense to scatter at the last moment. The truck leaped the curb and rammed into the door, slamming Loomis hard into the wheel.

Stunned for a moment, he was puzzled by a strange noise. He became aware that his chest was resting on the horn button. With the hood jammed through the door, the horn was sounding inside the building. Loomis slid back into the seat and put the truck into reverse, but the motor had died. He could hear bullets hitting the radiator. Fortunately, a part of the splintered door lay across the shattered windshield, protecting him. He restarted the truck, ran it backward six or eight feet, set the brake, grabbed his Schmeisser, and ran for the safety of the building.

The sergeant lobbed two grenades in through the splintered door. The explosions blew out the high front windows, frames and all, showering the street with glass and debris.

Loomis charged through the opening in the door, running hard.

In the semidarkness he collided with a folding wooden chair and clattered with it to the floor. The fall probably saved his life. A burst of bullets chewed into the wall behind him. Loomis jerked the Schmeisser around and returned the fire, aiming at the point where he'd seen the muzzle blast. After two quick bursts, he rolled away. There was no return fire.

As he became accustomed to the gloom, Loomis strained his eyes to determine the layout of the building. The room was long and narrow, apparently a former lodge hall. A platform ran the length of each wall. At the far end of the room, where he had seen the muzzle fire, a stairway led down. Loomis remembered that the terrain dropped away into a ravine behind the building; the stairs probably descended to the level of the alley.

The sergeant and two soldiers came in, hugging the floor. They all waited, alert, for the gunfire that did not come.

"I may have hit him," Loomis said quietly. "He was in that stairwell. Cover me. I'll go see."

Crouching, he zigzagged to the left, giving the soldiers a field of fire. He eased up to the stairway, the Schmeisser poised, but as he neared the top steps he saw blood splattered on the railing beyond. Cautiously, he peered over the edge. A crumpled body lay at the foot of the concrete steps.

From the back of the building, gunfire erupted again.

Loomis motioned to the soldiers. They came up fast. He led them down the stairway, stepped over the body, and kicked open the door with his boot.

The green Pontiac was parked in the middle of a large room. Half of it was painted black. Three men were crouched behind it, aiming machine pistols at the alley door. As they turned the weapons toward him, Loomis squeezed the trigger of his Schmeisser and traversed the length of the Pontiac, catching the last man just as he got off a burst that ripped into the concrete above Loomis's head.

Loomis stepped behind the door frame for protection and rammed in another clip. The sergeant went past him, his Colt .45 automatic poised. But the battle was over. Loomis's sustained burst had killed all three men. Two more bodies lay in the open doorway. Beyond, Loomis could see the soldier in the jeep, tense, still alert, with Bedoya deployed out to the right with his Schmeisser for perfect triangulation of fire.

"*Está bien,*" Loomis called to them. "We have them all."

Two in the doorway, three behind the car, and the one in the stairwell. Six dead. He walked out to meet Bedoya. "You all right?" he asked.

Bedoya nodded. Loomis put the Schmeisser into the jeep and rubbed his shoulder, now beginning to hurt from his hard fall.

"I'm getting too old for this shit," he said to Bedoya.

"It took you a while to get down here," Bedoya agreed. "I thought you'd stopped for another beer."

"I'm either going to have to cut out this crap or else start getting some sleep at night," Loomis said.

He walked over to study the tire tracks on the damp ground. A dozen Dominique chickens, driven from their grazing by the shooting, were edging back toward the shade at the rear of the building. One, bolder than the rest, began pecking experimentally at the spent brass. In the garage, the soldiers were working off tension by joking, laughing, and shouting around the blood and carnage. Loomis watched them in disgust. He walked back to the jeep and climbed in to rest, to catch his breath, and to hide his shaking hands. The first hesitant faces were appearing at windows and doors up and down the alley. A group of half-naked children came up the drive and stood, silent, staring at the soldiers and the bodies. Bedoya came over to lean against the jeep. He unbuttoned his shirt and flapped it, trying to dry the stain under the armpits.

"I've been thinking," Bedoya said. "El Jefe probably will be very concerned over that half-million pesos. He should have a big reward posted by now."

"Probably," Loomis said. "But I wouldn't count on collecting it." He pointed to the tire tracks. "Unless I miss my guess, that money is long gone. We hit the transfer point too late."

He was right. A thorough search of the building failed to find a single peso.

Ramón El Rojo had obtained another half-million pesos for his revolution.

Chapter 2

The sultry, oppressive atmospheric inversion over Washington remained stationary throughout the eighth straight day, blocked by a high-pressure ridge at sea beyond Cape Hatteras. On Capitol Hill, and in the residential sections, tensions rose with the temperature. Two police cars were overturned and burned in a renewed outburst of violence along 14th Street, and in one weekend six grocery clerks died in robbery-murders. In Congress, debate on inflationary increases in Social Security benefits dominated headlines from the House, and the Senate continued to stall over approval of the new Secretary of State. The *Washington Post* predicted that Congress easily would override an expected presidential veto of the foreign aid bill, jeopardizing the chief executive's chances for a second term. The President was assumed to be considering all the political ramifications of using the veto. The White House press corps was awaiting his decision.

These matters normally would have been of deep concern to President Robertson. But on this Thursday morning in early July he was only marginally aware of routine crises. Instead, his full attention was devoted to a twenty-one-page report on his desk in his hideaway cubbyhole in the Executive Office Building.

Travis J. Robertson loved the power of the presidency but hated the pomp and ceremony of office. His nature required a considerable measure of privacy. Occasionally he needed to escape to a quiet place, smoke a cigar, and think.

The White House was hell for a man who required solitude. He couldn't move without a posse of Secret Service agents in tow. The guy with the black satchel was continually underfoot in case the United States suddenly needed to bomb the piss out of Russia. Aides, secretaries, and advisers gave him no peace. Nor could he find refuge in the living quarters. His wife claimed artistic interests and habitually held court for important people who talked incessantly about some perverted dead Frenchman or other. Robertson's preferences ran to poker, good bourbon, and fast cars. He no longer had time for poker. If a man couldn't drink seriously, Robertson saw no use in drinking at all. He occasionally downed the swill served at political functions, but he hadn't communed with a good bottle of bourbon in years. His Ferrari was on blocks in a garage back in Lincoln, Nebraska, gathering dust.

Yet Robertson had won a measure of privacy. He had located the twelve-by-fourteen-foot room in the Executive Office Building. It was separated from most of the rampant confusion by a storage space. His hideaway was an open secret among White House staff members, but no one dared violate his demand for seclusion.

So while political pundits all over Washington speculated freely on what he would do about the foreign aid impasse, the President calmly lit his second cigar since breakfast and opened the report from Langley. He had read the entire manuscript a dozen times. Yet he turned back to the beginning.

That was the one overriding factor in his success: a passion for painstaking analysis. President Kennedy's major talent had been calculated charm, a knack for constructing a political machine around his own carefully created image. Lyndon Johnson's forte had been persuasion, the ability to bring key people around to his viewpoint despite all logic. President Robertson knew he possessed neither of those techniques. He had no charm, good looks, or friendly ways. A stand-up comedian had claimed on national television that, during the presidential election campaign, one poster depicted a topographical map of the Dakota Badlands instead of the face of the candidate and that no one had noticed. Robertson wasn't sensitive about his heavily lined face, but he wasn't especially

amused by the joke. He knew he was generally considered
the most laconic President since Cal Coolidge. He had developed a certain public style. By mentally shifting gears he
could perform for audiences when necessary. But such
efforts went against his nature. However, no one was better
at analyzing his fellow men. All through his political career
Robertson had spent long nights determining the exact nature of his friends and opponents. He usually knew others
better than they knew themselves. He often stayed up all
night, thinking. He worked while most of Washington slept.
After midnight, there were fewer interruptions, and he
could get more done. He also found that when he phoned
people at 4:00 A.M., they tended to be more candid. At dawn,
when the city stirred, the President went to bed. He limited
himself to a few hours of sleep, a practice that probably
accounted for his wrinkled face. He had been called "Old
Pickle Puss" on the floor of the Senate, where even early in
his career he had been chided a few times for his tardy
arrivals. A reporter once irritated Robertson into an explanation. "It's been my observation that nothing interesting or
worthwhile ever happens before noon," he had told the reporter. The remark had returned to plague him during campaigns, but even his worst enemies conceded that on occa-
sion he possessed a dry wit.

He now turned his full analytic powers on this new problem and on this strange man, Clay Loomis.

The report was woefully incomplete, despite its length.
Robertson read through the manuscript once more, then
tossed it aside as worthless to his purposes. He would learn
more, no doubt, when he talked to the men from Langley.
He still had thirty minutes before the appointment.

He carefully relit his cigar and opened the packet of photographs. He pulled out the one that had intrigued him most.

Shot four days earlier in Santo Domingo, the color photograph showed Loomis standing at the side of a jeep. The
depth of field indicated that a telescopic lens of considerable
power had been used. Loomis's face was in sharp focus. A
young Dominican standing beside Loomis was laughing, but
Loomis was unsmiling.

Robertson reached for a magnifying glass and examined the face.

There was a solidarity to the features that Robertson liked. Loomis obviously was a big man, six-three or four, and well proportioned. The jawline was firm, with no extra flesh along the jowls—a mark of drive and determination. The muscles around the mouth were strong, with deep lines circling outward and downward from the nose. A sign of forcefulness, self-expression, Robertson believed. The scars over the left eye and along the left cheek were mentioned in the military records contained in the report. The nose had been broken enough to lend it individuality, and Robertson envied Loomis that thick thatch of dark hair. But what held Robertson's attention were the eyes. They were electric blue, a surprising contrast to the dark features and tropical tan. The eyes fascinated Robertson. He sensed that they revealed depths sufficient to challenge his talents.

With his left hand he moved the magnifying glass experimentally, altering the image slightly. With his right hand he rolled his cigar, thinking, searching for the elusive truths he felt the eyes contained.

Here was a man who kept much locked up within himself, he concluded. A man who could wait as well as act. Who felt things deeply, yet who maintained a certain you-be-damned, go-to-hell attitude toward the world. And clearly, here was a man used to having his own way. Robertson didn't know how he knew these things. He simply knew them. Life had sculptured those features, and Robertson read their meaning.

He also sensed in Loomis something else he couldn't quite define.

The crow's feet definitely were not laugh lines. They seemed to stem from a narrowing, a guarded wariness. Robertson searched for a word. Distrust? Suspicion? Disillusionment?

Cynicism, he decided. The mark of a man burned by experience. Loomis would not be a man to commit his emotions lightly.

Yet, Robertson somehow would have to gain Loomis's confidence.

He rolled his cigar thoughtfully for a moment, closed the folder, and pressed a button on his desk. He asked his appointments secretary to escort the men from Langley into the Oval Office. Gathering all the material and his notes, Robertson left the hideaway office and was halfway down the corridor before he remembered his retinue. He waited impatiently for the Secret Service men and the guy with the satchel. Properly flanked, Robertson walked rapidly across the drive and into the White House.

As he entered the Oval Office, he nodded a greeting to the two men from Langley, and dismissed his appointments secretary. "We'll be more than an hour," he said. "Hold all calls. Stack appointments. I don't want to be disturbed."

He escorted the visitors to the conference couch, again taking their measure.

The Director, Delbert Wallaby, was tall, well built, even athletic. The thick, graying hair, fashionably long over the collar, lent him an air of distinction. A Harvard man, an eminent attorney, Wallaby was politically oriented and motivated. His appointment had been forced on the Administration, but Robertson had not objected strenuously. Wallaby was intelligent and experienced. Robertson knew that Wallaby often foresaw the shifting tides in the world's storms long before the so-called experts at State.

His Deputy, Cyrus Ogden, was another matter. Short and heavyset, even chubby, with high forehead and thinning hair, the pipe-smoking Deputy could have been mistaken for a professor of philosophy at some small, remote college. In a city fascinated by power, the Deputy remained virtually unknown. But Robertson was in a position to know that this quiet, outwardly affable little civil servant was one of the most powerful men in the world. Directors came and went at the whims of politics or presidential fortunes. But the Deputy, as chief of the agency's Clandestine Services throughout the world, toppled budding empires, murdered potential Hitlers, and made the world safe for American investments. There was a reticence, a smugness about the little bastard that Robertson didn't like.

Robertson motioned them to the couch, walked to his facing chair, and carefully placed the report on the small table within easy reach.

"This is the goddamnedest thing I've ever read," he said. Neither man smiled.

"Why in hell wasn't I told about this earlier?" Robertson asked.

Wallaby was not fazed. "First, we had so little information that we hardly put credence to it," he said. "Then, when more became known, and the facts established, we thought we had the matter solved. Naturally, when the affair got out of hand, we made you aware immediately."

"Are you certain of your information?"

"Absolutely," Wallaby said.

Robertson tapped the report with a forefinger. "The nuclear capabilities they claim. Is such a thing possible?"

Wallaby nodded emphatically. "Yes, sir. Not only possible, but even probable, we're told. Our nuclear people say we're overdue. They've long been expecting something like this."

"And this so-called Hamlet Group. You have no idea who they are? What they want?"

Wallaby shifted in his seat and glanced at his Deputy before replying. "No, sir. Not at the moment. It's all in the report there."

Robertson clamped his cigar in his teeth and fixed the Director with a gray-eyed stare that had become an anathema to the White House staff. He then whipped out the cigar and spoke with heat. "I don't like this, Wallaby," he said. "I don't like this at all. Your agency has been a pain in the presidential ass for some time, a source of constant embarrassment. Yet you take on something of this scope without alerting me, or anyone. What in God's name possessed you?"

Wallaby glanced uncomfortably at his Deputy, who seemed to be enjoying the exchange. "As I said, Mr. President, we had so little information, initially . . ."

"All the more reason we should have gotten right on it,"

Robertson interrupted. "We've been wasting valuable time."

"There's really not much we can do at this point, Mr. President," Wallaby said. "Our hands are tied. Everything hinges on what happens in Santo Domingo."

"We have the alternative you mentioned," Robertson pointed out.

"If the ship is destroyed, Mr. President, we will lose what few pieces of evidence we have."

"So you recommend that we depend on the Dominican Republic, and on this man, Clay Loomis?"

"Yes, sir."

"I also infer, from your rather incomplete report of our deteriorating relationships there, that we do not enjoy the admiration of Loomis."

"No, sir."

"Why not?"

Wallaby hesitated. "It's a long story, Mr. President," he said.

Robertson glared at him. "We have time," he said. "I have the feeling you're holding out on me. There's obviously something fishy about our situation with Loomis. I want the full story."

Deputy Ogden coughed, his device for interruption. "Perhaps I could help," he said. He glanced apologetically at Wallaby. "I have known Loomis longer. Twenty years or more. But it's all rather complicated. I would have to go back to how he came to us, how he came to leave . . ."

"Please do," Robertson said.

Ogden shifted in his chair and frowned at the floor for a moment, reflecting. "First, let me say that he is a remarkable man," he said. "Fantastic career, even in our trade. He enlisted in the Marine Corps when he was fifteen. A big, raw-boned kid from West Texas. He was at Tarawa, and in several other Pacific campaigns. Made a name for himself in the Corps. Later, there was a captain who took an interest in him, helped him get his high-school equivalency certificate, talked him into going to college on the GI Bill. He earned his B.A. in romance languages, of all damned things, in 1950, just in time for Korea. He accepted a commission and made two combat tours."

"Won some medal, didn't he?" Wallaby prompted.

Ogden nodded. "His company was cut off when the Chinese came into it. The C.O. was killed, Loomis took charge and brought the company back to Hungnam, fighting their way, carrying their wounded. It was one hell of a thing. I read his colonel's report. He was recommended for the Congressional, but MacArthur, or someone, didn't want the publicity. It was reduced to a Silver Star. Afterward, he got shore duty, Guantánamo Bay, Cuba. Good duty, in those days, I'm told. Plenty of rum and beer, and whorehouse liberties up to Guantánamo City in the mountains."

"I've been there," Robertson said.

He remembered how it had been, when he visited Guantánamo as a lieutenant commander on a battlewagon, the liberty parties crossing the bay by launch to Caimanera and the railroad, then the two-hour jolting ride on wooden seats, naked children running alongside at every hamlet, fighting over coins tossed out the open windows by the sailors and marines. And he remembered Guantánamo City in Batista's Cuba, dirty, poverty-stricken, baked in the sun, hopeless.

"Somewhere along in there," Ogden said, "Loomis made contact with some of Fidel Castro's rebels and was recruited."

"He had leftist leanings?"

"Idealistic, perhaps, but not left. If you remember, Mr. President, our own State Department also was fooled to some extent by Castro's intentions. We couldn't very well condemn Loomis for the same mistake."

"I suppose not."

"He fought alongside Castro in the Sierra Maestra. After Batista fell, Loomis had a difference of opinion with Castro but managed to get out alive. He became associated with a group preparing to invade Cuba. Our people got wind of it. His old C.O.—the one who talked him into college—was by then at Langley, recognized the name, and recommended him as a potential intelligence officer. With his background, he sailed right through, and was involved in the training program for the Bay of Pigs."

Robertson winced. "We've managed to find him some good duty, haven't we?"

"It gets worse, sir. He went into 'Nam with the first teams, working with the Berets. Laos, Cambodia, the whole tour. It was in Laos that something happened. I'm not sure yet we've got the straight of it. Loomis objected to some of the things we were doing. He developed a highly independent attitude, defied orders, and actually blocked one of our major operations." Ogden paused. "He was dismissed with extreme prejudice."

He waited to see if Robertson was familiar with the phrase. Robertson was. "And he's still alive?"

Ogden smiled. "He killed the first man we sent against him. And the second. Then he dropped out of sight. We know he served in Biafra, as a mercenary. And perhaps in another African war or two. He was in Guatemala, and maybe Chile. We knew vaguely where he was. Frankly, we lost interest in fulfilling the contract."

"I can see why," Robertson said.

"He surfaced in Santo Domingo during the last revolution as right-hand man to El Jefe. After the fighting, he was commissioned to set up the palace guard and the national security force. Now it has grown into more than that, we understand. He has no title to indicate his exact status, but in effect he is the number-one presidential adviser. And as you may know, Mr. President, the Dominican Republic has been extremely dependent upon the United States in the past, both politically and economically. Some of our best men have handled our affairs there—Edwin Terrel, Dan Mitrione, Anthony Ruiz. Then of course there was our stance during the Trujillo assassination in 1961 . . . ."

"Don't bring that up," Robertson said. "I don't want to hear anything about it."

Ogden smiled again, unperturbed. "Point is, we had a very strong operation there. Loomis has managed to shut down our whole station. He convinced El Jefe to 'go it alone,' to ignore U.S. aid. This policy was popular with the people for a time, but now the shoe is beginning to pinch. From all indications, the country is on the verge of another major revolution."

Robertson scowled. "That would screw things up good, wouldn't it?" He sat for a moment, pondering another possibility. "Would we receive more cooperation there—would our job be made easier—if Loomis were removed?"

Ogden didn't hesitate. "No, sir. Without Loomis, it would be chaos."

"I agree," Wallaby said.

Ogden explained. "Loomis is a very complex person. He can work on a certain level with his men, drinking and whoring around. He is extremely popular with the police, the military, and his men. Yet, he has this intelligence, this experience, and he is very adept at expressing himself. He has a tremendous influence on the higher echelons of Dominican government—and especially with El Jefe. If we can convince Loomis, win his cooperation, we figure he will be our ace in the hole in this operation."

Robertson shook his head in disbelief. "And this man Loomis—the man you've attempted twice to kill—is the one we now must go to for help. I don't like it. I don't like it at all."

Wallaby pointed to the folder. "When he has the information in that report, he'll have to help us," he predicted. "He has no choice."

Robertson pushed back his chair, turned, and walked to the window beyond his desk. He stood for a moment, his back to his visitors, looking out across Washington, slowly rolling his cigar. He hated to be the man to put Loomis on the griddle once more, but he could see no other way. Simple elimination would be kinder than what Loomis might have to face before it was all over.

After a full minute of thought, he turned back to the men from Langley.

"You've underestimated Loomis twice," he said. "Let's pray to God you haven't this time. It's a gamble we have to take. This Hamlet Group's got us by the balls. Go ahead. Put your plan into operation."

Chapter 3

El Jefe stirred his coffee slowly, watching the rich cream mix with the luxurious black blend. He sipped from the cup, taking time to savor the results of six years of study and experiment. "Too much *arábica,* don't you think?" he asked.

They sat at the glass-topped table in the kitchenette off El Jefe's apartment. The coffee sampling had become a ritual during the last few months, providing an excuse for their long discussions.

Loomis sampled the coffee in his own cup. The *arábica* was a departure from El Jefe's long preoccupation with African *robusta.* Loomis couldn't find much difference in the taste. Still, there seemed to be a lingering quality of faint bitterness. "It has a slight bite," he said.

"Surely there is an *arábica* bean of softer quality," El Jefe mused.

Loomis knew that if a softer bean existed, El Jefe would indeed find it. He currently had buyers stationed in Ethiopia, Brazil, and Kenya.

"Five hundred thousand pesos," El Jefe said with an ease that indicated the two subjects—money and coffee—were not far removed in his mind. "Eleven men for five hundred thousand pesos. I think Ramón must be very happy with the exchange."

"Probably."

"Colonel Escortia responded very well this morning," El Jefe said. "He anticipated their movements, and was waiting. Your work of course was even more exemplary. Yet, five hundred thousand pesos are missing. Tell me, what did we do wrong?"

Loomis never knew for certain what was in El Jefe's mind

26

during these conversational rambles. "I don't think we did anything wrong," he said evenly. "You just can't win them all."

El Jefe frowned. "I can't accept that philosophy. A man in my position *must* win them all."

He studied Loomis for a moment in silence. Loomis sipped his coffee, trying not to show his irritation. He waited, wondering where the discussion was headed. Oblique ploys were a part of El Jefe's stock-in-trade.

He was a handsome man, big, almost as tall as Loomis, and of heavier build. He weighed close to three hundred, and there was little fat on him, Loomis happened to know. They often worked out together in the gym, and El Jefe easily handled weights that gave Loomis difficulty. His skin was deeply tanned—a golden brown—for he spent much of his time in the *palacio* pool, now well protected by high brick walls.

El Jefe abruptly took the conversation off on another tangent. "You are, for all practical purposes, a stateless soldier of fortune," he said. "Have you ever wondered why I have trusted you with my life?"

Loomis *had* wondered, from time to time. He voiced the only conclusion he had reached. "Because I'm a professional, I suppose."

El Jefe considered the answer. "Not just that alone," he said. "True, I must have experienced men about me. And your job certainly requires professionalism, a toughness that your background supplies. But there's more to it. You have been betrayed many times, and in each instance you have fought back—sought revenge—for those betrayals. Against Castro, your own government. Every instance. I believe you have a deeper appreciation of honesty than most men. Do you agree?"

"Perhaps," Loomis said.

El Jefe leaned forward to peer intently into Loomis's face. "Tell me, *amigo*. Do you trust me? Do you believe that in the moment of truth I will protect your interests as well as my own?"

Loomis also had often pondered that question. "I wouldn't be here if I hadn't reached that conclusion," he said.

He knew that El Jefe was an emotional man. Yet he was surprised at his impulsive shoulder punch of affection. "Good," El Jefe said. "It's imperative that we trust each other." He crossed to the silver service and poured more coffee. "I have a fear that this incident this morning—the bank robbery—has a deeper significance than the act itself. What do you think?"

Loomis nodded. "It's a new wrinkle."

"Not just another nuisance raid or act of terrorism," El Jefe said. "A well-planned, well-executed feat. Clearly, Ramón needs money. But for what? More guns?"

"No," Loomis said. All reports from well-placed sources indicated Ramón had plenty of weapons.

"Then what? Men?"

"Perhaps."

El Jefe watched Loomis's face intently. "Could he buy many men?"

"He wouldn't need many," Loomis said. "A half-dozen of your generals would do."

El Jefe's gaze didn't waver. "Can he buy them?"

"Not now," Loomis said. "But if he should appear, even momentarily, to be winning . . ."

"Then he *would* be successful," El Jefe said, completing the sentence.

"We're as ready for him as we'll ever be," Loomis said. He didn't add that, in his own assessment, the sooner Ramón made the effort, the better. El Jefe's support was slipping, week by week.

El Jefe finished his coffee and slowly poured another cup. "I no longer know what to expect from the people," he said. "If fighting should break out in earnest, which way do you think they would go?"

"Fifty-fifty," Loomis said. "Half the population will barricade themselves in their houses and sit it out. The other half will be split right down the middle."

"A cold-blooded assessment," El Jefe said. "And probably

accurate. In other words, I can expect support from only one-fourth of my people."

"I prefer to think positively," Loomis said. "Let's say that only one-fourth will oppose you."

"That is a more comforting view, I suppose," El Jefe said. "And it has been my experience that at least a quarter of the human race is against anything. Looking at it that way, I don't have to take it personally." He frowned, hesitated, and for a moment seemed to be searching for words. "Are we in agreement that Ramón's raid on the bank this morning may signal a new phase of his preparations for revolution?"

Loomis nodded.

"I think, then, that there are certain precautions we must take," El Jefe said. "I have a job for you that requires trust and delicacy. I wouldn't ask just anyone to do this thing. It will not be pleasant for either of us."

Loomis waited, apprehensive.

"It concerns my brother. I don't believe you've met him."

"No."

"But you understand that our political philosophies differ."

Again, Loomis nodded, waiting.

"I believe it would be to his interest, and to that of his family, for me to consider placing him under my protection. Despite his wishes, if necessary. I want you to go to Santiago and to bring him back here. My brother, and his whole family."

El Jefe didn't like to receive unsolicited advice in some areas. But Loomis felt he should point out something. "That might not be politically expedient at the moment."

"I'm well aware of that," El Jefe said. "My brother may be more popular with—shall we say—self-styled intellectuals than I. If I'm forced to place him under virtual house arrest, and if that action is misinterpreted by some, then that's their problem, not mine. I have far greater concerns. There is the possibility that Ramón may try to get to me through him— or through his family. My brother and I may be different breeds of cats, politically, but he *is* my brother. That fact at the moment is a liability to both of us."

"What if he refuses to come?"

"Bring him anyway."

"Bound?"

"If necessary."

"By helicopter, or by plane?"

"By car. As you may know, my brother's wife, Juana, was in a plane crash and critically injured several years ago. She thinks she survived only through divine intervention. Apparently she doesn't want to trouble the Lord to perform any more miracles on her account. She has vowed never to fly again. I will respect her wishes."

Loomis hesitated. He was trained in helicopters and preferred their effortless efficiency. A 175-kilometer trip through country plagued by rebel guerrillas offered unnecessary complications. But El Jefe obviously had taken that into consideration. Loomis searched his mind for the files on the Manuel de la Torre family: a daughter, twenty-eight, and a son, fifteen, by a first marriage, and two children by the second, a boy and a girl, five and six. The second wife was known as a religious fanatic. The older daughter, María Elena de la Torre, was a movie actress and political activist.

"We'll need two cars," Loomis said. "And some sort of heavy weapons group."

El Jefe nodded impatiently. "I have intended to bring Colonel Rodríguez down to the *distrito*. For the last two months, he has had the difficult duty of protecting Manuel's family, against their wishes. He will understand our problem. We can now kill two birds with one stone—relieve Rodríguez and move the family here for better protection. Rodríguez can provide your escort."

The plan made sense. There would be no need to drain troops from the capital at a crucial time. Loomis had worked with Rodríguez. He was a competent man.

"When?" Loomis asked.

"Tomorrow night, I think. We should move rapidly. You will go as my personal emissary to impress upon my brother the necessity that he accept our hospitality. Manuel is not a realist, but if he is faced with the inevitable, I don't think he will resist. María Elena may give you the most trouble."

"And how far should I go with her?"

El Jefe frowned. The reason for Loomis's question was plain. María Elena de la Torre commanded a world press. She could raise a tremendous stink if she chose to do so.

"Her safety is paramount," El Jefe said. "You have a blank check."

Loomis looked ahead to the problem of having the De la Torres in the *palacio*. María Elena de la Torre would be a prize hostage for Ramón, focusing worldwide attention on his movement.

"With the family, we probably should increase protection here at the *palacio*," Loomis said.

"What do you suggest?"

"I think it'd be best if, outwardly, we keep things as normal as possible, to indicate to Ramón that we're not scared yet. We might increase the guard at the gates. That'd be natural, after the robbery. And I'll have Bedoya place a few machine guns on the balconies at strategic places not visible from the street."

"An excellent idea," El Jefe said. "And tell me. What did you think of our friend Colonel Escortia?"

"I was impressed," Loomis admitted.

"Do you trust him?"

"Hell, I just met him."

El Jefe persisted. "What's your inclination?"

Loomis shrugged. "My inclination is to trust him."

He hoped the question wouldn't be asked about some of the other army brass.

"I also tend to trust him," El Jefe said. "I plan to promote him. And to place him in command of the Distrito Nacional. What do you think?"

Loomis had found no fault in Escortia. He rather liked him. But the promotion would jump Escortia over at least four men who presently outranked him—men whose support El Jefe might need during the next few days. Loomis chose his words carefully. "I hope the disadvantages don't outweigh the advantages. There are some who would advise against it."

"If I worried about what people thought, I wouldn't have

brought you into the *palacio,*" El Jefe said. "I don't know whether you know it or not, but half the staff thinks you are a CIA plant."

"What makes you think I'm not?" Loomis asked.

El Jefe laughed. "You couldn't be that deceitful if your life depended on it." He put his arm around Loomis's shoulder, escorted him toward the door, and then grasped his hand. "Have a pleasant trip," he said. "And take care. I have the feeling I will be needing you in the days to come."

Chapter 4

Santo Domingo slept during the heat of midday. Shortly after noon, the exact time depending upon whim, most shops closed their doors. The city lay quiet more than two hours, baking in the tropical sun. In mid-afternoon, with the first fresh breezes from the Caribbean, traffic again stirred. By two-thirty or three, most shops were reopened. Narrow Calle El Conde, the main street through the business district, again was crowded. The poor came to stroll along the sidewalks, window-shopping the many boutiques that displayed a dazzling array of wealth tantalizingly close, yet light-years away for those subsisting on 180 pesos a year. The *descamisados*—the shirtless ones—found what satisfaction they could in splurging a few *cheles* on a "New York" chocolate bar or a few Swiss cookies. So ingrained was the pastime of strolling El Conde that a phrase, *darse un Condazo,* had become a part of the nation's language.

A measure of entertainment was offered the poor by the wives and daughters of the *tutumpotes,* who arrived throughout the afternoon in their Mercedes-Benzes and Buicks. Striding firmly into the exclusive shops with heads held high, they tactfully ignored their audience. Their military chauffeurs remained at the curb, guarding the cars, until summoned to carry out the packages.

Later in the afternoon, with temperatures dropped from the nineties to the more reasonable lower eighties, a few American tourists arrived from the hotels to *darse un Condazo,* winding their way amidst the poor, the clamoring black-market moneychangers, the pathetically young prostitutes, the heavily armed soldiers, and the professional beggars with their rented, often maimed children.

Not until the relative coolness of early evening did Calle El Conde fully come to life.

Shortly after sundown on the day of the bank robbery, Loomis backed his Olds Regency from the *palacio* garage, wheeled through the gate without stopping, and set out on one of his periodic tours to gauge the mood of the people. The robbery had left him more deeply troubled than he cared to admit to El Jefe, although as yet he had no confirmation of his intuition. He sensed some meaning in Ramón's move beyond the obvious.

Loomis always had believed that he could detect any brewing political change by a look at the people. In his experience he seldom had been wrong.

He first drove southward, past Parque Independencia, into Ciudad Nueva, a section of lavish homes devoted to a wide variety of architectural styles—mostly Mediterranean, Bermudan, and Spanish colonial. Some gardeners were still at work in the wide expanses of lawns and roses, gardenias, irises, gladioluses, bougainvillea, and other tropical flowers beyond Loomis's range of knowledge. He left the car windows down, enjoying the mingled aroma of the flowers and of the ocean front a few blocks away. As he drove, he studied the homes. He knew the owners, and had been a guest in many of them. Yet he had never quite felt at ease in such luxury, knowing the desperate poverty of Santo Domingo's extensive *barrios*.

He then turned eastward toward the mouth of the Ozama, where, almost five centuries ago, Christopher Columbus once anchored his fleet. Two blocks past the Convent of the Dominics, the first university in the New World, he turned northward to *darse un Condazo* with his Olds. He drove slowly, watching the faces of the people.

In the narrow Isabel la Católica, just north of the Biblioteca Nacional, a line of young homosexuals leaned against the centuries-old walls of golden stone, smoothing their long, oily hair, waiting in vain for the aging *turista norteamericano* who would make them rich. On the streets to the east, Loomis could see the sentinels with submachine guns, blocking the way to the military zone of the fortress. Built in 1505, the place was still in use.

All the faces Loomis saw were controlled, devoid of expression.

At the intersection of El Conde, Loomis turned left and inched through the heavy, two-lane traffic. Ahead of his Olds, a military pickup truck cruised the street, its horn sounding almost constantly as the driver cleared the way. Four soldiers were sitting on the truck bed, legs dangling out the back. Their automatic weapons were pointed carelessly at the crowded sidewalks. The pedestrians pretended not to notice. Occasionally, the soldiers yelled anatomical comment to prostitutes, who did not respond. Gray-clad Dominican marines and drab-green uniformed *policía nacional* guarded each intersection. They saluted and waved Loomis through.

At the corner of Santome, Loomis braked. A white Mazda was stopped at the curb. A hand reached out from the open car window and seized the wrist of a young prostitute. She was struggling, but the hand pulled her toward the car. The crowd around her stepped back, watching silently. The soldiers did not intervene. The police document on the windshield of the Mazda identified the young hippie-hoodlums as members of *La Banda,* responsible for thousands of beatings, robberies, kidnapings, and political murders in recent years —all with sanction of high police protection. Members of *La Banda* were kissing cousins of the fascist *paleros* of the Trujillo era and of the *tontons macoutes* of Papa Doc Duvalier. The driver wore an Apache headband. The hoodlum wrestling with the girl wore a floppy black hat. He was pulling her into the car through the open window.

Loomis stepped from the Olds. *"Hola! Un momento,"* he called to the one in the floppy hat.

"Ten cuidado, señor," a sergeant of the *policía nacional* said at his elbow. "Be careful. That's Franco Loco. Crazy Frank."

Franco Loco was known for his abilities with a 9-mm parabellum.

Loomis slammed the door of the Olds and moved forward.

Crazy Frank turned, saw Loomis, and released the frantic girl. Still facing Loomis, he laughed and said something to the driver. With a screech of tires, the car sped away. The girl glanced at Loomis, then hurried into the crowd and disappeared. Loomis was left encircled by wooden-faced Dominicans, who stared at him without comment.

Loomis returned to the Olds. He drove on west. Circling Parque Independencia, he turned northward, into the *barrio* of San Carlos de Tenerife. Driving slowly around a block, he monitored his rear-view mirrors carefully. He then parked and sat, lights out, on a side street to watch his back trail. As darkness closed around him, he could hear a pig rooting in the yard behind a nearby clapboard shack. A baby was crying somewhere. A goat bleated from farther up the block. Twice Loomis heard rats scurrying in the trash along the gutter.

His tour of the city had left him deeply disturbed. The tension, the smoldering anger of the people were increasing every day. His worst fears had been confirmed. Santo Domingo was a pressure cooker, ready to explode under the strain of constant seething resentment.

After twenty minutes, Loomis was convinced he had not been followed. He fired up the motor and drove fast out the Duarte Highway to the north.

More than an hour later, well into the plantation country, he slowed as he spotted the marker he sought, then whipped the car off the highway into a narrow dirt road. For a time he sped between fields of tall, sweet-smelling sugar cane, his tires purring in the soft earth. He drove until the road came to a dead end, stopped, and switched off the lights.

He sat motionless in the darkness for more than five minutes before a shadow emerged from the cane field and approached the car. Loomis placed his .380 in his lap, turned on a faint dash light, and tapped the button that released the door catches. Richard Allen Johnson slid in and closed the door. Loomis pushed the button again, throwing all the latches.

"Hello, shithead," he said.

"I'll sure say one thing for you, Loomis," Johnson said.

"You really know a remote rendezvous when you see one." He saw the pistol in Loomis's lap. "Well, honk if you love Jesus! Don't tell me you think I've taken up that old contract on you!"

"How in hell would I know?" Loomis said. "It's been damned near fifteen years since I've seen you. People change."

"Well, if you don't mind my saying so, you seem like the same old asshole to me," Johnson said.

"I can't see that Washington duty has given *you* any polish," Loomis said. "Are you certain you lost my man?"

"Three blocks from the hotel," Johnson said. "I sure hope he can find his way back all right. And you don't have to worry. I've got three men out there. No one will interrupt us."

Same Johnson. Cocky, overconfident, impatient, completely fearless, a 225-pound bundle of nervous energy constantly threatening to erupt. A man who lived for danger. Johnson had weathered the years well. In the dim light, Loomis could see patches of gray in the hairline over his temples, but his body apparently was as lean and tough as it had been in the early fifties when he made All-America as a halfback at Ohio State, or in the sixties when he and Loomis were laying waste in Southeast Asia. Loomis had not expected to see him again. They once were the best team in the Far East. Loomis had assumed those days were gone forever.

"You're risking your health and mine," Loomis said. "I hope you've got a good reason."

"The best," Johnson said. "I'm what's so popularly in demand these days: a man with a message. And here's the message: you are in a unique position to perform a very valuable service for your country."

"I hate to sound crass," Loomis said. "But what's my country done for me lately outside of trying to kill me?"

Johnson sighed. "I tried to tell them that'd be your attitude. Not a bone of forgiveness in his whole body, I told them. No sense of charity whatsoever. So they have empowered me to offer you a proposition. You play along with us on a little project, and we'll see that those old charges against you are wiped off the books. Full restoration of citizenship. Clean files."

Loomis had learned, long ago, to hide his true feelings. For years, he'd accepted the fact that he probably would never be able to go home again. Johnson's offer awakened thoughts, images he'd long blocked from his mind. But as these thoughts came, they were shackled to another: nobody offers something for nothing.

Loomis waited until he was certain he could keep his voice level. "Who's 'we'?" he asked.

"Consider who could make that offer," Johnson said. "Then you'll begin to get some idea of what's involved."

"I have. But who sent you? Are you here representing the company?"

"I really don't know," Johnson said. "And I'm not being evasive. It started out as one thing and evolved into another. There's an awful lot of people connected with it now."

Loomis believed him. But it wasn't enough. "I have no guarantee, then?"

"Oh good Lord, Loomis! Is there ever, in our kind of life? But this obviously comes from the top. And I personally think it's a very generous offer. After all, you killed two of the company's best men."

Loomis couldn't control a sudden surge of anger. "What the fuck am I supposed to do? Apologize?"

Johnson turned in the seat to face him. "Listen, Loomis. I'll level with you for old time's sake. There's something big afoot. I don't know what it is. But it involves you and this flea-bitten country. I think you'd be damned foolish not to take advantage of it. That's my personal opinion. But they gave me a long, prepared script. Want to hear it?"

"Why not?" Loomis said. "It's your show."

"O.K. Here it is: I spent some time in your old home town last week. You probably wouldn't recognize it. The Interstate cuts through the west edge, and the house where your maternal grandparents lived is gone. The house you grew up in on the ranch is still standing, but no one has lived in it since your dad died. It's deteriorating rapidly. Your high-school sweet-heart is married to a rancher and has a daughter seventeen that looks a lot like she did at that age, if her high-school graduation picture was a good likeness."

Loomis knew that the monologue was calculated to stun him emotionally.

It did.

"The superhighway has put San Antone twenty minutes away, and most people now go there to shop," Johnson went on. "Half the stores along Main Street are closed, and the windows of most are boarded up. Your old home town is practically a ghost town. The drugstore's still open, but they've taken the soda fountain out, so I doubt if you could get your old job back. The movie theater closed in sixty-two. Your Uncle Pete stores hay in it. And incidentally, he's doing real well. He's what? Seventy-two now? The ranch seems in good shape. He pastures about four hundred head of cattle on it—red cattle with white faces and no horns, I forget what the fuck they're called."

"Polled Herefords," Loomis said. "All right. I'm impressed. You and the company have gone to a great deal of trouble. But you're talking about thirty-some-odd years ago. If you know that much, you know I left at fifteen. And I've never been back."

"And now you can't go back," Johnson said. "Not unless you send in your boxtops and accept our generous offer. According to the script, along about here you're supposed to start weeping, swear you'll do anything to go home again, and break into 'America the Beautiful.'"

"Shit, just my luck," Loomis said. "I've forgotten the words."

"Your mind tends to rot in two-bit tropical revolutions," Johnson said.

"Since it's old home week, how about some company news? What ever happened to Smitty?"

"He bought it. About sixty-eight. Chopper lost a blade in the Delta."

"Tompkins?"

Johnson laughed. "He's out. A millionaire. The company set him up in a Delaware corporation as cover. He's apparently more businessman than spook. The cover grew too lucrative. Now he's running an airline."

"Melana?"

"You're not going to believe this. I flew back from Beirut and married her. Three kids now. Two boys and a girl."

"Son of a bitch. That must have jolted the folks at Langley."

"For a time. But it's all right now. Gooks are in fashion and I've got a houseful."

"Somehow, I never figured you for a family man."

"Melana knows the score," Johnson said. "She knows my work. She knows me. We just carry a lot of insurance and don't think about it. She's young and still beautiful. If anything happens, she'll make out."

That was Johnson. The complete realist.

"I suppose you heard about Susy," Johnson added.

"Yes," Loomis said, fighting to hold back his anger. "They didn't have to do that."

"The company wasn't involved," Johnson said quickly. "I made certain, later. It was local talent. The company had nothing to do with it."

"Well, it happened," Loomis said. "She's ten years dead. And you've made your point. What is it they want me to do?"

"First, go on the payroll."

"In place?"

"In place."

"No," Loomis said emphatically. "I'm old enough to be old-fashioned. I only work for one country at a time."

"Better think it over. The pay's good, and you're no spring chicken."

"I've had better offers, and from nicer people."

"All right," Johnson said. "That was the first proposal. This is the second: There's no reason we can't work with you in your present capacity."

"That's for me to say," Loomis pointed out.

"All you have to do is fly to Washington for a briefing. That's what they really want."

"No. Washington can come to me."

"Christ!" Johnson exploded. "Who in hell you think you are? This is top-level. The White House. National Security Council. Joint Chiefs. Do I make myself clear?"

Loomis thought out his answer carefully. "Anything Washington has to say to me, they can pass on through you or through someone else. I'm busy. I've got problems of my own. I don't have time to play grabass in Washington."

"You're crazy!"

"Maybe. But at least I know who I'm working for."

"They'll pull strings."

"Let them pull strings. I'm not going to Washington. That's final."

"All right. I'll deliver your answer. But I'm sure that won't be the end of it. You'll be hearing more from me." Johnson fumbled to find the door release.

"Wait," Loomis said. He reached beneath the steering column and punched the emergency flasher button. After three flashes, he turned it off.

"What the hell was that for?" Johnson asked.

"That was permission for you and your men to leave," Loomis told him.

"You're putting me on."

"Twelve men," Loomis said. "A thousand-yard perimeter. They let you in. And they wouldn't have let you out without my signal."

"In darkness?"

"Sniperscopes," Loomis explained. "We may run a backwater operation down here. But we run it right."

He punched the button opening the door latch for Johnson. The sound was loud in the silence of the night. Johnson stepped out and closed the door. Loomis wheeled the Olds around and headed back toward the highway, leaving him standing at the edge of the cane field.

Chapter 5

After the third assassination attempt against him, Ramón had developed sleeping problems. Each time he dozed off, he tended to relive the stark terror of that night when bullets and grenade fragments filled the house and he lay helpless on the floor, splattered with gore from what had been his brother. His insomnia was beyond solution. He would not allow himself the luxury of sleeping pills, heavy wine, or other conventional remedies. So, he was wide awake when the message came shortly after midnight.

Ramón was certain that his year-long campaign to mount a successful revolution was near fruition. All signs pointed to it: growing unrest in the streets, increased repressions from the administration, mounting dissension in El Jefe's own party. But Ramón knew, from his copious reading, that a revolution must be plucked at the right moment. A day too soon, or a day too late, and all might be lost.

The message indicated that perhaps the moment had arrived. El Jefe's hired gunman, Loomis the *norteamericano*, would be leaving for Santiago de los Caballeros within hours to bring the De la Torre family back to the capital. The information came from a good source and Ramón did not doubt it. He had thought, several times, of using the kidnaping of Manuel de la Torre as the kickoff for the revolution. From his studies, he had learned that the principal danger in any revolution is the rise of a third, moderate force as a haven for defectors from both combatant sides. Manuel de la Torre was a logical rallying point for such a group. He was personable, held the respect of many intellectuals, was well known from his writings, and was well separated, politically, from his brother. His kidnaping would at least delay the organization of a political haven for noncombatants. And Ramón was sufficiently imaginative to realize that the kidnaping of De la Torre's film-actress daughter would make bigger headlines abroad, focusing international attention on his revolution.

The fact that the De la Torre family would be in transit, protected only by a company of soldiers, seemed to present an opportunity too great to be ignored. True, in their home in Santiago, the De la Torres ostensibly were virtually unprotected. But Ramón had learned that the Santiago police and special army units kept them under constant surveillance, with a radio net that in moments would seal streets and summon hundreds of well-armed men to the scene.

In the *palacio,* the family would be even more inaccessible. Ramón knew he must prepare the first major operation of his revolution for execution within the next eighteen hours.

He awoke his aide, Juan, and prepared messages for delivery throughout the city. Juan was reluctant to go.

"La Banda," he explained.

The irony of the situation was not lost on Ramón. He was preparing to launch a revolution, and his men were terrified by street hoodlums. His Paul Revere was afraid of being mugged. There was reason for the concern. *La Banda* had ruled the streets after dark since the Balaguer regime in the late sixties and early seventies.

Ramón sent Juan out into the night armed with a quotation borrowed from the great Latin revolutionary José Martí: "It is better that a man die young for an ideal, than to live all of his life without one."

While he waited for Juan to deliver the messages, Ramón went into the kitchen of his heavily guarded compound and prepared an elaborate salad for himself, using exotic cheeses, fruits, and seafood in proportions he'd determined after long experiment. He now seldom ate anything else, and he carried only 126 pounds on his six-foot frame. His gaunt build, thin face, and high cheekbones, combined with dark, sunken eyes ravaged by insomnia, had led some of his men to call him *La Calavera*—"The Skull"—a word that in their idiom carried the added connotation of "daredevil." This nickname disturbed Ramón. He hoped he had courage, but he did not intend, ever, to be reckless.

He returned to his study and continued his work, correlating the revolutionary thoughts of some of the world's great thinkers—Leo Tolstoy, Henry David Thoreau, Ralph Waldo Emerson, George Bernard Shaw, Seneca. The difficulty was that some of the best material was the less familiar, rarely printed. He had devoted every spare moment during the last five years to this work.

After two hours of reading and writing, he heard voices in the outer corridor. He switched off the light and went to meet his advisers.

His council of war had arrived.

They argued until daylight.

Ricardo Morales, the hatchet-faced lawyer from Santiago, agreed that the revolution's affairs had reached the pinnacle. He urged immediate action. "The northern provinces are ready," he said. "Our men are trained, they are psychologically prepared. If we wait much longer, they will become bored, lose their enthusiasm."

Julio Paredes, the portly, asthmatic doctor from San Francisco de Macoris, was less certain that the moment had arrived. "El Jefe is losing prestige and support every day," he pointed out. "His generals are feuding. The economic reprisals from his anti-U.S. policies are beginning to hurt. The longer we wait, the easier he will be to overthrow."

"The outbreak of revolution will bring even more severe economic pressure to bear," the lawyer countered. "Tourism will dry up overnight. Even the quick-divorce flights from New York probably will be halted."

Ramón listened to the arguments with a detached air. Nothing was being said he had not explored, evaluated carefully. There was only one opinion he really wanted to hear: that of Professor Mario Salamanca. "What do you think, Professor?" he asked.

Horn-rims askew, his beard untrimmed and awry, his suit soiled and rumpled, the Professor hardly seemed the type one would select as a councilor. But no one was more thoroughly informed on Latin American politics, past and present. The Professor spread his hands in a helpless gesture.

"The matter simply boils down to a question of opportunity," he said. "The kidnaping of the De la Torre family could serve as the classic *grito* of revolution, proclaiming that we are at last committed. I frankly don't know when a better opportunity might occur. Another factor to consider is that it would require only a small force, leaving our organizational charts intact for the opening phase of the revolution for every major town in the north. I believe we could control the entire Cibao within a week or two, and with it the country's breadbasket. I believe we should strike."

The Professor's analysis was recognized as the final argument. Yet the decision clearly was Ramón's to make. The group watched his reaction, waiting, expectant.

Ramón rose and faced them. "I agree," he said. He turned to Doctor Paredes. "I also agree with the doubts, the misgivings you voiced. But I think Professor Salamanca has put the issue into words. We are ready. We can't afford to let this opportunity go by."

They hurriedly made plans. Forty rebel soldiers would be moved from San Francisco de Macoris to Rincón in a stake-bed truck, with both men and weapons concealed under a load of sugar cane. A frame to provide adequate space under such a cargo had been prepared months ago. Another thirty men would drive south from La Vega in private cars, their weapons hidden beneath seats or in auto trunks. A traffic search on that short distance of road was a minimal, calculated risk. Sixty men from a group of rural guerrillas encamped along the Río Yaque del Norte would march eastward to a rendezvous where the Duarte Highway crossed the Río Yuna.

Near that point, with more than 130 well-trained men and plenty of weapons, Ramón would organize the ambush to start his revolution.

Ramón could see no way that his plan could fail.

He had hopes of taking the De la Torre family alive, but this was not essential.

Their deaths also could accomplish his major objectives.

Chapter 6

Loomis made the three-hour, 175-kilometer trip to Santiago alone in his private Olds. He thought of taking Bedoya, but he felt that his *segundo* might be needed in the capital.

He drove fast on the long, open stretches of the Duarte Highway, curving northward and westward around the eastern slopes of the Cordillera Central. To the west he could see the peaks rising to more than ten thousand feet. He passed through fields of sugar cane, cocoa, and coffee and, at times, long expanses of virgin hardwood timber. The highway, rebuilt during Trujillo's last years, was good, one of the best in the country. In general, it followed the route of the first highway, built during the 1916 American occupation, connecting the capital with the country's breadbasket, the rich, fertile Cibao valley along the Río Yaque del Norte.

Three days of rain had cleared the air along the slopes, and from the higher places it seemed he could see all the way to the coast. The sky was cloudless, but the rains had cooled the land and tempered the effect of the strong sun. Loomis drove with the air conditioner off, the windows lowered. He often passed fields of workers tending the crops. Some waved as he passed. He wondered what was on their minds. He knew what would be on his mind, if he were in their place, trying to live on 180 pesos a·year.

In 1869, during one of the half-dozen times the United States seriously considered annexing the Dominican Republic, U.S. Senator Charles Sumner, in a celebrated opposition speech, warned that the United States would be linking itself to "a dance of blood." As proof, he merely cited Dominican history.

The phrase was apt. Neither the Vietnamese, nor the Koreans, nor any people Loomis knew had endured so much. In the months when he had little else to do, he had read deeply in Dominican history.

He passed through the town of La Vega, where—with divine assistance, it was claimed—a handful of Christopher Columbus's armored Spaniards murdered thousands of helpless Indians. And within a generation, all Indians were gone in a classic case of genocide. Slave ships, beatings, disease, unaccustomed work, the sword, and the gibbet destroyed a peaceful, gentle people.

Blacks, other Indians, other peoples were brought to the island, but in five hundred years the philosophy had not changed.

Loomis wondered, at times, how El Jefe would be rated among the scores of dictators who had ruled the Dominican Republic. There had been excesses during the last few years. El Jefe didn't condone the use of *La Banda,* but he regarded it as a necessary evil. Strong, unpalatable measures had to be taken to control some elements, he said. Loomis had been powerless to stop the practice. It was beyond the limits of his authority.

There were no simple answers to the problems of the Dominican Republic. One former president, Juan Bosch, had his initial enchantment with democracy tempered by experience. Bosch now believed that the Dominican Republic was without a political solution in the institutional sense. He advocated a benevolent, responsive dictatorship.

El Jefe was far more benevolent than most in the country's history.

Loomis arrived in Santiago de los Caballeros well before dark. He drove past the tree-shaded squares and the Trujillo era's overly modernized buildings to the Trujillo-built luxury hotel, the Matum. Checking in, Loomis shaved, showered, and changed from slacks and pullover to a light tan suit and tie. With yet another hour to kill, he went down to the dining room for dinner. Shortly after dark, as young couples began to gather at the Matum for a night of dancing, he checked out and drove to army headquarters.

Colonel Felipe Rodríguez Prado met him in the outer offices with a warm *abrazo.* Not yet thirty, Rodríguez was the best-known hero of the revolution that had elevated El Jefe to office. Although severely wounded, he had led the charge that had breached the walls at the military center, an action that had been witnessed by El Jefe himself. After the battle, Rodríguez was commissioned by El Jefe while a doctor worked to recover stray bits of metal from his wounds. Now, Rodríguez not only was in charge of the entire Santiago Province, but also was the eyes and ears of El Jefe in Santiago.

He took Loomis into his inner office and closed the door. "Let's go get drunk and talk of old times," he said.

Loomis laughed. He felt affection for few people. Rodríguez, with his easy smile and direct manner, was one. "El Jefe would tack my balls to the nearest wall," Loomis said. "But after this assignment, we will have to have a serious *borrachera."*

Rodríguez walked to his desk, took a cigarette from a silver case, and lit it thoughtfully. "A delicate assignment," he said. "Señor De la Torre won't go unless forced."

"Maybe we can convince him it's for his own safety," Loomis pointed out. "And for that of his family."

"He's blind to the danger," Rodríguez said. "I've had hell with him—and that daughter of his. El Jefe has insisted on close security. But if De la Torre sees one of my men on his property, he complains to me personally. And the daughter makes a game of shaking her protection."

Loomis had hoped there would be no difficulties. But Rodríguez confirmed his premonitions.

"What do you suggest?" he asked.

Rodríguez smoked in silence for a moment, considering. "We know he'll refuse. Yet, we'll have to ask. So I propose that you ask him, politely, with a company of my best men behind you."

"You're a genius," Loomis said. "Those were my exact thoughts."

At 8:30, Loomis knocked at the front door of the huge, rambling De la Torre *estancia,* hoping to catch the family finishing dinner. From long surveillance, Rodríguez knew that they dined late. Apparently the timing was perfect. When the butler, a big Indian peasant, showed him into the high-ceilinged study, Loomis caught a glimpse through a distant doorway of the entire family seated at the table.

The house was in traditional Spanish style, with heavy wooden furniture, exposed beams, and thick paneling throughout. The somber tone of the dark wood was relieved by the bright weavings and tapestries.

The De la Torres were an enigma to Loomis. He knew many details of their private lives. And none fitted.

María Elena de la Torre Ibañez and her fifteen-year-old brother, Raul de la Torre Ibañez, were Manuel's children by his first wife, who died of a ruptured appendix on a yacht cruise to the South Pacific. A year later, Manuel married one of his graduate students, Juana Velcz Gutiérrez. Juana was not much older than María Elena.

Juana believed in miracles and experienced visions. Some said she was a mystic. Others said she was a religious nut. Juana and María Elena rarely spoke to each other.

But María Elena was the most intriguing mystery. Trained in music, drama, and ballet from an early age, she became a film star overnight with a remake of *Joan of Arc*. After a brief, intensive career, she quit Hollywood following six films. She became a political activist, first traveling, making speeches, then dropping from sight to pursue academic degrees. She completed work for her master's and Ph.D. during the era of militancy on United States campuses. Her dissertation, a firsthand study of revolutionary politics, was scheduled for publication by a university press. And now she had just as mysteriously returned home to live. No one knew why. She had long refused to talk to the press.

De la Torre kept Loomis waiting less than two minutes. He was a smaller man than El Jefe, almost a head shorter. But in the prominent nose and deep-set eyes Loomis could see a strong family resemblance. He entered the study with his puzzlement evident in a slight frown. "Señor Loomis," he said. "The name is familiar. But forgive me, I cannot put it into place."

Loomis didn't waste words. He shifted into flowing, formal

Spanish. "With your permission, Señor De la Torre, I have
the honor to be chief of security to El Jefe. He has sent me
with a cordial invitation for you and your family to visit him
in the capital for an indefinite stay."

"Of course. The *norteamericano,*" De la Torre said. "Have
you dined?"

"Thank you, yes."

"Perhaps you will join me in a brandy . . ."

Loomis knew that De la Torre's typical Latin cordiality
was also a stall for time, while he sought to compose a reply
El Jefe might not find offensive, yet one that would leave no
doubt he meant what he said. Loomis declined the drink.

De la Torre took his time pouring his own.

"Please convey to my brother my regrets," he said. "As I
have explained to him many times, we simply cannot leave
Santiago. The children are in school. And I have my classes
at the university . . ."

"I hope there will be no unpleasantness," Loomis said.
"But El Jefe has instructed me not to accept your regrets.
I've been told to put this in the strongest terms. He has valid
reason to believe your life—and that of your family—is in
danger. El Jefe feels that since the danger exists because of
his position, he is responsible for your safety."

"I don't wish to be rude," De la Torre said. "But I have no
intention of going to Santo Domingo. Please consider our
conversation on this subject ended."

"You're making my job difficult," Loomis said. "You know
your brother. You can appreciate the position I'm in. Please
ask your family to be ready to leave for the capital within two
hours. They may take only essentials. Your property here will
be well guarded until you return."

"I'll take this up with my brother," De la Torre said. He
crossed the room and tugged at a bell cord. The big Indian
entered. "Please escort Señor Loomis to the door," he said.

The Indian stood for a moment, uncertain, then moved
toward Loomis. Taking a step backward, Loomis pulled his
revolver.

"I'm sorry," he said. "You've made this necessary. The

house is surrounded by soldiers. Please tell your family to pack. If you don't, I'll call the soldiers in to do the packing for you."

As Loomis stood, pistol in hand, he saw movement to his left. Turning, he brought the .357 to bear on the loveliest girl he'd ever seen. Dark thin face, large intelligent eyes, and an abundance of long dark hair. For a moment, he didn't recognize her. He was used to seeing those delicate features ten feet tall on a movie screen. They now were reduced to a compact package no more than five-feet-four. But there was no mistaking that mouth. Prim one moment, full and generous the next, and with a smile and laugh that bordered on wanton, the mouth gave the face a kaleidoscope of constant, unself-conscious emotion. It was a face that had left critics ecstatic through six films. Clay had seen them all, some two or three times. El Jefe had prints of each and proudly screened them for visitors.

If the sight of the pistol fazed her, she hid it well.

"Papa! What's happening?" she asked.

"Hector has ordered us to take refuge in that fortress he calls a home," he said. "This gentleman is conveying the invitation."

She glared at Loomis. "You're not a gentleman," she said. "You're Loomis. I've read a lot about you."

"And you're María Elena," he said. "I've read a lot about you, too." He could have added that much of what he'd read was in his top secret security files.

"Please don't say you liked my films. I think I might throw up."

The vocal inflections, the facial mannerisms, he had seen hundreds of times. But no screen image had conveyed the awesome delicacy of that clear olive skin, the natural richness of that thick, dark-chestnut hair. He was puzzled and disturbed by his reactions. A decade had passed since his last infatuation. Occasionally a new girl would hold his interest for a while. And pretty girls were not exceptional in his life. The beach hotels usually were full of women combining a quick divorce with a brief vacation. Many seemed to need

more than an ornate Dominican gold seal before restoring
themselves, mentally, to freedom. Loomis had done what he
could to help repair broken psyches from time to time. Some
resulted in extended liaisons. A few of those women were
well known in the entertainment field.

But dry mouth, accelerated pulse, a feeling of awkward-
ness?

He thought he'd put that twenty years and more behind
him.

"To the contrary," he said. "I didn't think a single one of
your films had enough substance to merit your attention, or
mine."

Her eyes widened in mock surprise. She gestured to the
pistol. "I knew film critics were hired mercenaries," she said.
"But I didn't know hired mercenaries were film critics. This
is the first time I've ever been reviewed at the point of a
gun."

"Please," Loomis said. "I'm only emphasizing the urgency." He holstered the pistol.

"You don't have to apologize," María Elena said. "Hitler
didn't. El Jefe doesn't."

"María Elena! My brother hardly deserves to be compared
to Hitler."

"Trujillo, then. If we had constitutional guarantees, hired
mercenaries wouldn't be able to come into our home waving
a pistol."

"We're wasting time," Loomis said. "I don't want to call
the soldiers in. But I will."

De la Torre sighed. "Señor Loomis is right," he said. "We
really have no choice. I know my brother." He turned to the
house servant. "Please inform the señora we will leave in two
hours for an extended stay in Santo Domingo."

María Elena didn't move. "I want it clearly understood
that I'm going under protest, that I consider myself a political
prisoner."

"Your uncle has invited you to be his honored house-
guests," Loomis said. "You can call it what you want."

Chapter 7

By midnight, they were well past La Vega. They drove rapidly through the darkness, the Commando V-100 armored car in the lead. Loomis came next in the Olds, and Rodríguez was behind him in his Buick. Two army six-by-sixes packed with troops brought up the rear. The lieutenant beside Loomis in the front seat was relaxed, yet alert. In the back, the older boy, Raul, was dozing. De la Torre and his wife were awake, but silent.

Raul was thin and frail, just short of effeminacy. But he had his father's quiet poise, dignity, and direct manner.

Juana was a larger woman than Loomis expected—not fat, but rather attractive and possessing an earth-mother plumpness. She wore her long, straight, black hair loose, adding to the image.

María Elena, the younger boy Fredrico, the girl Nina, and the maid were riding with Rodríguez. After the initial encounter, María Elena chose to ignore Loomis's existence.

Loomis was unable to relax. Some sixth sense kept his tension high. He concentrated on the driving, focusing on potential trouble spots.

They had entered a stretch of forest along the rugged slopes of the Cordillera when it happened.

As they rounded a curve, the Commando V-100 armored car ahead suddenly erupted into a brilliant ball of orange flame.

Instinctively, Loomis knew there were no survivors. He doused the Olds headlights and skidded off onto the shoulder, taking the car deep into the wide barrow ditch. Behind him, Rodríguez's reactions were equally fast. The Buick skidded to a stop behind the Olds. One truck shot past, then

skidded crosswise the road with a squeal of brakes. The other
halted behind them as a rear guard.

"What happened?" De la Torre asked. His voice had a
trace of excitement, but no panic.

"Probably a bazooka or recoilless rifle," Loomis said. "An
antitank weapon." He punched the switch that unlocked all
the door latches. "Everyone pile out behind the car and lie
flat."

The soldiers were leaving the trucks, jumping from the
endgates, deploying for positions. The rebel automatic weapons opened fire. Machine pistols and something heavier,
probably a BAR.

The soldiers, illuminated by the burning armored car,
made good targets. Loomis saw at least six fall.

Rodríguez came running up to the Olds. Loomis hunkered
down with him beside the car. "We can fall back," Rodríguez
said. "We're only about six kilometers beyond the *estancia*
of . . ."

"No. I think that's what we're expected to do," Loomis
said.

He walked to the back of the car and opened the trunk. As
the lid swung up, he reached in and unscrewed the bulb. He
took out his Schmeisser and a half-dozen clips, jamming them
into his jacket pockets. He loaded the gun, levered a round
into the chamber, then stepped up onto the trunk of the car
to study the road ahead. The Commando V-100 was still blazing furiously. The roar of the flames filled the night with
sound and illuminated the edges of the forest around them.
Loomis was certain the eight men inside the car were dead.

Beyond the burning vehicle, he could see a network of logs
and brush. The sporadic gunfire was coming from each end
of the barricade, and from positions flanking the road. The
soldiers were returning the fire, but probably without much
effect. From what Loomis could see, Ramón's men seemed
dug in well.

Loomis figured that the main force was on the road behind
them, waiting in ambush. He was so certain, he thought it
best not to send a probe in that direction. The longer

Ramón's main force remained uncommitted, the better the odds.

For a moment, Loomis considered flanking the barricade and circling through the trees to attack from the rear. With that small force wiped out, perhaps they could run the barricade. But the maneuver would take time. Ramón's other group no doubt would hear the fire-fight and come up to take part. There also was the threat of the bazooka-type weapon.

Loomis remembered the advice of a general long dead: if you're ever in doubt between two courses of action, they're probably both wrong; think up something else.

He stepped down from the car and took Rodríguez to one side. "I figure Ramón's got us blocked fore and aft," he said. "We can't risk a pitched fight. Not with the family. We can't get help here in time. Not at night. We'll have to do the unexpected. I'll take the family straight into the woods. You can keep Ramón busy about thirty minutes, then pull in behind me. You know the location of the old Navárez Plantation?"

"Roughly."

"I figure it's about six miles from here. I'll radio and get some birds in there to dust off at daylight with the family. By then, we should have help by highway from either Santo Domingo or La Vega. We'll turn back on Ramón, and our relief will be behind him. Maybe we can sandwich him like he's trying to sandwich us."

"Beautiful," Rodríguez said.

"I'll take six men with me, if you're agreeable," Loomis said. "Along with your radioman and a couple of BARs. If we run into anything, we'll lay down a barrage, and you can come running."

The De la Torre family huddled in the ditch behind the Olds. Loomis squatted beside them while he waited for Rodríguez to send the soldiers. The light from the burning armored car had faded, but Loomis could see Rodríguez running along the far side of the road, positioning his men. The firing was now scattered.

"We're moving into the forest," Loomis told De la Torre.

"We could probably hold out here until help comes, but I don't want to risk it. There's a clearing about six miles from here. We'll have helicopters waiting there."

De la Torre nodded. His eyes showed concern, but no fear. Behind him, María Elena and Raul were nestled together, their arms around each other. Juana was holding the younger children flat, protecting them with her body.

When the soldiers assigned to point reported to him, Loomis gave them instructions to move out and break trail, with the BAR men flanking. He told them that if they made no contact after two or three hundred yards, they could risk flashlights held low to the ground.

"And you stick with me like glue," he told the radioman.

Rodríguez and his men opened a diversionary barrage, and the soldiers trotted into the woods. Loomis waited with the family until the soldiers disappeared. He figured that if Ramón had them flanked, the perimeter would be less than a hundred yards. When the soldiers apparently met no opposition, Loomis followed with the family, carrying the younger boy piggyback. De la Torre carried Nina.

Loomis let the soldiers stay well out in front, the faint glow of their hooded flashlights barely visible. The radioman, Loomis, and the boy led the second group, with María Elena, Juana, and the maid in the center. Raul, De la Torre, and the girl followed. Three soldiers lingered back as rear guard.

Once they were away from the road, and their eyes became accustomed to the night, they made good time. Although the quarter-moon was low on the horizon behind them, the sky was cloudless, and enough starlight penetrated the trees to distinguish shapes. There was no wind. Despite the relative coolness of the night, they soon were sweating from the exertion. Loomis stuck his extra ammo into his belt, peeled off his light jacket, and threw it away. As they moved farther from the road, the ground became more level, but fallen limbs and underbrush made footing difficult.

A little more than a mile out, Loomis called a halt. He handed the boy to Juana and knelt by the radioman. Through army headquarters in Santo Domingo, he managed a tele-

phone link to Bedoya at the *palacio.* He switched to English.
"Listen, Squirt, I'm in a jam," he said. "Ramón hit us in
force."

For once, Bedoya seemed worried. "Where are you?" he
asked.

Loomis gave him the coordinates. "Get three birds into the
old Navárez Plantation at daylight," Loomis told him. "Bring
Rodríguez's men some ammo. I think the site will be clear,
but they better check it out before they go in. They can hose
it down with a gunship or two. Tell Colonel Escortia I suggest
moving a company toward us from the capital along the road.
They'll find a burned weapons carrier where we were hit.
There should be a plain trail for them to come in behind us."

"El Jefe has ordered that the army not leave the capital in
less than battalion strength," Bedoya pointed out.

"Well, Escortia can bring a whole fucking battalion, then,"
Loomis said. "I don't care. Right now we could use them."

"Hokay, Captain," Bedoya said. "The cavalry is on the way.
See you at daylight."

Loomis secured the radio. María Elena was watching him.
"Why don't you wave your pistol at Ramón?" she asked.

"I plan to," Loomis told her. "Just as soon as I get you
people on that whirlybird."

The woods behind them were now silent. Loomis fought
his inclination to turn back to find out what had happened.
They moved on westward.

After they had walked another mile, they began to hear
intermittent firing again some distance behind. It continued
off and on for the next two hours. From the sounds, Loomis
estimated that Rodríguez was doing his job, harassing
Ramón's advance with occasional solid stands at strategic
points, then retreating.

Less than a mile away from the clearing Loomis heard two
explosions. Claymores, or reasonable facsimilies, he guessed.
Since Rodríguez wasn't equipped with heavier weapons,
Loomis feared the worst. After a breathless moment of silence, the night erupted into a sustained battle no more than
a thousand yards away.

Ramón obviously was making a determined effort to inter-
cept them before they reached the landing zone.

They arrived at the clearing thirty minutes before dawn.
Loomis spread the soldiers in a close perimeter. He gathered
the family in a shallow ditch where they lay flat, ready to
make the dash to the helicopters.

Then they waited.

The gunfire to the rear hadn't slackened perceptibly. Loomis was certain that Rodríguez would be running low on
ammunition. He wondered how long he could hold out. They
badly needed the help of the gunships.

Loomis waited impatiently, often checking his watch.
Then, through the canopy of trees to the east, he saw the first
solid pink tinge of daylight. And no helicopters were in sight.

The gunfire seemed to be growing nearer.

Loomis moved to the radioman, knelt, and put through a
call to Bedoya. "We're here," he said. "Where are the fucking birds?"

"On the way, Captain," Bedoya said. "Sorry we're late.
We've had some complications. Nothing serious. Just a small
war."

Loomis had suspected that Ramón's attempt to kidnap or
kill the De la Torre family might be a part of a bigger plan.
But he hadn't allowed his mind to dwell on it.

"The *palacio?*" he asked.

That, as his responsibility, was his first concern.

"Safe so far," Bedoya said. "We've only had terrorist stuff,
but plenty of that. Sniping all over town, and satchel bombs.
Some kind of plastic, C4, maybe. One at the main gate of the
palacio. Another at the Palacio de la Policía. Two at armed
forces headquarters. And another here and there. We've got
about fifty dead and twice that many injured, probably."

"No solid fighting anywhere?"

"Not in the *distrito*, unless snipers are trying to control
some sections. But we've had reports of pitched battles in San
Francisco de Macoris, and some activity in Santiago. Everything's still sketchy."

"Escortia have help on the way here by road?"

"If they don't run into anything, they'll be there within three hours. Escortia's afraid of a trap—an ambush or mines. He has told them to take it slow and careful."

The sounds of battle were definitely much closer. Loomis could see Rodríguez and his men retreating toward him through the trees.

"We can't hold out here much longer," Loomis told Bedoya. "The gunships might make the difference."

"We should have you in sight within two or three minutes," Bedoya said. "There's only two of us. We lost one gunship right after takeoff—clogged fuel lines, probably sabotage. But the pickup bird and this gunship seem all right."

"What about the ammo?"

"Right here," Bedoya said. "I see something—smoke—up ahead. I think we're coming up on you."

Loomis saw them before he heard them. They approached rapidly, low over the distant trees.

"We're in the shallow ravine at one o'clock relative," Loomis told Bedoya. "Take your gunship and hose down the area seventy meters or so beyond that big dead tree. Might make your trip worthwhile."

"O.K., Captain," Bedoya said.

The copters chattered over, so low they raised dust. The pickup bird banked back to assess the landing zone, hovering. Bedoya's big Huey opened up, pouring .50-caliber machine gun bullets into the trees, the gunners walking the fire streams with tracers.

Rodríguez and his men took advantage of the barrage and fell back once more, hunting better cover. Rodríguez came toward Loomis, running low, limping. His right leg was bathed in red from thigh to ankle. He sprawled beside Loomis. The stench of cordite hung heavy in the air.

"They flanked us," he said. "Hit us good with Claymores. I've only got about thirty men left."

Loomis watched the gunship as it swung in close to the target area. He knew the Huey's heavy firepower would be devastating at such short range. He called to the bird hovering over the landing zone, telling the pilot to come in for the pickup. "Get ready!" he yelled to the De la Torre family.

He turned to Rodríguez and shouted over the clatter of the rotor blades and the roar of the machine guns. "I've got to go in with the family," he said.

Rodríguez looked at him and said nothing. Loomis wanted to explain. The De la Torres were his responsibility. If the bird were crippled on takeoff, went down in the forest, or if the *palacio* grounds were under fire on landing, he *had* to be there.

"I'll be back as soon as I can, with as much help as I can round up," he promised.

They both knew that Loomis was talking in terms of more than an hour's trip.

"Good luck," Loomis said.

Afterward, Loomis sought to remember the subtle inflections in Rodríguez's tone: if there were hidden barbs in his reply, Loomis didn't detect them. But he always wondered.

"Y buena suerte a ti, también, compañero," he said.

As the helicopter touched down, Loomis picked up the boy Fredrico, urged the rest of the De la Torres to their feet, and led them as they ran for the bird. Raul carried Nina, and De la Torre had his arms around Juana, who was screaming, holding back, frozen with fear.

They were halfway to the Huey when their eardrums were assaulted by a terrific explosion. Loomis dropped to one knee, still holding the boy, and turned to see a huge ball of orange flame where the gunship had been. It plunged to earth with an awesome roar.

"Bedoya!" Loomis yelled, rising to his feet to run toward the wreckage.

But there was no way anyone could have lived through that explosion. He watched helplessly as the burning remains of the gunship settled into the trees.

The bazooka. Some persistent idiot had lugged that tube and projectiles all the way from the highway for one fantastic, lucky shot.

Or had it been lucky? Could he do it again? At slightly longer range, but with a more stable target?

"Into the chopper, quick!" Loomis yelled.

As he ran for the bird, he tried to remember the time required to reload and fire a bazooka. Not long, he recalled.

He literally tossed the boy to a crewman, then turned to help De la Torre with Juana, now screaming and fighting in earnest. A waist gunner grabbed her wrists and she was lifted into the ship.

Loomis could hear Rodríguez and his men expending precious ammo in a sustained fire to keep the bazooka man's head down. But he also heard bullets hitting the Huey as Ramón's rebels concentrated their fire on the bird. Raul, María Elena, and the maid scrambled aboard, aided by crewmen. Loomis dived into the chopper, landing on his stomach.

"Pull pitch!" he yelled at the pilot. "Lift!"

The pilot needed no further urging. The De la Torre women screamed, not from the constant slap of bullets hitting the ship, but from the express elevator takeoff and the stomach-freezing tilt as the pilot swung away over the trees.

Loomis checked to make certain no one was hurt and that there was no serious damage to the Huey. He then took a headset and reported the loss of the gunship. He gave instructions for preparation of a relief force.

But as he suspected, the effort was futile.

By the time he returned to the clearing with help, Rodríguez and his men were dead. And Ramón's rebels had simply vanished.

Loomis found Rodríguez's bullet-riddled, decapitated body beneath a tree. His machine pistol was empty, as were his bandoliers. Bedoya's body was burned beyond recognition.

It was then that Loomis began remembering Rodríguez's words which, literally translated, said, "And good luck to you, too, Old Buddy." And he began to wonder how Rodríguez meant that.

Loomis knew that his decision to go with the family had been right.

But the knowledge didn't help at all.

Chapter 8

MINUS 9 DAYS, 23:57 HOURS

President Robertson first learned of the outbreak of revolution in the Dominican Republic from his regular morning situationer delivered by State. The report was brief, almost hidden amidst the lengthy accounts of the latest developments in the Middle East, Asia, and the new hot spot, the Bering Strait. The news from the Dominican Republic obviously was based on confused, incomplete data. Before leaving his 10:00 A.M. breakfast, Robertson summoned an aide and requested that all information on the revolt be fed to him minute by minute, as it arrived at State.

By 11:00 A.M., enough information was in hand to define Administration policy. Although the morning papers had carried little more than bare bulletins on the revolt, the early afternoon editions contained far more extensive stories, inspired by accounts of the narrow escape of the De la Torre family. Most front pages carried photographs of María Elena de la Torre, gleaned from their files.

Robertson assumed that with this dramatic aspect to what would seem to be a routine revolution, the matter of United States policy would arise at his 1:00 P.M. news conference. He was not mistaken. He was prepared.

The situation in the Dominican Republic was being watched carefully, Robertson told the press in the serious, thoughtful manner that had become so much a part of his political image. No, he did not at this time anticipate United States intervention. If the Dominican authorities should ask for aid, and if the lives of United States citizens and other nationals should be adjudged in danger, then of course a new evaluation of the situation would be made. But he wanted to stress most strongly that the best information available was that the administration in the Dominican Republic was in control of the situation, and he had complete confidence that the authorities there would do their utmost to protect the lives and interests of United States citizens.

He fielded a carefully loaded question from the *Washington Post:* No, he saw no reason to attempt to draw parallels between the present situation in the Dominican Republic and any prior situation that had instigated United States occupation. Those interventions were for the judgment of history. Not being in full command of the information that had led to those actions, he would not make second guesses as to whether there had been sufficient provocation. He was concerned only with the present situation.

He even managed to end the issue in a light vein—another technique that fast was becoming his trademark. He shifted to his droll, wrinkled, deadpan manner and offhand tone of voice. He was happy, he said, that the De la Torre family was safe, for he long had been a great admirer of María Elena— for her acting, not her politics, he added in mock haste. He thought hers the best interpretation of Joan of Arc he'd ever seen. And, he reminded the reporters, he was old enough to remember Wallace Reid and Geraldine Farrar in the silent version.

In the polite, indulgent response, Robertson managed to turn attention to a safe, planted question.

But his aides, by necessity perceptive of such things, noticed that there was no levity in Robertson's mood as he emerged from the press conference. He secluded himself in his hideaway office and placed six phone calls to his most select confidential advisers, allocating twenty minutes for each call.

He was still on the phone when the men from Langley arrived. His appointments secretary knew better than to interrupt, but he also frequently and emphatically had been made aware of Robertson's penchant for promptness. So he sent a memo in by the President's personal secretary, reminding him of the appointment. The reply came back scrawled across the bottom of the memo: "Keep them waiting. Urgent I see them. Will be over in a few minutes."

There was a belief, prevalent among the President's aides, that his walk often conveyed his state of mind. While pondering an issue, he often walked with head lowered, his steps methodical and plodding. Those who saw him cross the drive from the Executive Office Building to the White House that Wednesday afternoon were certain that Robertson was in the throes of indecision on some matter.

He met the men from Langley with a curt, almost distracted nod. He waited until they were seated in the Oval Office and he had a fresh cigar going before he broached the question.

"State thinks El Jefe can hold out. What do you people say?"

Wallaby glanced briefly at his Deputy before replying, a habit that was beginning to irritate Robertson. "As you know, sir, Loomis rolled up our operations there some time ago," the Director said. "So we don't have a wide base on which to make an assessment. But Johnson is an experienced man, and he has been on the scene four days now. He believes El Jefe will retain control through the next few days, at least."

"How will the fighting affect our problem?"

"Obviously, it complicates things," Wallaby said. "But it might be a blessing in disguise. It would provide the cover for intervention which, sir, we recommend most strongly."

Robertson wasn't surprised. He had his own sources at Langley. And he knew the past histories of the agency and its role in interventions. He had known what Wallaby wanted. And the President knew his response might be the biggest decision of his administration.

"What are your reasons?" he asked quietly.

"It would give us a handle on the situation," Wallaby pointed out. "We would gain control—if not the entire cooperation—of El Jefe, and of Loomis."

"But under duress," Robertson said. "Do you think that would be wise?"

Wallaby's mouth opened in surprise. "But—I thought that in your news conference you carefully left the door open for intervention."

"I didn't close the door. But I didn't open it in the first place," Robertson said. "I'm not eager to have my administration remembered for another Bay of Pigs, another Vietnam. And I might add that I'm fully aware of the role of the CIA in past administrations. In my view, Kennedy and Johnson both received highly inaccurate estimates of crucial situations. I must warn you now. I will not allow my administration to be influenced by such tactics."

Wallaby's face slowly flushed beet red. He made a move to rise from his chair. Robertson could see the muscles in his jaw working as he fought for control. "Mr. President," he said. "May I respectfully remind you that *no* administration in history has been faced with a problem of such dangerous ramifications."

"All the more reason we should handle this thing in the right way," Robertson said evenly. "Don't get your hackles up. I'm not blaming you for past mistakes made by others. But you're running the same outfit over there that made those mistakes. You've got to be aware of it. I've got to be aware of it." He paused for a moment, stoking his cigar. The more he thought about the matter, the more firmly convinced he became that his first instincts were right. He tried to put them into words. "As I see it, intervention would probably create new problems, not solve the one we've got. Why not deal direct, and in a straightforward way, with the Dominican government? We might see where that gets us."

"Loomis wouldn't cooperate with us," Wallaby predicted. "He'd want to retain full control down there."

Everything kept coming back to Loomis—the unknown factor. "What exactly did Loomis say?" Robertson asked.

"Mostly, that he was too busy with the new revolution to come to Washington for the briefing. 'To play grabass,' was his exact terminology, I believe."

"Well, I can understand that," Robertson said. "He doesn't know our problem." He considered the matter for a moment. "Does Loomis work well with Johnson?"

Wallaby glanced at Ogden, signaling him to field that one.

Ogden stared at the bowl of his pipe and took his own sweet time about answering. "They used to be inseparable," he said. "They were one of our best teams. If we assigned one to a mission, the other would find some way to bring himself in on it. Then they had an ideological falling out over the operation in Laos. We even took the precaution of sending Johnson to head the station in Beirut before we dismissed Loomis. We were concerned that Johnson might learn of the extreme prejudice situation and attempt to stop it."

Robertson studied Ogden. He was developing a genuine dislike for the smug little bastard. Why couldn't he answer a question straight out and in fewer words? "Then they are close friends?"

"I wouldn't say that, sir."

"Then what *would* you say, presuming that someone really wanted to know the answer to that question?" Robertson demanded.

Ogden smiled easily. "Well, the truth is that a fist fight they had over the Laos operation was one of the factors that strongly influenced our decision to eliminate Loomis. He broke Johnson's nose and jaw. That made it much easier for us to get Johnson out of the way and off to Beirut. I don't think they have communicated with each other since, not until this operation. In summing up, I would say they retain a healthy respect for each other's talents. But they are no longer close friends."

"What was the fight over?"

Ogden hesitated, and glanced at the Director, who gave a slight shrug.

"It was just one of those things," Ogden said. "We needed some information in a hurry. We had some prisoners—a half-dozen Pathet Lao—who had the information. Loomis, at some point in his career, had received helicopter training and became very adept. He and Johnson simply took an interpreter and the prisoners up several thousand feet— bound hand and foot, by an open door. When the first man refused to answer, Johnson kicked him out. By the time he got to the third man, we had all the information we needed. Loomis apparently hadn't intended to go to that extreme."

"My God," Robertson said.

And Johnson was still on the payroll.

Ogden seemed to sense Robertson's thoughts. With raised eyebrows, he spoke in a tone that struck Robertson as a bit haughty. "I would estimate that Johnson saved at least two hundred American soldiers, and maybe more, by sacrificing only two of the enemy," he said.

"Of course," Robertson said wryly. "A nasty war. And Loomis objected?"

"Later, while drinking, they started a discussion of the incident. And one thing led to another."

Robertson had heard nothing that altered his view of the matter. Yet, he felt he should give the men from Langley one last opportunity. "Do you people have any serious objections to giving Johnson the authorization to apprise Loomis of the full situation?"

"Yes, I object most emphatically," Wallaby said. "Loomis would not cooperate with us. He'd want to retain total control of the operation."

Robertson sighed. "Mr. Director, I'd trade with the Devil himself on this if I thought it'd do any good. Right now, it looks like we're stuck with Loomis. And maybe he's the man we *need* to run this operation. Frankly, from what I've heard about the man so far, I like his style."

"May I remind you, sir, that Loomis is not covered by the Secrets Act," Wallaby said. "We don't know what he'll do, what sort of compromising situation he might put us into."

Robertson snorted in disbelief. "My God, Wallaby. Doesn't that strike you as a trifle absurd? Here we have a man you've twice attempted to kill. We have two old murder charges against him we can't possibly prosecute. He has served, is bearing arms for foreign governments, and has lost all rights of American citizenship. But now we need him. And you're worried about his security clearance."

"There's one other possibility," Ogden said quietly.

"What?"

"Renew the contract on Loomis. With him out of the way, we could move into Santo Domingo in force with a clandestine operation to handle the matter."

"I suppose we should keep that option open," Robertson said. "But at the moment, it seems to me we can work better with Loomis than without him."

"I still recommend intervention," Wallaby insisted. "With marines in Santo Domingo, and the navy offshore, we would be able to do whatever we want."

"Again, I suppose we should keep that as an option," Robertson said. "But I have polled my advisers on this, and I concur with their judgment. We must try for cooperation. Please instruct Johnson to inform Loomis of the full situation."

Wallaby hesitated. "Mr. President, if this ever becomes a public issue, I will be forced to reveal that I protested most vigorously."

Robertson clamped his cigar in his teeth and stared Wallaby down. "That's your prerogative, Mr. Director," he said. "And it's mine to make the decisions."

Chapter 9

After two nights of fighting, El Jefe's generals were congratulating themselves, confident that they had defeated Ramón thoroughly in his first efforts. Loomis thought otherwise. He granted that by day Santo Domingo remained deceptively normal. Unless one happened to notice the number of army vehicles at the major intersections, the dramatic decline in the number of tourists on the streets, and a subtle, apprehensive air throughout the city, he might not know that he was in the midst of a revolution.

But at night the streets became another world, inhabited for the most part only by soldiers, policemen, snipers, and elusive terrorists armed with explosives. El Jefe and his generals put into effect a plan for "safe corridors" along El Conde east and west, and along Duarte north and south. These corridors were heavily defended day and night. Consequently most of the sniping and hit-and-run battles took place along them. More than two dozen soldiers or *policía nacional* were killed each night, along with a few unlucky civilians who happened to get in the way. The hospitals were swamped with wounded.

The generals insisted that Ramón had failed in his primary objectives—the kidnaping or killing of the De la Torre family and the establishment of a foothold in Santo Domingo. Although Ramón held essential areas in the northern provinces, they believed that the revolution had entered a stage of stalemate that in time would defeat Ramón, who had fewer resources.

Loomis offered a different assessment. He argued that despite the setback with the De la Torre family, Ramón had succeeded in his basic objectives. The family's narrow escape brought worldwide attention to Ramón's revolution. He held vital regions and warehouses in the nation's breadbasket. Loomis argued that the stalemate would benefit Ramón, not the regime.

He pointed out the factors in Ramón's favor: the more military pressure Ramón forced the administration to apply in the streets, the more resentment and resistance would be created among the people. Overnight, most tourists had fled Santo Domingo, inspired by a satchel bomb in the lobby of the Hotel Embajador. Two tourists and four hotel employees had been killed. There now were few new arrivals. The quick-divorce flights from New York had been suspended. The country simply could not endure the economic loss indefinitely. Loomis had intercepted messages to Ramón from several leftist countries pledging recognition and support for the revolutionary government when the proper moment arrived. And, if further proof were needed, there was the testimony of the few rebels captured. All insisted they were held back from fighting in the capital by Ramón's standing orders. This information made sense to Loomis. Ramón didn't want his followers to dash into the streets to die foolish deaths. His plan clearly called for control in the north and strong pressure against the capital, never allowing a night to pass without a carefully measured battle or two, and at least one devastating explosion in a place considered well protected.

Harassment was Ramón's game, Loomis argued. And Ramón was winning. His losses were negligible, and his forces were growing daily while morale among the government troops was dropping.

El Jefe listened to Loomis, but he found the argument of his generals more convincing. He boiled down his doubts to one question: "If Ramón's so strong, why doesn't he come out and fight?"

Loomis repeated his belief that Ramón was gathering his strength until the right time.

El Jefe couldn't accept the theory. He only knew of one way to run a revolution. His way.

"If he is certain of winning, now is the time for him to

strike," he said. "He'd win more troops over by doing it. He *already* has more than I did when I started. If he'd declare himself, take a stand, they'd fall out of the trees, spring up out of the ground. No. Inaction kills revolutions. Ramón is too inactive."

Loomis gave up on the argument. He was confident that developments soon would prove him right.

María Elena continued to ignore Loomis's existence, a fact he found unsettling.

On the morning after the rescue, the *palacio* was besieged by more than a score of reporters who had flown in overnight to cover the revolution. They wanted to interview María Elena. She refused to see them. At El Jefe's request, Loomis went to the De la Torre quarters that afternoon to urge María Elena to cooperate. El Jefe wished to prove to the world that María Elena was safe and that she was an honored *palacio* guest, not a political prisoner thrown into some dungeon.

Loomis talked to her briefly in a small parlor in the family quarters. She came into the room pale, distraught, obviously still shaken from the battle of a few hours before. Yet she faced Loomis with the same defiance she had shown in Santiago. She did not sit or offer Loomis a chair. "I see no need to discuss the matter," she said. "I haven't talked to the press in two years. There's no reason to do so now."

Her delicate, soft features made her seem vulnerable, belying her firm stance and strong words. Loomis had an almost overwhelming impulse to put his arms around her, to give her whatever assurance he could. He was irritated by the inclination. He told himself that he was only intrigued and fascinated by the mystery of her. He knew, perhaps better than anyone, that impulses arising from the emotions are dangerous and that affairs of the heart are the worst kind. Surely, he had learned that lesson by now.

"El Jefe places no restrictions on you," he said. "You can tell them anything you want."

Her eyes blazed up at him in anger. *"What* could I tell

them? That I'm a political prisoner? Held here against my will? No, thank you. I won't give Ramón that satisfaction, even if it's what my uncle deserves."

"El Jefe has only your best interests at heart," he told her.

"He had no right to bring us here," she said. "We were perfectly safe in Santiago."

Loomis spoke with some heat of his own. "You were safe in Santiago only because your uncle kept you and your whole family under discreet but close surveillance. Three companies of troops were assigned to guard you. That was their sole duty. They were in constant radio contact, literally around the corner. Believe me, lady, there are plenty of reasons for El Jefe to be concerned for your safety. And may I remind you that a lot of good men died last night because of those reasons."

Her eyes wavered for the first time. Loomis saw her hands tremble and instantly regretted he had been so blunt.

"Well, anyway, I will not talk to the reporters," she said.

Loomis made one last effort. "It would only take a minute," he said. "They are just men doing their job."

She gave him one final, scornful look. "There are already too many people around here operating on that philosophy," she said. She turned and walked out of the room.

Loomis faced the reporters alone. He described the night's assault, placing heavy importance on the heroic delaying tactics of Rodríguez and his men and on Bedoya and the men in the gunship.

That evening, he dressed as usual and went down to dinner. El Jefe seldom left the *palacio,* and his social life centered around quiet evenings with small gatherings invited in for drinks, dinner, and a movie. The guest lists varied—senators and ambassadors, newspaper publishers and plantation owners, his generals and advisers, and, always, their wives. El Jefe had made plain to the *palacio* staff that Loomis held a standing invitation. Loomis only had to advise the social secretary each day of his intentions. He usually accepted. The food was better than most available elsewhere in the country. And he liked the company, most of the time.

Loomis also enjoyed the dinners in that they revealed a side of El Jefe he otherwise wouldn't have known existed. The old warrior apparently was starved for feminine attentions. There were stories that when El Jefe's wife died young, he had grieved for years and vowed never to remarry. In his quiet, genteel attitude toward the women, El Jefe showed a debonair, suave self that seldom surfaced in other surroundings.

By the time Loomis entered the lounge, a dozen or more guests had arrived. He nodded greetings to a general and his wife, to an industrialist and his daughter, and moved toward the bar. Drink in hand, he turned to find María Elena de la Torre staring at him. She was standing alone in a corner of the room. Her gaze dropped to his shoes, then slowly and frankly sized him up, conveying as clearly as spoken words her shock and disbelief that he would dare to be in dinner jacket, presuming to mix with civilized people as an equal.

Then she pointedly turned away.

Throughout the cocktail hour, Loomis couldn't keep from stealing glances in her direction. She was wearing an understated black sheath, V-necked, with a white linen jacket. Her long dark hair was loose. An ivory cameo necklace was the only trace of jewelry. Loomis was convinced he had never seen a lovelier woman in his life.

At dinner he was seated next to a senator's wife, the daughter of a prominent Dominican family. Educated in Europe, she was extremely well read. Loomis had discussed books with her many times, so they naturally fell into a lively comparison of the relative value of Russian and American authors. Loomis was expounding his theory that Russian writers, from Dostoevsky to Solzhenitsyn, had profited artistically from their harsher experiences—intellectual rebellion, revolution and warfare, arrest, penal servitude, and their eventual return, older and infinitely wiser, to a troubled society. In mid-sentence he looked up and caught María Elena watching him intently. She quickly looked away. Yet Loomis sensed that she continued to listen to the conversation.

The disturbing eye duel persisted through dinner. Loomis would feel her gaze on him. But when he turned casually in her direction, she would be looking elsewhere. By the end of the evening, concluded with the screening of a French comedy, Loomis was hardly aware of anything other than María Elena. After the guests left, and as the De la Torres walked toward their quarters, María Elena paused in the doorway and gave him one last, lingering glance. Loomis could read no meaning on her face.

He found the whole evening disconcerting.

The next night, annoyed with himself over his foolish eagerness, he went down early for cocktails. After taking a drink from the bar, he turned and walked straight across the room to María Elena, who regarded his approach without a sign of expression.

"I'm sorry, but I live here, too," he said. "You'll just have to put up with seeing me around."

He was rewarded with the barest hint of a smile. "You seem absolutely naked without your guns," she said. "And I've been wondering where you learned to read. I thought you more of the simian type."

"I'm full of surprises," Loomis said. "You really haven't seen any of them yet."

Her eyebrows lifted in mock surprise. "A film critic, a gunman, and an authority on world literature. What next?"

"I play a mean game of tennis. You care to try me?"

"How do you know I play tennis at all?"

"I told you I was full of surprises."

"My security file," she guessed, accurately. She seemed disturbed by the thought. "What else is in there?"

"You're full of surprises, too," he said.

She laughed, then. A rich, throaty laugh that struck Loomis as pure music.

"You should laugh more," he said. "It does things to your eyes."

"Political prisoners don't laugh much," she said.

He gestured with his drink to their surroundings, the huge crystal chandeliers, heavily framed oil paintings, the wide brocade draperies, marbled floors, and elegantly gowned and jeweled women. "You'll have to admit that this beats those Nazi ovens."

She made a face. "As long as I'm penned up, I'd just as soon be on bread and water. Two days in this place, and I'm already half crazy."

"Crazy enough to play tennis with me?"

She laughed again. "All right," she said. "When?"

"Morning is best. The *palacio* courts are in shade. Eight o'clock?"

"Eight o'clock," she said.

El Jefe led the way into the dining room. María Elena was seated to Loomis's left. She remained strangely quiet through the early portion of the dinner. Across the table, De la Torre, his wife, and Raul also seemed subdued. From the strained atmosphere, Loomis assumed that a confrontation had occurred between El Jefe and the family over their enforced residence.

El Jefe seemed to be making an effort toward amends. He was especially attentive to Juana and María Elena, recommending certain dishes, making sure their every need was met.

The conversation centered around El Jefe at the head of the table, ranging from the latest American and Italian films to the sad way tourists were ruining the best places in Spain and the south of France. News of the destruction of an airliner by terrorists in the Middle East was discussed, leading El Jefe to turn the topic of conversation to Dominican politics —usually a taboo subject at *palacio* dinners.

"I don't know the solution to this terrorism," he said. "There's only small consolation in the fact that we are not the only country in the world having such difficulties. I must confess that I don't understand what is in the terrorist's mind. I simply don't know how to deal with him."

He paused, and directed his attention to María Elena. "It has occurred to me that I haven't asked the opinion of the one person present who is an authority on the subject. As some of you may know, María Elena wrote her doctoral dissertation on the Tupamaros—lived with them, went along on missions with them."

A murmur of surprise swept the table. Loomis wondered how María Elena's affiliation with the Tupamaros had been kept so secret. Although there was considerable information in his files—including a terrific picture of her in jungle fatigues and crossed bandoliers—her career in South America hadn't been discovered by the press.

El Jefe seemed to enjoy the reaction. "Perhaps you could tell me, María Elena. What is in the terrorist's mind?"

María Elena considered her answer carefully. "I think the most difficult thing to understand is that the terrorist is a person driven to the most extreme desperation by what he considers oppression, political, spiritual, poverty, or whatever. His setting becomes a world unto itself—a world that feeds on itself to the point that all logic is lost. The illogical becomes logical. He and his group become convinced—convince themselves—that if enough innocent people are endangered, killed, the government will accede to their demands and that the general population will applaud the result. The terrorist may be crazy, to our way of thinking, but he has his own logic."

El Jefe nodded slowly, thinking. He seemed genuinely impressed with María Elena's answer.

"If you were in my place," he said, "how would you deal with him?"

María Elena didn't hesitate. She spoke with an intensity that went beyond the best of her screen roles. "I would disarm him by removing his oppression. I would restore constitutional guarantees. I would hold free elections. I would improve his wages so that each year he could see that he is better off than the year before."

"A very heavy order," El Jefe said.

"You promised those things when you took office," María Elena pointed out. "And you haven't delivered them. That fact is what sends your terrorist into the streets."

A tenseness had settled over the table. The food was forgotten. The moment hung on El Jefe's reaction.

He slowly shook his head. "María Elena, you are so young. There are so many things that are not in your books. In my youth, there was not the slightest feeling of national unity in this country. Now, at least, we have that. We *have* made progress. But *which* constitution would you restore? There have been thirty-nine—an unholy mess from the standpoint of attempting to establish traditional law. And how can you conduct elections when fifty percent of the population is illiterate? When there are more than seventy political parties and splinter factions?"

He paused. "No, I haven't called free elections. There would be chaos. You are looking at the only stability this country has at the moment, and I must recognize that fact. I *must* take strong measures. I have no choice."

There was a gentleness, almost a pleading quality, in El Jefe's tone. But María Elena was not swayed by his argument.

"Don't you see?" she demanded. "Those repressions were the very thing *you* opposed when you made your revolution. The issues remain. If you continue to use Trujillo's methods, then to the terrorist in the streets, your government is identical with Trujillo's."

"María Elena!" De la Torre said.

El Jefe waved a hand. "It's all right, Manuel. María Elena has a valid point, and the courage to make it." He turned back to María Elena. "*Vida,* I hated Trujillo with my every breath. I can never forgive him his excesses. My friends died, many of torture, in La Cuaranta. I apologize to my dinner guests for bringing up this topic. But I must admit, María Elena, I understand Trujillo better every day."

"He knew how to govern," Maria Elena said, repeating the popular street joke.

El Jefe refused to be baited. "Yes, Trujillo knew how to govern. He was very, very good at what he wanted to do. But he was not benevolent. And that is my problem. How *can* one be benevolent? How would you hold elections with ignorant, illiterate voters who haven't the slightest inkling of the issues?"

"You could set up literacy programs."

"And how are you going to educate a man who earns less than a peso a day in the cane fields—and who needs that peso to live?"

"You could set up adult schools, and rotate the workers."

"If one-fourth of the workers are in school, the Gross National Product, already one of the lowest in this hemisphere, would drop by twenty-five percent."

"Night classes, then."

"How is a man going to study after spending fourteen hours in the cane fields or in a factory?"

"He could be inspired into doing it."

"Now you have come to the core of the matter," El Jefe said. "How can you give a man hope, when there is no hope for him in this life?"

"That's just my point," María Elena said. "You've underestimated people. Haven't you realized that this man who spent fourteen hours in the cane field, or in the factory, is your sniper, your terrorist with his explosive? That's why your men can't find Ramón's army. It's all around you. Your men pass his soldiers on the street every day, think of them as workers, and never recognize them as the enemy. That's why Ramón is winning. He offers them hope."

"You think Ramón is winning?"

"Please read my dissertation, Uncle. Today's guerrillas are far more dangerous than the full-time fighters of your day. They strike and melt back into their environment. Perhaps not even their own families suspect. They subsist on your economy. The longer Ramón can survive, forcing you to repressive measures, the greater his strength."

El Jefe glanced at Loomis, who shrugged elaborately. María Elena turned to look at Loomis, puzzled.

"You sound exactly like my friend Loomis," El Jefe explained. "He has been upsetting my generals by telling them they are losing. That is his argument."

María Elena looked at Loomis. "Well, he's smarter than I thought," she said.

After dinner, the other guests followed El Jefe into the theater for the screening of a new Italian film. María Elena seemed upset, so Loomis proposed a drink on the terrace. She accepted.

They sat in the moonlight and talked until long after the film was over, the guests had left, and the other *palacio* residents had gone up to bed. Under María Elena's persistent questioning, Loomis revealed a bare outline of his life. She seemed intrigued. "Talk about an odyssey!" she said. "What are you hunting for?"

"If I knew, maybe I would find it," he said.

"Maybe you ought to sit still for a while and see if you can figure it out," she said. "And I thought I'd racked up some mileage! You make all my knocking around sound like nothing."

"What are *you* searching for?" Loomis asked.

"You ought to know," she said. "You have my files."

"They only have facts," he explained. "They don't tell why."

"Then your files are worthless," she said. "The 'why' is the important part."

When they at last went to their rooms, María Elena hesitated at the door. "I've enjoyed it, Loomis," she said. "I haven't talked like that in a long time."

"I thought I did all the talking," he said. "I still know almost nothing about you."

"Maybe there's not much to know."

"That *would* surprise me," he said.

She laughed and looked up at him. "Well, let's not rush it, Loomis. Things are complicated enough as it is." She squeezed his hand and went in, leaving him with a vague sense of a promise unfulfilled.

Loomis lay awake for a time, torn between logic and his emotions. He had made his decision years ago: no more entanglements. He now wondered if he would be able to live up to that decision.

María Elena's files were accurate in one respect: she was an excellent tennis player. Loomis had a big advantage with his reach, yet he lost the first two sets before rallying on the third. María Elena's small build gave her a quickness Loomis couldn't match. They quit after an hour because of the heat.

María Elena watched Loomis towel off.

"My God, Loomis, you're big as a house," she said. "How much do you weigh?"

"Too much," he said.

"Well, you get it around all right," she said. "Maybe it's not all blubber."

That evening, El Jefe served a new Alsace white wine that was a resounding success and lent a special glow to dinner. When the guests went in to view the film, Loomis and María Elena again headed for the terrace. Almost without his prompting, she began telling about her life.

"I don't think anyone who hasn't been through it could realize what it's like," she said. "You have to want, to need, success terribly to do all that's required to achieve it. Long hours of voice lessons, dance lessons, diction, dramatics. There isn't any harder work in the world. The discipline has to be unbelievable.

"Then when you start, you have to take shit off so many people, the little people that stand in the way. You work and drill. You hunt for the part that's got one good line, one good song that might make somebody, somewhere, sometime, remember you at the right moment.

"And you think that when you move up, things will be better. They're not. The further you go, the more false the world becomes around you, the more you have to depend on others. That's what happens to the real talent—the Marlon Brandos, the Montgomery Clifts, the James Deans. You have to battle every step of the way to hang onto what's you, and only those that put up a good fight survive. Most don't. I once heard a psychiatrist say that with most people, he could peel away the outer personalities like the layers of an onion, until he reached the core, the real personality, shorn of all superficialities. But he said that with actors you just peel away all the facade, all the layers, and you find nothing at the center. That's what happens to your Marilyn Monroes, your Judy Garlands, your Diana Barrymores. They are overwhelmed by the superficialities of their lives to the point they no longer know themselves, or what they're supposed to be. Some, Shirley MacLaine, Jane Fonda, Marlon Brando, me, start hunting for causes, something real, to find our way out of the falseness.

"I wish them luck. For me that was no answer. For a time, I thought it was. Join the Robin Hoods. Rob from the rich and give to the poor. What a crock of shit it all was. The guerrillas claim to be fighting for the rights of individuals, then tromp on everyone's lives. They rob, kidnap, kill, and call their crimes justified because they're done for the poor, the down-trodden. Well, I've seen the poor, and most of them aren't worth the effort. Move them into a mansion and you'll have a slum tomorrow. They don't know any better and are inca-pable of learning. They're lazy—maybe not physically lazy, but lazy in imagination, in planning, foresight. They'll trade their future for a bottle of wine and a good screw. I'm sorry for them, and I believe in making things available to them. But you can't force-feed them.

"Hollywood. Nothing can convey the falseness. There's no friendship you can trust, no contract that can't be broken. Egos. Greed. Backbiting. Maliciousness. I had to get out.

"And the academic world isn't much better. Totally out of contact with reality. They have their theories. That's all they can talk about, theories. But if they had to put them into practice they'd starve. They're wrapped up in their own little insular world, involved in their own petty politics. Who has the biggest office, the biggest desk? Who has first choice of graduate assistants? Who caught the dean's ear at what committee meeting? If the sun came up in the west some morning, most of the academic world wouldn't notice.

"I'm twenty-eight years old, and I've spent twenty of that hunting the real world, the real me. Maybe I found a certain reality in the beginning, in the sweat of hard work. But it got lost in all the falseness. And for the first time, I really became scared. I felt that what was me was being scattered to the four winds. And I know that when you lose yourself, you lose everything. I've seen it happen to too many people."

Loomis yielded to his long-harbored impulse and put his

arms around her. The warmth of her response was unexpected. They remained more than two hours on the terrace, exploring with kisses the depth of their mutual involvement, confirming with touch and word their mutual need.

At last, Loomis led her to his room. He put an album on the tape deck, and they made love to the light of distant magnesium flares being lofted near the Duarte Bridge, where the army was searching for a sniper.

Chapter 10

At 2:00 A.M., the phone rang. Loomis reached across María Elena and picked up the receiver. A phone call at that hour couldn't be ignored.

Johnson was on the line. "Loomis, I've got to see you. Now. Tonight." Loomis sensed desperation in Johnson's voice. He felt a twinge of alarm. Johnson wasn't prone to panic.

Loomis rolled over and lowered his feet to the floor. "This won't keep till morning?"

"Loomis, I'll level. This thing is four days overdue now. It's big. We've got to get on it."

"All right," Loomis said. "Give me thirty minutes."

"Where?"

Loomis didn't want to bring Johnson to the *palacio*. And Johnson obviously didn't want to meet in his room. Loomis tried to think of some place that would be open at 2:00 A.M. He could think of only one that was suitable. "Club Carioca," he said.

"That sounds like a nightclub," Johnson protested. "We need a quiet place."

"We'll find a quiet table," Loomis said. He promised to send a car; Johnson would need an escort through the streets.

"And Johnson . . ." he said.

"Yes?"

"This better be worth the trip."

"It will be," Johnson said. "That I can guarantee you."

Loomis borrowed El Jefe's Mercedes 450SL from the *palacio* stables and drove through the quiet, almost deserted streets to Club Carioca. He parked half a block away from the high wooden door, monitored the street for several minutes, then left the car, taking the Schmeisser with him.

Tony was behind the bar, his sleepy eyes monitoring, missing nothing. He watched Loomis approach without changing expression.

A quick survey told Loomis that this was not one of the Club Carioca's livelier nights. A dozen girls loafed by the bar. They glanced at Loomis, then away. He knew them all.

He walked to the bar and nodded to Tony. "I'll need a fifth of Jack Daniel's," he said. "A *norteamericano* is coming to see me. We need a quiet place to talk."

Tony grunted almost imperceptibly. He spoke quietly to a Chinese waiter. Loomis turned and crossed the heavy tile floor to a round table in the corner. He placed the Schmeisser against the wall behind him and sat, facing the bar so he could see its full length, the patio that extended out into the open air, and the walkways to the cribs that surrounded the patio on the other three sides.

Loomis had seen all of them worth seeing: the Grand Shima in Yokasuka, Paris's Pigalle, London's Soho, and the boys' towns along the United States-Mexico border. The Club Carioca was not without charms, as such places went. In the Trujillo era, the Generalissimo himself saw to it that the place was well supplied with fresh talent, it was said. Young girls, twelve to fourteen. At sixteen, they were veterans. By eighteen, they were ready to move to the lesser clubs, the streets, or to marry some young *hijo* who appreciated their talent and capabilities.

Now, the girls were mostly in their late teens; Trujillo's penchant wasn't a national affliction.

When Johnson entered, he seemed confused and uncertain. He stopped at the door. Loomis waved and Johnson came toward the table, looking back at the bar, still puzzled.

"What is this? A whorehouse?"

"That must be a prime factor in America's resounding success in world politics," Loomis said. "The perception of its intelligence officers."

"Come on, Loomis, knock off the shit," Johnson said. He turned to look at the stucco walls, the cane-bottom chairs, the bare wooden tables. "Is this place clean?"

"If you mean electronically, I'm certain it is," Loomis said. "If you're worried about the clap, I wouldn't guarantee anything."

"Look, Loomis, don't be a smart-ass. Frankly, you look pretty flabby to me. I think I could take you now. But there's a lot of stuff I have to unload on you, and it's serious. I can't emphasize how serious. Just bear with me. O.K.?"

"O.K.," Loomis said.

"If it's any satisfaction to you, your stupidity and bullheadedness have impressed everyone concerned. Your invitation to Washington for briefing has been canceled. I have been authorized to fill you in on the whole mess."

Johnson studied the bar and courtyard for a moment, then lowered his voice. "What I'm about to tell you is known to not more than two dozen people in Washington. My people had to go right to the top to get clearance for this talk. Do you understand what I'm saying? Right to the top."

Loomis nodded, feeling a tremor of apprehension. With all the events of the last few days, he'd almost managed to push from his mind a vague sense of foreboding over Johnson's earlier visit. Now, he knew that concern had been justified.

"Do you happen to know the story of Theodore B. Taylor?" Johnson asked.

Loomis shuffled through his mental file. "Never heard of him," he said.

"Few people have, outside the world of physics," Johnson said. "For some reason, Werner von Braun and a few others have received all the publicity. But Ted Taylor is a theoretical physicist who has been behind just about every major nuclear development during the last twenty years. Nuclear-powered space ships, if we ever have them, probably will be based on his designs. The nuclear warheads in our missiles, from the thirty-megaton jobs right down to cannon shells, are mostly his designs."

Johnson poured himself another shot of Jack Daniel's and sipped. Loomis waited.

"Ted Taylor is a remarkable fellow," Johnson said. "During

the last several years, he has literally scared the shit out of a few strategic people in Washington by pointing out a dangerous situation. An atomic bomb, or practically any nuclear weapon, is surprisingly easy to construct, if you're not especially concerned with maximum efficiency. Now, I don't mean that your average graduate student could go right into the business. But during the last ten years or so, enough information has been declassified that it's available for those interested enough to track it down."

Loomis felt a chill start at the base of his spine and move upward. He sensed what was coming.

"Your plain, garden-variety atomic bomb is rather simple," Johnson said. "It conceivably could be constructed by one man, working alone. There are many men in the world who probably could do it. Hundreds, perhaps thousands. There's no list. If there were, it probably wouldn't be complete. There's always your fifteen-year-old scientific genius to consider. Now, I don't mean a kid adept with Tinker Toys could do it. But you take an unusually bright one, he probably could."

"Since everyone else seems to know, you might tell me," Loomis said. "What exactly is involved?"

"A shaped charge. Three pounds of plastic explosive could serve as the trigger. Or an old navy gun. Up to now, the main problem has been the fission material, Uranium-235 and Plutonium-239, produced in expensive, complicated processes at Oak Ridge, Tennessee, and Hanford, Washington. But we've been turning out the stuff like crazy for thirty years. We've built atomic bombs, scrapped them, built atomic missiles and warheads of all descriptions, scrapped them for newer gadgets, then replaced those with thermonuclear devices. We've even lost a few of the damned things, as you may remember. And, with breeder nuclear power plants going into operation all over the world, making more of the stuff, there's plenty of nuclear material loose. It's not all weapons grade, but Ted Taylor says any physics student worth his salt could turn most of it into weapons-grade stuff with readily available materials. There's now enough uranium and plutonium in private hands to make several thousand atomic bombs. To put it bluntly, we no longer have control of the situation. Am I boring you?"

"I'm sweating the punch line," Loomis said.

"The punch line is that we know that someone has been buying up nuclear materials, presumably has devised the means of assembly, and the makings for one atomic device are on the way here to Santo Domingo."

"Oh shit," Loomis said. "Ramón?"

"We're not certain. But we don't think he's involved. We only know it's en route to this country. A Liberian tanker left Lisbon six days ago, bound for the docks here. The nuclear material was loaded from a fishing boat downstream from Lisbon on the Tagus, after the ship cleared the harbor channel. Nighttime operation."

"And all your people, with all your facilities, couldn't stop it?"

Johnson shrugged. "There were suggestions that the ship might simply disappear to become another tantalizing mystery of the Bermuda Triangle. But I assume there was too much risk of an international incident. Besides, we have a man aboard."

"What's the ETA?"

"Day after tomorrow, about noon, we believe. It's now a little more than four hundred miles out from your east coast. We have it under constant high-altitude surveillance."

"Mid-ocean rendezvous?"

"No way. Surveillance is around the clock."

"All right," Loomis said. "What do you want me to do?"

"Impound the ship and cargo. Find the goods. Rescue our man."

"Just like that."

"Just like that. We've made inquiries. You've got the clout."

Loomis thought ahead to the problems. "Assuming I'm able to impound another nation's ship, what'll I be looking for?"

"A half-dozen oil drums, probably. They'll look like a thou-

sand other oil drums on board. We understand there's a hold
somewhere on board for container cargo, and that they'll be
there. We're hoping they'll be marked in some way. We're
also hoping our man will have them located by the time the
ship arrives."

"Will a Geiger counter help?"

"We're told that's not positive. If the people know what
they're doing—and we'll have to assume that they do—
there'll be virtually no radiation."

"Just enough material for one bomb?"

"That's the word we have. Our best information is that
forty-nine kilos are aboard the tanker—intended for one
large bomb."

Loomis sighed. "Johnson, I think you better level with
me."

"What do you mean?"

"I can't work with you people until I know as much about
this as you do. And I have the strong feeling you know much,
much more than you're telling."

"Not a great deal more. We first got wind of it in Greece.
An anonymous tip. I'll spare you all the doubletalk details of
the trade—the 'an analysis based upon events substantiated
by a thorough investigation indicated that the information
probably was valid' sort of thing. The information was that
an international cartel is involved. They call themselves the
Hamlet Group. We managed to infiltrate a man into the
second or third level on the organizational chart. He ascertained that the information was accurate. But something
happened. As far as we know, he no longer exists."

"What kind of an international cartel? If your man infil-
trated, surely he came up with some names."

"He did. Two of the people he worked with are dead. The
others have disappeared. Maybe they're dead, too. All trails
have run out."

"Why Santo Domingo?"

"We don't know. Our information simply is that one device
will be detonated in Santo Domingo. You heard me. Detonated. Frankly, and I hope this doesn't hurt your feelings, the

consensus at Langley is that they don't give a shit about Santo Domingo, one way or another. It will just serve as a horrible example. Like the old bad joke about the farmer who hit his mule over the head with a club, just to get his attention. This group only wants to get our attention. At least one other bomb will be secreted in a major city in the United States. *After* the bomb is detonated here, certain demands will be made upon the United States."

"What demands?"

"We don't know. We have no idea who these Hamlet people are. So we have no idea what they want."

"But I still don't understand why they picked Santo Domingo."

"Oh, come on! You've got to admire the psychology of it. If an American city were hit first—San Francisco or New Orleans destroyed, for instance—the nation would react like a wounded animal, more in anger than in panic. Santo Domingo is physically close, well within our sphere of influence, yet emotionally remote. Reaction will be horror, panic, exactly what the Hamlet people want."

"Hamlet. Does that have any covert meaning?"

"Possibly. They may be trying to tell us something. Hamlet is the code name for the most efficient atomic bomb ever made. They may be indicating to us that they know the secret of Hamlet."

"God almighty," Loomis said.

"Precisely. I'm glad I've managed to impress you," Johnson said wryly. "May I inform my people you'll cooperate?"

Loomis sat for a moment, thinking. He had spent time as a merchant seaman; there were a million places on board a ship to hide contraband. The holds might have to be emptied. A tanker would pose special problems. The tanks could have false bottoms. Cutting torches couldn't be used until all fumes were removed. And that was a complicated procedure. Obviously, anyone with enough know-how to make an atomic bomb should be able to do a fair job of hiding the materials. With a small, Mickey Mouse security force, he was faced with an international organization undoubtedly far more sophisticated. He would need all the help he could get.

"I'll cooperate," Loomis said. "But on my terms."

Johnson grimaced. "And what are those?"

"We'll be far too busy here to deal with sixteen agencies in Washington. They can feed us their information. We'll keep them advised, but we'll initiate all procedures here."

"Just between us, I agree," Johnson said. "I'll pass it on with my recommendation that under the pressure of time, we accede to your unreasonable demands. For the record, consider that I have protested vigorously."

"And another thing. We don't want a planeload of Washington people coming in here every hour on the hour. We'll ask for specific help. In other words, they don't call us, we'll call them."

"Again, you're right, of course," Johnson said. "But frankly, I doubt they'll agree."

"If they give you any trouble, just ask them one question," Loomis said. "What the fuck they been doing for four days?"

"I hope you don't mind if I quote you verbatim."

"I hope you do."

"Actually, they *have* been working on it," Johnson said. "But all leads ran out."

"We could have used that time," Loomis fumed. "Now, we may not be able to do all we should."

"You have any ideas?"

Loomis nodded. "Possibly. Let me check on it, talk to El Jefe. I'll get back with you in the morning."

"I can't emphasize enough," Johnson said. "We've got to keep that ship under wraps."

"I assume you'd also like to keep this thing out of the General Assembly of the United Nations," Loomis said. "Which is where it'd wind up if we simply clamp the crew in irons."

"For whatever it's worth, the Russians are cooperating one hundred percent on this," Johnson said. "They're as worried as we are. All our defenses—all their defenses—are based on retaliation. Mutual wipeout. But a mobile, free-lance nuclear power, no matter how small, upsets things tremendously. If we don't know who they are, where they are, there's no way to retaliate."

"How heavy is this gear we're hunting?" Loomis asked.

"The nuclear materials, possibly a few hundred pounds, packing and all. Probably not much more than that. We suspect that the hardware, the mechanical parts, may be coming in by more conventional means. Also, of course, there will be some personnel coming in. How many, and from where, we don't know. But there's the possibility that if we set up a computer scan on all incoming people, Octopus might turn up something."

Octopus, Loomis knew, was one of the company's many elaborate computer systems. It contained complete information on dissident people throughout the world. Thousands upon thousands of complete dossiers, available for instant readout.

"How big a blast do your experts figure?" Loomis asked.

"Depends almost entirely on the bomb maker. If he really knows his stuff—and we have to assume he does—there is the definite possibility of something in the well into the kiloton range, about five times the size of Hiroshima. That's at the outside, they say. If he's a rank amateur, he may not be able to do much better than Hiroshima, a hundred thousand dead, maybe. Our people say blast effects are hard to figure because of wind direction, amount of fallout, other intangible factors. If the wind is blowing toward the Cibao and the heavily populated country to the north, and it's an especially dirty bomb, it could mess up the whole interior, too."

Loomis sat for a moment, fighting back his emotions, making his mind block out all personal feelings, forcing his attention to the problem at hand. It was a mental trick he'd learned long ago, and it saved him much anguish through the years.

"What's the target date?" he asked.

"That we don't know. We're working on it."

"And who are these Hamlet people? Come on! Level. You've got some leads, some suspicions."

"Only theories, at this point," Johnson said. "An international oil cartel connected with the Middle East situation is suspected. The international Mafia has been suggested. Dope traffic may be involved. It might be some nutty terrorist group that has acquired money, or some other group of a dozen or so rag-tag hippies. And, I don't know whether you know it or not, but there's been a highly placed group at work in the United States attempting to seize permanent political power so they can control the economy. There's even a theory this already has been accomplished. Certainly, they've made inroads. This may be their next step. And if you tell anyone I've told you all this, I'll renew your contract, personally."

"While we're talking off the record, let's clear the air on something else," Loomis said. "I assume that the only reason the United States didn't blow that tanker out of the water, and all the nuclear gear along with it, was because they lost all other leads to Hamlet, and to the other bomb."

"You're a fairly perceptive fellow," Johnson said. "Otherwise, I have no comment on that."

"They planned to destroy the tanker, then decided they couldn't afford to eliminate their one known link to the Hamlet people. *That* was the reason for the delay—while the decision was debated."

"Take the long view," Johnson said. "You've got to admit it makes sense. We'll seize the ship, grab the goods, and someone on board surely knows something." He glanced at his watch. "I've got to report in to Langley. You have any word to pass on to them?"

Loomis considered for a moment. His plan was only half-formed, but there wouldn't be much time.

"Tell them to get some extra men into Lisbon," Loomis said. "We may need help from the Lisbon station."

"You'll contact me in the morning?"

Loomis nodded. "We'll set up a safehouse first thing. I'll call in my people and we'll get to work."

After Johnson left, Loomis sat for a while at the table, sipping Jack Daniel's, thinking.

He then returned to the *palacio* and over the protests of the domestic staff awoke El Jefe from a sound sleep.

Chapter 11

Once each day, shortly before noon, Otto Zaloudek left his rooms in the Garden Suites and waddled down through the coconut trees to the porous rock overlooking the sea. For an hour he stood on the edge of the golf course, watching the waves break on the cliffs. Twice each day he walked laboriously through the arched passageways to the dining room, where for breakfast he usually ordered mangu, and for dinner lobster tails sautéed in anisette sauce. Only once did he come down to the Bar Piscina. He ordered one drink, a *cocoloco,* and sat for a time at the half-moon mahogany bar under a thick thatch of palm, watching the swimmers in the salt water pool. But his mind remained on other things. After a few minutes, he again returned to his room, leaving his drink untouched.

Zaloudek knew he posed an enigma to the hotel staff. Most of the guests who endured the seventy miles of dirt and washboard roads from Santo Domingo came for the famous Pete Dye golf course, swimming, and the Sadie Thompson atmosphere of Hotel La Romana. He was aware of the curiosity he created among the other guests. But he had no patience with the small talk he heard in the dining room or at the bar as they discussed the cloying sweetness from the sugar refinery across the road, planned their boat trips to Río Chavon, or stared through binoculars across the water to the flat profile of Isla Catalina.

All of each day, and most of the nights, he spent with his diagrams and pocket calculator, rechecking his figures, making certain that his design was the best possible under the circumstances.

He would have preferred to use plutonium. They had given him his choice, and plutonium presented the biggest challenge. But there would be obstacles in working with plutonium in the less than optimum conditions. Neither plutonium nor uranium presented significant radiation hazards. But plutonium was far more poisonous. One air-borne particle, lodged in a lung, could be fatal. Uranium contained no such dangers.

And there were certain design considerations. A plutonium device normally is detonated by a shield-shaped charge that turns the radiation back on itself to the point where the mass goes supercritical instantaneously. If the bomb is to achieve maximum yield, the shape of the charge must be perfect and the detonation uniform. Hours upon hours of delicate work would be required to assure uniform depth of the plastic explosive. Moreover, the pre-ignition balance in a homemade device would be hazardous—just below the edge of criticality. A solar flare, cosmic rays, radiation from any unexpected source such as radar, conceivably might push the balance over the margin to ignition. A slight miscalculation on the part of the designer might accomplish the same result.

At times, Zaloudek found himself wishing he had chosen plutonium. There would be greater yield—a larger fireball—with less material. He would be working with a mass the size of a baseball, instead of something on the order of a grapefruit. The machinery would be more complex, more sophisticated. Every artist likes to show his skill to the fullest, and Zaloudek was no exception. But each time he imagined himself painstakingly shaping the C_4 charge over an aluminum shield, carefully inserting wire to measure the uniform depth, only inches away from the mass of Pu_{239} hovering just below criticality, he broke into a cold sweat.

And logic told him there wasn't that much difference. Uranium could be brought to criticality by a device ridiculously simple by comparison. While there might be far less personal satisfaction in tinkering with such Model-T mechanics, there were the compensations of far more safety and dependability. He knew for certain that the device would work and that it would be more than adequate for its purpose. His design was far more advanced, and several times more effective, than that of the bomb that destroyed Hiroshima. If he only achieved a fraction of the design's potential—a "fizzle yield," as it was termed in the trade—the blast still would be well into the kiloton range.

The trick was to attain maximum yield, to bring the mass to supercriticality uniformly and at the same instant. He was confident he had the best possible means under the circumstances, incorporating some of the best features of Hamlet. Yet, he continued to check and recheck his figures, to make certain he had not made a mistake at any point in design.

Zaloudek by nature was cautious, plodding, painstaking. That was his overriding talent: he was methodical. Besides, there was nothing else to do to keep his mind occupied while he waited.

He had feared for a time that the project might be delayed by the revolution breaking out in the country. Although there was little evidence of the revolution at the Hotel La Romana, Zaloudek heard much excited talk among the other guests, and there were cancellations as some fled. But on the day after the outbreak of fighting, word was sent that despite possible complications, the project would be carried out. Zaloudek was to continue to wait.

There remained a few details that disturbed Zaloudek.

The first was the fact that no one, at any time, had asked for an estimate of effects. Zaloudek was clear in his own mind. Little Boy of Hiroshima produced a yield of thirteen kilotons and killed a hundred thousand people. He was certain that his own device would produce eight times that: a little more than one hundred thousand tons of TNT.

He had studied—and witnessed—nuclear weapons effects. There was one rule of thumb he had remembered: a nuclear explosion can vaporize its yield in mass. Zaloudek figured most of a square block in downtown Santo Domingo would simply vanish.

From that point, the effects became complicated. Gamma rays would spread death throughout the vicinity of ground zero; the exact distance would depend on the shadow effects of buildings. The visible light and heat would cook an even wider area. Neutrons would follow, dealing more destruction. Air shock waves, carrying lethal missiles, concrete blocks the size of automobiles traveling at the speed of a rifle bullet, would batter down all structures for more than a mile in each direction. Smaller shrapnel would reach for miles. The fallout, perhaps the most devastating of all, would rain radiation far inland. All these factors were very difficult to assess exactly, but Zaloudek could conceive of half a million dead, especially if the prevailing winds succeeded in carrying the fallout into the thickly populated Cibao to the north.

Yet, no one had asked for Zaloudek's estimate. The only request was for a fireball—and the bigger the better, they said.

Zaloudek couldn't understand their lack of interest in the carnage.

His Santo Domingo atomic bomb would be the greatest man-made disaster in all human history.

He had no inkling of what was in the minds of the Hamlet people. He suspected, but he didn't know.

But it didn't matter, for he was using them for his own purpose—which was more important, and would be more far-reaching.

Zaloudek had waited at the Hotel La Romana almost two weeks. On Saturday morning, just after dawn, the message at last arrived: a car would pick him up at noon Sunday for the next phase of the operation.

His wait was ended.

PART TWO

Chapter 12

MINUS 7 DAYS, 05:33 HOURS

For the first time since the revolution began, the sniping failed to end at daylight. If anything, the tempo increased. Shooting erupted at several points along El Conde and throughout the Old Town, with snipers firing brief bursts from balconies and rooftops, then disappearing before government troops could retaliate, only to pop up again and repeat the performance in other places. Grenades and plastic explosives were lobbed into the streets from windows and balconies by unseen terrorists.

Just before dawn, Colonel Escortia moved six French-made AMX-13 tanks into the business section, between El Conde Gate and the Tower of Homage, hoping to cut his losses. But the snipers were elusive. They were almost impossible to catch in the act. They went unarmed on the streets, to all appearances mere frightened civilians scurrying for safety. But once inside buildings, they raced upstairs to designated rooms. From beneath mattresses, secret panels, and carpet-covered trapdoors they took weapons and joined in the battle. When the return fire became too intense, they hid the weapons and fled down the stairs or over the rooftops, once again mere frightened civilians.

Immersed in his own problems, Loomis was only vaguely aware of the intensified fighting. He'd spent most of the night with El Jefe and the generals, mapping a plan of action. When they reached agreement on basic strategy, he went to the phone and made arrangements for a temporary headquarters, with tight security, and the various communication setups they would need.

An hour after dawn, he set out for the Hotel Embajador with a driver and the jeep. A soldier rode shotgun on the air-cooled Browning M1A6 machine gun.

The route out Avenida Bolívar took them within two blocks of the United States Embassy, and Loomis was relieved to see that all seemed quiet there. They heard sporadic firing from the vicinity of the university to the south as they passed. As they drove through the Botanic Gardens, Loomis swung his Schmeisser up, alert for an ambush, but the entire stretch seemed deserted. They made the trip without incident.

The lobby of the Embajador was jammed with newspapermen and television crews who had flown in from all over the western hemisphere. The Embajador by tradition served as press headquarters during Dominican revolutions. Most of the foreign correspondents were veterans. Many had covered Dominican revolts before. Some had requested their favorite rooms. All undoubtedly had done their homework, Loomis figured. He knew many from past wars—a few dating back to early Vietnam.

As Loomis entered, they swarmed across the lobby toward him.

"What's the situation, Loomis?" asked the man from the *Washington Post,* his voice rising above the din.

The group crowded around Loomis, blocking his way. Hand-held television lights flared, and he squinted against the glare. He slung his Schmeisser and held up his hands for silence. "Shut those fucking things off," he told the cameramen. The lights went out. The group stood quiet, expectant.

"You probably know as much as I do," Loomis told them.

"Bullshit," said the lady from the *New York Times.* "We happen to know you practically sleep with El Jefe."

Loomis looked at them for a moment, as if reluctant.

"All right," he said. "This is from 'a well-placed source within the administration,' or whatever cliché you people are using these days. Don't quote me direct. I'm just a fellow doing his job. I'm willing to let the locals have all the credit for their little wars."

He paused, making certain no pen had yet moved, that no camera or tape recorder was whirring.

"I talked with Colonel Escortia by phone a few minutes ago," he said. "I *can* give you some background information. So far, there's been no fighting in force here in the capital. It's still all hit-and-run. There's just more of it today. Most of the fighting has been in the old section, back over by the river. About fifty rebels were killed during the night. Government losses were about the same, with another forty or fifty wounded."

"What about civilians?" the *Washington Post* man asked.

"I don't have a count on that."

"What measures are being taken by the government?" the man from Montevideo asked.

"Colonel Escortia has moved tanks into the old city," Loomis told them. "But let me stress that he did so for the protection of his men, not for the additional firepower. As far as I know, only light weapons have been used."

"What about the situation in the rest of the country?" someone asked. "Is the revolution widespread?"

"There have been reports of heavy fighting in San Francisco and Santiago," Loomis said. "You could say the issue is in doubt in both cities. But we have no firm figures."

"Is the De la Torre family safe?" the *New York Times* woman asked.

"They are in residence at the palace," Loomis told her.

"Are they in custody?" she demanded.

Loomis hesitated, regretting the tone of candor he'd established. Although he trusted these professionals to protect their source when asked to do so, he also knew they were capable of providing their own slant.

"They are palace guests, under the protection of El Jefe," he told her.

"Have you had any contact with Ramón?" asked the *Post*.

"Unfortunately, no," Loomis said.

The reporter's eyebrows lifted. "Why 'unfortunately'?"

Loomis carefully planted his bombshell. "Because, if the government were in contact with Ramón, certain negotiations might be possible. Not from any position of weakness on the part of the government. Let me stress that—not from a standpoint of weakness. Ramón hasn't caused that much damage. But the government might make certain concessions to him, from a sincere desire to restore peace in the Dominican Republic."

There was a brief silence while the reporters recorded and assessed that information.

"Is that official?" the *New York Times* woman asked.

"That's from your same famous, anonymous and well-informed source within the administration," Loomis said.

As the reporters scattered to phones and typewriters, Loomis hurried on through the lobby to the elevators and to Johnson's room on the third floor.

Johnson answered the door, pointed to a carafe of coffee, and returned to the phone. Loomis closed the door, latched it, tossed his Schmeisser onto the rumpled bed, and poured himself a cup of coffee. He also helped himself to a jelly roll from Johnson's unfinished breakfast—and eavesdropped.

Johnson's end of the conversation seemed to consist mostly of affirmative grunts. But after several minutes, he grew impatient.

"Loomis is here now," he said. "I'll let you know as soon as I find out." He hung up the phone.

Loomis reached for another jelly roll.

"Want me to order you up a breakfast?" Johnson asked.

"No thank you," Loomis said. "I'm not very hungry. The folks at Langley up early this morning?"

"Nobody, including me, has been to bed in a week," Johnson said, rescuing his ham and eggs. "Somehow, they just don't share my confidence in you."

"They should have been with me during the last four or five hours," Loomis told him. "I've even built some confidence in myself."

"I take it, then, that you *do* have a plan."

"Do indeed," Loomis said. "But first things first. Why don't you call up all those brand-new forty-thousand-a-year file clerks over at your embassy? Tell them to be over at the Jaragua by ten o'clock. We'll set up headquarters there. Arrangements are being made now. We'll get the show on the road. Miles to go and all that crap."

"What in the world would make you think we've got any new company men planted in the embassy?" Johnson asked.

"An axiom of the trade," Loomis told him. "CIA intelligence officers always act like file clerks. The file clerks always act like CIA intelligence officers. But we're giving you carte blanche. Call in all of them you need."

"How will they get over there?"

"An escort will pick them up at the embassy at nine-forty," Loomis said. "Most of the fighting is back toward the river. They shouldn't have any trouble."

"Your exact words last night, as I recall," Johnson said. "And I almost got creamed three times on my way back to the hotel. Once by rebels and twice by your people."

He went back to the phone and put a call through to the United States Embassy. Loomis spotted a tell-tale bulge in Johnson's luggage. He went to it and pulled out a fifth of bourbon. He poured some into his coffee. Johnson cupped a hand over the mouthpiece.

"Help yourself," he said.

Cup in hand, Loomis crossed to the dresser, where he picked up a leather case that had caught his eye. The Oriental girl who looked back at him from the frame was familiar, yet unfamiliar. He had difficulty matching this well-coiffed, fashionable, anglicized matron with the painfully thin waif he had known a dozen years ago. The children beside her were more exotic than Oriental. An attractive family. Beside the case was a stack of travel brochures. Johnson, always the tourist, saw the sights and absorbed local lore wherever he went.

And he had seen most of the world.

Johnson cradled the phone. "Listen," he said. "The people at Langley are shitting little green apples. They want to know what you plan to do about the tanker."

"I guess we can tell them now," Loomis said. "Did they move some backup into Lisbon?"

"Half the force in Europe, apparently. That's a big station to begin with. Now there must be a hundred men there. That enough?"

"Depends on how bright they are." Loomis thought back

over his plan. He still could find no hole in it. "All they've got to do is to find an authentic case of bubonic plague and check same into a Lisbon hospital within twenty-four hours or less."

Johnson stared at him for a moment until comprehension came. "Im-fucking-possible!" he exploded. "You're crazy!"

"That's the trouble with you Civil Service types," Loomis said. "No sense of challenge."

Johnson considered the idea. "It might work," he said. "It just might work. But there's not enough time. Couldn't we fake it?"

"No. We can't risk the Hamlet people suspecting we're onto them."

"Can't be done," Johnson said. "Not within twenty-four hours."

"Fifty bucks says it can."

"You're on. What's the secret?"

"No secret. Just ingenuity and a lot of hard work."

"Maybe you better tell me," Johnson said. "Langley may be a little short on ingenuity this morning."

"Think it out," Loomis said. "We don't want a registered case. This patient has to be completely unknown to authorities such as the World Health Organization. A patient that can't be traced. So we can forget about most of civilization. But it'll be found where bubonic plague is indigent. Any guesses?"

"India?"

"Close. Might do in a pinch. But I'm counting on Africa. That's closer to Lisbon."

"How will we find this patient? Put classifieds in all the papers?"

"Oh, Lord, Johnson, you're supposed to be the expert on clandestine operations. Think, now. Who would have charge of a case of bubonic plague in some remote region of Africa?"

"A medical missionary?"

"Right. Some contemporary Doctor Livingston, a thousand miles out in the bush. Now, what do you suppose would entice such a man to make us the gift of a bona fide terminal case of bubonic plague?"

"How would I know? A new choir loft, maybe?"

"O.K., you're dumb, so I'll tell you. Only one thing would work: a good supply of medicine to salve his professional conscience. Advancement of science and all that. Isn't there a pharmaceutical company among the Delaware corporations?"

Johnson nodded. After the CIA failed in its early efforts in the late forties and early fifties to plant intelligence officers among foreign news correspondents and the overseas ranks of existing commercial firms, special corporations were formed solely to serve as cover for agency men abroad. At the time, the State of Delaware offered the simplest and easiest route to incorporation. The many worldwide commercial operations of the CIA eventually became known in the trade as "the Delaware corporations."

"Also, we'll need a company man who knows medical jargon well enough to pass for an M.D. If you have an M.D., so much the better."

"This is beginning to sound dirty."

"I've had good teachers. Have Langley locate the headquarters of all churches and organizations that send missionaries into the outback. Put out the word through the pharmaceutical company: they've found a superdrug that just might cure advanced cases of the plague. It might stop this scourge of mankind once and for all, and so forth. They need a terminal patient to test the stuff on. The drug is extremely unstable, which is the reason for speed. They've just made up a fresh batch of it, and they hate to waste it. As far as the bush doctor is concerned, the drug—and the patient—are being flown to Lisbon for the most expedient rendezvous possible."

"I'll sure say one thing for you, Loomis," Johnson said. "You've really got one hell of a devious mind." He started toward the phone, but hesitated. "Does the patient necessarily have to be a terminal case? Wouldn't a tolerably sick one work just as well?"

Loomis shook his head sadly. "Johnson, you've just got no class. That's the key to the whole thing. The doctor is happy to get the dying man off his hands. After the damned drug doesn't work, all we have to do is bury the patient and send the doctor a letter saying that was tough titty about his patient, but he has made a tremendous contribution to medical science."

"I see," Johnson said. "No loose ends dangling."

Loomis nodded. "You're learning," he said.

Chapter 13

Loomis opened the meeting two hours later in a hastily prepared suite at the Jaragua. The site was a compromise. Loomis wanted to get away from the *palacio* and the routine traffic of government. Obviously, the Embajador was out. The press immediately would grow suspicious of the activity. And Loomis didn't want to meet in the United States Embassy, for he knew that would be the first step toward losing control of the whole operation.

The suite was stripped of all furnishings except tables and chairs. All pictures, vases, and ornaments were removed in the interest of electronic sanitation. A plain green felt cloth covered the big table in the largest room. Ordinary saucers served as ashtrays. When the suite was ready, Loomis had his staff make one final electronic search. They found no indication that the suite was not clean.

The entire wing of the hotel was then sealed. Loomis placed well-tailored, well-armed men at strategic points. Any remaining tourists—or newspapermen—who happened to be strolling down the corridors would see nothing to arouse curiosity. To all outward appearances, the guards could be native businessmen waiting for their wives or local executives quietly conferring on some matter. But if a tourist or newspaperman happened to make a wrong turn, attempted to enter a wrong room, he would be guided politely but firmly in the right direction.

Communications to the suite were jerry-rigged, but sufficient. Three lines were patched into the switchboard at the embassy to maintain continuous contact with key offices in Washington and Europe.

At 9:45 the first of the group arrived. By ten all were

present, seated solemnly at the long table. Of the entire group, only Loomis and Johnson—and perhaps Johnson's two men—knew the purpose of the meeting. Only Loomis's use of El Jefe's name had convinced most of the Dominicans to attend on such short notice.

Facing them, Loomis experienced a strong sense of *déjà vu*. He'd been through this so many times—the planning before committing the troops.

He thought back to the major's talk on the mess decks of the APA wallowing off Tarawa, when he was not yet sixteen, scared, positive that with all the gear he'd never make it down the cargo nets and into the Higgins boats. And there had been the colonel, Loomis couldn't even remember his name, who'd delivered the pep talk in the snow above the Chosin Reservoir. And Fidel, before they came down out of the Sierra Maestra to move on Havana. That had been a good one. A lot better than the one the big shot from Washington had made to the brigade in the jungles of Guatemala before the Bay of Pigs.

Loomis shoved the thoughts aside. He studied the faces of the men around the table.

Most seemed more irritated than curious. Loomis knew he would encounter varying degrees of hostility among them. That was natural. He wasn't worried about it. But he *was* concerned that the hostility might stand in the way, that they might not accept his word on the urgency of the problem. The Dominican Republic had been so totally immersed in its own affairs for so many years, and the Dominicans had faced so many crises, that such an abstract, faceless danger would be difficult for them to accept.

Loomis rose. He opened in English, aware that all in the room spoke the language well enough to follow his meaning. "Most of you know me. Some don't. I'm Loomis, chief of security to El Jefe. I'll introduce you quickly, for we have little time to get acquainted. To my right is Colonel Escortia, who is here representing the army in the Distrito Nacional."

He continued on around the table. Johnson and his two agency men. Dr. Ricardo Espinosa, chairman of the physics department at the university, who, Loomis had been surprised to learn, was one of the leading scientists in the world in his specialty of molecular structure. Admiral Manuel Marquez of the Dominican Navy, who had weathered a number of rough political seas to keep his post. Navy Captain Luis Martínez, superintendent of Santo Domingo's dock facilities. Juan Camacho, in essence director of Dominican foreign affairs. Dr. Francisco Limantour of the medical systems at the university. José Galíndez, chief of the Policía Nacional.

With the introductions completed, Loomis paused. He lowered his voice to a confidential tone. "Last night, Mr. Johnson, representing the United States Government, informed the Dominican Republic of a critical situation. I spent the night discussing the matter with El Jefe and his advisers. He has assigned me to bring the matter to your attention."

As he talked, Loomis made eye contact with each of the Dominican leaders, attempting to break through their antagonism, their natural resentment that he, a foreigner, had been selected to become the confidant of El Jefe, to convey orders to the country's administrators.

"Before I go into the matter, let me make plain the structure of this meeting," he said. "I am acting for El Jefe. He has made me responsible for the decisions, subject, of course, to his approval. You have been asked by El Jefe to be my advisers. Your counsel and expertise are urgently needed. The next two or three days will probably be the most memorable in your lives. I hope they are not the last days of your lives."

Loomis gave the words time to take effect. The faces around the table were now a study in contrast.

He saw anger, curiosity, amusement, contempt, and surprise.

But he had reached them.

"Everything you are about to hear is in the utmost confidence," he said. "Nothing revealed here is to leave this room. If you must divulge anything to an assistant, or if I feel I must, to my staff, we will all make the evaluation to do so."

Loomis glanced at his watch. "I won't keep you in suspense any longer. Less than forty-eight hours from now, a Liberian

tanker is scheduled to arrive in Santo Domingo. She is scheduled to tie up alongside the docks in La Francia to off-load
crude and some container cargo. The United States Government has information—has evidence—that a party or parties
unknown have placed aboard that ship nuclear materials
sufficient to construct a homemade but effective bomb well
into the kiloton range. The United States believes that device
will be detonated in Santo Domingo, probably within a week
of the arrival of the material, unless we make a successful
interception."

Loomis waited patiently through the exclamations from
around the table, then raised his hands for silence.

"I know this is a lot to absorb on such short notice. But we
all have a lot of work to do. I hope you'll keep this thought
foremost in your minds: this is but one of two bombs to be
constructed by this group. It'll be set off without preamble,
not as an attack on the Dominican Republic, but as an example to lend weight to an extortion attempt against the United
States. We are not in a bargaining position, even if we knew
who they are. We've *got* to find that bomb."

He called on Johnson to fill the group in on the details.
While Johnson talked, Loomis jotted down ideas on a legal
pad, outlining the plan he'd mapped out with El Jefe.

Johnson described events leading up to the loading at the
mouth of the Tagus, the aerial surveillance, and the various
theories as to who might be behind the plot.

Colonel Escortia kept shaking his head in amazement, and
Loomis made a mental note. Escortia, a man of action, might
become a problem in a game of watch and wait. Dr. Espinosa, the molecular authority, was staring at the table, lost
in thought. Of all the group, he alone had shown no surprise.
The others listened to Johnson in stunned silence.

"We have no knowledge of what this Hamlet Group
wants," Johnson concluded. "But obviously, the United
States and the Dominican Republic are in this together. My
government offers every facility for your use in our mutual
problem."

He sat down, unbuttoned his collar, and loosened his tie.

Loomis leaned back and braced his boots on the rungs of an empty chair. "Any questions so far?" he asked.

Dr. Espinosa looked up from his preoccupation with the table top. "Uranium or plutonium?" he asked.

"Our information is that uranium will be used for the Santo Domingo device," Johnson told him. "Our man who managed to infiltrate the Hamlet Group learned, before he was killed, that the group also possesses plutonium. Their bomb maker chose uranium."

"A mixed blessing," Dr. Espinosa said. "And an understandable decision on his part. It perhaps would be less deadly in yield, but it would be much easier to construct and more certain, mechanically, to perform."

"Why are you so certain Ramón isn't connected with this?" Colonel Escortia asked.

"Primarily, because this is out of his league," Loomis said. "We can't be positive he doesn't know about it. But for the moment I think we can assume he doesn't. On the advice of El Jefe, I have leaked word to the press that the government would be receptive to dialogue with Ramón. We may need his cooperation on this. Obviously, his revolution will complicate matters. We may have to ask him for a cease-fire."

Sharp glances told Loomis that the possibility didn't sit well with the Dominican leaders.

But no one protested.

Galíndez of the Policía Nacional fixed his sleepy, heavily lidded stare on Johnson. "I have been to Langley for training by your agency," he said. "I know of your computer, Octopus. I was told it contains names, descriptions, and *modi operandi* of thousands of criminals and political terrorists. Can't Octopus help us on this?"

"We will call on Octopus," Johnson said. "But a computer is only as useful as the information you can put into it. With this case, we have so few data. Perhaps, with developments, Octopus will be of some use."

Loomis waited patiently while Johnson handled the questions, giving them time to grasp the problem, allowing them a few minutes to consider the possibilities. He still sensed

their resentment toward him but, as yet, resistance was un-
formed. He brought the questioning to a close.

"We've got a lot to do in the next twenty-four hours," he
told them. "Each of you has a room or suite on this floor. You
can set up shop here, have your staffs and assistants bring in
whatever you need. For the most part, we can allow your
staffs and the press to assume our work is connected in some
way with the revolution. I see no reason to tell anyone otherwise, except on a need-to-know basis. Obviously, secrecy is
mandatory. If this Hamlet organization learns we're onto
them, they'll probably put another plan into operation."

"What about our families?" Dr. Limantour asked.

"Presumably, we *will* find the material," Loomis told him.
"If we don't—if it comes to that—we'll map out some plan
of evacuation. But at this point, it hasn't been discussed."

"What right, under international law, do we have to seize
the ship?" Captain Martínez asked.

"None," Loomis said. "So we've taken the trouble to manu-
facture a reason." He turned to Dr. Limantour. "Have you
ever treated a case of bubonic plague?"

Dr. Limantour smiled slightly. "No. And if that was a polite
way of asking how much I know about it, I'll answer that
question, too. I know about as much as you could expect of
any outstanding chief of diagnostic studies—just the bare
basics."

"We're planting a case of bubonic plague in a Lisbon hospital," Loomis explained. "Naturally, the patient will have had
extensive contact with someone aboard the tanker. We'll
quarantine the ship for a thorough medical study of the crew,
fumigation of the holds for carrier rats, whatever we're allowed to do under international law. This will, of course, give
us the opportunity to conduct a thorough search of the ship.
I hope that you, and Captain Martínez, will explore the medical and legal aspects and determine our limitations."

The two men nodded agreement. Loomis turned to the
foreign affairs director.

"Señor Camacho, seizure of a ship naturally involves our
foreign politics to some extent. El Jefe would like for you to

monitor—and of course to participate in—our discussions and to offer your opinions on any potential hazards you might foresee."

"With a clear-cut case of a communicable disease, I do not believe there will be complications," Camacho said.

Loomis went to the next item on his list.

"Dr. Espinosa, I've been advised by the U.S. Government that the materials aboard the tanker probably will be hidden in oil drums identical to thousands of others on board. They say we probably wouldn't be able to find it by radiation. Do you agree?"

Dr. Espinosa toyed with his pen a moment before answering. "Not necessarily," he said. "The United States has achieved considerable sophistication in this field. Their shipping methods have been evolved over a long period, utilizing much experience. If this is a homemade container, the techniques are perhaps far less accomplished. I would presume that there might be a fair chance of a measurable degree of radiation—enough to merit the effort. But we will need equipment more precise than any we possess in the Dominican Republic."

"All right," Loomis said. "Give Johnson a list of everything you need. It will be flown in on orders from Washington. Also, perhaps you can confer by phone with Mr. Johnson's experts, and advise us on what we'll be hunting."

Loomis went rapidly to the next item. "Admiral, the United States has the tanker under aerial surveillance. Its position now is two hundred miles or so northeast of the entrance to the Mona Passage, moving at fifteen knots. How soon can we put the ship under surface surveillance?"

The admiral figured briefly on a scratch pad. "The *Duarte* is in harbor," he said. "She could put to sea within the hour. At thirty-three knots—that would be forty-eight knots closing—she would be able to make rendezvous about daylight tomorrow morning."

"Good. It would be best if the *Duarte* approached the tanker from the west, as if entering the passage from another direction. It would then be natural for the *Duarte* to fall in astern and follow the tanker on into Santo Domingo."

"The *Duarte*'s radar is probably superior to that on the tanker," the admiral pointed out. "She could keep watch on the tanker's movements without revealing her presence, if so desired."

Loomis considered the suggestion. "I would prefer visual contact, as long as we're not too obvious with it," he said. "I think we should guard against any rendezvous with a small boat, or possibly a cargo drop by raft, along our northeast or east coast."

"And if that occurs?"

"Then they can intervene, under the assumption that illegal contraband is being handled. We'll play it by ear."

Loomis moved to the next item on his list. "Señor Galíndez, I realize that the Policía Nacional has many problems at the moment. But we have no other facilities to conduct a massive manhunt. And this search will be complicated by the fact that we don't know who we're looking for. We only know that he exists."

"The man who will construct the bomb?"

"Yes. With the ship due, there's a good chance he'll be arriving within the next day or so. Or, if he's in the country now, he may move toward a rendezvous. I suggest, Señor Galíndez, that we monitor every passenger that arrives by ship or air and every motorist who crosses the island."

"The airports and ports of entry would not be too difficult," Galíndez said. "But checking out all motorists would be a tremendous undertaking."

"You can borrow what personnel you need from the military," Loomis told him. "I suggest we arrange a well-publicized jailbreak in Santiago or one of the northern cities. Roadblocks on all major highways would then be considered natural. Since we don't know who we're hunting, arrests are unlikely. But a license number, a name, a brief notation on all foreigners and of the time and circumstances might be a good thing to have. Our bomb maker probably will be on that list. And his name might set bells to ringing on Octopus."

Galíndez again fixed Loomis with his sleepy, blank stare.

"Señor Loomis, with your permission. I must say I do not understand all of this. Why go to all this elaborate subterfuge? Why not simply seize the ship under any pretext, find the nuclear materials, and arrest and question the crew?"

The room fell silent. Loomis felt all eyes on him. Galíndez at last had put the opposition into words. Loomis hesitated, knowing that most of the Dominicans in the room were allied with Galíndez. Loomis felt their strong resistance, and he *had* to have their cooperation.

"Señor Galíndez, you have gone to the core of the matter," Loomis said. "I wish it were that simple. I *also* like direct action. My first impulse is to seize the ship. I also hate subterfuge. As some of you may know, I once was a member of the CIA." Loomis saw glances exchanged around the room. He had confirmed some rumors. "I left the agency thoroughly disgusted with the clandestine practices. But in certain instances, I am forced to acknowledge the necessity of their use, and I think this is one such instance. The seizure of the ship without some due legal process would be international piracy per se. It would be condemned throughout the world. If the materials are *not* aboard, if the Hamlet people have tricked us, then we would have alerted them to our search, and they would take appropriate measures."

Loomis paused. The faces were thoughtful, absorbed. He was reaching them.

"Yet it goes deeper than that," he added. "These are clandestine, covert people we are dealing with. We have to fight them with their own weapons. Of course, this is nothing new. Intrigue is as old as politics. But now the stakes are higher, and the methods are more sophisticated. I sincerely believe this is the first confrontation of a new era—a dangerous time of free-lance nuclear threats. If the Hamlet people fail, someone else will try. For the first time, a small group of people has the means to challenge entire governments, whole nations. As long as nuclear materials are available, someone, somewhere, will make the effort. They know our techniques, so they simply circumvent them. We must learn *their* techniques, if we are to survive."

The room was silent. Loomis knew that he had convinced them.

He glanced at his watch. Noon. Countdown had started on the last forty-eight hours.

"Anyone have further questions, suggestions, or comment?" he asked.

There were none.

"We'll stand adjourned for the moment, then," he said. "We'll meet back here at six tonight to map final details."

Chapter 14

In mid-afternoon, reports of heavy fighting in the Cibao were confirmed. Government forces were definitely losing ground in both Santiago and San Francisco.

In the capital, sniping became so prevalent that by late afternoon all stores and offices were closed. The streets were deserted.

"My back is to the wall," El Jefe complained to Loomis. "The tourists are gone. Commerce has stopped. The sugar mills are closing down."

Preoccupied with the Hamlet affair, Loomis hadn't realized that Ramón had made such inroads. For the first time, he wondered if perhaps Ramón might be moving too fast. If his revolution became overextended, overcommitted, it might be difficult to sustain. However, there was no denying the pressure he was applying on the government.

"In another two or three days, there will be complete chaos in the streets," El Jefe said. "The people will become hungry, desperate. I've got to do something. But anything I can do is wrong. Colonel Escortia wants to issue new identification cards and to place strong checkpoints all through the *distrito.* Like in Trujillo's worst days. I can't bring myself to do that."

Loomis suggested placing troops on the rooftops downtown to discourage sniping. El Jefe said he would pass the suggestion along to Escortia.

"Are you prepared for the arrival of the tanker?" El Jefe asked.

"With any luck, we will be," Loomis said.

"I keep wondering about this Hamlet thing," El Jefe said. "There is a thought that bothers me. If the Hamlet people are intelligent enough to acquire the materials, and to arrange for the bomb's assembly, why would they make it so easy for us to catch them?"

"That's the thought that keeps bothering me," Loomis admitted.

"I fear this ship may be a diversion," El Jefe said.

"I agree, that's a strong possibility," Loomis said. "But the fact remains, the ship is all we have to work with."

Loomis went to his room, showered, sprawled across his bed naked, and slept for the first time in thirty-six hours. When he awoke, María Elena was beside him, cradling his head in her arms.

They lay for a time without moving, listening to the occasional faint, far-off chatter of automatic weapons.

Then, without a word, Loomis pulled her under him. A frantic desperation drove them through steadily building momentum toward a climax that left them both breathless and shattered.

They rolled apart and lay for a time in the darkness without talking.

María Elena at last broke the silence. "Loomis, I knew something was wrong the other night when you didn't come back. Why didn't you tell me about the atomic bomb?"

Loomis reached to turn on a lamp beside the bed. "Who told you?" he asked.

"El Jefe."

Loomis was unable to keep his irritation from showing. "He shouldn't have worried you with it," he said.

María Elena's tone turned defensive, defiant. "Well thanks a lot, Loomis, you male chauvinist pig. As it so happened, my uncle thought I might have enough intelligence to have some idea of who is behind Hamlet."

Loomis rolled onto one elbow, facing her. "Do you?"

"What do you care?" she said with an elaborate shrug. "I'm nothing. My opinions aren't worth anything."

"All right," he said. "I stand corrected. Tell me. I really want to know. I'm humbly begging."

She laughed. "That's better." She put a hand on Loomis's

chest and let it roam while she talked. "I don't think Hamlet is a terrorist group, anyone fighting for causes," she said. "I feel they're completely without principle. They're driven by greed. Their demands will probably be to put them in a position of power."

Loomis reached to take her hand. "That takes in most of the human race," he said.

"Oh Loomis! How can you say that? Sure, the world's full of shitty people. But I can't keep from admiring all those fighting for causes—even the wrong causes."

"If you scratch them, you'll usually find that the cause is number one," he told her.

She looked at him, concerned. "I can't believe you really think that. What about all the grand causes of the past—your American Revolution?"

"A good case in point," he agreed. "In the English version, all our heroes come out traitors. It's all in the viewpoint. Most people alive then had a vested interest, one way or another, that turned them loyalist or revolutionary."

She made a helpless gesture with her hand, then bit her lip in thought. "O.K. I suppose this would be the supreme test for a Texan," she said. "What about the Alamo?"

"Another example," he told her. "When I was a kid I was taught that the men in the Alamo died fighting for Texas independence. No one questioned it. More rose-colored glasses. At the time of the Alamo, Texas independence hadn't even been declared. They died fighting for restoration of the Mexican Constitution of 1821, under which they had land grants."

"All of them?"

"Well, maybe some of them just didn't like Mexicans," he admitted.

María Elena seemed disturbed. She lay silent for a moment. "If you feel that way, I don't understand how you can fight other people's wars for them."

"Everybody likes to do what he's good at," Loomis said. "I happen to be good at it. It's an honorable profession—maybe the oldest."

"Then you *are* a cynic," she said. "But if you don't trust people, how can you form deep relationships?"

The question jarred Loomis more than he wanted to admit. He thought his answer out carefully.

"Nothing is forever," he told her. "The good times are few and far between. You just hang onto the good times as long as you can and try your damnedest to live through the bad. That's all you can hope for in this old world."

María Elena lay for a time, staring at the ceiling, absorbing the thought. "Well, I guess I've discovered the flaw in the big rough diamond," she said. "Maybe it's up to me to fix it. I guess I'll just have to prove to you that there are good things —lasting things."

She moved over to him and they began again. He soon had her in good humor, laughing. He thought her small, firm breasts the most perfect creations he'd ever seen, and told her so.

"Oh Loomis! Don't tell me you're another tit man," she said.

He pulled her to him, nuzzling. "A tit man, an ass man, a bottom man." He moved over her, holding her head in his hands. "And," he added, "a great admirer of feminine intellect."

"Oh goody gumdrops," she said, putting her arms around him. "A Renaissance lover!"

They made love with a strange, unhurried leisure.

Afterward, she snuggled against him. "Hold me, Loomis," she said. "That's what I really need."

They lay entwined throughout the night, listening to the sounds of the growing revolution.

Chapter 15

Mike Elliott spent the afternoon sailing on Oslo Fjord with the tall Norwegian blonde from Scandinavian Airlines. Elliott normally liked small women, but he liked variety even more. The blonde almost matched his six-foot-two, but she was well proportioned and kept him laughing with her terrific sense of humor. They capped the sail with four rounds of beer at the open-air Pernille. There they made plans to go dancing that evening at the Rosekjelleren, one of Elliott's favorite places. The sunken dance floor, the suggestive decor, and the nude floorshow were always a turn-on. And Elliott had learned that the blonde lived alone in her own apartment near Holmenkollen, liked American men, and had an open mind about sex. Elliott was looking forward to a terrific night.

Then he returned to his room at the Continental and found the cable waiting.

The first surprise was that the whole cable was a message. Usually, Langley risked only cryptic notes tucked away in long blocks of text. These notes in turn were encoded into five-letter groupings to be decoded against Langley's twenty-seven-column square, a device tradition claimed had never been broken. The key to the square was hidden in the third of a sequence of numbers buried in the text. The key to the location of the message was indicated by variations in the signature.

Elliott looked at the signature on the cable. Andrew L. Latham. The full meaning didn't hit him for several seconds.

ALL?

It was a long cable.

Making certain the door to his room was latched and

bolted, Elliott set to work. He unscrewed the back of his watch, lifted out the special bit of glass designed to masquerade as a jewel in the movement, and carefully placed it on the desk. Searching in his bag, he found the penlight—a common tool among world travelers for reading street maps in dim light and counting unfamiliar money in ancient taxis. After screwing the fake jewel into the penlight tip, Elliott projected the twenty-seven-column square onto the wall. Then, with pad and pen, he began the long chore of ferreting out the message.

Elliott had never been adept at code. The five-letter groupings, designed to prevent educated guesses by outsiders, further confused him. Once he had the full text decoded, he had to study it for several minutes before finding the meaning:

> PROCE EDLIS BONSO ONEST AVAIL ABLE CARRIE RASSU MEGRO UNDHO GCONT ACTBR OADSW ORDEF BAHID TOEST ABLIS HREND EZVOU SSAFE HOUSE RUAJO SEVIA NAFUT MOSTC AUTIO NADVI SEDDA NGERI MMINE NT.

By dividing the words, he came to the message:

> PROCEED LISBON SOONEST AVAILABLE CARRIER. ASSUME GROUNDHOG. CONTACT BROADSWORD EFBAHID TO ESTABLISH RENDEZVOUS SAFEHOUSE RUA JOSE VIANA F. UTMOST CAUTION ADVISED. DANGER IMMINENT.

The "groundhog" gave him pause until a vague memory stirred that the name was his own deep cover. He'd never used it, and he'd almost forgotten it. The "EFBAHID" was a puzzler, until he recalled that numbers often were given simple letter count—A=1, B=2, C=3, etc. This translated into a phone number, 562-1894. Similarly, the "F" after Rua Jose Viana translated into house number 6.

The "danger imminent" advisory aroused all of Elliott's latent paranoia. He'd always assumed there were certain risks involved in his line of work. Caution was standard operating procedure, deemed too obvious for comment. He'd never seen, or heard of, a similar warning encoded with instructions. Did Langley know something? Was the blonde involved?

He remembered how readily she'd agreed to a date.

Had he been set up?

He forced himself to quit thinking of such vague possibilities. That was the route to insanity.

Instead, he immediately phoned the airport and put himself on standby for the first flight to Lisbon. To make certain a seat would become available, he switched to his role of travel agent and phoned four of his clients, informing them that they'd been bumped from their overnight flight to Lisbon. The clients—two women schoolteachers from Ohio and an elderly farm couple from Nebraska—were not surprised. Most American tourists are aware of the airline practice of overbooking flights. They also know that American tourists are the first to be bumped. Elliott's CIA self had no qualms over the trick, but his travel agent's conscience bothered him. He phoned the airport and booked them for a later flight.

He then called the blonde and cancelled the date, explaining that his home office in New York had scheduled three flights of important conventioneers into Paris, the Paris manager was down with the flu, and they'd called on him to take up the slack. From the tone of her voice, Elliott judged that she didn't buy the story. But he was too disturbed to be concerned. Let her think he had found a bigger, better blonde.

He packed carefully but rapidly, wishing he could carry more in the way of weapons. Electronic surveillance at airports posed a problem for clandestine warriors. His .38 pen would set off alarms, but at least it seemed innocent to outward appearances. He could carry it in his hand going through the gate. But his 7.65 autoloading cigarette lighter was too much of a curiosity to risk taking along.

On the night flight to Lisbon, he had trouble sleeping. The "utmost precaution, danger imminent" phrase kept ringing

in his mind. His seatmate was a German auto parts specialist.
Or at least the man said that's what he was; he did seem to
know a great deal about the anatomy of Volkswagens. Across
the aisle were two American schoolteachers, almost exact
replicas of the two Elliott had bumped from the flight. They
had spent the day in Frogner Park and were discussing the
wonders of the Vigeland statuary. Or at least they said they
had spent the day in Frogner Park.

The flight arrived on time. Elliott managed his way
through customs in less than forty minutes, switched a hundred kroner into escudos, and found a public telephone. Inserting a coin, he held the receiver to his ear while he monitored the lobby. Then he dialed Broadsword's number,
hoping he could remember the crazy doubletalk they had
taught him at Langley.

He let the phone ring twice, hung up, waited a moment,
then dialed again. Someone at the other end picked up the
receiver.

"Hello. Is this 562-1894?" Elliott asked.

"It is," a flat voice answered. "With whom do you wish to
speak?" ("The meeting is on; give me the right response, and
I'll tell you when.")

"Arthur, please." (King Arthur handled a mean broadsword, let us both remember.)

"Arthur isn't here, right at the moment. But you might try
reaching him at 562-0030." ("Be here at 0030—thirty minutes
after midnight.")

"Thank you, I will," Elliott said. He hung up the phone and
glanced at his watch. He had less than two hours; he was
thankful that he knew Lisbon well from many visits while
serving out of the Madrid station.

With another coin he dialed the Infante Santo. All four of
his bumped clients had been booked into the colorful old
hotel down by the Tagus. Rooms in Lisbon were at a pre-
mium in season, and with four reservations lapsing, Elliott
figured the Infante Santo would be his best bet. He was right.
A room was available. He asked them to hold it for him. He
knew that the place was noisy from nearby rail and highway

traffic, but he was in no position to choose.

He went to the hotel by taxi, carefully watching his back trail. As far as he could determine he was alone, but he wanted to make certain before heading to the safehouse.

After a quick shower and change of clothes, he asked the hotel doorman to summon a taxi—a minor precaution to make certain a special taxi wasn't waiting for him. He gave the driver the address of A'Cave on Avenida Antonio de Aquilar.

On arrival, he quickly walked down into the noisy cellar and moved through the crowd to the bar. A teen-aged prostitute joined him, and he ordered drinks, keeping a careful watch on the entry. While the girl whispered into his ear the delights she had readily available, Elliott concentrated on the doorway so intently that he almost overlooked the fat German at the far end of the bar. Elliott couldn't put a name to the face, but he knew he'd seen that round moon countenance before, either in the company files, or on a briefing somewhere. Langley had taught Elliott an elaborate system of identification, but he had devised his own, based on movie stars. And he had the man pegged. Sydney Greenstreet.

Elliott put his drink on the bar. "Let's go," he said to the girl.

He rushed her through the crowd, up the stairs, and into a taxi waiting at the curb. As they pulled away, bound for the girl's flat, Elliott turned to watch the German emerge from the club.

Single tail?

He had no way of knowing.

"You not like me?" the girl asked, puzzled over his distraction.

Aware that she had moved her hand into provocative territory, Elliott really looked at her for the first time. A Latin Lolita, not more than fourteen or fifteen. Thin, waiflike, and strangely appealing. Back home, her delights would bring a ten-year stretch in the slammer. Here, she was available and a veteran.

"I like fine," Elliott said, patting her thigh affectionately.

"But tonight, I want you to entertain a friend. It's his birthday."

"Pardon?"

Elliott reached into his pocket and gave her thirty escudos. "When we turn the next corner, I'll jump out," he said. "You go on to your flat, and wait in the doorway, hidden. My friend is in the Fiat behind us. When he walks up to your door, tell him you are my birthday gift to him."

The girl didn't know whether to be insulted or flattered. Elliott didn't give her time to decide. As they turned the corner, he gave the driver a handful of escudos and instructions. When the taxi slowed, he jumped to the pavement and sprinted for a doorway as the taxi roared away. He reached the shadows just before the Fiat rounded the corner. He watched it disappear after the taxi.

Elliott waited in the doorway five minutes, but nothing stirred. He walked two blocks to a main thoroughfare and hailed a passing cab. He reached the safehouse on time.

"I was tailed," he told Broadsword.

"At this point, I'd be surprised if you weren't," Broadsword said. "This has turned into one hell of a hot operation."

Elliott appreciated the fact that Broadsword didn't bother to ask if he'd lost the tail. Broadsword wasn't a worrier. He trusted his men to carry out their assignments as true professionals.

Elliott had known Broadsword at Langley by the name of Brad Jordan. Always stocky, Jordan had gained weight but still seemed solid. And the new patches of gray at his temples added a look of maturity.

"We're all here," Broadsword said. "Come join the party."

He led Elliott into a large, dimly lit room, lined with shelves and workbenches that gleamed curiously white. As they moved nearer, Elliott saw the reason. The shelves were filled with row upon row of false teeth, hundreds, perhaps thousands. The safehouse was a dental laboratory. Elliott forced his eyes away from the macabre array. Six men were waiting at a long table.

"This is Groundhog, surfaced at last," Broadsword said. "If today were February second, we'd have six more weeks of winter. Groundhog saw his shadow on the way here."

Broadsword introduced the group. Elliott knew three of them. One was the hippie operative assigned to monitor the youth-drug culture around Torremolinos on the Costa Brava. He was known as Peter Rabbit. Dr. Thomas Segal was a bona fide medical doctor attached at various times to various embassies and who doubled in brass as a company man. The third, Ralph Webb, dated back to the Office of Strategic Services during World War II and the formative years of the CIA. As a cover he'd launched an import-export business that soon, even without his help, doubled and tripled his company salary. Webb ostensibly resigned. But he remained available for special assignments. He was known as Tycoon.

The other three were introduced as Archer, Bowman, and Shield. Elliott didn't know them. He shook hands, and sat down facing them.

Broadsword glanced at his watch. "We're on a tight schedule," he said. "Please pay attention."

He paused to light a cigarette. "Briefly, here's the situation: the company needs to search a tanker somewhere in the Caribbean. Where, and for what, I don't know. But to make the search feasible, we will plant in a Lisbon hospital, within twenty-four hours, an authentic case of bubonic plague. This case will provide the *raison d'état* for seizure and search."

"Far out, man," the hippie said.

Elliott was aware of the intensified interest around the table. Company operatives for the most part lead relatively dull lives. They dote on challenge. Elliott knew this assignment might become a part of company legend. Every company man had his repertoire of wild assignments. Elliott once flew to Rio to take a leak. As he stood before the designated urinal in Rio, he was jostled, and a deft hand planted a small packet in his coat pocket. He zipped up and flew back to Oslo, stopping only briefly for another leak at Heathrow. He'd tossed the packet into a designated dustbin without ever knowing what it contained. He'd had other unusual assignments. But as far as he knew, no one had ever been ordered to hunt up a case of plague.

"We have found a case," Broadsword said. "A black male, forty-two years of age, at a Protestant mission in Zaire, Africa. Our job is to transport the patient discreetly into Lisbon and into a hospital. The mission is complicated by the fact that efforts are being made to monitor, and presumably to stop, our every move."

"Russians?" Archer asked.

"No," Broadsword said. "At this point, we don't know who. We have reason to believe it isn't a nation, but some sort of international cartel."

"Why don't we pick one up and see how he bounces?" asked the hippie.

"That's being taken care of," Broadsword said. "Our job is to concentrate on the mission."

"This plague," said the hippie. "Aren't we apt to waste a lot of people? Ourselves included?"

"Negative," Broadsword said. "But I think we should all have our minds put at ease on that. Doctor, would you please explain?"

Dr. Segal swung his horn-rim glasses idly by one earpiece and smiled benignly at Peter Rabbit. "Contrary to popular belief, the plague isn't readily communicable," he said. "And man is incidental, even accidental, to the natural cycle of the disease. Normally, the cycle goes from rats to fleas to rats. It's only when the rat population dies that the fleas turn to other hosts—squirrels, gerbils, and humans. The disease is not transmitted from human to human without the right species of flea."

"What about your garden-variety Torremolinos sand flea?" Peter Rabbit asked, scratching himself ostentatiously.

"Only about a hundred of the fifteen hundred known species of rodent fleas are able to transmit plague," Dr. Segal said. "But to be on the safe side, we'll disinfect you along with the patient and the plane."

"If the disease is so difficult to transmit, why all the panic over it?" Elliott asked.

"Partly psychological—a holdover from the Middle Ages," Dr. Segal said. "But medically, the plague is a persistent disease, indigenous to many areas, only awaiting the right conditions to emerge. The bacillus remains alive in dried sputum for three months and may exist indefinitely in certain soils. It can survive in dry flea feces for five weeks at room temperature."

"I'm home free," Peter Rabbit said. "I keep my flea shit in the refrigerator."

"How ill is the patient?" Tycoon asked. "Is he apt to crap out on us?"

"Possibly," the doctor said. "Actually, bubonic is a misnomer in this case. There are three types—bubonic, pneumonic, and septicemic. Our patient is septicemic. Recovery is rare. The patient may die within twenty-four hours, but more commonly on the second or third day."

Broadsword again looked impatiently at his watch. "You can continue this seminar on the plane, Doctor," he said. "We have to get moving. Here are your assignments: Groundhog, Peter Rabbit, Tycoon, and the Doctor will fly to Zaire to return the patient. Dr. Segal holds credentials as the director of a drug research team. He has been briefed and will handle all negotiations with the mission hospital. Tycoon has prevailed upon his African connections to facilitate transportation, and the mission will be flown in his Lear jet. He is in charge of logistics. Groundhog and Peter Rabbit will, under the Doctor's supervision, prepare the patient for passing as a businessman of Moorish ethnic origin. Archer, Bowman, and Shield will assume charge of surface transportation here and—last but by no means least—security of the operation. Any questions?"

"Arms?" Elliott asked.

"I've managed a Walther P-38 for each of you," Broadsword said. "But please bleed a little before you use them."

"I gather we're not traveling on passport," Elliott said.

"Definitely negative on that. This is a covert action, all the way." He stood up and handed out the pistols. Each contained a full clip. More ammo was placed on the table. Elliott pocketed a handful of cartridges.

"Have a pleasant flight," Broadsword said. "I'll be expecting you back here sometime early tomorrow night."

"One thing," Peter Rabbit said. "What if that black cat does croak on us?"

"Bring him back anyway," Broadsword said. "We'll just play like he's alive long enough to see the mission through."

Chapter 16

Four hours later, they landed at Yundum Airport outside Banjul, the Gambia, on Africa's west coast. Elliott had slept most of the way, and he awoke vaguely disturbed by a dream. The motion, the physical confinement of air travel, often tended to inflict him with erections and erotic thoughts. Although he couldn't remember all the details of the dream, he had the impression he'd been with the girl in Lisbon. Her presence lingered. Fully awake, he could conjure up a vivid mental picture of her face. That was unusual. He seldom could remember women so well. Experimentally, he thought of the girl he'd spent hours with yesterday in Oslo Fjord. He could form only a faint image of a large build and blonde hair. He switched to the waif in Lisbon. She came into his mind as clear as television, all on the basis of that brief glimpse in the taxi.

Strange.

Only twenty minutes were allocated in Banjul for refueling. Tycoon left the plane, but everyone else remained aboard. Elliott glanced out at the whitewashed, bougainvillea-covered cottage that served as the terminal, then rolled over and returned to sleep. When he awoke three hours later, they were over water, flying into a brilliant red dawn. Elliott moved forward to find out where they were.

"Just nearing the coast of Gabon," Tycoon said. He had the plane on autopilot and was half-turned in the seat. "In another hour, or little more, we'll land in Kinshasa for clearance. I'll have to pull a few strings."

The Doctor was reading Homer. In Greek. Peter Rabbit was studying Elliott with amusement. "Hey, man. You always sleep with a hard-on?" he asked. "A thousand miles. You must've set some kind of record."

Elliott grinned, mildly embarrassed. He'd never served in the military. He always felt unsure of himself around barracks humor.

"I was supposed to spend the night with a girl in Oslo," he said. "And I wake up in Africa. What a crazy life."

Peter Rabbit nodded agreement. "You should see the two chicks who rolled into Torremolinos last week in a Volks camper. Coeds from Louisiana State. They're living on the beach. I don't think they've got a complete dress between them. I'd just been invited to move in when word of this thing came. If they're gone when I get back, I think I'll cut my throat."

"I feel for you both," Tycoon said. "But I can't reach you."

"Rough to be over the hill, huh?" Peter Rabbit asked.

Tycoon laughed, but said nothing. The Doctor looked up from Homer, irritated. Peter Rabbit turned in his seat to face Tycoon.

"What do you suppose this thing's all about?" he asked. "What's aboard that tanker, anyway?"

Tycoon shrugged. "I assume that if they thought we had a need to know, they'd have told us."

"At least they could tell us who these people are we're up against," Peter Rabbit said.

"I really believe they *don't* know," Tycoon said. "I've never been involved in anything like this before. Broadsword was upset. He tried to hide it. But I know him well. I wouldn't be surprised if there isn't a small war going on back in Lisbon right now."

"You think there may be a reception committee waiting when we get back?" Peter Rabbit asked.

Tycoon shrugged again. "I have the uncomfortable feeling there's going to be a lot more to it than just wheeling this fellow into the hospital," he said.

They landed at Ndolo Airport at Kinshasa, a private field three miles from the city center. Again only Tycoon left the plane. Plates of *moamba*—chicken cooked in palm oil—and rice were sent aboard. With the plane's air-conditioning system off, the heat built up rapidly. More than an hour passed before Tycoon returned. He came aboard in a jubilant mood.

"We're in," he said. "A little trick they call the *matabiche*. Or, to put it crudely, a bribe."

"How much?" Peter Rabbit asked.

"Five thousand zaire—ten thousand dollars."

Peter Rabbit winced. "For that kind of money they should throw in a couple of lepers."

After another thirty minutes of delay for refueling and safety checks, they left Kinshasa and flew due eastward, following the general route of the huge river curving through the jungle. Elliott was fascinated by the wild country below. He could see no evidence that man had ever been there.

Doctor Segal came to sit beside him. "Ever read Joseph Conrad's *Heart of Darkness?*" he asked. "There's one line in it I've never forgotten: 'Going up that river was like traveling back to the earliest beginnings of the world, when vegetation rioted on the earth and the big trees were kings.' Down there is where it took place. The Zaire River. The Congo, they called it in Conrad's day."

"In my day, too," Peter Rabbit said. "I was down there with it in sixty-five."

Tycoon turned around, surprised. "I didn't know that," he said. "Broadsword didn't mention it."

"He may not know it," Peter Rabbit said. "That was before I joined the company. Pierre Mulele and his Simbas were killing a lot of people. Me and about twelve hundred other guys hired out to the Belgians to put a stop to it."

"Did you know Loomis?" Tycoon asked.

Peter Rabbit waited a couple of heartbeats before answering. "I knew him," he said. "He was there."

Elliott had been isolated on station so long that he seldom heard much company gossip. But he knew about Loomis. Everyone knew about Loomis.

"I knew him in Vietnam," Tycoon said. "Way back early. I was there when it all happened."

"Loomis was one tough son of a bitch," Peter Rabbit said. "He was suspicious, kept to himself. And nobody messed with him. I can tell you that."

"Johnson was tougher," Tycoon said.

"Not the way I heard it," Peter Rabbit said. "Johnson was company all the way. Loomis wasn't. He was his own man. Nobody ever bought him."

"I won't argue the point," Tycoon said. "I wouldn't want to go up against either one. If they'd left the war to those two, they might not have had to call in a half-million men."

"Whatever happened to Loomis?" the Doctor asked.

"He's riding shotgun for some dictator in South America," Peter Rabbit said.

"The Caribbean," Tycoon corrected.

"The company ever drop the contract?" Elliott asked.

"A long time ago," Tycoon said. "In fact, I understand that when the top brass heard what was going on, all sorts of hell was raised."

"I worked with Johnson once," Elliott said. "He seemed all right."

"They were a hell of a team," Tycoon said.

Peter Rabbit was standing up, looking out the window. "Where exactly are we going, anyway?"

"A small Protestant mission up beyond Kisangani," Tycoon said. "I doubt if it even has a name."

Elliott was watching the jungle slide by below. "Is the country there any different from this?"

"Not a hell of a lot," Tycoon said. "It looks pretty much the same from the Atlantic to Lake Tanganyika a thousand miles to the east. There are more than ten thousand missionaries down there. The Catholics alone have six hundred missions. God knows how many Protestant."

"Will we have to travel far from the plane?"

"Not if things go right. There are more than two hundred landing strips hacked out of the jungle. We'll set down at one and pick up our man."

"How did the company find him in all that country?" Elliott asked.

"Shortwave radio, most likely. There isn't much of any other way of doing business out here."

"I suppose they were lucky to find a good case," Elliott said.

The Doctor looked up from Homer. "Not necessarily. I've looked up the figures. They average more than four hundred cases a year."

In mid-afternoon they landed on a narrow strip surrounded by jungle. The turf was rough, and the Lear jet veered sharply as Tycoon rode the brakes to bring the speed down. The end of the runway rushed toward them, but Tycoon didn't seem perturbed. He was amused by Elliott's nervousness. "You should be along when we *really* have a short runway," he said.

As they taxied up to the edge of the trees, Elliott could see a small group waiting around a Land Rover. Tycoon cut the engines, and the group came toward the plane. Two blacks carried a stretcher, and two white men walked a few paces behind.

Tycoon placed a hand on Dr. Segal's shoulder. "Time to make some medical noises," he said. Dr. Segal moved toward the door. Tycoon turned to Elliott. "You and I will go out with him. Let him do most of the talking. Just play it by ear. He'll introduce us as executives of the drug firm that has found the miracle cure."

Peter Rabbit was peering out the window. "Looks like that cat's gonna need it," he said. "He hasn't moved. He may be dead already."

"You keep out of sight," Tycoon said. "If these natives get a good look at you, it might set primitive religion back a hundred years."

The Doctor went down the ladder first and walked out to meet the group. Tycoon hung back, giving him time. Dr. Segal shook hands with the missionaries, exchanged a few words, then knelt to examine the patient. Tycoon seemed to accept the movement as a signal. He walked down the ladder. Elliott followed him.

"An excellent test case," Dr. Segal said as they walked up to the group. "Well advanced, but still retains all the vital signs."

"We're extremely grateful for your cooperation," Tycoon told the missionaries.

Dr. Segal made the introductions. Elliott missed the

names, including his own. The tall missionary was a Robert Mitchum type. The short one resembled Peter Lorre.

"We would be honored if you would care to visit our mission," the Peter Lorre said. "It's only five miles away."

Dr. Segal declined politely. "Perhaps another time," he said. "As you can understand, minutes may make the difference in our septicemic studies."

While Dr. Segal discussed the medical history of the case, going over the records, jotting down notes, Tycoon and Elliott helped the blacks load the patient. Then farewells were said, the doors closed, and Tycoon started the engines.

The whole loading operation had taken less than twenty minutes.

Tycoon devoted his full attention to the takeoff. Aligning the plane at the end of the strip, he brought the engines to maximum power before releasing the brakes. The plane gathered speed rapidly. But Tycoon held it just off the ground, gathering more air speed, until the end of the runway, then he climbed steeply into a shallow bank, circling back westward. When they reached cruise altitude, he set the automatic pilot and left his seat.

"Now the work begins," he said. "We've got to prepare the patient for admission to the hospital. As Dr. Segal told you, the disease risk is minimal. But we'll still follow antiseptic procedures, as a precautionary measure. We'll all do as Dr. Segal says."

"We've brought medipaks," Dr. Segal said. "Sterile gowns, surgical masks, gloves. And we'll all scrub thoroughly afterward. That should be sufficient."

They moved the patient to the center of the cabin space and released the stretcher straps. Dr. Segal peeled back the blankets, and they were able to study the patient for the first time.

He was big and jet black. The skin of the arms, neck, and upper torso was leathery and wrinkled. The face was broad, the nose flat, and the mouth negroid. The hair was bona fide Afro, as big as a medicine ball, and filthy. The legs were scarred from years in the brush, and the man obviously had

gone barefoot most of his life. He was breathing, but seemed
to be in a deep coma.

"I suppose we can look at the bright side," Peter Rabbit
said. "He doesn't have a bone through his nose. But who'll
ever take him for a European?"

"We'll have our own doctor at the hospital," Tycoon said.
"I doubt that anyone will check closely. But we're to do all
we can. And we're counting on you for the biggest part of his
cover. Broadsword said you once trained as a tailor."

Peter Rabbit stared at him in amazement. "How the fuck
did they know *that?*" he asked. "I've never told *anyone.*"

Tycoon shrugged. "I suppose it's in your record, somewhere. And that's how you came to be on this mission instead
of screwing a couple of chicks. It's true, isn't it? You have
training as a tailor?"

"Affirmative," Peter Rabbit said. "When I was growing up
in Brooklyn, my old man apprenticed me out to an uncle in
a tailor shop. But I thought I was through with that needle-
and-thread shit years ago."

"This won't take long," Tycoon said. "We'll help you measure him. In the compartment behind the head, you'll find a
half-dozen suits, and you can alter one to fit. I think we have
all the gear you'll need." Tycoon looked up at Elliott. "Think
you can turn that real-McCoy Afro into a continental clip? I
understand you once did some barbering."

Elliott had worked in a barbershop one summer to earn
extra money while in college. "I haven't cut hair in fifteen
years," he said.

"It'll come back to you," Tycoon said.

Dr. Segal broke out the medical packs. They donned the
sterilized gowns and strapped the black upright. After Peter
Rabbit took measurements, Elliott went to work, honing the
wire-tough Afro down to a reasonable facsimile of a European trim.

Afterward, they washed the black thoroughly. Dr. Segal
used an electric buffer to scrape away callouses from the feet
and hands. On the last part of the flight, after they cleared
the Gambia, they carefully dressed the black in his new

finery: silk underwear, over-the-calf hose, blue pastel shirt and coordinated tie, continental-style suit, and English jodhpurs. To Elliott's astonishment, a wallet filled with pocket litter—a well-used passport, credit cards, and such—established a new identity.

"How did they do all that on such short notice?" he asked.

"I suppose they always have some identification waiting for people who need it," Tycoon said. He set up a Polaroid camera and began fitting special lenses. "All we need now is his portrait to complete his passport."

Dr. Segal used tiny surgical clips to hold the black's eyes open. They propped him up and Tycoon snapped his picture.

"I just thought of something," Peter Rabbit said. "What if this cat wakes up in the hospital and starts talking whatever language he uses?"

Tycoon and Dr. Segal exchanged glances. The Doctor seemed mildly embarrassed.

"We've thought of that," he said. "I've given him a massive shot of novocaine at the base of the tongue. The muscles won't function very well for the next twenty-four hours or so."

"And after that?"

Dr. Segal reached for the black's wrist. He measured the pulse against his watch. "I doubt if there will be any 'after that,' " he said.

Chapter 17

The landing in Lisbon seemed anticlimactic. An ambulance was waiting as they taxied to the end of the runway at the small, private field off Campo Grande north of town. An unobtrusive but sizable fleet of small cars lurked in the darkness along the edges of the field.

A Mercedes pulled up and stopped beside the ambulance. While attendants loaded the patient, Elliott, Dr. Segal, Peter Rabbit, and Tycoon joined the silent driver in the Mercedes. Two cars pulled out ahead of them and two behind. The caravan drove southward into the older part of town. Turning off on Gomes Freire they headed to St. Joseph's Hospital. They were met at the emergency room door by a platoon of nurses and orderlies. A tall, lanky Portuguese doctor came out to shake hands with Dr. Segal. They conferred briefly. Broadsword emerged from the shadows and climbed into the Mercedes.

"We were lucky," Broadsword said. "We've managed to sucker them out of position. But it's taken a lot of doing, and I'm still worried. It's a big outfit. Very intense. Half our European force is keeping them occupied out toward Estoril."

The driver started the car, and they drove rapidly back toward the safehouse.

"Any idea who they are?" Tycoon asked.

"No. I've tried to keep from blowing the whole thing by making contact with them. But if I can get you people out of town safely, we'll see if we can't find one who's talkative."

Broadsword seemed pleased with the way the mission had gone. "We're well within our time margin," he said. "Langley should be satisfied."

They remained at the safehouse only long enough to complete the debriefing.

They then left at thirty-minute intervals. Peter Rabbit went first, heading for Portela de Sacavem and a flight to Barcelona. Tycoon went back to his jet, bound for Rome. Dr. Segal's flight was to Madrid, where he was scheduled to switch to a military jet for a quick trip to Washington.

Elliott was the last to leave.

"Be damned careful," Broadsword said. "I'm still worried. Go straight to Oslo, check in with Langley, then lie low until all this blows over. This organization seems to have fantastic resources. When they realize we've had them on a false scent, they may get rough. They'll want to find out what in hell has been going on."

Elliott's baggage had been packed and sent ahead. A car and driver picked him up at the safehouse to take him to Portela de Sacavem. Preoccupied with his thoughts, Elliott didn't see the collision ahead of them on the expressway. His first inkling of danger was the driver's sudden braking. He glanced up and saw a car flipping end over end thirty yards away. Another creamed on the right-hand barriers. Elliott's driver put the Mercedes into a skid and managed to miss the wrecked cars by scant inches. They came to rest on the shoulder beyond, jammed against the guard rail. Traffic screeched and crunched to a halt behind them.

They were unhurt, but they were forced to wait twenty-five minutes while the road was cleared. The delay was enough for Elliott to miss his flight. The next was two hours and fifteen minutes away.

The driver studied his watch in indecision. "I was supposed to see you off," he said. "But I'm due in Estoril in a few minutes for a pickup. And I'm already late."

"Go on," Elliott told him. "I'll be all right."

Reluctantly, the driver left. Elliott stood in the terminal for a few minutes, watching faces. He was certain he hadn't been spotted. And he had no intention of remaining conspicuous in a public terminal for two hours. He had no trouble in deciding what to do.

He walked to the taxi ramp and hired a cab. "A'Cave," he said.

The girl wasn't in sight when he entered the crowded bar. He ordered a drink and sat waiting, his back to the wall. He declined offers from other prostitutes, and watched the door. He had spent the better part of an hour toying with the drink and was on the verge of giving up when he saw her come down the stairs with an American sailor. They were in a heated discussion. Elliott moved closer.

"No suckee suckee," the girl was saying. "Fuckee fuckee. Twenty escudos."

"No fuckee fuckee," the sailor said. "Suckee suckee."

Elliott tapped the sailor on the shoulder. "I hate to interrupt such intelligent conversation. But if the lady doesn't want to blow you, why don't you blow?"

The sailor swung around unsteadily to face Elliott. "What the fuck's it to you, mate?"

"If you're not going to do anything but argue with her, I'd like to take her off your hands," he said. He turned to the girl. "Fuckee fuckee is fine with me," he said.

She smiled at him tentatively, uncertain.

"Well, it's not with me," the sailor said. "You better shove off, mate."

"I plan to," Elliott said. "But I'm taking the girl with me. And I believe you're too intelligent to try to stop me."

The sailor blinked at him. His eyes shifted to the width of Elliott's shoulders, to Elliott's loose stance. He stood for a moment in indecision.

"Ah, fuck it," he said, backing away.

"That's precisely what I intend to do," Elliott said.

Pushing the girl ahead of him, Elliott moved through the crowd and up the stairs. No taxis were in sight as they left the club, but in the distance Elliott saw one dropping a passenger. As the taxi came toward him, Elliott raised an arm and the driver pulled to a stop at the curb. Elliott and the girl climbed into the back seat. The girl gave the driver an address that meant nothing to Elliott. As they settled into the soft leather upholstery, Elliott wrapped his arms around the girl.

"You remember me?" he asked.

"Sure, I 'member you," she said. But she didn't. Her answer came too fast.

Elliott knew his childish hope was pathetic—that she would recall one brief encounter, when she no doubt screwed a dozen men nightly. Yet, she was everything that had haunted him throughout the African trip. Small, deliciously compact body. Rich, dark hair worn in a gamin cut. Delicate cleft chin, thin waif face, and childlike innocence to the eyes.

She moved her hand to his crotch. "You like?" she asked.

"I like," he said, bending for a long, tongue-searching kiss. Her hand moved experimentally. He had wild thoughts of taking her in the back of the taxi.

And in that moment, the doors of the taxi flew open and four men piled in, guns drawn.

The taxi had slowed for an intersection. The driver didn't acknowledge his new passengers or miss a beat in the handling of the wheel as he moved on through the intersection. Elliott knew, with sickening certainty, that he had been set up in a fashion any amateur should have recognized.

One unseen gunman sat behind Elliott, pistol pressing into his ribs. Two more faced him from the far side of the seat. The fourth was up front with the driver, facing to the rear. And the girl was practically in Elliott's lap, hindering any move he might make.

"Don't mind us," the one in front said. "Go right ahead with what you were doing."

He held a pistol leveled at Elliott, resting on the top of the seat: a Colt Python, .38 or .357 magnum. Elliott's mind registered the fact with trained detachment. The man's English was slightly modified BBC, with the bare hint of an accent. Hungarian? German? Czech? Elliott couldn't be certain. The man was square-built, muscular, forceful. A Rod Steiger.

"At least let the girl go," Elliott said. "She has nothing to do with this."

"Of course," the Rod Steiger man said. "We'll let the girl go."

Something in the way he said it, and in the deadly silence

that followed, brought home to Elliott the full situation. He understood that they couldn't under any circumstances let the girl go. They couldn't risk her going to the police with the story of an American being kidnaped by four armed men.

Nor did they intend to let him go, either.

Accepting these facts realistically, Elliott began to make plans.

His single-shot .38 pen was useless against such odds. He pushed it out of his mind. He would have to try something else. He kept silent, orientating himself to each man's location, watching their movements with an eye toward their degree of expertise, evaluating their relationships, and estimating his chances. He still couldn't see the man pressing against him from behind, but he had the two across the seat pegged. Lee Marvin and Ernest Borgnine.

The driver had turned westward. Elliott recognized the entrance to Monsanto Park, and he knew they were on the 24 de Janeiro Road that led to the old fort. At a bend of the road, they stopped.

"We will leave the girl here," the Rod Steiger said.

The girl looked at Elliott, dubious, searching.

"Go ahead," he said.

The Lee Marvin and Ernest Borgnine stepped out on the far side, and Elliott knew they were to be the girl's executioners. He waited until they helped the girl out of the door and moved away from the car.

Then he made his move.

He wheeled to his right, bringing his right elbow high in a vicious arc that caught the man behind him low on the jaw. He felt it crunch just as the pistol went off. A searing, white-hot iron lanced his side, but he was certain he'd managed to escape with only a flesh wound.

Without pause, he brought his left hand back, reaching for the Rod Steiger's Python, hoping the man would be too confused, too cautious to shoot.

He was. Elliott's hand closed on the gun, holding the hammer immobile, as he brought his right hand across in an open-handed chop to the throat. The blow landed perfectly.

Elliott felt the carotid bone and windpipe collapse. He had time for a fleeting sense of satisfaction. The man would do no more breathing unless someone thoughtfully performed a tracheotomy within the next four or five minutes.

Switching the Python to his right hand, Elliott plunged out of the car, hunting a target as he fell headlong. Both the Lee Marvin and the Ernest Borgnine had turned back toward the car, leaving the girl, who stood frozen by fright.

"Run!" Elliott screamed at her. Rolling frantically to one side, he squeezed off a shot at the Ernest Borgnine, and heard the bullet hit flesh. The man dropped. Elliott shifted his fire, but he was too late. The Lee Marvin fired, and in the same instant a tremendous blow to his chest slammed Elliott back into the side of the car. His head struck the left rear tire. Holding the Python firm in both hands, he fired. The .357 bullet knocked the Lee Marvin flat.

Elliott lurched to his feet and began staggering toward the trees thirty or forty yards away. Ahead, in the dim glow from the distant lights of the park, he could see the girl, awkward in high heels in the soft ground, running for cover. She looked back, saw him, and stopped.

He tried to yell, to tell her to go on, but he had no breath. His chest was an agony of fire and he was certain a lung was collapsed. He stumbled, almost fell, and she moved back toward him. At that instant, the shotgun blast hit him, sending him full length on his face. As he fought to hold onto consciousness, he heard the shotgun fire again and knew that one was for the girl. When he managed to raise his head, he saw her crumpled in the grass a few feet away, her arms and legs askew like a broken toy.

Elliott was overwhelmed for a moment with the sadness of the senseless waste. He was then swept by a consuming anger, giving him enough strength to turn, bringing the .357 around.

The driver was approaching him, the shotgun at port arms. A Maurice Chevalier. Elliott struggled to bring the pistol up, but he knew there wouldn't be enough time. And there wasn't. The unsmiling Maurice Chevalier calmly raised the shotgun, sighted at Elliott's chest, and fired from less than fifteen feet. Elliott hardly felt the buckshot hit. He was wondering, vaguely, if he should have taken time to shoot the driver before he plunged out of the car, in the hope he would still have enough time to drop the executioners.

He was still pondering the question as he sank back to the grass, and oblivion.

Chapter 18

The tanker overshot the Mona Passage. That was the consensus of Johnson's experts. Simply poor navigation, they said. The ship's track, monitored in the suite at the Jaragua as reported from Langley, showed that the ship maintained a steady west-southwest heading 22.3 nautical miles beyond the point where a turn to port normally would be expected. The experts assumed that the ship's captain, uncertain of his exact fix, made landfall to confirm his navigation with visual or radar sightings.

Loomis suspected otherwise. He pointed out that the ship was equipped with Loran. He believed the ship's eccentric course might have been for another purpose. But Johnson sided with the experts.

"They say Loran isn't all that accurate," Johnson argued. "Sometimes returns from the ionosphere confuse things. Captains who depend on Loran sometimes wake up lost. Among younger crews, celestial navigation is becoming a lost art. They depend on Loran. And we checked. The ship doesn't have the more accurate short-ranged Decca system."

"What exactly is your constant aerial surveillance?" Loomis asked. "Satellites?"

"Loomis, if I knew I probably couldn't tell you. And if I could, you probably couldn't understand it. My impression is that it's some sort of infrared, heat-seeking gadget. The experts swear by it."

"And you trust the experts."

"Don't you?"

"The experts told the people in Johnstown that if that old dam did break, it'd only raise the level of the river eighteen inches. The experts told the thirty thousand people in St.

Pierre that if old Mount Pelée did blow her top, there was no threat to human lives. The experts . . ."

"All right, I get your point. So sometimes the experts are wrong. You have some other way of watching that ship?"

"What do those surveillance scans look like? You ever see one?"

"No. But I imagine they'd be gibberish to us common folk —swirls of color and so forth, requiring a high degree of interpretation."

Loomis examined the tracks on the plot map and measured distances. "They weren't far from land here, and here," he pointed out. "I'd feel much better if we asked your people for a recheck of those two points."

"The ship maintained speed each place," Johnson said. "I don't see how they could have off-loaded cargo underway at fifteen knots."

"Johnson, as an intelligence officer, you have a few short-comings," Loomis told him. "Any third-rate deck crew in the navy could do that trick in their sleep."

"But the track of any other vessel would show."

"Maybe. Maybe not. I'm guessing. A wooden-hulled diesel, with exhaust discharge under water, moving into the track of a large ship, might not show up very well. Not unless the interpreter were looking for it specifically."

"All right," Johnson said. "I'll ask Langley for a restudy of those points. I'll tell them the Dominican Republic's resident expert doubts their competence."

With all preparations made, Loomis left the Jaragua suite for the night and returned to his quarters. He showered and sprawled across the bed. When he awoke, María Elena was beside him and the telephone was ringing. Loomis turned on the bedside lamp and picked up the receiver.

El Jefe's voice came to him strained and tired. "Both Santiago and San Francisco have fallen," he said. "La Vega has extremely heavy fighting and may not hold out long. For all effects, Ramón now controls the entire Cibao. He may move on the capital at any moment. We must make preparations."

Loomis sat up, struggling against sleep, wondering how much of El Jefe's panic was from fatigue. He checked his watch. Just after 4:00 A.M. From the open balcony came the faint sound of far-away shooting, and Loomis could see the glare of distant flares floating to earth. "What's the situation here?" he asked.

"Relatively quiet," El Jefe said. "There's some action the other side of the Duarte Bridge. Ramón thus far has concentrated his full attack in the Cibao. He has drawn our strength. We have nothing left for the *distrito*."

"Ramón may be moving too fast," Loomis said. "He may not be able to secure or supply what he's gained. Things may not be as bad as they seem."

"I've told myself that," El Jefe said. "But I must face facts. My army consists of only nine thousand men. Three infantry brigades, one artillery battalion, and one antiaircraft battalion. Ramón has engaged one brigade in Santiago, another in San Francisco, and inflicted twenty percent casualties in less than two days of fighting. The survivors of both brigades are demoralized, totally without spirit. The government forces are collapsing. And for the defense of the capital, Colonel Escortia has at his disposal only one infantry brigade and one artillery battalion."

Loomis again felt restrained by the limitations of his job. Under the government's organization charts, his sole concern was palace security and investigation of subversive activities. By law and common courtesy, he was supposed to leave the fighting to the military. Yet, he had far more combat experience than most of El Jefe's generals. Once more he felt compelled to speak up.

"Ramón still has a long way to go," he said. "And thus far, his most important gains probably have been psychological. Your men didn't expect heavy opposition. They got it. Now, they're disorganized and confused. Ramón's men are high and maybe without much reason. Ramón can't possibly have the logistics established to supply them with food and ammunition for sustained fighting."

"What would you propose?"

"I would make more use of the air force," Loomis said.

"Ten old F-51 Mustangs, twelve Vampire jets, and three B-26 bombers," El Jefe said. "One Huey gunship. Valuable, but practically worthless under the present circumstances. If there were some way of giving close support to the ground forces, I would be willing to risk a few civilian casualties. But the pilots are not well trained, and even on the ground the fighting is chaotic, confused. I simply cannot bring myself to order heavy bombing, to murder innocent people caught in the combat zones."

"The planes could be used as a psychological weapon," Loomis pointed out. "You could fly in supplies to the government forces, right over rebel rooftops. The more trips, the better. Far more trips than necessary. That would convince them government troops are not lacking supplies. You could send the Vampire jets over to rock Ramón's men with sonic booms. After a warning pass or two, a little light strafing wouldn't do much damage, but it'd scare them, remind them they're mortal. And I'd print up some leaflets. It doesn't matter what the printing says. The real message would be that they *could* be bombs. I think all that would give your men a much-needed psychological boost, and time to prepare a counterattack. And it'd give Ramón's men some second thoughts about the whole thing."

The intensity of his voice had awakened María Elena. She lay looking up at him, listening.

El Jefe considered the suggestions. "That might be very effective," he agreed.

"There's something else," Loomis said. "We may still need to contact Ramón, to inform him of Hamlet."

The line was silent for a moment. Such a thought was contrary to El Jefe's principles; one never dealt with the enemy. El Jefe had been reluctant in approving Loomis's earlier efforts to contact Ramón.

"Will that really be necessary?" he asked.

"I'm half-convinced the material isn't aboard the tanker," Loomis told him. "And if it's not, we may have to appeal to Ramón for help in finding it. Conceivably, it might be in rebel-held territory. And if he moves on the capital, he'll hamper our search here."

"But how do we know Ramón himself isn't involved?"

"Logic. The CIA claims its tangle with the Hamlet Group in Lisbon was one of the biggest confrontations with a clandestine force since the Berlin blockade. Ramón simply isn't in that league. And there is no evidence that the Hamlet people need him."

"I'm not so certain," El Jefe said.

"Hamlet has money, power, position," Loomis said. "It's obviously international in scope. The company just lost a man in Lisbon. He managed to take four Hamlet operatives with him. The Lisbon station picked up two live ones in a caper at Estoril. Octopus had complete dossiers on all six—every one was a veteran mercenary. The two live ones knew nothing except that they'd been hired, and at good pay, to do a job. Look at the logic. Why would the Hamlet people risk their whole worldwide operation by tying it to Ramón's back-country revolution? It makes no sense. I'm positive Ramón is not involved."

"Even so, I still don't see why we need to bring him into the matter. What could he do?"

"If the bomb is planted, and we can't find it, we may have to ask him to agree to a cease-fire."

"I don't think he would listen. He would suspect a trick."

"We could convince him. He's not stupid. If he sees that the country, or at least the capital, is in danger, he would understand that this is his problem, too."

The line was silent while El Jefe wrestled with the matter. "I once tried to get in touch with Ramón," he said. "At one point, I thought he might listen to reason, that we might find common ground, resolve our differences. I could find no trace of him. I sent word and received no reply."

"All the news correspondents are trying to arrange interviews," Loomis said. "The *New York Times* and the *Washington Post* have made contact with him. I'm keeping watch on both. They may lead us to him."

"I'll have to think about it," El Jefe said. "We can cross that bridge when we come to it."

Loomis called the Jaragua suite for a situation report. The tanker had reached the lower end of the Mona Passage and was now heading westward. The *Duarte* was two thousand yards in her wake, keeping close surveillance. All seemed normal.

María Elena stirred from the bed and shuffled through Loomis's music collection. She selected a tape, threaded the machine, and turned up the sound: Segovia playing Villa-Lobos. She came back to bed.

"I could do it," she said quietly.

"Do what?"

"Contact Ramón. I could walk right out the front door of this place and fly right to him, just like Mary Poppins. I wouldn't even need the umbrella."

"But you couldn't fly back. Ramón would see to that."

"I could get the message to him, though. And he'd believe me. There'd be no other reason for me to go to him voluntarily."

"Don't even think about it," Loomis said. "We may not need to contact him at all. I just wanted El Jefe aware of what we might have to do. I'm just keeping the options open."

"Damn it, Loomis, you're always spoiling my big scenes," María Elena complained. "If you hadn't been along, I might have been martyred there in the jungle. Headlines all over the world. Front page. It would have been a glorious funeral —you've probably never seen the dramatics these Latins put into something like that. It would put a crack in the foundations of the Vatican, but the church might have restored me to a state of grace. I would have been buried in white!"

"The way you describe it, I'm sorry I missed it," Loomis said.

"I might have had a theater named after me: the María Elena de la Torre National Theater. I might have made the cover of *Time* magazine again. They might even have gotten a few facts right. And all my movies would have been rereleased. I might have become a cult! Oh shit, Loomis, why do you do these things to me?"

"You've got a cult," Loomis said. "Me."

"Anyway, I could do it."

"There's no need at this point," Loomis said. "Maybe I'm imagining things. Maybe the materials *are* aboard the tanker."

"And on the other hand, maybe they're not," María Elena said.

Chapter 19

By 11:00 A.M. the tanker was hull-down on the horizon to the southeast, a faint, dirty smudge against the cobalt-blue sea. Johnson stood at the window of the Jaragua suite, oversized binoculars to his eyes, trying to see the ship through the haze of its own stack gas. Loomis didn't bother with the binoculars. He now knew everything he needed to know about the ship. The search itself was the problem.

"I can't see the destroyer yet," Johnson said.

"It's in place," Loomis told him. He had just received word that the destroyer would overtake the tanker five miles out to demand that the tanker slow to five knots and drop anchor one mile offshore. Loomis moved to the window and looked down at the Jaragua pool, where two fashion models from New York were supplementing quick divorces with Caribbean sun. A retired army couple from Virginia sipped rum and Coke beside the beds of poinsettias under the palms by the pool. Through the motionless upper leaves of the palms, on a level with the third-floor headquarters suite, he could see the approaching tanker, eighteen miles out. In little more than an hour the search would begin. He went back to the tables to study the charts.

The Newport News Shipbuilding and Dry Dock Company had provided the complete plans for the ship down to the last rivet and plate. And from various sources throughout the world the CIA had assembled information on the ship and crew. All the material, gathered in Washington and flown by jet to Santo Domingo, was now spread on the hotel tables. Loomis had spent hours digesting the information. Yet he had the uncomfortable feeling that somewhere something had been overlooked.

He spread out the blueprints once more. The tanker was typical, no different from hundreds turned out during and after World War II in the years before the oil-shipping industry learned the economics of supertankers. In its early days the tanker had been considered a giant itself: 887 feet long and sixty-five thousand tons deadweight. But the tanker was now twenty-three years old. Most modern tankers were twice its size.

The layout of the ship also was conventional. Ten huge center tanks occupied most of the space amidship. Each center tank had wing tanks on both port and starboard, totaling thirty bulk cargo spaces. The fittings were old style, with high-suction lines to within a few feet of the bottom on each tank. Separate, low-suction stripping lines were attached to the bottom of each tank to drain sludge. And each tank was equipped with heating coils to facilitate cold-weather pumping.

The search teams had been divided into four groups. Each was assigned to a specific area of the ship. The teams were now receiving final briefing in separate rooms.

"A" Team would search the tanker's bow: a maze of dry cargo spaces, pump rooms, deep tanks, boatswain's stores, and the chain locker. "B" Team, responsible for the midship tanks, had received spur-of-the-moment training to handle the special equipment required. "C" Team would search the engine spaces and boiler rooms housed in the stern section along with more pump rooms and the ship's fuel tanks. "D" Team would search the main deck and ship's superstructure: the crew's quarters, galley and cargo spaces aft, and the three-deck bridge superstructure slightly forward of midship.

And every space would have to be combed inch by inch.

Yet Loomis had the persistent feeling that he was walking into a trap. And long ago he had learned to trust his instincts. He studied the blueprints, analyzing what clues he could dredge up from his subconscious.

The more Loomis thought, the more all the unknowns narrowed to one question: Who were the Hamlet people?

The Lisbon incident as described by Johnson still disturbed
him. He felt that if he knew where to look, the Lisbon operation might provide some indication.

"Who was the man who got wasted?" Loomis asked.

Johnson placed the binoculars on the windowsill and
rubbed his eyes. "Mike Elliott," he said. "I don't think you
knew him. He came in later. I worked with him, a time or
two."

"Good man?"

"In his own way. But shy on discipline. He had a weakness
for women."

"Imagine that," Loomis said.

"We think they used a girl to suck him in. She was a known
prostitute. But we haven't been able to learn why he went
from the airport directly to a nightclub. He was seen there
alone, then later leaving with the girl."

"Maybe he knew her," Loomis said. "Maybe the opposition
had her staked out, hoping he'd show."

Johnson considered the theory. "Possible," he said.

"Probable," Loomis said. "And that may mean they're
ahead of us, anticipating."

"You have a sneaky mind," Johnson observed.

"It's the company I keep," Loomis said.

The tanker refused to obey or acknowledge signals from
the *Duarte*. Ordered to slow to five knots, she maintained a
steady fifteen, steering straight toward harbor. The *Duarte*
repeated the order and issued coordinates for mandatory
anchorage. The tanker refused to reply. Two miles from
shore, the *Duarte* sent a five-inch shell across the tanker's
bow. The shell splashed less than two hundred yards off the
tanker's starboard bow, raising an instant column of water
fifty feet high. Perceptibly, the tanker slowed. The *Duarte*
moved in closer and repeated the coordinates for anchorage.

Loomis and Johnson watched the action through binoculars, standing in the bow of a fifty-foot motor launch. The
thirty Dominican marines with them would serve as the
boarding party. As they watched, the dull boom of the

Duarte's five-incher came to them across the distance, a full fifteen seconds after the shell splash had disappeared.

"I think that did it," Johnson said, studying the ship. "He seems to be altering course, moving out of the channel."

Their launch was tossed by deep swells. Loomis had difficulty keeping his binoculars trained on the ship, but he could see a half-dozen men moving toward the bow. "They've called away the anchoring detail," he said. "They're going to drop the hook. We might as well go on out there."

He turned and motioned to the coxswain of the launch, who nodded and rang his bells for more power. The launch turned sharply to starboard as the coxswain steered for the opening in the breakwater.

As they came abreast of the ancient cannon at the mouth of the muddy Ozama, the tanker dropped anchor. The roar of the anchor chain playing out through the hawse pipes sent seabirds along the breakwater scurrying into the air. The *Duarte* didn't anchor but stood by less than five hundred yards off the tanker's beam. Loomis could see that the *Duarte*'s quad-forty mounts amidships were manned and ready.

They rounded the breakwater jetty. The coxswain turned the launch sharply to port to meet the first full swells from the open sea and steered straight for the ship.

"Bigger bastard than I thought," Johnson said.

From their vantage point, low on the water, the high sides of the tanker loomed like cliffs. The coxswain maneuvered the launch around to the starboard side. Loomis couldn't see anyone on deck or in the ship's superstructure. But as the coxswain slowed, turning the boat in a circle toward the ship's side, a head appeared at the railing. As Loomis watched, the man raised a loud-hailer.

"What the hell is this?" the amplified voice boomed in English. "What the fuck you cocksuckers want?"

"Well, they sure sound like our kind of people," Johnson said.

Loomis motioned, and a crewman brought him a hailer. He put it to his mouth and pulled the trigger. "Lower a ladder," he yelled at the man. "We're coming aboard."

The head disappeared. For a full minute, Loomis thought his demand might be ignored. Then three crewmen went to work, swinging out a small boat boom. When it was secured, a thirty-foot Jacob's ladder tumbled out and dangled from the boom to the surface of the sea.

"Christ, are we going to climb that?" Johnson asked.

"We might try going up the anchor chain," Loomis said. "But I think the ladder would be easier."

"I'll sure say one thing for them," Johnson said. "They don't believe in making anything easy for anybody."

The tanker rode high in the water, the Plimsoll well above the surface. As the coxswain brought the boat in under the boom, Loomis studied the huge, raw red patches of lead paint protecting the metal from rust. Little of the original color—black—remained. Various exhaust lines along the ship's side spewed sewage, bilge pumpings, and deck drainings into the sea, raising a strange mixture of smells. Even in the context of most tramp freighters, this one was filthy.

A boathandler moved past Loomis, carefully walking the gunnels, and snared a dangling boom line with his boathook. As the coxswain killed the engine, the boathandlers pulled in slack on the lines and held the launch in place under the swaying Jacob's ladder. With the swells running four and five feet, the bottom of the ladder couldn't be anchored. Loomis slung his Schmeisser, grabbed the ladder, and went up first. There was a trick to it. The ladder was stiffer when approached from the side. Otherwise, one's feet tended to shoot skyward.

Oddly, there were no curious faces at the rails. Loomis climbed rapidly up to the boom. As he pulled himself up onto the hardwood, catching his breath with short gasps, he could see three officers and a group of seamen waiting on deck. No one moved to help him. Sweating heavily from the exertion, Loomis waited until his breathing returned nearer to normal. He then inched his way across the boom to the steel deck. As he walked toward the group, he singled out the officer wearing a cap with a tarnished scrambled-egg insignia.

"Captain Larson?" Loomis asked. "I'm Clay Loomis of . . ."

"I don't give a fuck what your name is," Larson interrupted. "What you mean, firing that fucking gun? What do you want?"

Loomis measured him for a moment. Larson stood six-feet-three or four. He would weigh close to three hundred pounds, with more muscle than fat. And he was one of the ugliest specimens of humanity Loomis had ever seen. A long scar gave the left side of his face a ribald leer. His nose was flat, and his pale blue eyes and blond hair seemed strangely obscene and out of place in company with the swarthy, pock-marked face.

Loomis kept his voice level and unemotional. He didn't bother to unsling his Schmeisser.

"I'm aboard this ship as the personal representative of the President of the Dominican Republic," he said. "Anything you say to me will be considered said to him."

Larson remained silent, waiting. The ring of misfits around him looked as if they'd been salvaged from Devil's Island. Loomis kept his eyes on Larson. He could hear Johnson and the boarding party coming up behind him.

"A man aboard this ship was exposed in Lisbon to bubonic plague," Loomis said. "You and the ship are in quarantine under International Sanitary Regulations of the World Health Organization, third annotated edition, and the International Health Regulations, as adopted by the twenty-second World Health Assembly in 1969. You and your men will be taken ashore for thorough physical examinations."

"I'll be goddamned if we will," Larson said. "I'm not leaving this ship. I'm captain. Nobody tells me what to do."

"That's your privilege," Loomis told him. "But you'll be going against explicit orders from your owners. And you can't go in to dock and off-load here until you comply. If you put to sea, you'll have the same problem anywhere you go, with any country or port in the civilized world."

Larson looked past Loomis to Johnson and his men. "Who are all these people?" he asked.

"World Health Organization and a half-dozen other agencies, all working with Dominican Republic Public Health Service," Loomis said. "As you may know, the plague is transmitted by a rat-flea chain. These professionals and their crews will fumigate the entire ship. A medical team is waiting ashore for you and your men. The whole thing will take less than forty-eight hours. It's been cleared with your owners."

Larson stared at the boarding party. His mouth worked several times before he could form words. Loomis had a strong feeling that Larson was reacting more in fear than from surprise and anger.

"Impossible," Larson said. "I've got dock space in Houston Friday. And there's a load waiting in Aruba."

"You know maritime law as well as I do," Loomis said. "Houston would put you in quarantine."

"Which one of my crew is supposed to be sick?"

"Not sick. Exposed. An able by the name of Stanislaus Boleslaw."

Larson laughed as if he had found the solution to his whole problem. "Shit, Boleslaw's dead," he said.

Johnson walked up beside Loomis. His face showed no surprise at the news. "Not from vomiting, diarrhea, and high fever, I hope."

"Naw. Fell over the side. Third day out. No loss. A boozer. Never did a lick of work."

"Just for the record, did anyone see him fall?" Johnson asked.

"Shit, nobody there to see. He wasn't missed until he didn't show for morning watch. We held an official inquiry. It's all in the log. You'll find I keep good books."

"We'll take a look, if you don't mind," Johnson said.

Larson led the way forward to his sea cabin. The ship was incredibly dirty. Lead-based paint, oil smudges, rusted plates, and welding slag covered the decks. Below, the clutter was even worse. Tools and equipment lay scattered and rusting wherever someone had tossed them the last time they were used. The passageways showed no evidence of having been cleaned since the ship was built. And the tanker was permeated with the smells of crude oil, engine fumes, stack gas, stale urine, and cooking grease. Larson seemed right at home amidst the mess. He showed them into a small wardroom.

From a shelf over a writing desk Larson took down a heavy journal. He was right in one respect. He kept good books. Their neatness was dramatically out of context with the rest of the ship.

The *Captain's Inquiry into the Death of Able Seaman Stanislaus Boleslaw* was typed into an impressive document bearing the signatures of all ship's officers. Included was extensive testimony from those who last saw Boleslaw alive and from those familiar with his habits.

The *Inquiry* found that Boleslaw spent most of his off-watch time back on the fantail smoking his pipe. The *Inquiry* even noted that the smoking area on open deck was restricted to a small portion of the fantail. According to the testimony, Boleslaw was feeling his way aft in the dark. The cook's helper had just dumped a load of garbage over the fantail and had gone back to the galley for another, leaving the safety chain down in front of the garbage chute. Boleslaw went aft, feeling for the chain in the darkness, and walked right over the side. Attached to the *Inquiry* was a list of Boleslaw's personal effects. Among them, Loomis noticed a detailed description of a half-dozen pipes.

Johnson read the *Inquiry,* impatiently tapping a pencil on the metal desk. "Well, it certainly seems to be in order," he said. "But Boleslaw's death really complicates matters. May take a week to clear this up."

"I can't wait a week," Larson said. "My owners don't pay me to fuck around."

"I assure you that you in no way can be held responsible," Johnson said. "A full report of the circumstances will be filed with your owners. Thus far, they have been most cooperative."

Larson now definitely seemed unsure of himself. He was worried. Loomis was certain of that. Larson was good at hiding his fear, but he now had all the appearances of a man trapped, hunting desperately for a way out.

"If Boleslaw's dead, what's the problem?" Larson asked.

Johnson shrugged. "For all we know, Boleslaw was out of his head with fever, went to the rail to vomit, and fell over the side from vertigo—all caused by the first symptoms of the plague. And if that happened, then every member of your crew has been exposed."

"I can't leave the ship untended," Larson insisted.

"Your owners have suggested that you sign responsibility for the ship over to the Dominican Republic until the matter is cleared up. The ship is safely at anchor. We will have plenty of experienced shiphandlers aboard. If any weather should develop, we can have you back aboard in twenty minutes."

"What outfit you with, anyway?" Larson asked belatedly.

"World Health Organization," Johnson said without blinking an eye.

Larson sat lost in thought, idly tracing the long scar across his face. Loomis could understand a certain amount of concern. The delay would rearrange his schedule of docking for loading and unloading. The time lost might be even more valuable than the cargo involved. Time had been the owners' chief concern. But Loomis sensed that Larson had on his mind some other, far more important problem.

For the first time, Loomis began to have hope that he had been wrong, that the nuclear materials were on board.

"I'll have to talk to the owners," Larson said.

He spent almost thirty minutes in the radio shack. He emerged a defeated man.

"All right," he said to Loomis. "Let's get this shit over with."

Loomis and Larson signed the papers that had been prepared. The ship's crew was mustered on the main deck and transferred to motor launches for the trip to shore.

As Larson left the deck he hesitated at the rail for a moment, looking back, visually searching the ship.

It could have been the natural reaction of a captain leaving his command, ascertaining that all was in order before going over the side.

But Loomis felt there was something more in the gesture.

Larson went over the side with the demeanor of a man heading toward the gallows.

Loomis and Johnson stood at the rail, watching the motor launches heading toward the opening at the end of the breakwater. The launches were to return immediately with the remainder of the search teams and the sophisticated electronics equipment flown in from Washington.

"Think Larson knows what we're after?" Loomis asked.

"I'm not certain," Johnson said. "But if he doesn't, there are plenty of people aboard who do."

Loomis watched the seagulls sailing around the stern, searching for garbage. "How you figure that?" he asked.

"Larson told me. You see, I knew Boleslaw." Johnson sat down on a bollard, leaned back on the life lines, and stretched out his legs. "In his own way, Boleslaw was a strange one. I worked with him. He had a Polish background of some sort but was reared in Hungary. Something to do with the war, I suppose. He was one of the young heroes in the Hungarian revolt during the fifties. He had to flee the country and made his way to America. He joined the U.S. Army. With his background, he shot up through the ranks, received a good education on the GI Bill after a hitch in Vietnam, returned to duty, and was a captain in G2 when he transferred over to the company. He was a linguist, specializing in Slavic languages."

"All very interesting. But what the hell does that have to do with this?"

"As I said, he was a strange one. A health freak. Worked out with weights, kept in top shape no matter where he was, what he was doing. Never polluted his body with poisons such as alcohol, coffee, or tea."

Johnson paused to watch the motor launches disappear around the head of the breakwater.

"And he didn't smoke," he added.

Loomis pondered all the ramifications of that bit of intelligence. "If Larson fabricated Boleslaw's death inquiry, then he must have known—or suspected—he was CIA."

"I don't know," Johnson said. "The whole mess puzzles me. Larson is scared shitless about something. He didn't seem worried about Boleslaw. In fact, he even bordered on bragging about that. But when it became plain we were taking the ship, he really turned worried. I think now the stuff is on board. I just hope Boleslaw managed to leave us some message or clue, before they killed him and threw him over the side. Sure would save us some work."

After rigging the accommodation ladder on the starboard side, the special teams brought aboard their equipment and started the search. Loomis and Johnson wandered throughout the ship, monitoring progress. The job was marvelously complicated.

The forepart of the ship contained a maze of cargo spaces both above and below the waterline. To make certain nothing was missed, all goods were removed from the two huge dry cargo spaces under the fo'c'sle. Nothing was left to chance. The entire anchor chain was hauled up from the chain locker to ensure that no nuclear birdcages were stored beneath. All of the bos'n's stores were brought to the main deck and examined. The forepeak tanks and deep tanks forward were probed electronically and physically.

The cargo tanks amidships proved less difficult than Loomis had expected. After the first few efforts, the searchers fell into a routine that scoured all thirty tanks within ten hours.

The stern section was another matter. The engine rooms, the after-engine rooms, the boiler spaces, and the pump rooms contained hundreds of inaccessible areas where physical search was hampered, and thick metal thwarted the radiation monitors. Closed-circuit television probes were brought in to search crevices no man could enter. The work was tedious and painstaking, continuing after other areas had been secured.

The crew's quarters yielded nothing of interest, aside from an impressive mass of clutter and an interesting collection of

pornography. Boleslaw's bunk was located and searched. No
hidden message was found.

With the search entering the twentieth hour, Loomis had
spread the ship's blueprints on the steel deck. He was kneel-
ing, tracing measurements in the pumping rooms against his
notes, when a hollow, popping noise seemed to come up
through the ventilator shafts on the after part of the ship.

"What the hell was that?" Johnson asked behind him.

Loomis reached for his Schmeisser. "I don't know," he said.
"But I sure as hell think we better go find out."

On the third level below the main deck, they met four men
from "C" Team fleeing topside in panic. Loomis tried to stop
them.

"Gunmen!" one of them yelled. "They're killing everybody!"

As if to prove him right, another burst of gunfire sounded
from below. Loomis grabbed the man's arm and held him.
He was one of the specialists, flown in from Washington.

"Where are they?" Loomis demanded.

"In the engine spaces," he said, pointing.

"How many?"

The man seemed confused. "I don't know," he said.
"Three, maybe four."

"What happened?"

"We opened the drive-shaft housing. They were inside.
They started shooting. They killed Smitty and Joe."

He was pulling away. Loomis turned him loose. He scur-
ried on up the ladder. Johnson worked the action on his
Schmeisser to chamber a round. "No wonder Larson was
worried," he said. "Apparently he has some passengers not
carried on the ship's papers."

Loomis tried to remember the layout of the engine spaces.
From what he could recall, a narrow hatch opened onto a
catwalk that made a square figure eight through the main
engine room. The engines were in the center. On the outside
of the catwalk were boilers, evaporators, and a maze of machinery. At regular intervals ladders led down to a steel deck
and the engine bedplates. Loomis had no idea where the

drive-shaft housing was located. Logically, it should be some-where at the rear of the engine spaces.

He led Johnson down to the main engine room hatch. It was standing wide open. None of the fleeing search team had bothered to dog it. Loomis moved cautiously to the opening.

Twenty feet away, crawling slowly toward them on the catwalk, a member of the search team was calling for help. He had left a trail of blood along the catwalk.

"Cover me," Johnson said, moving past Loomis. He trotted out onto the catwalk, picked up the man, and brought him back. There were no sounds from the engine room.

Johnson put the man on the deck. Loomis recognized him as one of the radiation specialists from Los Alamos. He had been hit in the stomach, groin, and thigh. He wasn't bleeding much; Loomis figured he would live. The man was conscious, eyes bright with pain.

Johnson knelt beside him. "How many of them are there?" he asked.

"Four," the man said, gasping for breath. "Smitty's down there. I think he's dead."

"Well, we'll go see," Johnson said. "Where exactly are those four fellows?"

"They were in the drive shaft. The housing. But I think they've moved."

Six Dominican marines came down the ladder, guns ready. Loomis motioned for them to stop where they were.

Johnson edged to the hatch and peeked in. "I've never seen so many places for bullets to bounce," he said. "I think the fewer people we have shooting in there, the better."

Loomis nodded agreement. He saw movement at the far end of the main engine room. He held his fire, on the outside chance it was a search-team member.

"My time to move," Loomis said to Johnson. "Cover me."

Crouching, he ran down the catwalk. He made it past the first engine. A stream of bullets spanged off the metal around him. Johnson fired one long, sustained burst that put heads down. Loomis rolled off the catwalk and dropped the eight feet to the steel deck. He took up the firing so Johnson could make his advance. When Johnson reached the crosswalk, he took up the firing, giving Loomis time to hunt cover.

The old team was working again. Loomis jammed home a fresh magazine with a feeling of exhilaration. They had established triangulation. With any luck, they should be able to cover each other through the advance.

"This is Interpol!" Johnson yelled from the catwalk. "You fuckers are under arrest!"

Johnson was just making noise, hoping to rattle them, make them get careless.

The ploy worked. Loomis saw a figure move, trying to spot Johnson. Loomis cut loose with a burst. The man dropped.

Then all hell broke loose. Two guns sprayed the area around Loomis, the bullets ripping into the boiler behind him with an uncannily loud clamor. Live steam roared through the bullet holes. Loomis had to move. He dashed across an open space to the after-engine, hearing Johnson's gun above covering him. He dropped beside the engine, taking what protection he could from a brace beam. For a full minute he heard nothing except the roar of the steam.

He became aware of a tingling in his left arm. A ricochet had caught him below the elbow. He was bleeding profusely. An artery had been severed. He slipped off his belt and was preparing a tourniquet when he heard Johnson's signal—a three-round burst. Loomis quickly stepped around the brace beam and sprayed the end of the engine room while Johnson moved up. Loomis then dashed to the next brace while Johnson covered him.

Loomis waited impatiently, watching. He glanced down at his arm. He was losing a lot of blood. Figuring he couldn't wait any longer, he cut loose with a three-round burst, signaling Johnson. When Johnson's gun took up the fire, Loomis plunged into the aisle shooting, advancing. He saw a muzzle blast and shifted his fire. A dark shape sank to the deck. He heard Johnson charging on the catwalk, firing down on the gunmen at close range, bouncing the bullets off the heavy bulkhead behind them. They attempted to flee in a desperate gamble. Loomis saw their target: a hole fifteen feet beyond them, where the deckplate had been removed to pump the bilge. He knew that if they reached the bilge spaces, they'd be difficult to hit. He cut the last two men down. They fell, sprawling, their machine pistols cartwheeling across the steel deck.

Johnson came clattering down the ladder. "This all of them?" he asked.

"All I saw," Loomis said.

Gun at ready, Johnson checked the bodies. "All four dead as lead can make them," he said. "I guess that's Smitty over there. He's dead, too." He noticed Loomis's sleeve. "What the fuck happened to you?"

"Nick," Loomis said. He put his Schmeisser down and reached for the pressure point above his elbow.

"Well, I'd sure hate to see you get a real wound," Johnson said. "You might bleed a little." He turned and yelled for the marines to send down a medic. He pulled a knife and ripped Loomis's sleeve, exposing the wound. "Doesn't look too bad," he agreed. "I guess you'll live, if you've got enough blood."

Feeling suddenly weak, Loomis leaned back against the engine. Johnson walked over to the bodies. "Those fellows sure are funny-looking Latins," he said.

"Maybe it's because they're Arabs," Loomis told him.

"Arabs? No shit?" Johnson rolled one over with his boot. "If that don't beat all," he said. "I thought we were wrapping up this can of worms. Now it looks like we've just opened another one."

Johnson was right. Octopus quickly identified the four Arabs as the terrorists who had destroyed the Israeli airliner at Tel Aviv ten days before. Larson apparently was transporting them to safety. He was well known in international crime circles as the man to see for smooth smuggling operations. Langley surmised that the Arabs were to be landed by raft on the coast of South America.

The ship search was concluded. No trace of the nuclear material was found.

"It went aboard in Lisbon," Johnson said. "It isn't aboard now. There's only one way to find out in a hurry what happened to it."

"What do you have in mind?" Loomis asked, knowing.

"I've taken the liberty of bringing in three interrogation specialists. Let's give them a crack at Larson."

"What sort of subtle, sophisticated interrogation techniques are in vogue these days?" Loomis asked. "Drawing and quartering?"

The sarcasm was wasted on Johnson. "Larson will walk out without a mark on him," he said.

"And probably not enough brains left to piss in his pants without help," Loomis said. "All right. Take him. But spare me the details."

They returned to their headquarters at the Jaragua. While Johnson reported the results of the search to Washington, Loomis called El Jefe, who didn't seem surprised over the failure. He had been following its progress, hour by hour, and had concluded much earlier that the material was not aboard.

And now, he had news of his own.

"María Elena is gone," he said. "She walked right out the front door and apparently just disappeared."

Loomis felt his last bit of energy draining away in an overwhelming sense of helplessness.

"Just like Mary Poppins," he said.

Chapter 20

The planes came over San Francisco de Macoris on the average of one every ten minutes. The C-47s continued on across town to the airfield to land supplies, but occasionally an F-51D Mustang or jet Vampire Mark 1 returned to strafe. The rebel forces were well protected, for the most part, and the strafing did little damage. Ramón knew that the whole operation was psychological. But he didn't know what to do about it.

He sat at a long teakwood table in the basement of the huge old church, waiting impatiently for his advisers to arrive, certain that each hour of indecision brought his entire movement closer to disaster.

Ramón was fearful that his revolution had moved too rapidly, too successfully. Sniper teams he had dispatched merely to harass and to worry government forces instead had engaged and won battles. Strategic enclaves he had envisioned as strong points had been expanded through sheer enthusiasm, and now the very size of his holdings endangered the whole revolution.

The victories had come too soon. He wasn't prepared for the tremendous responsibilities. His program had called for a campaign of several months, gradually building his strength in the north, allowing him time to assimilate supply sources before moving on the capital. His orderly plan of advance included step-by-step occupation of plantations, factories, food plants, and warehouses. Now, the map of conquest was inflated, hodgepodge, and dangerously out of balance. He had entire cities at his disposal, but the price of victory was beyond his means. He had to find some way of feeding and supplying thousands.

Ramón held his breath as a Vampire Mark 50, more aggressive than most, passed low overhead, strafing the streets. He heard .50-caliber shells splattering against the old church walls, and the rain of glass and plaster on the tile floors above. For a heart-stopping moment, he feared that his exact location was known and that a cluster of bombs might follow the bullets. But reason told him his whereabouts could not possibly be known. He himself had not chosen the site of his strategy conference until a few minutes ago. His advisers hadn't been informed. They had been ordered to report to various safehouses around town, where they would be picked up by a single driver, who alone would know the meeting place.

Dust and powdered plaster drifted down from the ceiling, blanketing the surface of the table with fine debris. Alfredo came hurrying down from the sanctuary above to make certain Ramón was safe. Ramón forced a smile of reassurance. He calmly checked his watch.

"It is time," he said. "Send the car. Tell the driver to watch the planes and to stop for cover when necessary. But we must hurry."

Alfredo trotted back upstairs. Ramón wiped the dust from the table and noticed with irritation that he had a tremor in his hands. He couldn't remember when he'd last eaten. He waited impatiently until Alfredo returned.

"See if the good father has food," Ramón said.

Alfredo returned a few minutes later with rice, beans, and the father's apologies that there was not more.

"This will do," Ramón said. "Perhaps we can feed the multitudes later."

By the time the first of his advisers arrived, he had finished eating. After drinking two cups of strong black coffee laced with rum, he felt much better. Within thirty minutes, the eight members of his general staff had assembled. The ninth, he was informed, had been killed during the final assault on the police barracks in Santiago.

Ramón called the meeting to order.

"We have arrived at a crucial point in our revolution," he

told them. "If we go ahead, we risk all. We're not prepared. Yet we can't wait. We can't sit back and hold on to what we've won. And if we retreat, pull back, we will lose momentum we may never regain. I would like to hear your views."

"We can't stop now," said Ricardo Morales, the hatchet-faced lawyer from Santiago. "We have El Jefe reeling. Let's move on the Distrito Nacional."

"That's exactly what El Jefe would want us to do," said Julio Paredes, the portly, asthmatic doctor from San Francisco de Macoris. "Most of his forces are concentrated in the *distrito*. There he has tanks, air power, artillery. And he knows that as long as he holds the capital, he holds the government."

"We also have stronger forces in the *distrito*," Professor Mario Salamanca reminded them. "And the discipline is better. Our snipers have remained snipers. Our sappers have been content to hit and run. And we are still living on El Jefe's economy. No one has to feed us."

Ramón moved to block the haggling. "Has your staff devised the battle plan I requested?"

"In detail," the Professor said. He hunted in his briefcase, unfolded a large map of the *distrito*, and stood to spread it on the table. Adjusting his heavy horn-rims and brushing an errant mop of unruly hair out of his eyes, the Professor spread his feet into his lecturing stance. "Instead of concentrating on the Duarte Bridge, as was done in past revolutions, we propose to focus instead on the Old Town, from here to here, along El Conde from the Gate to the river," he said. "The approaches to the bridge will be blocked to the east, halting traffic from the military base at San Isidro. We will concentrate strong forces at this point here, on the Boca Chica highway, and here, on Las Americas at this junction."

"The sea on one side, the river on the other," Doctor Paredes said. "It would be a trap."

"All our forces would be concentrated on two fronts," Professor Salamanca pointed out.

"The gunboats and destroyers could shell from the river, or from the sea," Doctor Paredes said.

"That possibility remains wherever we fight in the *distrito*," the Professor countered. "If El Jefe chooses, his destroyers can stand at sea and shell the entire town."

Ramón again stepped into the debate. "What are the chances for assassination?"

All eyes turned to the Professor. He hesitated, adjusting his horn-rims carefully, smoothing his scruffy beard. When he spoke his voice was firm. "Minimal. El Jefe never leaves his quarters. Never. But we have options. El Jefe has placed the entire *distrito* defense under command of Colonel Escortia. If we remove him at the opening of the battle, El Jefe's defense structure will be thrown into confusion. There is much infighting, much jealousy, in the upper echelons of his military. El Jefe would lose valuable time in re-establishing line of command. And there is another possibility. The *norteamericano*, Loomis, has become something of a security blanket for El Jefe, psychologically as well as in fact. Loomis travels freely in the streets. An ambush could be arranged. His death would contribute much toward El Jefe's eventual decision to abandon the fight. And the country."

Ramón was impressed. If one couldn't reach the kingpin, the destruction of the props might suffice. Yet he hadn't thought of that possibility himself.

"Can you kill them?" he asked.

"Colonel Escortia is careless," the Professor said. "He moves on a schedule, and his daily routine varies little. He can be killed. Almost in any time-span. Loomis would be more difficult. But not impossible. His activities are erratic. He used to spend much time in the whorehouses. But he hasn't been there much lately. He once shunned other *norteamericanos*, excepting now and then one of the women from the divorce flights. But now he seems to have invited some *norteamericanos* into the country. He has set up a sort of headquarters in the Jaragua and spends time there with them and with other members of El Jefe's staff. But he is also careless, and perhaps arrogant. He could be watched and killed."

Ramón felt a vague stirring of prescience. For some time

he had sensed that some unknown factor was affecting the government, altering decisions. The Professor's words provided the first solid clue.

"Tell us more about these headquarters," he said.

Professor Salamanca shrugged and spread his hands in a helpless gesture. "It is something new," he said. "Security around the Jaragua is tight. We do know that they've installed special communications equipment of some kind. There is a lot of activity. At least a dozen *norteamericanos* have flown in by commercial jet, and we've had reports of unmarked planes setting down briefly to unload both passengers and cargo. Yesterday, a tanker anchored out past the breakwater. There are reports that the *Duarte* fired a shell across the tanker's bow, but I cannot confirm this. As you know, the *Duarte* often fires its guns in practice. And I understand that with the five-inch gun, once you have loaded, the only practical way to unload is to fire it. But we do know that Loomis, some of the *norteamericanos,* and two dozen or more Dominicans went aboard. The ship's crew was taken to the university, and as far as we can determine, they are still there. We don't know what's happening."

Ramón allowed his anger to surface. He struck the table with his fist. "Why wasn't I informed of this?"

The Professor seemed undisturbed by the outburst. "It happened only yesterday," he said. "And we didn't know where you were."

"But the headquarters, the *norteamericanos* landing. You should have reported these things."

"We weren't certain of anything," the Professor said. "If I reported all the vague rumors that come to me, I would have time for nothing else."

"Do you suppose they're preparing for intervention by the United States?" Doctor Paredes asked.

"The *norteamericanos* undoubtedly are CIA," Ramón agreed. "But what could the tanker have to do with it? I don't understand that at all."

"If El Jefe has opened the door to the CIA, intervention won't be far behind," Doctor Paredes predicted.

"My information from Washington is that they won't intervene, no matter what the provocation," Ramón said. "Criticism was heavy after the last occupation—in sixty-five. Much has been written that President Johnson received bad information from both State and the CIA and that the occupation was unnecessary. And of course the intervention in Vietnam almost wrecked the country. I personally don't think any American president would risk it, no matter what pressures he might be under."

"Well, they're up to something, apparently," Doctor Paredes said.

"We may be jumping to conclusions," lawyer Morales pointed out. "It might be something that has nothing to do with the revolution."

Ramón considered that possibility. "The communications equipment worries me," he said. "The tie-up undoubtedly is to Washington."

"Special Projects Division, CIA, perhaps," Doctor Paredes said. "Maybe they're preparing to direct El Jefe's military operations and provide so-called specialists, as they did in the earliest days in Vietnam."

"I don't think so," Ramón said. "El Jefe has resisted them for years. Why would he suddenly do a complete about-face?"

"It must have something to do with the tanker," Morales said. "Perhaps a smuggling operation."

"That is likely," Ramón agreed. "I think there is a strong possibility that it has nothing to do with the revolution."

"But we must keep it in mind," Doctor Paredes said. "We must not forget the possible ramifications."

"Agreed," Ramón said.

"I don't think we should let it deter us from our path," Professor Salamanca said.

Ramón smiled. "And what is our path, Professor? The capital? Let's examine the pros and cons. What would be the worst thing that could happen if we move on the capital?"

"Failure," Doctor Paredes said. "Total defeat."

"Impossible," Professor Salamanca said. "Absolutely impossible. We'll never be more ready."

"We can't hold out here long," Morales said. "And if we fall back, the government troops will increase the pressure on Santiago and in Santo Domingo."

Professor Salamanca nodded. "And by the same token, if we move on the capital, the government will pull troops from both Santiago and San Francisco, relieving pressure on both. Our forces in the Cibao would then be able to hold until the issue in the capital is decided."

Ramón tended to agree. "Let me recapitulate," he said. "We concur that we cannot hold indefinitely the ground we have gained. The pressure is too formidable. And we cannot retreat. The psychological setback would be too severe, perhaps disastrous. Our only recourse is to maintain our forward momentum by moving on the capital with an all-out attack. Is there any disagreement?"

There was none.

"On the whole, Professor, I endorse your proposed plan of battle," Ramón said. "I appreciate the element of surprise. The government forces will be expecting pressure at the Duarte Bridge. This plan will isolate their strong points. Yet, by controlling the eastern approaches, we can control the bridge. I only see one serious disadvantage. Once fighting begins in earnest, our troops will be isolated, boxed in by the river, the sea, and the two fighting fronts. How do you propose to supply our forces throughout sustained fighting?"

"By controlling the tidal basin and the docks," the Professor said. "We would move supplies in from the east, here, then cross the river, perhaps under cover of darkness, at this point here. If the government moves strong forces across the bridge to hit our supply route, pressure would be relieved on the fighting fronts."

Ramón immediately grasped the daring ingenuity of the plan. There was a calculated risk in dividing forces. But if the tidal basin were controlled, the government forces would be spread along a lengthy front.

Ramón laughed. "Marvelous. My congratulations, Professor. Does anyone object to the basic premise of the plan?"

There was no response.

"Then we are in agreement," Ramón said. "We will attack,

using this basic plan. And the sooner the better, as we cannot
long hold out here. Would daylight, day after tomorrow, be
satisfactory, Professor?"

"We will be ready."

"Good," Ramón said. "Let's prepare the details."

The battle maps were spread, and for two hours the rebel
commanders drafted assignments, prepared orders, and
designated sector responsibilities. Ramón found that he had
little to do but listen. His commanders were thorough, experienced men. Most had survived previous revolutions, and
were now putting into practical use the valuable lessons they
had learned.

The work was interrupted by Alfredo's soft knock at the
door. Ramón excused himself and went out into the stairway.
A runner from divisional headquarters stood waiting. His
message was brief: María Elena de la Torre had been captured by rebel forces in Santo Domingo and was now being
brought by car to San Francisco.

Ramón returned to the conference, walked to a cabinet,
and broke out the priest's communion wine. He filled nine
chalices, and signaled to Alfredo to distribute them at the
table.

Ramón proposed the toast. "I have a feeling, gentlemen,
that the revolution has entered a new phase." He lifted his
chalice. "To our success, gentlemen."

Before the silver chalices returned to the table, Alfredo
opened another bottle in preparation for the second toast.

Chapter 21

Loomis put every available man and every waking moment into the search for María Elena. He led four raids on known rebel assembly points. More than two hundred suspected rebels were rounded up and thoroughly questioned. Every informant listed in the secret books of the Policía Nacional was alerted to the ten-thousand-peso reward posted personally by El Jefe.

But results were meager.

The best information came from a minor rebel official who collapsed under interrogation. He confirmed Loomis's fear that María Elena had been taken into rebel-held territory. He didn't know where.

Loomis at last had to admit that without more information he was helpless. If he could ascertain Ramón's exact location, a surprise raid into rebel territory might succeed. Or an infiltration might prove effective. But under intensive questioning, the rebel consistently denied he even knew what city Ramón presently was using as his headquarters. The rebel offered his own private view that one of the weaknesses of the revolution was Ramón's practice of never remaining long in one place. Even members of the headquarters staff often were unable to reach Ramón, the rebel said.

The *palacio* was besieged by news correspondents and television crews. María Elena's disappearance was major news, and the reporters were desperate for follow-up stories. In the light of the *palacio*'s fortresslike aspects, most reporters quickly surmised that María Elena had left government protection voluntarily. Their main concern was the question: Had she gone over to the rebels of her own free will? On this the government maintained an official silence. Some of the reporters left, hoping to make contact with the rebels. Loomis placed them under close surveillance with the same hope. He kept his men probing into rebel activities on the chance that some stray bit of solid information would come his way.

The Hamlet search also seemed to be at a dead end. A check of dock areas along the north shore failed to turn up anything unusual. A sustained, detailed search was beyond the capabilities of Loomis's staff. Rebels held many of the major roads in the north. Most fishing boats were at sea and for the moment inaccessible. Any of a hundred quiet, sheltered coves along the north or east shores of the island could have served as a site for transfer of a few barrels from boat to waiting truck.

Interrogators were at work on Larson and his crew, but as yet there had been no report.

For the first time Loomis and Johnson were forced to consider that they might not be searching for nuclear materials, but for an atomic bomb.

Johnson suggested that the search should now be concentrated on the bomb maker. Loomis could find no fault with his logic. Considering the dead ends, the bomb maker might offer the best opportunity for a new lead.

Complete data from more than a hundred roadblocks erected early in the search were fed into Octopus. Loomis set up a special office, containing computer terminals for direct access to Octopus. The electronic search continued on a twenty-four-hour basis.

Acknowledging that the search now must consider the possibility of a completed atomic bomb, the United States Government, at Loomis's request, sent in an outstanding nuclear authority, Dr. George C. Coon, a small, affable man who wore a perpetual grin. Johnson had worked with Coon in the past and seemed to regard his arrival as a stroke of luck.

"Now you might think, just to look at him, that he doesn't have enough sense to come in out of the rain," Johnson said by way of introduction. "Well, he does. I mean, if it was raining, and he was getting wet, I really think Coon would come in out of it. Unless, of course, he happened to be thinking of something else."

Coon grinned broadly at Johnson's gibes and said nothing.

"He's talented, too," Johnson said. "Coon can stand and stare at a blank wall all afternoon and never blink."

Coon went to work preparing a prospectus. He took many things into consideration. The Atomic Energy Commission's MUF lists—Materials Unaccounted For—of the last twenty years were analyzed in detail. Santo Domingo's terrain and physical features were studied. Time limitations, required hardware, and many other factors were postulated. From his contrived scenario Coon emerged with some probabilities and presented them at a conference in the Jaragua headquarters suite.

"I think the nuclear device will be placed on a roof," he said. "Altitude is preferable. They might try for an airplane, but a nuclear drop involves a sophistication undoubtedly beyond their capabilities. I would guess that the device will be prepared at another site—some small workshop, perhaps. A home garage might do. The individual components could be manufactured elsewhere, even in another country, and assembled here. Our man undoubtedly would want to make a final check of the components, however. Or, it could be that some or all of the actual construction may be done here. My point is that he probably will spend some time, somewhere, fitting and shaping components before moving to the actual detonation site for final assembly."

"How long will he spend at the detonation site?" Loomis asked.

"Probably a minimum of four to six hours," Coon said. "I'm assuming, of course, that the site would be the most vulnerable factor in the whole operation. He would want to keep his time there to a minimum. But the very nature of a homemade atomic device undoubtedly would preclude merely taking it intact to the site and leaving it. First, there's the weight to consider—several hundred pounds, at best. Some bulk, four or five feet by two or three feet, most likely. And the mechanism might be somewhat delicate. There would be the risk of jarring something out of kilter. No, I think our man would prefer to assemble the device at the detonation site. I certainly would."

In late afternoon the first new lead arrived. Johnson returned from the Octopus terminals with a sheet of paper and in high humor.

"I've just received an interesting readout," he said. "Two names. One is Clay Loomis. Served with various insurgents throughout the world, now known to be in the Dominican Republic. Might do anything if the price is right."

"Oh for Christ's sake. Come on, Johnson," Loomis said.

"I can't help it. That's what the machine said. But the other name is more interesting. A man passed through your Boca Chica roadblock two nights ago. Gave his name as Sam Ledbetter of New Orleans. But his physical description and passport data cross-check to Otto Zaloudek, a nuclear physicist who once worked on the fringes of the scientific communities at UCLA and Los Alamos. I think Zaloudek's our man."

"What's your reasoning?" Loomis asked.

"One, Zaloudek has dropped completely out of sight. A thorough search doesn't find him anywhere. Two, he is known to have been in Europe—two trips recently, six and eight weeks ago. Three, he became disenchanted with the U.S. nuclear setup a couple of years ago and was canned. It seems he became concerned that the two great powers were about to blow up the whole world, or something. He had a plan for disarmament. Both sides were to shoot all their nuclear goods into space."

"I remember something of that," Coon said. "He had some followers. No one prominent. But there was some concern over security."

Johnson nodded. "Zaloudek apparently never had complete access to bomb design. But he was on the fringes. He saw a bit here, a bit there. The feeling is that he has the capability."

"Most any student of physics knows the basic theory," Coon said. "If he has an inventive mind, it's child's play."

"What kind of man is he?" Loomis asked.

"A complete profile is being prepared. And we'll be getting photos on the Photofax for distribution. But so far, we know he's a tinkerer: slow, methodical, drives everyone around him to distraction with his plodding ways. He'll be easy to spot."

"How?"

"Easy. We can't miss him. He's short and round. He walks like a duck. And he'll be busy building an atomic bomb."

Chapter 22

The machine shop was far better equipped than Zaloudek expected. He had asked only for welding equipment, cutting torches, calipers, a few other tools, and a simple lathe. His conservative requests had been ignored. The Hamlet people included an elaborate drill press, complete die equipment, and a huge chest of precision tools, along with a forge and other metal-working gear.

"I won't be needing all this," Zaloudek told the man called Arnheiter. "It's only in the way."

Arnheiter shrugged. "That's what they sent," he said. "They even gave me a floor plan. I just did what I was paid to do."

Zaloudek ran a hand along the edge of the drill press. "A terrible waste," he said. "This building, everything here will be vaporized. Maybe, when we're through, we can take some of this with us."

"I think not," Arnheiter said. "We'll be damned lucky to get out ourselves. You don't know what it's like, up in the north, in the Cibao. Santiago was a battlefield. San Francisco is held by the rebels but is under siege. La Vega has heavy fighting."

"But you got through," Zaloudek pointed out.

"Only because I know the roads," Arnheiter said. "I dodged the roadblocks."

If Arnheiter had encountered so much trouble, Zaloudek couldn't understand how the other people would manage to move the nuclear materials. "Are you certain the goods are safe?" he asked.

"I'm positive they were as of three hours ago," Arnheiter said. "Of course in this fucked-up country, anything can happen. But I think they'll reach here just after dark. We thought there would be a better chance of bringing the truck in without trouble in the early evening."

"We don't have much time," Zaloudek said. He was impatient to start work. There were so many things he would have to check.

"We can't do anything but wait," Arnheiter said. "No use sweating it. You want a beer?"

"No," Zaloudek said. "I will be needing steady hands, if the goods come."

Arnheiter shrugged. "Suit yourself," he said. He went into the back room, where Zaloudek earlier had seen a small kitchenette.

Zaloudek still wasn't used to Arnheiter's brusque ways, despite their two days together. He knew little about him. In odd moments, Arnheiter had mentioned service with the French Foreign Legion in Algeria. He also seemed familiar with Uruguay, Honduras, Chile, and other hot spots. The man appeared completely devoid of humor and imagination. Zaloudek was by nature impatient with delay, and thus far there had been nothing but delays. Arnheiter had been six hours late at the rendezvous—a bar near the Duarte Bridge. And now, the truck with the goods was more than twenty-four hours overdue. A cryptic message had arrived: the material was safe and on its way. Zaloudek liked to keep his mind occupied. Waiting rankled him greatly.

Arnheiter had arranged a room for Zaloudek a block away. But Zaloudek said he would prefer a cot in the shop, explaining that he expected to be working day and night, with only a few hours of sleep, until the project was completed. In one of his few concessions, Arnheiter had agreed.

The shop was on Duarte Avenue just off El Conde. Ostensibly a new firm not yet open for business, the shop was kept locked. A sign out front informed the curious that "El Mickey" Air-Conditioning Repair would soon have a grand opening. The building itself was small, no more than thirty feet across the front and perhaps sixty feet in length. Large, overhead double doors at the front were connected to a high-speed chain lift that opened and closed the entrance within seconds. Inside, the concrete floor was clean and un-cluttered. Zaloudek had assumed that his working conditions would be much worse.

Arnheiter returned with his beer. He pulled two cane-bottom chairs up to a small drafting table. "We better get our shit together," he said. "There may not be time, later."

He explained that there were three options for their es-cape route after the blast. A small boat was waiting in Boca Chica. With any luck, they could head east by car, put out to sea, and there await word whether to sail for Puerto Rico, the Virgin Islands, or possibly a mid-ocean rendezvous.

"This fucking revolution may queer that," Arnheiter said. "If fighting breaks out around the Duarte Bridge at the wrong time, we're screwed."

"The roads in that direction are not good," Zaloudek said.

"There's that, too," Arnheiter agreed. "I'm not too keen on the boat. Even after we get to sea, we're still a long way from home."

Zaloudek nodded agreement.

The second option, Arnheiter explained, involved a back-road trip to the Haitian border, where arrangements had been made for seclusion in Petionville. The third plan called for flight by small plane to Port-au-Prince for connection with a commercial flight to Jamaica.

"I don't like the idea of the small plane," Arnheiter said. "If one of those Dominican Vampire jets sees us, we'll never make the border."

Zaloudek felt the same way. He didn't like to fly, especially in small planes. But he also disliked mountain roads. "Is the highway through the mountains dangerous?" he asked.

"Highway, hell," Arnheiter said. "It's no more than a cow-path. And it's all mountain. Real rough country. But there're no soldiers up there. And once we're over the Haitian bor-der, we're safe. We can spend two months or more holed up, drinking and screwing."

Zaloudek didn't like any of the plans. He couldn't imagine putting to sea in a small boat, vulnerable to pursuit by both sea and air. He was terrified of small boats. And big ones, too. He would feel naked and exposed on the open sea.

The idea for escape by small plane was even worse. He was certain that with the blast, American jets would soon be monitoring the area. Even if Dominican jets failed to find them, the American planes with their better equipment were certain to notice a private plane scooting for the Haitian border. And the thought of a desperate trip by car over mountain roads left him nauseated.

Spreading a map on the table, they debated the plans throughout the afternoon.

Eventually they decided on the dash by car to the border. Arnheiter's preference for the plan seemed closely linked to the probability of two months in seclusion. Zaloudek also found the prospect held appeal.

"All right," Arnheiter said. "I'll send the word that we'll take that route. But of course if anything happens, the other options are still open."

After a light supper brought in by one of Arnheiter's men, Zaloudek napped on his cot in the corner of the shop. He was awakened shortly after midnight by the arrival of the truck.

Arnheiter opened the big front doors and the two-ton Ford stake-bed backed into the shop. The doors were hurriedly closed and locked.

Zaloudek laced his shoes, walked to the back end of the truck, and watched as Arnheiter and his three men lowered the power loader, exposing the cargo. Seven green fifty-five-gallon oil drums were stacked neatly in front, a light chain snaked through the tops to hold them in place.

A chill of anticipation went up Zaloudek's spine.

A nuclear engineer for more than twenty years, he'd never before worked with weapons-grade uranium. He knew all about it in theory. He'd seen parts of designs for many nuclear weapons. But he'd never seen the raw materials.

"What'll we do with the stuff?" Arnheiter asked.

"How about putting it over there?" Zaloudek said, pointing to the far corner of the room. "You might have them put the barrels a few feet apart."

"Why?"

"A simple precaution," Zaloudek explained. "If uranium beyond a certain amount is brought together, the mass turns critical. That's why it is shipped this way, in small bottles, suspended in barrels. In the trade, they're called birdcages."

Arnheiter looked at the barrels with renewed interest. "You mean that shit might go off?"

"Conceivably," Zaloudek said. "I'm speaking in terms of an accident—barrels knocked over, bottles broken open. Of course the result would be a fizzle yield, a sort of messy dud. But forty-nine kilos of uranium would make a considerable disturbance, even with inefficient detonation."

"You hear that, you fuckers?" Arnheiter yelled. "Take it easy with those things!"

Zaloudek waited patiently while the men unloaded the trucks. With a counter, he then carefully checked each birdcage for leakage.

The material apparently was still in the original Crescent, Oklahoma, conversion plant packing. He could find no damage. Each barrel contained a ten-liter bottle placed in a length of five-inch pipe, which was centered by welded braces. Each ten-liter bottle contained seven kilograms of uranium.

Each barrel weighed less than a hundred pounds, easily handled by one man.

"How big a bomb can you build with this stuff?" Arnheiter asked.

Zaloudek eased one barrel out into the center of the floor, well away from the others.

"The question isn't how big, but how efficient," he explained. "The Hiroshima bomb had sixty kilograms of uranium. We've got forty-nine here. But the Hiroshima bomb was very, very crude. Terribly inefficient. A stupid bomb, really. I've seen figures estimating less than one percent of its fuel was utilized. I'll be very disappointed if we fail to achieve a ten percent yield."

"Then it will be bigger than Hiroshima?"

"Somewhere in that range," Zaloudek said, taking refuge

in evasive nuclear weapons terminology.

"How much bigger?"

Zaloudek spread his hands in a helpless gesture. "Who knows? Again, there are so many factors to consider. Much of the efficiency also is contained in the situation. We don't have a B-29 or B-52 handy, and our device will be impractical for a private plane. So an air burst is out. That means we'll lose some efficiency to shadow effects. On the other hand, a ground burst will kick up more dust and debris—all full of deadly radiation. Chunks of concrete and steel will fly out like artillery shells for miles. It's difficult to predict exactly what will happen."

"Where'd you learn all this stuff? Working for the government?"

"No. Not all. You or anybody can find the essential material if you know where to look. The *Los Alamos Primer* has all the basics. It was declassified ten years or more ago. You can get it from the government for a couple of bucks. There is a book called *Manhattan District History* that explains all the technical problems they ran into with the Trinity, Hiroshima, and Nagasaki shots. It was Top Secret when written, but then declassified in the sixties. There are others."

"Is that where you got all these charts and figures?" Arnheiter asked, pointing to the drafting table.

"No, those are mine. I made them up from the *Los Alamos Critical Mass Summaries.* They cost three dollars, and you can get them from the National Technical Information Service. Not everything is in there. But all heavy metals are very similar. You can get some idea of the critical mass, the shaping of the metal, reflectors, and so forth. I think I could manage if I'd never seen a bomb design. But I *have* seen the essential details of Hamlet, a very good design. I have incorporated some of Hamlet's best features into my own device."

Arnheiter seemed to be growing nervous. He looked at the barrels with mounting concern. "How do you know the damned thing won't go off before we get our asses far enough away?"

"I don't," Zaloudek said. "But I can assure you I'll do my

best." He reached for his white coveralls. "I might as well get to work," he said. "Let's move a cage over by the workbench."

With the barrel in place, Zaloudek lifted out the bottle, opened it, and poured out into his open palm some dull brown grains resembling instant coffee.

He could hardly believe his eyes.

"This is uranium oxide!" he shouted.

Arnheiter eased over to look, keeping a respectful distance. He seemed confused by Zaloudek's distress.

"They said it was weapons-grade stuff," he said.

"It may be," Zaloudek said. "But it's uranium oxide. I told them I wanted metal—what we call broken buttons."

Arnheiter seemed on the verge of panic. His voice trembled. "They probably didn't know the difference. I didn't. I thought uranium was uranium. Can't you use this?"

"I could," Zaloudek said. He tried to explain the problem. "You see, efficiency is a matter of mass, of compactness. Uranium oxide is loose—too much wasted space. It would work. But it'd be far, far less efficient. I would have to redesign everything, completely. I couldn't obtain anywhere near the yield I want."

"Maybe that's just one barrel," Arnheiter offered. "Maybe the rest of the stuff is all right."

One by one, they opened the other birdcages.

All contained uranium oxide.

Zaloudek knew of no way to convey to Arnheiter his terrible disappointment. He could use the uranium oxide. Criticality could be achieved. He could find ways of surmounting the inherent problems. Several ideas came to mind immediately —various methods of using explosives to bring the uranium oxide into a more compact mass at the crucial instant.

Yet, the results would be bush league—equal to no more than a few hundred tons of TNT.

Zaloudek wanted more.

He wanted much more, for he had a purpose of his own that required the awakening of the world's scientific community.

And that would not be accomplished by a fizzle yield in some remote tropical setting.

Zaloudek stood for a long time, rolling a thimbleful of the brown grains around in his palm with an index finger, thinking.

Vaguely, he recalled a lengthy process of conversion. In the commercial world, the method was complex and time consuming. Yet . . .

He walked to the drafting table and jotted down some formulas. For more than an hour, he pitted figures against formula, remembering, hoping.

At last, he turned to Arnheiter.

"I have an idea that might work," he said. "It'll take a lot of effort. But I may be able to turn this oxide into the form I want."

"How?"

"A chemical process. I'm not certain I can do it with our limited facilities. You'll have to buy some laboratory equipment, chemist's-shop material. Or steal it. Everything I need should be available somewhere in Santo Domingo."

"O.K.," Arnheiter said impatiently. "What do you need?"

"I'll make you a list. First, and most important, a lab furnace. A small one, the kind used in schools, would do. It won't cost more than a hundred dollars or so, probably. You can say it's for classroom use. Or for firing ceramic pottery, maybe. I'll also need a vibrating tray, but I can make that from the machinery here. I'll use the motor from the drill press. I'll need some graphite crucibles—might as well get a dozen or so. They're only a few dollars each. Hydrofluoric acid—several quarts. And some powdered magnesium. That ought to do it."

"How much money, all told?"

"No more than three hundred dollars, probably."

"But it'll take hours," Arnheiter fumed. "And we're already behind schedule."

"While you find the equipment, I'll be working on the trigger mechanism," Zaloudek said. "The only time we will lose will be that converting the uranium. And it has to be done."

Zaloudek examined the remainder of the gear. Everything he had requested was neatly packed in six heavy crates. The metal work had been done to his exact specifications. The quality of the material and workmanship far exceeded his expectations. Laying out all his equipment, he set to work.

By the time daylight arrived, he had succeeded in honing the old three-inch navy gun to his specific needs. Much of the preliminary work had been done. His only remaining concern was the precise fitting. While he experimented with the firing mechanism, making certain all was in order, Arnheiter left with the truck and two men to hunt the laboratory equipment.

When he was confident that the navy gun conformed perfectly with his designs, Zaloudek went to work shaping other parts for his device, carefully taking the measurements from his drawings, checking and rechecking the figures against the prepared equipment.

Arnheiter returned in late afternoon, signaling his success with a broad grin. The laboratory furnace was rented from the university, ostensibly for use in a ceramic art gallery. Arnheiter had given the name of an existing art gallery but forged the signatures. The crucibles and hydrofluoric acid were easily located, and bought without arousing suspicion, at a wholesale pharmacy. But the powdered magnesium had required considerable search. Posing as a manufacturer of signal flares, Arnheiter had at last located a supply in a pharmaceutical warehouse. Arnheiter had hinted the flares were for use in the revolution.

"Good work," Zaloudek said. "Let's see what we can do with it."

Working intently, with Arnheiter helping, Zaloudek jury-rigged a vibrator tray and fitted it inside the furnace.

After pouring four and a half kilograms of uranium oxide onto the tray, he turned on the vibration mechanism.

Over a Bunsen burner, he heated hydrofluoric acid in a flask fitted with stopper and tube. The resulting hydrogen-fluoride gas he fed into the furnace, which he allowed to heat to five hundred degrees centigrade. As they watched, the consistency of the uranium began to change.

"What the hell's happening?" Arnheiter asked.

"The hydrogen fluoride gas and the uranium oxide are forming water and uranium tetrafluoride," Zaloudek explained. "We're going to have some fun with that."

He cooled the uranium tetrafluoride and mixed the residue with metallic magnesium powder in a six-to-one ratio. He then added some potassium chlorate and poured the material into a graphite crucible. With an electric coil he'd contrived, he heated the crucible to six hundred degrees centigrade. At that point the magnesium ignited.

"Jeez!" Arnheiter yelled, jumping away from the harmless shower of sparks.

Zaloudek laughed, taking care to hold the crucible steady while the spectacular fire consumed the last of the magnesium.

"I think it worked," he said. "With any luck, we have magnesium fluoride on top and uranium metal on the bottom. In foundry jargon, this is called a derby."

Cooling the crucible in a soft spray of water, he knocked the unwanted material away to reveal four and a half kilograms of bright new uranium metal.

"That ought to work," he said. "Most of the success of a nuclear shot lies in the shape of the mass. I should be able to reshape this exactly the way I want it."

The relief of knowing that his conversion process would work left Zaloudek drained of energy. He had not slept in more than thirty hours. He went to his cot, napped for four hours, then began a routine that varied little during the next three days. He worked stretches of nine to ten hours, with alternate three- to four-hour intervals of rest.

He painstakingly converted the remainder of the uranium oxide to metal. Taking great care always to keep the pieces of subcritical uranium separated, he shaped each, using precision calipers to ensure a perfect fit. Together, the components of uranium would form an interlocking cylinder, one fitting inside the other as a sort of plug. When fired from the navy gun, the plug would penetrate with tremendous pressure to form one supercritical mass—instantaneously.

The result, he was certain, would surpass the devastation of the device at Hiroshima.

Zaloudek then went back to work on the various parts of the firing mechanism, the foundation, the frame, and the cover. He patiently joined the parts. He fitted the neutron shield. He installed the navy gun. He checked and rechecked alignments. And he tested and retested the ignition gear.

When he was satisfied with the results, he carefully disassembled the device, packed all the components in the wooden crates, and reported to Arnheiter.

"We're ready," he said.

"How long will it take to put that thing together at the site?" Arnheiter asked.

"Six hours," Zaloudek said. "Maybe less."

"Then I can send word we'll be on time?"

"We'll be on time," Zaloudek said.

Arnheiter summoned his men together beside the truck, handed out the special weapons, and issued his last-minute instructions.

The project then entered its final phase.

PART THREE

Chapter 23

The battle that eventually centered on the Primate Cathedral and the Tower of Homage began at daylight. Loomis was at breakfast when the first explosions rattled the *palacio* windows. From the volume and intensity of fire, he knew immediately that Ramón had launched his all-out attack on the capital.

Loomis hurried to a phone and tried to reach Colonel Escortia, hoping to move a heavy-weapons company into the *palacio* compound. An aide reported that the Colonel had just left his quarters.

A few minutes later word came: Colonel Escortia was dead. As his driver opened the rear door of the Colonel's Chevrolet for him to enter, an unseen lanyard attached to the door pulled the pins from three grenades secreted beneath the rear seat. In his last moments, Escortia apparently sensed what was happening. But before he could escape, the car was blown apart. The mangled body was found a dozen paces away. The driver lost both arms but was still alive.

El Jefe summoned Loomis to his quarters. "Everything is in a mess," he said. "I'm taking tactical command. I need you here."

Loomis fought down his protest. El Jefe was right. The issue of the revolution might be decided within the next four or five hours. Although the lines of command were plain, the organizational structure of the military was riddled with jealousies and backbiting. Clear, decisive action had to be taken.

Loomis was worried to distraction over María Elena, but logic told him that she was safe, at least for the moment. His sources had learned that she had reached Ramón's headquar-

ters in San Francisco, but that the headquarters had since
been moved. No one knew where. Loomis found some comfort in the knowledge that Ramón wouldn't risk the life of the
most important political hostage that could possibly come his
way outside of El Jefe himself. And if Ramón happened to
accept María Elena's plea for a cease-fire, he would carefully
guard the life of the enemy's emissary.

Logic also told Loomis that the battle for the capital took
precedence over the search for the atomic bomb. With
firefights raging throughout the *distrito,* a thorough hunt
would be impossible. And a block-by-block, house-by-house
search was the only practical method left.

The revolution had to be quelled so the bomb could be
found.

For the next six hours, Loomis shoved all other thoughts
from his mind and concentrated on the battle.

He quickly ascertained that no immediate effort would be
made to storm the *palacio*. All of the rebel forces seemed to
be concentrated along the Ozama River, centering at the
Tower of Homage and the Primate Cathedral.

At first, Loomis failed to see the reasoning in the plan of
attack. But later reports brought word of rebel buildup along
the Real Carretera Bocachica across the river, and Ramón's
tactics became more apparent.

"They're using the river to make us disperse along a broad
front," Loomis explained to El Jefe. "They knew we'd defend
the bridge heavily. They're making us waste use of our troops
there. I don't think they intend to attack the bridge at all."

"But we have them bottled up, with lines here, and here,"
El Jefe said, pointing on the map. "How will they get supplies
to their men if fighting is prolonged?"

"Across the river, I think. They'll use the river, and the
tidal basin, for rafts and small boats."

In the silence that followed, Loomis knew that El Jefe was
groping for a possible alternative in positioning government
troops. "I wish we could use the gunboats," he said.

The range inside the harbor would be too short for the
gunboats' main batteries. It would be like using a cannon in
a crowded room. The destroyer's main batteries could not be

deflected enough to be brought to bear. And they'd be vulnerable to recoilless rifle fire from shore.

"They might stand off, several miles at sea, and shell the tidal basin," Loomis said.

"I gather you don't think that would be effective."

"Probably not," Loomis admitted. "If I had a choice, I'd try to get tanks along Avenida 30 de Mayo here, to where they could effect a field of fire across the tidal basin.

El Jefe ordered the plan put into action. Three AMX-13 tanks were sent rumbling up Avenida George Washington and Avenida 30 de Mayo, taking heavy small arms fire. Personnel carriers in the wake of the tanks moved troops into the rocky shoreline below the boulevard, where they were able to return the heavy fire. The rebels fell back, and for a time the tanks were near Pointe Bellini, commanding both the mouth of the river and the approaches to the opposite banks. But in early afternoon, rebels flanked the tanks, knocking out two with recoilless rifles. The remaining tank retreated.

By nightfall the rebels held more than thirty blocks of the Old Town, from within a stone's throw of El Conde Gate to the river and south toward the sea. More than two hundred government soldiers were dead and a like number wounded. The hospitals were jammed. Rebel casualties were believed heavy but perhaps somewhat lighter than those of the government. Shortly after dark Loomis received reports that rebel reinforcements, brought down from San Francisco, were being moved across the river to relieve those who had carried the fight all day.

With daylight, the combined forces would no doubt advance westward toward Parque Independencia and, possibly, the *palacio.*

"We've got to hold them," El Jefe said. "Ramón is overextended, going for broke. If we can move them back tomorrow, the whole thing will collapse. Do you have any ideas?"

Loomis found armchair fighting a frustrating experience. All day he had chafed over the confusion. Now, he might help restore some semblance of order.

"Maps, reports are one thing," he explained to El Jefe.

"The situation may be another. I'd like to go look at things firsthand."

"Do you really need to take the risk?" El Jefe asked. "You're undoubtedly a marked man."

Loomis shrugged. "If I am, it isn't the first time. I doubt Ramón will do anything significant tonight. I would guess he's preparing for a daylight assault—probably on the *palacio.*"

"All right," El Jefe said reluctantly. "I'll await your reconnaissance. Then we'll talk. When will you be back?"

"I should make it a little after midnight," Loomis said.

El Jefe was silent for a moment. "Do you think there's any hope of getting María Elena back before the assault?"

"No," Loomis said. "I doubt Ramón will act on her plea for a cease-fire until he knows, one way or the other, how things are going to go. He will doubt her story. He won't risk his revolution."

El Jefe nodded. "That is the way I see it," he said. He massaged his temples, fighting fatigue. "I don't mind telling you that all this is beyond me. I don't know what to do. I'm in an embarrassing position. I've resisted the United States for years. And now I must raise the question: Should I call upon them for help?"

Loomis didn't want to make a recommendation either way. "I'm probably the last person in the world who could give you the right answer to that." he said.

El Jefe nodded his understanding. "I wouldn't think of asking them for help under normal circumstances. But my God! María Elena in the hands of the rebels! The nuclear bomb! And the Hamlet people—something we can't even find or fight! And on top of everything, Ramón is now showing twice the strength we anticipated."

"Twenty thousand U.S. Marines might make a difference," Loomis agreed.

"How do you think Washington would respond to a call for help?"

Loomis considered the possibility. The new President was an unknown quantity. In the past, there would have been no question. But Vietnam, as well as lingering repercussions from the 1965 Dominican occupation, not to mention the Bay of Pigs fiasco, to some extent had soured political inclinations for meddling in other people's affairs. And of course the CIA, the military, and various United States corporations had come under considerable fire for manipulating foreign governments and elections.

"I really don't know," Loomis admitted. "I've been out of contact too long."

"I've had reports that a U.S. Navy task force has been assembled at Guantánamo Bay. It could be a precaution, or perhaps even a routine fleet exercise. But they are reported to be headed this way. In the light of that, I'll hold off on any request, for the moment. But you might feel out your friend Johnson on the possibility of intervention. If worse comes to worst, just the bare hint of intervention might make the whole revolution collapse."

"I wouldn't count on the United States," Loomis said. "From what I've heard, without me the whole country's gone to hell."

Loomis returned to his quarters, changed into old Marine fatigues, and called Johnson at the Jaragua.

"I'll sure say one thing for you people," Johnson said. "You really know how to run a noisy war."

"Good local talent," Loomis said. "Lots of experience. What did your people learn from Larson?"

"Just confirmation of what we suspected. The material was off-loaded to a shrimper at the north end of the Mona Passage. Seven barrels of stuff. Four wooden crates. Larson doesn't know who hired him, what was in the barrels, or who they went to. All he had was a recognition signal."

"You believe him?"

"No. But I believe the crew that took his brain apart and studied all the little pieces. Larson thought he was handling heroin. He set his price accordingly."

"Bullshit. That cargo must have weighed several hundred pounds. There's not that much heroin in the world."

"Well, Larson's not the brightest fellow alive, either. He was told that the crates contained art objects. He didn't open them."

"Where is he now?"

"Awaiting your pleasure. I suggest holding him on suspicion of smuggling until we find out which way the wind blows."

"I'll recommend it to our government tomorrow, if we still have a government. Any description on the shrimper?"

"Negative. Larson says it was a dark night. The calendar confirms it. Aerial reconnaissance in Washington is doing some backtracking to see what they missed. They might come up with something. But I wouldn't lay odds."

Loomis thought of the many small towns and fishing villages along the north coast. The boat could have landed cargo most anywhere. There were hundreds of coves and freshwater creeks where a small boat might put light cargo ashore.

"I wish we could take a chopper and run up there," he said.

"I doubt it would do any good," Johnson said. "I would imagine the material is here in Santo Domingo by now."

"Look, Johnson, I'm fixing to make a tour of the lines. Why don't you come with me?"

"You always seem to put me in the position of pointing out the obvious," Johnson said. "Isn't there some shooting going on over there?"

"I'll bring an extra weapon," Loomis said. "We can have some fun."

"You don't understand, Loomis. I don't mind dying to keep some Latin dictator in office. But frankly, I'd be at a loss to explain to Langley if my body became an international incident."

"It'd raise the CIA's image from second-rate domestic political burglaries," Loomis said. "But don't worry about it. I promise. If you're wasted, we'll burn your body. You'll just disappear and become a great mystery. A *cause célèbre.*"

"Oh, in that case, I accept. I've always wanted to become one of those. But I think you better hear my news. Lisbon snared a runner a few hours ago. They picked his brain. All it contained was a simple message: 'One P.M. Saturday, Santo Domingo time.' Our people in their brilliance believe that means Santo Domingo is to be vaporized at one o'clock on Saturday."

"That's tomorrow!" Loomis said.

"Brilliant people all around me," Johnson said.

Loomis thought ahead, his mind racing to all the ramifications. If the city were evacuated by government troops, the rebels, not believing the bomb existed, would move in.

And María Elena was with the rebels.

But El Jefe probably wouldn't evacuate. El Jefe kept the revolution foremost in his mind. That would be his first concern.

Loomis had read psychological studies of a phenomenon: when people are faced with an overwhelming danger, they tend to ignore it. All over the world, villages cling to the sides of active volcanoes, cities mushroom on known earthquake faults, and houses are built on floodplains and beneath huge dams. Repeatedly, populations warned of impending disasters have chosen to ignore them.

Without Ramón's help, the city wouldn't be evacuated.

"We've got to reach Ramón," Loomis said, "We've got to arrange a cease-fire, an evacuation."

"I was afraid my news might upset you," Johnson said. "I even thought about not telling you. What have you heard from María Elena on the possibility of calling off this inconvenient little war?"

"Nothing."

"No news is bad news," Johnson said. "Frankly, unless we get things calmed down enough to conduct a house-to-house, I'm not optimistic. No firm leads, and only eighteen hours."

"I don't think Ramón is going to cooperate in any way," Loomis said. "He's really putting on the pressure."

"Ol' buddy, I think you'd better reconsider that offer from the company," Johnson said. "Look on the bright side. What you've got is a kind of shitty job, anyway."

"They all are, in our line," Loomis said. A plan began to

take shape in his mind. "I'll pick you up in twenty minutes."

"Back entry," Johnson said. "I don't want to be seen. If word gets back to Langley, they'll think I've lost my mind." He paused before adding, "And maybe I have."

Chapter 24

Loomis circled around past the bungalows to the back entrance of the hotel. Johnson wasn't in sight. Irritated, Loomis killed the jeep engine, prepared to wait.

From a hundred yards away came the sound of the surf. A band was playing somewhere in the hotel, and through the open doors at back Loomis could hear the chatter of the kitchen help. Otherwise, the night was quiet. Unnaturally quiet.

Within minutes his irritation turned to worry. Johnson was not a man to be late. Not unless there was a reason.

Loomis picked up the two Schmeissers and stepped from the jeep. Moving away from open moonlight, he edged into the darkness beneath the palms. He waited until he heard footsteps on the graveled drive, then eased around the trunk of a palm, his weapon ready.

"Hold it, ol' buddy," Johnson said softly. "Wherever you are, don't shoot. It's me."

Loomis stepped out. "What the fuck are you doing?" he asked.

Johnson put a forefinger to his lips. "Keep it down," he said. "There's a well-armed delegation out front. I have a hunch they're waiting for you."

"What makes you think *I'm* the target?"

"Adds up," Johnson said. "You leave your palatial pad, obviously headed for the hotel. A lookout phones ahead, and four men move into place. Come on. I'll show you."

He led Loomis to the third floor. Cautiously, they eased down the corridors to Johnson's room at the front. Without turning on the lights, Johnson moved to a window and parted the curtains. "Down there," he said. "Other side of the hedge beyond the pool."

For a moment, Loomis saw only pool, palms, and a row of orange and white deck chairs. Then he saw something move behind the hedge that screened the pool from the drive.

"Four?" Loomis asked.

"All I counted. They may have a hole card hid out in the trees."

"How long they been there?"

"Since about two minutes after I hung up the phone from talking to you."

"How'd you come to notice them?"

"That's the way I've managed to live these forty-some-odd years. By noticing things."

Loomis figured Johnson probably was right about the lookout and phone call. The timing jibed. But if the phones were tapped, they would have known to ambush him behind the hotel. He was seen leaving the *palacio,* and they had assumed he was headed for the front entrance. The assassination squad had moved into position.

The problem was what to do about them.

"We could go ahead, play like we didn't see them," Loomis said.

"We could," Johnson agreed.

"But they might just wait and ambush me some other time. Right when I was least expecting it."

"Probably," Johnson said with elaborate disinterest.

"You don't go out of your way to help anyone make a decision, do you?"

"What you ought to do doesn't matter," Johnson said. "What's important is what you're gonna do. I have the definite feeling you're gonna go out there and blow the living shit out of them."

"I'm thinking strongly in that direction," Loomis admitted. He now could make out the shape of another assassin in the trees behind the hedge.

Johnson sighed. "I sure wish I could help," he said. "It's a hard life, being a neutral in the middle of a war."

"I could use a good neutral," Loomis said. He was looking through the blinds, fixing the location of each man firmly in his mind. "I'll sneak down there onto the balcony above the entrance. You can move around to that pavilion on the east side of the swimming pool and practice your neutrality. When I open fire, you can neutralize anything that moves in your direction."

"Hot damn, I knew there was bound to be a loophole there somewhere," Johnson said. "Langley will be proud of me, working so hard to practice neutrality." He stepped to the window and studied the pool area, figuring the angles of crossfire.

Loomis handed him the Schmeisser and an extra clip. They backed out into the hall. Johnson stopped to check the load.

"Give me time to get down there," he said.

"Five minutes," Loomis said. "No more. They're probably already beginning to get nervous."

Johnson went out the back way to circle the hotel. Loomis walked down the long corridor of the L-shaped building, to the balcony that jutted over the front entrance. The swimming pool was nestled in the angle of the L, with the pavilion at the far end.

Fortunately the revolution had driven the few remaining tourists inside. The corridors were deserted, and despite the heat no one was using the pool.

The reinforced concrete railing of the balcony was slightly more than waist high. Keeping low, Loomis moved to the front of the building, directly over the entrance where, except for a bit of luck, he would have been assassinated.

He waited five minutes by the sweeping second hand on his watch, flipped off the safety on his weapon, and stood up abruptly.

None of the gunmen had shifted position. They turned, bringing their weapons up. Loomis killed two with short bursts before return fire chewed into the concrete behind him.

Ducking below the balcony wall, Loomis waited until Johnson started the crossfire. Confident his target was otherwise occupied, Loomis again swung his weapon over the balcony. He fired a dozen rounds into a man fleeing down the driveway. He was knocked sprawling, his weapon bouncing along the gravel.

Johnson's final burst sent the fourth man tumbling into the swimming pool.

Either there was no fifth man, or he had fled. Loomis walked cautiously down the first flight of steps, rounded the flagpole on the landing, then edged down the last half-flight. Inside the lobby, three hotel employees were flat on the floor, judiciously awaiting the outcome of the battle. No one was curious enough to come out and learn what had happened.

Loomis crossed the wide entranceway to the pool area. With his toe he rolled one of the assassins over onto his back into a spreading circle of blood.

He'd never seen the man before.

Johnson walked up, looking at the body in the water. "Shit, now I've messed up the pool for the tourist trade," he said.

With the shooting over, Loomis allowed himself the luxury of anger. "Four of them. With AK-47s. Sons a bitches weren't taking any chances, were they?"

"You should be flattered," Johnson said. "You must have one hell of a reputation in this part of the world."

"Let's go," Loomis said. "I feel like cracking a few heads tonight."

Johnson pointed to the bodies. "Shouldn't we tell the hotel people what to do with the debris?"

Loomis started back toward the jeep. "That's their problem," he said.

MINUS 15:32 HOURS

The streets of the Old Town lay relatively quiet and peaceful under a bright quarter-moon while both rebel and government troops made preparations for the battle anticipated at dawn. All electric power to that section of the city had been cut, and above the darkened buildings the stars were bright in a cloudless sky.

Loomis drove slowly toward the government headquarters at the old fort just north of the rebel lines. Johnson rode shotgun, keeping his Schmeisser at ready, watching the doorways and overhanging balconies.

"Tomorrow they'll move on the *palacio,*" Loomis said.

"What are the odds?"

"For El Jefe, not so good," Loomis said. "Not without help."

"What are *you* going to do? Don't you think it's about time to bail out of this mess?"

"I've got several alternatives working," Loomis told him. "What I'll do depends on what happens. We've heard that a U.S. Navy task force left Gitmo yesterday, headed this way. You know anything about it?"

"Your sources on that are probably better than mine," Johnson said.

"El Jefe may request intervention. Allowing for the bomb situation, what do you think are the odds on that?"

"My own opinion?"

"Yes."

"Your best estimate would come from somebody at State," Johnson said. "But since you ask me, I'll tell you. I wouldn't count on the President doing a damned thing."

"But it could happen?" Loomis insisted.

"Depends on how much pressure is brought to bear, and from what direction. If Alcoa needs the bauxite, that'd bring pressure. If the sugar is needed, that'd be more. There are a lot of little factors that are beyond my purview. The President might risk it."

"I admire a man with firm answers," Loomis said. "What about the atomic bomb? Doesn't that enter into it?"

"That's one of the little factors I mentioned," Johnson said.

Loomis parked the jeep on the sloping street in front of the old Santa Barbara Church. While Loomis lifted the hood, removed the distributor cap, and lifted out the rotor, Johnson backed into the street, looking up at the old church with its ancient arches, grilled windows, and impressive bell tower.

"That thing must be old as hell," he said. "When was it built?"

"Oh for Christ's sake, Johnson," Loomis said, irritated. "Do you always have to be the fucking tourist?"

"I'm serious," Johnson protested.

"Hell, I don't know. But it's fairly modern. Built some time in the seventeen-hundreds. Now the old fort, where we're going, is more your speed. It was built in fifteen-seventy-four."

They passed through a checkpoint manned by six government marines. Then they climbed the six tiers of steps leading up through a flowered park to the fortress. A row of ancient cannon, unused for centuries, still pointed out over the harbor. Loomis could see two of El Jefe's generals sitting on a cannon in the moonlight, deep in a heated argument. One of the generals, Eduardo Arango Jiménez, wanted to move artillery and tanks from the Duarte Bridge westward to form a wedge between El Conde Gate and the *palacio*. He pointed out that the rebels for the moment had little use for the bridge. He doubted any effort would be made to capture the bridge or its approaches. The other general, Jorge Gomez Franco, thought the rebel advance on the *palacio* could best be thwarted by a heavy attack on the flank. Gomez pointed out that tanks and artillery could sweep southward at daylight, diverting rebel attention from making any more efforts toward the west.

Loomis joined them and listened quietly to the debate, asking occasional questions to pinpoint troops and lines of contact. Johnson wandered away, examining the old fort.

The discussion continued more than an hour. At one point the generals asked Loomis for his opinion. He agreed that both plans had merit. A combination of the two might be best, he pointed out. If the rebels could be contained at El Conde Gate, only time might be gained. On the next try the rebels might succeed. But if they were contained at the gate, while a thrust southward along the river managed to cut their lines of supply, then defeat would be clear-cut.

The generals were dubious. They felt the government lacked the manpower for such a wide front. Loomis didn't argue with them.

The only person he had to convince was El Jefe.

Eventually, he tired of the talk. He felt he knew the lines and general dispersion of forces as well as could be expected. He only needed one more bit of information.

"Where is Ramón's center of operations?" he asked.

"The Primate Cathedral seems to be the staff headquarters," Gomez said. "But Ramón isn't there. We don't know where he is. We suspect he may be with a force somewhere in reserve."

"Who seems to be running things over there?"

"Professor Salamanca of the university."

"Formerly of the university," Loomis said.

They laughed. Loomis shook hands with them and wished them luck. After rounding up Johnson, he returned to the jeep, thinking.

The plan that kept nagging him was just crazy enough to work.

"You like to have some fun?" he asked Johnson.

"It all depends," Johnson said. "What's your idea of fun?"

"The rebel headquarters is in the Primate Cathedral, just a few blocks south of here. We might sort of reconnoiter, see what's going on down there."

Johnson made a silent whistle. "Look, Loomis, I know these rebel guys are amateurs. But I assume they know enough to post a few guards, load their rifles, and all that."

"You worry too much," Loomis said. "We can move right down the riverbank. We ought to be able to take care of anyone we happen to run into."

"Loomis, you're nuts. You know that? What would be the point?"

"They tried to kill me tonight. I'd like to stir up their shit a little."

"People have been trying to kill you for thirty years now. You've never taken it personal before."

"It's always personal."

"The girl. That's it. You must be worried about the girl. You wouldn't let a friendly little ambush upset you so."

Loomis let his irritation show. "Of course I'm worried about María Elena. Why not? She should be back by now.

There's only one explanation. Ramón doesn't believe her story about the bomb. He's holding her hostage. And he's going to use her in some way."

"I guess I'm just dense," Johnson said. "But what good would we do her over there blowing hell out of things?"

"I just want to bring back one of Ramón's stud ducks," Loomis explained. "The Professor, or some other *honcho*. Then I'd be in a position to talk about a hostage exchange. And it's the *only* way I know to talk to Ramón direct about a cease-fire."

"Well, why didn't you say so in the first place? That makes sense, even to me. What are the odds?"

"A battalion of U.S. Marines probably couldn't get it done before daylight," Loomis said. "I figure it might take you and me a couple of hours."

Johnson laughed and picked up his Schmeisser. He slowly but firmly slipped a cartridge into the chamber. "Loomis, I'll sure say one thing for you," he said. "You don't leave a fellow much room to say no."

Chapter 25

From the old fort they moved downriver, carefully avoiding where possible the open patches of moonlight, taking their time, frequently standing motionless for several minutes to make certain they didn't blunder into rebel troops.

They passed the Alcazar, tall and unreal in the moonlight. Johnson seemed far more excited over the Alcazar than at the possibility of running into soldiers. Loomis had to explain, in whispers, that the castle originally was built by Christopher Columbus's son, Diego, in 1510, and for many years served as the seat of government in Spanish America. Apparently the restored palace remained unharmed. Loomis literally had to pull Johnson away from it.

Moving with even more caution, Loomis edged closer to the river as they neared the docks. Twice they circled around rebel checkpoints, avoiding contact.

When Loomis sighted the Tower of Homage he turned away from the river, but Johnson was not to be denied.

"What is that?" he whispered.

"Oh shit, Johnson, why don't you buy a guidebook?" Loomis fumed. He explained that the old fortress, dating back to 1505, had been restored, and was still used by the military. He figured the rebels would be concentrated there.

They were. From a distance, Loomis could see a hundred or more soldiers bivouacking near the tower.

By contrast, the rebel headquarters in the Primate Cathedral appeared deserted. Two lone sentries stood at the heavy pair of wooden doors inset into the thick, flaking walls. Only two feeble lanterns lighted the courtyard. The faint light glinted softly off the ancient sunburst of stained glass over the doorway. Carefully, Loomis studied the bell tower to the

right of the doors. Each bell had a separate arch to protect
it from the weather. But the crumbling bricks sheltered no
snipers. He studied the roofline. He could see where the
original white walls were stained by streaks of rust from the
roof. But he could see no snipers posted on the roof. He
signaled to Johnson. They hunkered down by a wall across
the marble courtyard and watched the entrance.

After a quarter of an hour, they heard voices approaching.
Four men came out of the darkness talking, laughing. Loomis
gathered that someone had messed his pants during a crucial
part of the day's action. The rebels seemed to think the
subject funny. Loomis watched carefully as they walked into
the faint light around the doorway. The sentries gave them
respectful salutes as they entered the cathedral.

Johnson looked at Loomis.

Loomis shook his head.

Ten minutes later, five more officers came from the direction of the tower and entered the cathedral. Loomis recognized a familiar shape.

"The sloppy little one with the beard and glasses," he whispered. "That's the son of a bitch we want."

Johnson pointed to his watch. Five minutes until twelve.
The rebel brass apparently were attending a midnight
briefing to cover last-minute details for the morning attack.
Loomis waited ten more minutes to make certain the guards
were not being relieved at midnight.

"Let's go," he whispered to Johnson. "I'll take the one on
the right."

As they walked casually, confidently, across the courtyard
toward the cathedral door, Loomis began talking to Johnson
in a low voice.

"The colonel" expected him to do all the work, and could
never be found when needed, Loomis complained in Spanish. Johnson nodded and made sympathetic grunts. The
guards glanced in their direction, but seemed unconcerned.
Not until they were within ten feet, as the light from the
lanterns fell across their faces, did one rebel become suspicious. He was bringing his gun up, on the point of challenge,
when Loomis hit him.

His first blow, a horizontal chop to the trachea, stunned the youth. As he bent forward, choking, fighting for air, Loomis brought a vertical chop down across the base of his cranium. The cervical vertebrae parted with a sickening crunch. Loomis caught the soldier's rifle before it clattered to the pavement.

As Loomis turned, Johnson's man dropped onto the stones, his head rolling over to rest at an odd angle. Johnson obviously had not lost his touch with his favorite punch: a heel-of-the-palm jab to the chin. Loomis had never liked the blow. Too much depended on angle and timing. But the whiplash effect could be devastating. Johnson always achieved spectacular results. The man was dead.

"I hated to do that," Johnson said softly. "I think if I lived in this flea-bitten country, I'd be on *his* side."

Loomis handed the rifles to Johnson. He checked inside the doorway, then dragged the bodies inside while Johnson kept watch. Beyond the entryway the church was dark. Loomis propped the bodies behind one of the massive pillars.

He moved the lanterns to cast even more shadow on the doorway, put Johnson in position, and stepped back to estimate their chances. In their khakis, standing in the shadows, they might pass as rebel sentries. In any event, the element of surprise would be in their favor. He put his Schmeisser within easy reach and took up his post with the Garand M1 rifle.

"I just want the Professor," he explained to Johnson. "We'll let the rest leave, if we can. If not, we'll waste them. And if anything happens to me, head west, right up that street, until you reach Calle Piña. That ought to put you in the clear."

"I'm wearing my dogtags," Johnson said. "If anything happens to you, I'll just drop myself in the nearest mailbox."

They waited in silence for almost an hour before they heard sounds from inside the church. Loomis tried to estimate the number from the approaching footsteps before they came through the door, deep in an argument over the proper placement of rocket launchers. Six officers passed within an arm's length of Loomis, hardly aware of his presence. None fitted the rotund shape of the Professor.

Loomis breathed easier as the group walked across the courtyard and disappeared in the direction of the tower. Johnson grinned and tossed them a belated, mock salute.

The next group came so quietly Loomis didn't hear them until they were near the door. Three came through first, several steps ahead of the Professor and a companion. The five started across the marble courtyard. Loomis heard no sounds from inside the church. He reached for the Schmeisser.

"Freeze!" he called to the five. "Anyone who moves is dead!"

Exposed in the open courtyard, the rebel officers obeyed their better instincts. They stopped, motionless, hands well away from their bodies.

"Now, put your hands on top of your heads," Loomis said. "Move!" He gave them a few breaths to contemplate their vulnerability. He still heard no sounds from inside the church. "Now turn around, slow, and face me," he ordered.

He watched Professor Salamanca's face as recognition came, and in that moment Loomis was certain that the Professor was the one who had ordered him assassinated.

Johnson moved out, flanking. Loomis side-stepped to the doorway.

"Come in, gentlemen," he said. "One at a time, please."

The lanterns inside were of better design—Coleman's with mantles. But they were turned low. Beyond, the church was dark. The meeting apparently was being conducted deep within the building. Loomis motioned the rebel officers into a line along a wall, then knelt to turn up a lantern.

Johnson entered and stopped, staring up at the shrine. "Good God, what in hell is that?" he asked.

"The tomb of Columbus," Loomis told him. "His bones are in that lead box over there."

"No shit!" Johnson said. He went over for a closer look.

"Who's your friend?" the Professor asked Loomis.

"Just a tourist I picked up."

The Professor snorted. "He smells like CIA to me."

"Believe me, he's a tourist," Loomis said.

"You guys sure make it tough for a fellow to see the sights,"
Johnson complained. He moved in and took their sidearms,
a collection of Berettas, Llamas, and Colt automatics, taking
care not to interfere with Loomis's field of fire.

Loomis tossed him a roll of heavy nylon-threaded Scotch
tape. "Lash them all up except the Professor," he said. "The
Professor goes with us."

"You're insane!" the Professor said. "There are hundreds
of rebels, anywhere you turn."

"And all asleep," Loomis said. "You four, turn around and
put your hands behind your backs."

Johnson picked up his Schmeisser and paused, listening.
Then Loomis heard it, too.

Footsteps were approaching from somewhere deep within
the church. Normally, a barrier of metal rods separated the
church proper from the tourist area around Columbus's
tomb. But the rebels had removed several of the rods, providing direct access to the church.

Loomis knelt and turned down the nearest Coleman. Johnson backed into the darkness of the church. Loomis walked
quietly to a corner, under the huge frescoes beside the
shrine. He was still hoping the newcomers would walk into
the light unaware, that they could avoid shooting, but the
Professor saw his chance.

"Trap!" he yelled. "Go back! Get help!"

Johnson's Schmeisser opened up on full automatic inside
the sanctuary. The noise was unbelievable. The five captives
bolted for the door. Loomis cut four down, but he allowed
the Professor to run, certain he could stop him. The Professor
was at the door, in full stride, when Loomis caught him behind the ear with the butt of his weapon. The Professor fell
sprawling and lay still.

Again all was quiet in the church.

"I could use some light over here," Johnson said.

"You all right?"

"I'm O.K. It's these other fellows I'm worried about. I think
they're all down for the count, but I'm not sure. Be careful."

Holding a lantern well out to one side, Loomis checked the

damage. Johnson had killed four rebel officers and critically wounded two. Blood, brains, and chipped masonry covered the floor.

"I sure hope nobody hit poor ol' Columbus," Johnson said.

Loomis hurried back to the Professor. "We've got to get out of here," he said. "If we have to, we'll carry the son of a bitch."

The Professor was dazed but able to stand on his feet. Loomis found his glasses and handed them to him. A thin trickle of blood ran from his ear into his beard.

"How much time do we have before the whole rebel army comes swarming over here?" Johnson asked.

"About two minutes. You have anything you want to do?"

"Not especially."

"There's a cannonball from Sir Francis Drake's flagship buried up there somewhere in the roof. It's something every tourist ought to see. If you want to run up and take a look, I'll see if I can't hold off the rebel army for a while."

"I'll pass. If you've seen one cannonball, you've seen them all."

Johnson hurriedly extinguished all the lights. Loomis led the Professor and Johnson out into the night.

"How far do we have to go?" Johnson asked.

"Eleven or twelve blocks," Loomis said. "We'll try to come out somewhere around the Gate of La Misericordia. People in that direction will think the shooting was down by the river."

Keeping to the shadows, they made four blocks without incident.

They were nearing the intersection of Calle 19 de Marzo and Calle Padre Bellini when a burst of bullets passed within a yard of them and slammed into a wall, showering them with concrete chips and plaster. Loomis ducked to the pavement, pushing the Professor full-length. Johnson sprawled beside them.

"Alto!" a sentry yelled from the opposite side of the intersection.

"That guy has got it ass backward," Johnson said. "Isn't he

supposed to challenge first, *then* shoot?"

Johnson worked his Schmeisser into position. Loomis could see more rebels in the doorways beyond the sentry. He didn't want a firefight. He put a hand on Johnson's arm. "Hold it," he said.

"Well, it pisses me off," Johnson fumed. "Nobody does his job right anymore."

Loomis pulled his Colt .357 magnum and put the barrel against the Professor's temple. He cocked the hammer. "Professor, your life depends on how well you carry this off," he said. "Send those soldiers south, down toward the ocean."

The Professor nodded, swallowed carefully, and called out a stream of obscenities that immobilized the sentry.

Never letting up on the tongue-lashing, he rose and stepped into the moonlit intersection. He rattled out orders, dividing the men into patrols to scour the ocean front for government troops he said had penetrated rebel lines.

"Hang onto that fellow and you might win this war," Johnson said.

Loomis waited until the soldiers left, then led the Professor and Johnson on west. Near the Old City gate they found barricades manned by government troops. Loomis called for them to hold their fire.

Prodding the Professor, they crossed the street under government guns. Loomis identified himself to a captain and borrowed a jeep.

Loomis held his temper until they reached the Jaragua. He took the Professor straight to Johnson's room, pushed him into a chair, and let his anger flow.

"Listen, you son of a bitch," he said. "I know you put out the contract on me tonight. I'd just as soon blow your head off as look at you."

The Professor licked his lips, stared at Loomis through his thick glasses, and said nothing.

"There's only one reason you're still alive," Loomis told him. "You may be worth more to me alive than dead. I need to talk to Ramón. You know how to reach him." Loomis picked up the phone and tossed it into the Professor's lap. "Call him," he said.

The Professor slowly shook his head. "I don't know where he is," he said. "Ramón moves constantly . . ."

"Don't bullshit me," Loomis warned. "Don't take me for an idiot. You're Ramón's top man in the capital. You're bound to know how to track him down if you want to. And you damned sure better want to. I have a proposition for him. You might find it interesting. He has a hostage—the girl, María Elena de la Torre. I'll swap you for her. Fair trade."

The Professor looked at the phone but made no move. "I can give you Ramón's answer now," he said. "He will not trade. I'm not that important to the movement. The girl has considerable propaganda value . . ."

"There are other things that won't wait," Loomis said. "The war has to be halted. It's a matter of life or death to the entire city of Santo Domingo. If the war isn't stopped, there's a good chance neither you nor Ramón will be alive this time tomorrow night."

The Professor looked up. "The girl has told a crazy story," he said. "Ramón doesn't believe her."

"Maybe he'll believe me," Loomis said. "I can give him names, places, dates."

"Then there *is* a nuclear bomb in Santo Domingo?"

"You better believe it."

"Who is behind it?"

"If we knew that, we might be halfway to finding it. All we know for certain is that it's international. Men have died in Europe, maybe elsewhere, to put it here. This man is from the CIA. He'll confirm what I say."

The Professor frowned at the phone for a full minute. Johnson tossed him a towel to wipe his ear and beard. He then lifted the receiver and dialed so rapidly Loomis couldn't ascertain the number. But he knew the clicks could be determined on the monitoring tape, if need be.

The Professor asked to speak to Ramón. An underling apparently gave him some difficulty, but within two minutes he had Ramón on the line.

"The *norteamericano,* Loomis, wishes to speak with you," the Professor said. "I don't know what he is going to say, but don't let my safety be a consideration in your decision. The movement is too important. And I think you should be aware that this conversation is probably being recorded and your location traced. Have care. I wouldn't put you in this potential danger, except that Loomis has partially convinced me that the girl is telling the truth."

He handed the receiver to Loomis.

Ramón's voice was cool, distant. "Loomis, I'm trying to decide whether you are incredibly good, fantastically lucky, or just plain stupid. Which is it?"

"You tell me," Loomis said.

"If it's any satisfaction to you, eight of my best staff officers are dead. But I think it's going to work against you. My men are terribly angry."

"I got what I went after," Loomis said. "He's right here. You can have him back. All I want is the girl in exchange."

The line was silent for a moment. "I'm reluctant to let her go, Loomis. Aside from the publicity value, she has a lively, entertaining imagination."

"Her story isn't original. I first heard it from the CIA."

"And you believe them?"

"I believe the story. You better believe it, too. I can't do my job, track down that bomb, with your fucking war going on. Let's call a cease-fire long enough to find it. Then you people can fight for the next thirty years, for all I care."

Ramón snorted into the phone. "I've spent two years building this revolution. I don't think I'm giving away any secrets by telling you that the next twenty-four hours, maybe the next twelve hours, will be decisive. My men are ready, psychologically. If I hesitate now, I'll never get back to this point. How do I know this isn't a clever ruse to stall my whole revolution right at this critical time?"

"You don't," Loomis said.

"I'm supposed to trust you?"

"Trust your instincts. You're bound to know that something unusual has been going on. Surely you've had reports."

"All of your unusual activities could have been staged for my benefit."

Loomis sighed. "Ramón, I'm tired. I've had a rough night. I'm going to tell you once more, and if you don't believe me, you can go fuck yourself. A good portion of Santo Domingo will be vaporized at one o'clock this afternoon. I don't know what part. The bomb may be on your side of the lines, it may be over here. We need a house-to-house search to find it. There's no way to do that with a war going on. And you're the only man who can call a cease-fire."

Loomis listened to the faint hum of the open line while Ramón wrestled with his decision.

"I'll return the girl," Ramón said. "In exchange for the Professor, of course. He's much too modest. I do need him."

"And the cease-fire?"

"That will depend on you and on El Jefe. The girl will bring you a proposal. I'm not inflexible."

"A proposal for a cease-fire?"

"Perhaps. A compromise. It's rather complicated. I would prefer to allow María Elena to describe it. Actually, she first suggested the plan. We have been negotiating for two days."

"Where will we make the exchange? And when?"

"How about an hour from now at the northeast corner of Parque Independencia? You can bring the Professor out from your barricades there. María Elena will be escorted from our lines. The exchange can be made in the middle of the street, under both rebel and government guns."

"All right," Loomis said. "An hour from now."

The exchange was made without incident. Loomis walked Professor Salamanca out from behind the barricades toward the center of the street, well lit by battery lanterns. A uniformed rebel captain brought María Elena out. Her hair was disheveled, and Loomis could see lines of fatigue under her eyes. She seemed completely dazed and exhausted. He put an arm around her and walked her to El Jefe's Cadillac. She clung to him desperately but didn't talk until they were in the car, driving the few short blocks to the *palacio.* He felt a shudder pass through her body. "Being away from you was the worst part, Loomis," she whispered. "Hold me. Please hold me."

In the *palacio* driveway, she regained her composure. "Ramón has agreed to a coalition government," she said. "But on these terms: he will accept my father as President, with the provision that he be named First Secretary. He will accept the government generals in the coalition, provided they are matched in number and position by his own generals."

"And El Jefe?"

"He must leave the country before there can be a cease-fire."

"Then that's no compromise," Loomis said. "El Jefe might step down, accept some honorary title for the good of the country. But Ramón is asking too much."

"That's what I told him," María Elena said. "We argued for two days."

"And he still doesn't believe the bomb exists?"

"He's not thoroughly convinced. But he *is* concerned. You see, he's hedging his bets. He thinks that if the atomic bomb exists, El Jefe will resign. If the story isn't true, then he has lost nothing in making the offer."

Loomis was impressed with Ramón's shrewdness. But when the proposal was explained to El Jefe, the old revolutionary didn't see the maneuver in that light. He believed that Ramón had heard rumors of the United States Navy force leaving Guantánamo Bay and assumed that Ramón hoped to effect a partial victory before the landing of U.S. Marines.

Despite María Elena's exhaustion, El Jefe led her repeatedly through her arguments with Ramón, hunting some clue to Ramón's thought processes. Loomis put a stop to the interrogation by summoning the *palacio* physician, who declared María Elena near collapse. He gave her a sedative and ordered her to bed. "Come to me when you can," she whispered to Loomis. "I need you."

El Jefe and Loomis went to work planning the defense of

the *palacio*. El Jefe vetoed Loomis's plan for a tank assault downriver to sever rebel lines of supply. The tanks would be needed to support a final line of defense, he insisted.

Ramón's proposal plagued El Jefe.

"He must know something we don't," El Jefe reasoned. "What does your CIA friend say about the possibility of intervention?"

"He doesn't know, of course. But he's doubtful."

El Jefe frowned, thinking. "Ramón must have good information that the U.S. Marines are en route here. The United States must be seriously considering intervention. They know Ramón is a leftist. Perhaps they don't want another Cuba. What do you think?"

"I'm more concerned over the bomb, at the moment," Loomis said. "I think we should give it precedence." He checked the time. Two minutes after 2:00 A.M. Less than eleven hours remained. "But even if the Marines landed at sunup, they probably couldn't secure the downtown section by one o'clock. I think our only hope of finding that bomb is to accept Ramón's offer."

"I'll see him in hell first," El Jefe said.

"That may be sooner than we think," Loomis said.

El Jefe looked up, surprised by the impertinence. But his mind seemed to be occupied with another thought.

"We must make the effort," he said.

He picked up a telephone and summoned an aide.

"I am making a formal request for U.S. intervention," he said.

Chapter 26

Even in the dead waste of the night, the White House press corps was not without resources. Within minutes of the first arrivals at the White House, most of the veteran reporters were alerted to the unusual gathering of national leaders. By the time the reporters themselves arrived in the predawn darkness, enough of a roster had been assembled to ascertain that the National Security Council was meeting in emergency session.

Speculation ranged widely among the press. Those with early deadlines fished desperately for solid information. The wire services sent queries to correspondents throughout the world, seeking clues.

Rumors of a new crisis in the Middle East persisted. Reports confirmed that most of the Sixth Fleet was at sea in the Mediterranean, which could mean anything. But the tell-tale activities of auxiliary ships—oilers, tenders, and such—seemed routine. Longtime observers in that part of the world discounted any extraordinary developments.

A few believed a new crisis had surfaced in the Far East. But again, no movements of the Seventh Fleet in Pacific waters or of the Strategic Air Command offered confirmation. Key Military Air Transport commands across the continental United States provided no clues.

Inevitably, speculation returned to the situation in the Dominican Republic. Correspondents on the scene from the *New York Times,* the *Washington Post,* and the *Chicago Tribune* reported a rapid deterioration of the government forces in Santo Domingo. Yet no one seriously believed that the Administration might be considering intervention. El Jefe certainly was not a favorite of the State Department; he had blocked too many United States programs and had spoken out too often on United States interference in Dominican affairs. The Latin America experts among the press corps said intervention was inconceivable. They pointed out that Lyndon Johnson's 1965 occupation was now universally deplored by political authorities and historians.

A few persisted in believing that the Dominican Republic was involved. Reporters with high sources in the Navy Department learned that the aircraft carriers *Enterprise* and *Ranger,* along with escort destroyers, had left Guantánamo Bay, Cuba, on such short notice that liberty parties flown to Kingston and San Juan were left ashore. These sources admitted that marines from Little Creek, Parris Island, and the barracks at Guantánamo had been rushed aboard to augment fleet marines.

By 5:00 A.M., the speculation stories had jelled into a consistent summation: something extraordinary was afoot at the White House, leading the President to call the National Security Council into emergency session in the middle of the night. All evidence pointed to some action by the United States in regard to the deteriorating situation in the Dominican Republic.

This was the gist of stories prepared by television networks and the wire services to lead the morning news budget.

Inside the White House, in the Situation Room near the National Security Adviser's basement office, the President after a full night of work sat quietly smoking a cigar and sipping his bedtime brandy, listening to the stormy debate raging around him.

Although he was deeply disturbed by the anger and hostility flaring in the small conference room, he didn't take part. He wanted all factions to express their views freely, with no hint of influence from their President.

Afterward, he would make the decision. Until then, he intended to keep an open mind, unaffected by emotion.

President Robertson was aware of the speculation in the Press Room. He received constant feedback from his press secretary, and on the table before him lay two bulletin leads from the wire services. He knew that these stories of conjecture, if allowed to continue, could be damaging. But he also knew that most of the nation was still asleep. Within an hour he would take action generating bulletins that would supplant all the random speculation with solid news.

Draining his brandy, Robertson listened to the firm, unhurried Oklahoma drawl of the Vice-President, chairing the council. Vice-President Threadgill was raising his voice to quell the uproar.

"All right, all right, let's just stop right here and sum up this situation," the Vice-President said. He referred to notes he had been making on a scratch pad. "Let's take a look at what we know. One, we're piss-positive the bomb is there. Two, without adequate search, the bomb probably won't be found. Not in time, anyway. Three, unless this war is halted down there, either one side wins or the other, or we get us a cease-fire, there won't be adequate search. Four, there doesn't seem to be any way the war can be halted unless we intervene. Five, if the bomb isn't found and disarmed before one o'clock today, Dominican time, tens of thousands, perhaps hundreds of thousands, of people will die. Six, that disaster will throw the door wide open for the United States to be extorted, literally held for ransom, by whoever is behind this, if the other bomb isn't found. Now, does anybody have any quarrel with that assessment?"

"I think it is an excellent analysis," the Defense Secretary said in his clipped Boston accent.

"What we've got to decide here is if we can stop that chain of events, and where," the Vice-President said. "As I understand it, our people screwed up good early in the game, wasted a lot of time trying to bring this fellow Loomis up here and all, playing cops and robbers all over Europe and Africa. No use crying over spilt milk. That's all under the bridge. But as I see it, these mistakes have brought us down to our point four—intervention. We've got to decide whether to try and stop things at that point—and if it's worth the risk. All these other things, recriminations, backbiting, and conflicts of personality, are out of order here today. Does everybody agree with that?"

President Robertson never ceased to marvel at Vice-President Threadgill's rambling prose, devastating logic, and uncanny influence on other men. Easterners often were surprised to learn that the lanky Vice-President, with his relaxed, rough ways, was a Rhodes scholar, an authority on Renaissance art. They seemed to find inconsistency in these facets of his personality. Born a millionaire, he'd never doubted his position in the world or seen any need to be other than himself. By contrast, the Secretary of Defense spoke in restrained, formal terms but had come up the hard way, never completing high school, building a small factory into a corporate giant through three decades of relentless effort. He remained in constant fear that all he had built would someday collapse. He forever faced the world tense, on guard. President Robertson tended to like the Vice-President better. He never quite trusted the Defense Secretary or his motives. Yet, the Defense Secretary held a position that gave him a unique view of the world. His opinions would have to be considered carefully. Robertson closed his eyes, massaged the deep furrows on his brow, and listened to the man's argument.

"We *must* intervene," the Defense Secretary said. "We simply have no choice."

"Let's look at it from every angle," the Vice-President said. "What's the earliest time you could put Marines on the ground?"

"Nine A.M., Dominican time," the Secretary said promptly. "That's lifting them in by helicopter from a hundred miles out. They would have air cover, including helicopter gunships, but no firepower from the sea until near noon. Our experience in 1965 was that we can expect minimal opposition. The imbalance of power is obvious."

The Vice-President nodded. "What's the latest assessment of the military situation down there?"

A naval aide quickly pinned a map of Santo Domingo to the wall. The Secretary rose and picked up a pointer. "From all we can learn—and we have worked closely with Langley on this—the rebels hold seventy or eighty square blocks of the Old Town, roughly from here to here, and they control the eastern approaches to the river. They are within a few blocks of the national palace, here, and it is virtually certain that they will take the seat of government this morning, if we don't intervene."

"And how do you propose to do that?" the Vice-President asked.

"By landing our marines here, in the Polo Grounds, and in the Botanical Gardens, here. With light tanks, armored personnel carriers, and so forth, they would move rapidly up Bolívar Avenue here, cutting the rebels off from the palace, then push them back to the river along a front, here."

The Secretary of State lit a cigarette and reached for an ashtray. "Suppose we intervene, as you propose, but fail to find the bomb, and it goes off. Won't *we* be blamed?"

"Let us look at it another way," the Defense Secretary shot back. "Suppose we *don't* intervene, and the bomb goes. Most of the world knows by now that the National Security Council is meeting in emergency session—an extraordinary night meeting. The press is not completely stupid. They will know, with any reflection, that an ordinary decision to intervene in the Dominican Republic probably would have been made after a telephone conference of the President with his most trusted advisers. *After* the bomb blows today, there will be demands for an accounting from this meeting. The facts will be plain. We knew of the bomb beforehand but failed to act."

The table fell silent. Then the Vice-President chuckled.

"I think you just grabbed the issue by the nuts, Charlie," he said. "We're damned if we do, damned if we don't. Let's examine the alternatives. What about our spook group down there, and this bad boy Loomis? Is there any chance they'll produce?"

"We've been expecting too much out of Loomis," the Secretary of State said. "His government is collapsing, the whole organizational structure of the country has broken down. There's fighting in the streets. Early last night an attempt

was made to assassinate him. He's got his hands full. We can't
risk acknowledging that Johnson and his men are down
there. They must keep a low profile. Their hands are tied. I
don't think we can expect them to perform miracles in that
situation."

"Then we *have* to intervene," the Defense Secretary said.

"Not necessarily," State countered. "The Vice-President
has listed a number of steps, a progression of events. I believe
we are too late to stop those events at point four—intervention. I believe we must realistically acknowledge that we are
helpless in the present situation. Our only option is to devote
all our energies to finding Hamlet and the other bomb."

"I *don't* think you *are* looking at this realistically," the
Defense Secretary said. "When this nuclear extortionist
group—whoever they are—makes public its demands, with
fifty to a hundred thousand or more dead in Santo Domingo,
we will be faced in this country with unprecedented panic.
We've *got* to find that bomb."

An aide entered from the Communications Room and
handed a sheet of paper to the President's National Security
Adviser, who glanced at the note, then handed it to President
Robertson.

He stubbed out his cigar while he read the message. He felt
all eyes on him.

"Well, this is a new development," he said. "One that El
Jefe didn't bother to mention in his dramatic plea for intervention. I don't know that it clarifies the situation. First, the
De la Torre girl is safe. It seems Loomis and Johnson grabbed
a hostage of enough importance that Ramón agreed to an
exchange. Secondly, Ramón has proposed a coalition government, with himself as First Secretary and El Jefe's brother as
President, if El Jefe will leave the country. El Jefe has
refused."

A murmur of surprise swept the table. The Vice-President
chuckled. "He's banking on intervention, Mr. President."

"You're probably right," Robertson said. He reread the
message. There was one aspect of it that bothered him.
"What I can't understand is Ramón. Why did he make the

offer, right when he's on the edge of a clear-cut victory?"

"The bomb," the Vice-President said. "Ol' Ramón doesn't quite believe the bomb exists, but then on the other hand he doesn't quite disbelieve, either. This way, he hands El Jefe the option."

President Robertson nodded his understanding. He always tended to trust the lanky Okie's logic.

"I think we have defined all the issues," Robertson said, pointedly ending the discussion.

He knew that the time had come to act.

He had analyzed, assessed, judged until he was dizzy with thinking. And there were no good solutions. There were only good men to study. One could only derive what knowledge he could from their experiences, their mistakes. He never ceased to be amazed at the varieties of idealism that drove men. Loomis, continually seeking justice in a world without justice. El Jefe, striving through benevolence to gain public acceptance in a thankless position—the wrong job in the wrong country. Ramón, honestly seeking human dignity in the most dangerous corner of the political spectrum, following the deceptive lights that had led so many good men astray. The Vice-President, seeking a deeper meaning to life in public service. The Defense Secretary, seeking security in power . . .

There were so many lessons to be learned.

President Robertson sat for a moment, feeling the pressures of office as he'd never felt them before. On his decision within the next few minutes would rest the fate of hundreds of thousands of people. He was tired and sleepy. Dawn was arriving and with it his bedtime. He had pondered all the issues and he still couldn't decide. He felt the need of one more painstaking examination of the matter. Rising, he faced the council.

"Ultimately, of course, this is my decision," he told them. "Harry Truman defined my position. Harry faced the heat of the first two nuclear disasters in human history. I'm now feeling the heat of the third. There's no way I can pretend I didn't know or avoid facing the responsibility. Less than eight hours from now, we will have one of mankind's major disasters unless something is done. Before I decide what action our government will take, I would like to have the benefit of your thinking. A brief assessment from each one of you. Charlie?"

The Defense Secretary didn't hesitate. "Intervention," he said. He pointed to the map. "Santo Domingo is a relatively compact town. In four hours the bomb might be found. And in taking that risk, we might get a lead on where the other bomb is located, and possibly some clue as to the identity of the extortionist group."

"State?"

"We're too late," the Secretary insisted. "I say let's consider this a lost cause, seek whatever redemption we can in helping the Dominican Republic in the wake of the disaster, and bring everything we have to bear on finding the other bomb, in nailing the Hamlet people."

"Emergency Planning?"

"Nonintervention, Mr. President. Every time we've entered another country in the last twenty-five years we've lived to regret it. We've lost face, lost ground. I think the chances of finding the bomb are minimal, the risk excessive."

"Mr. Vice-President?"

"I'm afraid I'm for landing, Mr. President. I'm aware that the odds are against us, the risks overwhelming. But I don't see how we can sit back and do nothing, when we have an entire naval strike force within range. Now, I'll admit, Mr. President, that if you had a heart attack in the next ten minutes, flopped over right here deader'n a doornail, and the decision was then *mine* to make, I might feel completely different. But from where I sit, I move for intervention."

"You don't always have to be so candid, Hank," Robertson said. The Vice-President smiled, winked at the Defense Secretary, then laughed.

"Mr. Adviser?"

"Nonintervention, Mr. President. I feel that the scales are just about balanced pro and con. But my gut feeling is for nonintervention."

President Robertson nodded slowly, thinking. He toyed with his brandy snifter for a moment, then reached for a phone. His private secretary was not in her office yet, so he dialed her dictaphone. "Please have Ron inform the press I will speak to them at ten o'clock EDT on a matter of national security. Full television coverage approved. If the question arises as to whether it concerns the Dominican Republic, the answer is affirmative. But Ron is to say no more at this time."

He hung up the phone. "A gambit," he said. "Speculation beforehand might be damaging. This will provide a solid news lead for the early editions and hold off the pack until ten."

He rubbed his eyes, forcing himself to recheck every angle one last time. He felt the subject had been covered adequately.

"Thank you, gentlemen," he said. "As it so happens, I agree with everything you've said. You've helped me to define matters."

He paused, wondering if his decision was the wrong one. Time was the only true test. The man in the hot seat had to block all personal and emotional considerations, listen to his logic, then stick to his decision through all that would follow.

President Robertson again faced his advisers. "I have decided *not* to intervene," he said. He turned to State. "Please forward my regrets to El Jefe. Word it softly, but imply strongly that he simply waited too long to ask, that we are convinced our assistance at this time would not be of benefit to him, to us, or to the people of the Dominican Republic."

The President studied reactions. Around the table there were no signs of disappointment or of protest—only of relief that the decision had been made.

The President felt he should add one more thing. "There is no need to burden El Jefe with this thought, but my main concern in the decision is that I see no way of finding that bomb in time. And I do not intend to go down in history as the stupid son of a bitch who sent twenty thousand U.S. Marines marching into a nuclear blast."

Robertson again turned to State. "Let's get word to Johnson and Loomis: they're on their own. They'd better find that bomb. They're our only hope."

He turned to his assistant. "Have the staff prepare a simple statement to the effect that although unconfirmed reports have led us to consider seriously—and stress unconfirmed reports—the possibility of intervention in the Dominican Republic, I have decided not to take action on a request from the President of the Dominican Republic for military intervention. Add that a naval task force is standing by to protect, and possibly to evacuate, any Americans or other foreign nations who may be in danger, the usual shit. I'm going up to the Oval Office now. Bring me the first draft as soon as it's prepared."

As he walked toward the elevator, the Vice-President came and put an arm around him. "I sure hope you don't take my little jokes seriously," the Vice-President said. "I wouldn't want anything to happen to you. Why, I've got a red hot domino tourney going on over in my office, and I'm two games ahead!"

He walked on into the elevator with the President, roaring with laughter.

Chapter 27

One by one, the Vampires swept low over the *palacio*, engines, rockets, and cannon blending into an earsplitting barrage. The rebel targets were now so close that the rockets and cannon were fired well to the north of the *palacio*, the shells angling over the roof and plowing into the rebel emplacements near the Parque Independencia.

The government's ten French AMX-13 tanks were now arrayed along the Avenida Simón Bolívar, their 90-mm cannon steadily pounding rebel entrenchments south of El Conde Gate. From his balcony, Loomis could hear the chatter of the tanks' 7.62-mm machine guns. Tracers arced across the park and disappeared into the buildings beyond.

The battle was now an hour old. The lines had not shifted since daylight, but on the army's radio net the government generals seemed confident that the sheer pressure of firepower would soon push the rebels back.

Loomis had no such illusions. He remembered other bombardments, other wars.

At Tarawa, three battleships and four cruisers fired three thousand tons of high explosive into 291 acres of coral on Betio during an eighty-minute bombardment, the most concentrated shelling in naval history. Yet enough Japanese survived to litter the beaches with three thousand American dead. Loomis had seen further examples that man is among the toughest of animals: Saipan, Okinawa, Inchon, Porkchop, the Delta . . .

As the earth-shattering roar of a Vampire faded into window-rattling explosions, Loomis heard the ring of his bedside phone.

"What do you think now?" El Jefe asked.

233

"If we wait more than another thirty minutes, I can no longer be responsible for your safety," Loomis said.

"The tanks are not holding?"

"They're holding. But they're too concentrated. Ramón will flank. He will come in from the east."

"We have moved reinforcements there."

"Not enough. It's time to bail out, at least until the battle is decided."

"No, Loomis. If I leave the *palacio,* I will be admitting to four million Dominicans, and to the world, that Ramón has won. I simply cannot do that until I am convinced no other course exists."

"It's almost nine o'clock," Loomis told him. "We will have to evacuate within four hours, in any event. I think we will have to assume that we are close enough to ground zero to put the *palacio* in danger."

A shrieking Vampire interrupted the argument. El Jefe waited until after the explosions.

"We still have time," El Jefe said. "My generals are much more confident than you. We may be able to push them back. Even the hint of some U.S. Marines would make the difference. I still have not heard from Washington. Can you call your friend Johnson? Perhaps he has heard something."

"I'll try," Loomis promised. "But in the meantime, just in case your generals are wrong, why don't I institute Contingency Plan B, on a standby basis?"

El Jefe's reply was interrupted by a tremendous explosion. The first rebel rocket had penetrated the south wall of the *palacio.*

"Perhaps you're right," El Jefe said in the ear-ringing silence that followed. "Having the plane ready won't hurt matters."

MINUS 03:48 HOURS

Johnson was not at the hotel. Loomis reached him at the embassy.

"I don't have much time to talk, Loomis," he said. "We're about to haul ass over here."

"You're not waiting for the Marines?"

"What marines?"

"Haven't you gotten the word?"

"Sure, we've gotten the word: 'Get out of that stupid country while you can.' "

"Just personnel, or the whole factory?"

"Personnel. And all the factory we don't want to lose. How are things shaping up over there?"

"I think the roof's about to fall."

Johnson lowered his voice. "Loomis, I don't want to sound like an alarmist, but why don't you get out of there before you get your balls shot off ?"

"We're waiting word on intervention."

Johnson sighed into the mouthpiece. "Loomis, when loyalty becomes stupidity, it ceases to be a virtue. Come with us. Bring María Elena, if you want. We'll worry about legalities later."

"You know something I don't?"

"Only that we've got a 707 waiting on the runway, and this place is going up like a roman candle at one o'clock. But of course don't let your decision be influenced by the fact that I've jeopardized my career—maybe wrecked it—trying to get you out of this mess."

Loomis thought about the 707. And María Elena.

The offer was tempting.

But he would have to face his own conscience.

"I've signed on for the full cruise, Johnson," he said. "I've got to see it through."

Johnson didn't argue. "If you change your mind, let me know," he said. "You won't have any trouble recognizing me. I'll be the first one on the plane."

MINUS 03:37 HOURS

Loomis found El Jefe in his office, head lowered, tears rolling down his cheeks. He handed Loomis a yellow dispatch. Johnson's impression of events was now official: the President of the United States sent his regrets that after due consideration, the request for intervention in the Dominican Republic must be denied. However, a United States Navy task force was standing by to take whatever measures were necessary to safeguard the lives and property of United States citizens and other foreign nationals. The President begged El Jefe's cooperation in whatever assistance the Dominican government might be able to offer . . .

"The son of a bitch," El Jefe said.

Loomis put a hand on El Jefe's shoulder. "I think it's time to go," he said.

El Jefe sat without moving, his face expressionless. "You go ahead. Take my brother, his family. I will stay here and die as I should," he said.

Loomis suddenly was so angry he almost hit him. "Bullshit!" he said. "This is no time to give up!"

El Jefe showed no signs that Loomis's anger had reached him. "It's all over," he said. "I have failed."

"It's a long way from being over," Loomis said, almost shouting. "It may be just the beginning."

"What do you mean?"

"Look ahead. If that bomb goes, the country will be in shambles. Your people will need leadership. If the bomb doesn't go, if Ramón takes over, how long do you think he'll last?"

"Not long," El Jefe agreed.

"Accept Ramón's offer!"

"No," El Jefe said, shaking his head violently. "I will not give him that satisfaction."

"Look at the future," Loomis insisted. "Your brother is a theorist. He has no practical experience. He is not an administrator. And Ramòn's head is in the clouds. He's never done anything but talk. Your generals couldn't agree on which way is straight up. In six months the country will be begging you to come back."

El Jefe considered the possibility, then shook his head. "I can't believe that," he said.

"They asked Juan Bosch to come back," Loomis reminded him. "Perón was driven out of Argentina, and they brought him back. You owe it to the country . . ."

"You are right in one respect," El Jefe said. "They would make a mess of it. The generals are inept, jealous, quarrelsome."

"I think either of us could write the script," Loomis said. "And whatever you decide, however the battle goes, we will have to evacuate the *palacio.*"

El Jefe studied the knuckles of his right fist for a long moment. Through the halls of the *palacio* Loomis could now hear the machine guns on the balconies firing toward the east and the occasional *carumph* of a mortar shell taking flight.

"All right," El Jefe said. "You have convinced me. Get word to Ramón that I accept his terms. Notify my brother. I will make a statement to the press to the effect that I am leaving for the good of the country, to prevent further bloodshed. Notify my pilot. I will go pack a few necessities."

Loomis hurried to a phone and dialed Ramón's number. He heard the receiver lift at the other end, then silence.

"This is Clay Loomis," he said. "I was given this number by Ramón himself. I must speak with Ramón on a matter of greatest urgency."

"I do not know a Ramón," a voice said. "Are you certain you are calling the correct number?"

"Just tell Ramón that Loomis wants to talk to him."

There was a moment of hesitation, then Loomis heard the sound of the receiver being dropped on a hard surface. He held the phone impatiently for several minutes. Then he heard the scrape of the receiver as it was picked up.

"Ramón," a voice said over the wire.

"Loomis here. El Jefe accepts your terms as per our discussion last night. He only asks safe conduct to his plane. He will leave the country within the hour."

Ramón chuckled. "That was last night," he said. "At the time, I felt the odds were against me. I was ready to settle for part of the cherry. Now, things look much better. I can hear machine guns over your end of the phone."

Loomis tried to put as much conviction as possible into his voice. "Ramón, I know you only half-believe the bomb exists . . ."

"I don't believe at all."

"But you have doubts."

Ramón's silence was his answer.

"The bomb exists, Ramón," Loomis said. "We know how the material came into this country. We have established the identity of the scientist they brought in to put it together. We've intercepted communications on the time of detonation. One o'clock. We only have three hours and forty-five minutes left."

"Then tell me who is behind it."

"That we still don't know," Loomis admitted. "But the plot is directed against the United States. We're only peripherally involved. We're the horrible example, so they can say to the United States, 'Look what we did,' with forty, fifty, maybe a hundred thousand dead. *Then* they can threaten the United States from a panic situation."

"A hundred thousand?"

"We are told we may expect something on that order. Maybe more. Maybe many more. And you're the only person who can stop it."

Ramón's end of the line was silent almost a full minute. Loomis could hear muffled, heated argument. Ramón's voice was hesitant when he returned to the line.

"My men are mentally prepared for total victory," he said. "I don't see how I can settle for less."

"Ramón, damn it, there can be no victory for *anyone* unless we find that bomb," Loomis shouted.

Ramón was quiet for a moment. "Loomis, if you're staging this, if this is a trick, I'll see that you are paid in full."

"If this is a trick, the U.S. Government and a lot of other people have gone to elaborate lengths to fool *me*," Loomis told him.

Ramón left the phone again, apparently covering the mouthpiece with his palm. But Loomis could hear an occasional voice raised in anger. Loomis waited patiently until Ramón returned with his answer.

"My advisers believe this is a trap. But you have convinced me. You and María Elena. I accept the cease-fire, on the basis of a coalition government as outlined by María Elena. But

Loomis, it will be difficult to stop the fighting immediately."

"I understand that," Loomis said.

"What can I do to help?"

"You might pull your men back from the downtown section, to disengage, so there will be no clashes between our troops."

"I'm not certain that would be best, psychologically," Ramón said. "My men fought for those positions, foot by foot. If you're agreeable, I would much prefer to put them to work, searching. That would give them something to do, something to burn up the adrenalin flowing in their blood."

The suggestion made sense. Loomis found a new appreciation of Ramón's abilities. "O.K.," he said. "If you'll organize your men into search teams for the sectors they hold, someone will be back to you soon with the grids of the search plan."

"All right. I will issue the cease-fire order now, if El Jefe will do the same."

"Consider it done. I hope we can stop the fighting within thirty minutes—by eleven o'clock. That will give us an hour, maybe an hour and a half, to turn the town upside down. If we don't find it, we'll still have thirty minutes left to evacuate the downtown section."

"Impossible," Ramón said. "There's not enough transportation . . ."

"I know," Loomis said. "But we'll have to make the gesture."

MINUS 02:45 HOURS

El Jefe made the calls to inform the generals of the cease-fire. Loomis knew they would believe no one else. While El Jefe argued, pleaded, and cursed on the line, Loomis dialed the United States embassy and for five minutes was transferred from terrified secretary to terrified secretary until he learned that Johnson and his staff had left for the airport.

Loomis groaned. Las Americas International Airport was twenty miles from downtown.

Loomis dialed Pan Am and talked with a friend. A runner

was sent across the field. Several minutes later Johnson came
to the phone. "This better be good," he said, breathing heavily.

"Unpack," Loomis told him. "We've got the war ended."

"Oh shit, Loomis. Don't you understand anything? We've
got our orders. There's nothing we can do."

"Wait for me there," Loomis said. "I'll be out to get you in
thirty minutes. Pull your electronic gear and experts off that
plane."

Johnson sighed to catch his breath. "Loomis, this plane
leaves in fifteen minutes. It's the last train from Boot Hill.
The embassy is closed. The last of the personnel is on the way
out here now. Everyone has plans for a big night stateside.
I've wired my wife to bring the kids and meet me in Miami.
I don't see how I can ask any of these people to step off the
plane."

"Don't ask them. Tell them."

"Give it up, Loomis. We're too late."

"I've just talked to Ramón. His men are staying in place to
help. We'll have an hour, maybe an hour and a half."

"Not enough."

"But it *might* be. Coon said the thing's probably on a
rooftop. While the Dominicans hunt, we can take a chopper
and go right down on the deck."

"And get our balls shot off."

"The Dominicans will start the search within the hour, just
as soon as they get organized. They won't have time to cover
all the downtown section. But we probably can check every
rooftop from the air."

"Loomis, I've got my orders. I can't countermand them.
You know that."

"I also know you are given a lot of latitude in the field. This
is a new situation. And we need your expert to disconnect the
thing when we find it."

Johnson's end of the line was silent for a moment. Loomis
waited.

"All right," Johnson said. "I'll call for volunteers. Coon is
nutty enough to go with us. But I'm not conning anybody. I

personally think you're going to have one hell of a roman candle here in about three hours."

"Maybe. But consider this, Johnson. If we *do* find it, you may not have to worry so much about the next one."

"You've got a point there, ol' buddy. But I can't keep from remembering the old standing general order on what to do in case of an atomic attack."

"What?"

"Oh, hell, Loomis. That one has whiskers: put your fingers in your ears, put your head between your legs, and kiss your ass goodbye."

MINUS 01:56 HOURS

Long experienced in revolution, the residents of the Dominican Republic usually were as sensitive to danger as alley cats. But for once their built-in radar failed them. As word of the cease-fire spread quickly from the military to civilians, the population swarmed into the streets to celebrate.

El Jefe rode from the *palacio* toward exile through jubilant crowds waving Dominican flags. He sat with his brother Manuel and María Elena in the back seat of the chauffered limousine. Loomis was perched in the jump seat, facing them. The rest of the De la Torre family had been sent to safety in the home of friends near San Cristóbal, thirty kilometers to the southwest. Manuel and María Elena were to join them there after seeing El Jefe off to exile.

The brothers, never close, obviously were disturbed over the developments that now clearly delineated them as opponents. Loomis felt the strain between them. María Elena, studying her hands at rest on her knees, seemed unusually subdued, lost in thought.

Loomis felt concern for her. The strain of the last few days showed. She was thinner, and the darkness around her eyes was not from eye shadow. She looked up once, met his gaze, and smiled ruefully. They'd had little time alone since her return from Ramón's camp.

As the car made its way slowly through the narrow streets

toward the airport expressway, El Jefe kept his face averted, studying the crowds outside the window.

"Maybe we should go ahead and make a public announcement about the bomb," he said.

"Washington believes panic would take a considerable toll," Loomis told him. "They advise waiting until the last possible moment."

"Washington advises," El Jefe said. "Perhaps we have listened too much to what Washington advises. The whole world is operated on what Washington thinks. And no one stops to consider that the United States can't even run its own government properly."

"An announcement probably would bring the people in from the suburbs to watch," Manuel said. "They would rationalize that one doesn't have the opportunity to see an atomic explosion every day."

"Papa!" María Elena chided. "The people are not that *estúpido.*"

"They may be that bored," Manuel said. "Sometimes I think boredom contributes more to revolutions than principles."

El Jefe ignored the exchange. The car entered the expressway and picked up speed. They rode the rest of the way in silence.

At the airport, the car was driven straight to the plane, a Boeing 707 outfitted for presidential use. The flight plan called for a landing in Caracas, then a nonstop trip to Madrid.

El Jefe stepped out of the car, glanced at the plane, then turned to take one last look in the direction of Santo Domingo.

"What a beautiful day for such tragedy," he said. "If I never return, I will always remember the Dominican Republic for its perfect days, for all the flowers and greenness. The gods must have great humor, to place such poverty and suffering in such surroundings."

He shook his head sadly, and Loomis saw tears welling up. "I tried so hard," he said. "I tried to do right. I wonder where I did wrong. I suppose I shall always wonder."

He turned to Loomis. "I wish you would come with me," he said. "I still need you, as a friend, if not as a protector. If you change your mind, you only have to let me know. You will always have a place with me."

"Thank you," Loomis said. "I've never been one to look ahead. I don't know what I'll do."

"In the accounting from my regime, there will be a special gift for you," El Jefe said. "Consider it only a small gesture toward expressing my immense appreciation for all you have done."

Before Loomis could reply, El Jefe seized him in a warm *abrazo,* then turned to María Elena.

"I will be a lonely old man, wherever I am," El Jefe said. "Come see me."

"We will," María Elena said, kissing him.

The two brothers stood for a moment, words failing both. They shook hands solemnly and exchanged quick *abrazos.* El Jefe then climbed the ramp into the plane without looking back.

Within a minute the ramp was pulled away, the engines started, and the ship began trundling along the taxi strip. Loomis, María Elena, and her father stood watching until the plane was airborne, banking toward Caracas.

De la Torre walked back to the car. María Elena lingered for a moment. "Your job is done," she said. "You don't have to go back. Please, please come to San Cristóbal with us."

"You know I can't do that," Loomis said.

She put a hand on his arm. "That's what worries me. I do know you. I'm afraid you won't leave in time."

"I'll leave," he said. "I have a lot to live for."

They walked back to the car. María Elena kissed him with an intensity that took him by surprise.

"Be careful," she said. She turned and entered the car.

De la Torre reached out to shake hands.

"I don't know what is going to happen, Loomis," he said. "Find the bomb if you can. But don't take undue risks. Pass the word to those concerned to make the announcement to evacuate when most feasible. We can rebuild the city from the ashes. But we must save as many people as we possibly can."

He closed the door. Loomis watched the car move away, gathering speed. María Elena turned once and waved through the rear window. Then the car turned a corner and passed out of view.

Feeling in his stomach the old familiar tightness of impending combat, Loomis walked hurriedly to the helicopter pad where the crew was readying his bird for flight.

PART FOUR

Chapter 28

Several slats were missing on the west side of the old water-cooling tower. Through a gap at eye level, Zaloudek could see the National Palace less than a mile away. He wiped the sweat from his forehead with his sleeve and leaned against the wooden corner post. The inside of the tower was a furnace. Despite the height, no breeze stirred inside the louvered box. Zaloudek was tempted to remove more slats for ventilation, but each time he considered doing so he felt far greater concern for his own safety.

Thirty minutes ago the shooting had stopped, and from the roof they had heard yelling and cheering in the streets six stories below. For a time, Arnheiter had feared that the bomb plot had been discovered and that the war had been halted for a search. But the signs of celebration eased his mind. Now, Arnheiter was worried about the time, carping continually, driving Zaloudek to distraction.

With only thirty minutes remaining before noon and their departure for the border of Haiti, Zaloudek was beginning the final stages of assembly. He had fitted the components together in his mind a thousand times. He knew them by heart, each micromillimeter notch and bevel. But the long preparation was over. He now began the work of love.

The transfer of the nuclear materials from the shop to the roof had been surprisingly easy—aside from the work itself. Most of the fighting the night before seemed concentrated several blocks to the south. Shortly after dawn, Zaloudek, Arnheiter, and the four gunmen made several trips with the panel truck, carefully repainted and bearing a hand-lettered sign: *El Mickey, el Acondicionador de Aire.* Piece by piece, they had carried the material into the building. Since the

electric power was off, they were unable to use the old elevator. They had to carry the material laboriously up the stairway to the fifth floor. From there they struggled up the
narrow half-flight into the superstructure and the door that
led onto the roof.

Now the van was parked on the street below. Arnheiter's
gunmen, armed with automatic weapons and hand-held citi-
zen's band radios, were stationed at strategic points, guarding all approaches to the building. They were to remain on
watch until Zaloudek completed the bomb. Then they all
were to walk quietly to the van, return to the shop, change
clothes, and separate into three groups for the dash to the
Haitian border.

Zaloudek was tired. The heat was rapidly sapping his energy. He again mopped the sweat from his forehead, and
studied the mass of uranium at his feet. He had waited more
than twenty years to get his hands on that grapefruit-sized
chunk of metal. And now he would show the world what he
could do. Several of the scientific community's most illustri-
ous physicists would be reminded that this was the Zaloudek
that they had relegated to Bunsen burners and Kipp genera-
tors, while lesser minds were given choice assignments.

Those world-famous scientists had ignored him, and they
had ignored his warning. Now, he would show them the true
destruction of nuclear power—an example that would
awaken the world to the fact that mankind was moving relentlessly toward nuclear Armageddon. Unless the two great
powers disarmed, destroyed all nuclear weapons, and ceased
making weapons-grade nuclear materials, then small nations,
even small groups, would soon have nuclear capability. Once
that point was reached, there would be no turning back.
Zaloudek was convinced of that. He had to warn the world
before it was too late.

The old water-cooling tower was ideal for his purpose.
Zaloudek could not have asked for anything better.

The tower itself was obsolete. New equipment with air-
cooled coils had been installed several years ago on another
part of the roof. The building's owner had left the old tower

intact to avoid the expense of removal. It had not been used for years. Eight feet high, it was built on a platform six feet above the roof. Zaloudek would have preferred more altitude for his bomb—an airplane, perhaps—but the tower would tend to minimize the shadow effect of the surrounding buildings. The tower itself of course would be vaporized in the first millisecond of ignition. From his line of sight, Zaloudek could see that the resulting fireball would have access to a much wider section of the city than if the bomb were sitting on the roof. Peeping through a broken slat, Zaloudek attempted to estimate how far the fireball would reach.

Arnheiter's yell jarred him from his reverie. "What in hell are you doing up there?" Arnheiter asked.

"Catching my breath," Zaloudek said. "It's hot in this thing."

Arnheiter looked at his watch in exasperation. "It's eleven-thirty," he said. "We're not going to make it! And you just keep fucking around!"

"I'm on schedule," Zaloudek said. "There's nothing left to do but to put it together. Just like reassembling a rifle."

"Is there anything I could be doing while you piddle around?"

Zaloudek hesitated. Arnheiter was nervous, impatient, a constant source of irritation. He simply didn't understand the need for rigid safety factors and painstaking measurements. But if Arnheiter had something to do, maybe he would quit pacing the roof, worrying.

"You can drill the holes for the frame," Zaloudek said. "I've marked the places."

Arnheiter climbed the ladder and stepped over the coaming into the tower. Zaloudek handed him the brace and bit. While Arnheiter drilled the holes through the two-by-six floorboards, Zaloudek located and carefully distributed the bolts, lockwashers, and nuts that would secure the nuclear device to the tower.

By the time Arnheiter completed the last hole, he was sweating, too.

"I don't see why you have to bolt the damned thing down,"

he said. "You've already said that when it goes off, the tower will flat disappear."

Zaloudek had no logical reason. The bolts simply fitted into his orderly working methods. He liked everything nailed down. He quickly made up an explanation.

"When the cannon fires, the recoil might conceivably jar things out of kilter," he said.

The possibility even sounded plausible to himself, but he knew the logic was deceiving. Criticality would come virtually simultaneously with the gun's explosion. In the next instant there would be no gun barrel for recoil, nor framework to be jarred. The gun and the steel frame would be vaporized —along with the building and most everything for at least a block in each direction.

"We're ready for the frame," he told Arnheiter.

They struggled the heavy base into position. Zaloudek then sent Arnheiter down to the roof with a crescent wrench to hold each bolt while he tightened the nut. He then called Arnheiter back into the tower to help him fit the cannon onto the frame. The thick-barreled gun was heavy. They could barely lift it. They made three separate attempts before the holes were lined up and Zaloudek was able to slip the bolts through.

Arnheiter staggered to the side of the tower, fighting for breath. He removed a louver and put his face close to the opening.

"Eleven forty-two," he said. "We'll never make it."

Zaloudek wiped his face and hands on a grease rag. "We're past the most difficult part," he said. "We will be off the roof by twelve noon. I promise you."

He worked the uranium target into place, carefully checking the alignment. He then fitted the reflector onto its track, and began working it toward the uranium, centimeter by centimeter, monitoring the buildup of neutrons.

"What the fuck are you doing?" Arnheiter asked.

Zaloudek attempted to explain. "I've got to get this just exactly right," he said. "There's no margin for error. The trick is to hold the mass just below criticality without going over. That's why I must measure the number of free neutrons, every move I make."

The explanation did nothing for Arnheiter's nerves. "You mean that thing is about to go off ? Right now?"

"Almost," Zaloudek said, monitoring the radiation with his equipment. "Theoretically, at least, some unexpected external source could send it over the brink. A burst of radar waves from a passing plane. A burst of cosmic rays. Or a minor mathematical error on my part."

Arnheiter was scarcely breathing. Zaloudek marked his settings with chalk. He backed the reflector a few inches and measured the distance from the mark to the uranium target.

"My calculations are confirmed," he said. "Now I'll arm the device."

With Arnheiter watching nervously, Zaloudek loaded the cannon and carefully fitted its projectile into place. He maneuvered the shield back onto its track and began edging it forward again, carefully monitoring the free neutrons with each minuscule move.

"Christ, how do you do it?" Arnheiter asked. "I'm scared shitless."

Zaloudek paused for a moment. "So am I," he said. "Only an idiot wouldn't be scared. But by taking it slowly, measuring the return carefully, we will be all right."

"What do you mean, 'return'?"

"The uranium is giving off radiation," Zaloudek explained patiently. "But at the moment, each chunk is subcritical. This steel reflector is bouncing back neutrons toward the target, contributing to a buildup. When the cannon fires, it will send the projectile into the uranium mass at five hundred feet per second. The projectile itself is uranium. The projectile will plug the hole in the reflector. The shaped charges will meet instantaneously and interlock in a way that increases pressures tremendously. The result will be a fireball."

"Jesus," Arnheiter said.

"I've hedged the bet a little," Zaloudek couldn't keep from boasting. "A little wrinkle of my own. I have glued a wafer of lithium onto the nose of the projectile and some polonium on the target. That's to boost the level of free neutrons on contact. The idea is sort of like making certain your fireplace catches by pouring gasoline on it. Also, there is a trick to the shape of the charge, the interplay of the mass and projectile, increasing the pressures by several factors."

"What's keeping it from going off right now?" Arnheiter asked, his voice strangely subdued.

"My arithmetic, mostly," Zaloudek said. "If it went now, it would be what is called a fizzle yield, a very low percentile of effectiveness."

"Does that ever happen?"

"Not any more. Usually, anyone who works with atomic weapons knows what he's doing."

Arnheiter checked the time. "Twelve to twelve," he said.

"See? I told you we'd be off the roof by noon," Zaloudek said. "I'm ready to connect the timer and interlocks. Once I do that, there's no turning back. This baby's going to go."

"I better check and make sure everything is all right," Arnheiter said.

He picked up his walkie-talkie and clicked the button twice. One by one, the acknowledgments came in by return clicks. First the man in the stairwell on the first floor, monitoring the entrance. Next, the lookout in the apartment building across the way. Then the guard at the door to the roof. And last, the man on the balcony over the truck. The escape route was clear.

"Go ahead," Arnheiter said. "Set the timer."

Zaloudek made the first connection before he heard the sound. He looked up. Arnheiter heard it, too.

A helicopter was heading straight toward them, just clearing the rooftops.

Zaloudek leaped to his feet, and was heading for the ladder when Arnheiter grabbed his arm.

"Don't panic!" he said. "Maybe they're not hunting us. Keep working! We're air-conditioning repairmen! We have every right to be here!"

Zaloudek knelt by the bomb, feeling his heart lunging uncontrollably. He fought against instinct to keep from looking up. He picked up a wrench and pretended to be tightening the bolts on the frame, so upset that he stripped the threads on one. He was aware that Arnheiter had moved to the tool kits and was standing within reach of his 9 mm Israeli Uzi.

And the helicopter came toward them, the flap of the rotors filling the tower with sound.

MINUS 01:12 HOURS

As Loomis took the helicopter low over the main business district, Johnson was leaning forward, tense and intent on the search. Coon, relaxed and jovial, appeared to be enjoying the ride.

Through his headset, Loomis monitored the nets on army and police frequencies. The search was floundering. The celebrations in the streets hampered traffic. Stores and offices were closed, blocking vital search areas. Apartments were empty and the doors locked. The routes to many roofs could not be found. Janitors and building engineers had vanished. Under the circumstances, the searchers were authorized to smash doors and chop holes, but those measures simply took too much time.

The air search also seemed doomed. Loomis had never before noticed the number of downtown rooftops in use. Many were bare, but most were not. Although the majority of downtown buildings housed offices and stores on the street level, the upper floors usually contained apartments.

"You ever see so fucking much laundry?" Johnson fumed. "They must have saved up their dirty clothes all through the revolution so they could celebrate today by flying their drawers."

Coon chortled. Loomis eased back on the cyclic, lowering forward speed, and studied the rooftops. He moved slowly up El Conde, no more than a hundred feet over the highest buildings, carefully watching the telephone poles and the maze of overhead wiring.

Alerted by the distinctive flap of the rotor blades, a surpris-

ing number of people streamed out of the apartments and
onto the roofs to wave. The roofs of El Conde soon seemed
almost as well populated as the crowded streets below.

Loomis studied the individuals, one by one, classifying
them, dismissing them as suspects. Women hanging laundry
looked up in dismay, concerned over the effects of the wind-
storm created by the chopper blades. A man on one building
ran to help his wife control dancing lines of laundry and
stopped to shake a fist skyward. On a balcony of a commercial
hotel three prostitutes made obscene gestures. Two repairmen were working on the air conditioner of an office building. One looked up. The other didn't bother. Loomis eased
back even more on the cyclic, hovering. In the street below,
their panel truck was parked illegally. Already, in the wake
of fighting the *mordida*—the bribe—apparently had been
resumed with the police for such practices. All appeared
normal. Loomis moved on. Two young girls were sunbathing
on the next roof, halter straps undone. They reacted with an
appropriate mixture of hilarity, modesty, and indignation.

Coon chortled.

Johnson glared at him in irritation, then looked at his
watch. "Ten till twelve, Loomis," he yelled. "An hour. You
really ought to give these poor fucking people an hour."

Loomis nodded. The air search seemed hopeless. There
simply were too many things that should be checked from
the ground. Any vent on the roofs below could be false,
hiding the nuclear device. It might be secreted in any of the
many superstructures. Or Coon could be wrong. A water-
front blast might be planned to raise a deadly radioactive
spray over the city. Conceivably, an air burst might be the
method: a radio-controlled plane, a drifting balloon, or a
high-level drop timed to detonate the device at a thousand
feet or so.

They would have to evacuate the city.

Loomis radioed ahead for a jeep and turned the ship back
toward the polo grounds, canting the nose down for speed,
stepping up the power. He took the helicopter straight in,
braking the descent at the last instant.

He cut the engine and the rotor began windmilling toward a stop.

"I'll sure say one thing for you, Loomis," Johnson said, unbuckling. "You haven't lost your horrible ways with a chopper. There was a minute or two there I forgot all about that fucking bomb."

MINUS 01:09 HOURS

At army headquarters the generals were congregated in a conference room around a map of the city. The areas covered by the search were shaded in red. Less than a third of the downtown section had been marked off.

Galíndez of the Policía Nacional saw Loomis and crossed the room to greet him. "We've just had word through military channels," he said. "The United States Government has received a message that a major disaster will occur in a country in the western hemisphere at precisely six o'clock today Greenwich Mean Time. That, of course, is one o'clock here. The message said that although occurring in another country, the disaster will be for the edification of the United States."

"Well, that sure ought to make the people of Santo Domingo feel a lot better about it," Johnson said.

"Do they have any clue at all yet as to the identity of the group?" Loomis asked.

"Langley has now projected the theory that Hamlet consists of the younger generation of some of the world's most powerful families, trying to exceed the successes of their fathers. One suspected is the son of an Italian automobile maker. Two are of Arabian oil families. Another is in Greek shipping . . ."

"That theory has been around awhile," Johnson said. "I thought we had discarded it."

"Apparently your people at Langley have some new clues to lend it support," Galíndez said. "But at this point, as far as we are concerned, I suppose the matter is academic and has no real bearing on the decision we must make within the next few minutes." He turned to face Loomis. "I have just conferred with De la Torre in San Cristóbal. He wants to announce the bomb's probable existence, without further delay. There is some opposition here. What do you think?"

Loomis glanced at his watch. Almost noon. They were entering the last hour. And there now was little hope that the search would produce results.

"I think it has to be done," Loomis said. "I would call it a bomb *threat,* a precautionary evacuation, to keep panic to a minimum. With forty-five minutes of warning, and with proper instructions, most people will be able to walk westward out of the danger zone . . ."

"There is one major problem," Galíndez said. "Electrical service has not yet been restored to most of the downtown section. Even normally, that would be a time-consuming procedure, involving electrical grids, things I do not understand. To complicate matters, the rebels sabotaged transformers and other electrical equipment. Consequently, most radios and television sets are inoperative in the section where they are essential. Most people in that section will not get the word."

A vague, discordant impression nudged Loomis's brain.

He nursed the fleeting sensation of unease, fishing for the source.

Then he made the connection.

Air-conditioning repairmen in a section that had been without electrical power for three days?

He remembered that one of the repairmen had looked up, expressionless. Loomis recalled his stance, loose, yet poised, near a toolbox.

The other repairman had not looked up—not with a helicopter hovering a hundred feet overhead.

Unnatural.

And on reflection, that gadget on the floor of the cooling tower seemed too big for an ordinary pump.

"Give me a phone book!" Loomis said.

A lieutenant hurried into an adjoining room. He returned with a phone book. Loomis rapidly checked the listings.

No "El Mickey" air-conditioning service was listed. And Loomis was certain that was the name he had seen on the side of the panel truck parked in the street.

"Hold the announcement!" Loomis said to Galíndez. "Give me ten more minutes! I'll radio in!"

He started for the door, with Johnson following.

"Oh Lord," Johnson said. "We've got another one of those famous Loomis hunches."

"More than a hunch," Loomis said. "I think this is it."

Coon was in the hall by the vending machines, drinking a Sprite and eating potato chips.

"And grab your physicist," Loomis said to Johnson. "I have the feeling we're going to need him."

MINUS 01:04 HOURS

Zaloudek ran a thin strand of wire to the base of the cover and carefully attached the end with a drop of solder heated with his butane torch. He then measured the wire to make certain that he had not placed the solder in the wrong spot.

"For God's sake, hurry!" Arnheiter said from the foot of the ladder.

"I'm about there," Zaloudek said.

He fitted the timer into place and began soldering the connections. Arnheiter came up the ladder far enough to see over the coaming. Zaloudek ignored him, concentrating on what remained to be done.

Arnheiter had been beside himself with worry over the helicopter. He now began again.

"Didn't they look like Americans to you?" he asked.

"I don't know," Zaloudek said, attaching the wires to the energizer. "I didn't look up until they were gone."

"They had to be Americans," Arnheiter insisted. "Two big guys, looked like pro football players. And a professor-looking little fat guy with a pipe. They looked right at us for a long time."

"They looked at a lot of people," Zaloudek said. "It just seemed like a long time." Zaloudek had been terrified while the helicopter was overhead, but now that it was gone, his relief was so great he no longer felt concern.

He had worked too long and too hard for this moment to think of anything else.

Unstrapping his chronometer watch, he placed it beside the electronic timer. Five minutes after twelve. Thanks to the helicopter and Arnheiter's irrational worry, Zaloudek was five minutes behind schedule. But they still had fifty-five minutes, plenty of time to reach the mountains.

"How much longer?" Arnheiter demanded from the ladder.

Zaloudek didn't answer. He wasn't even breathing. He was setting the timer, giving it his full attention. Arnheiter came on up the ladder and stood behind him, blocking off the sun. That helped some. Zaloudek got the timer set precisely right, released the knob, and resumed breathing.

"The bomb is armed," he said. "All I have left to do is the cover."

"Leave it," Arnheiter said. "For Christ's sake, it's not going to rain."

"Won't take but a minute," Zaloudek said. "This may be the most important part."

Arnheiter waited impatiently while Zaloudek fitted the cover into place. The thin wire snared its track on the first attempt, a stroke of luck Zaloudek hadn't expected. The aluminum was light, yet tough, offering considerable protection. His ingenious interlocks dropped into place with loud clicks.

Arnheiter's nerves jumped. "What the hell was that?"

"The interlocks," Zaloudek explained. "The cover fits like a Chinese puzzle. And there's a trip wire. If anybody finds this thing and tries to disarm it, the wire will trip the trigger."

"Jesus," Arnheiter breathed. "A booby trap."

"Right," Zaloudek said, feeling his pride. "This is going to go in fifty-four minutes, no matter what. I couldn't stop it now, myself. And I designed it. *Nobody* can stop it."

"Christ!" Arnheiter said. "I wasn't told anything about that!"

"It wasn't in the plan," Zaloudek admitted. "I thought it up myself."

"Let's get the fuck out of here!" Arnheiter said.

They climbed out of the water tower, taking the guns but leaving the tools behind. Zaloudek laid his weapon on the graveled roof and climbed back up the ladder to replace the slats, hiding the bomb. He then hurried to catch up with Arnheiter, who was at the door leading into the building. Arnheiter was crouched down on one knee, cradling the walkie-talkie to his ear. Zaloudek assumed he was alerting the crew to return to the van, but when Arnheiter looked up, his face was drained of color.

"The police," he said. "Steiner can see them stopped in front of the van. They're coming in! They're coming in this building!"

Zaloudek and Arnheiter froze, staring at each other in indecision.

Then gunfire erupted on Calle El Conde below.

Chapter 29

The gunman may not have seen Loomis and Johnson pushing their way through the crowd until after he opened fire. Loomis had parked the jeep across El Conde from the El Mickey van, directly beneath the gunman's window, and below his line of vision. The first of the Policía Nacional arrived a moment later, their little Belgium FN4 armored car winding its way through the throng of jubilant Dominicans. They stopped in front of the van. Loomis and Johnson left Coon in the jeep and had started through the crowd toward the van as the three policemen stepped out of the armored car.

The police lieutenant had just opened his mouth to speak to Loomis when a burst from a machine pistol passed just over Loomis's head and made a crimson mess of the lieutenant's chest. Two sergeants scrambled for the hatch of the armored car. The gunman cut them down inches away from the FN4's two 7.62 machine guns.

"Dumb fucks!" Johnson yelled, diving beneath the van, bringing his Schmeisser around for use. Loomis landed beside him, painfully skinning both kneecaps on the rough pavement.

The crowd, screaming and yelling in panic, vanished within fifteen seconds. Then an eerie silence settled over the deserted street. Loomis studied the sprawled bodies beside the armored car. All three were apparently dead. He crawled across Johnson's legs to look back at the jeep. Coon was gone.

"I told you he had enough sense to come in out of the rain," Johnson said. "You didn't believe me, did you?"

"Where's the gun?" Loomis asked. "You have him located?"

"Roughly. Third floor, second window from the right, I think. You and your hunches."

"I can't imagine leaving only one gun to protect your rear on an operation like this," Loomis said. "There's probably more."

"And above us," Johnson said. "We better get out from under this thing. That clown may put a tracer into the gas tank. Or somebody might drop a grenade."

"If they had grenades, they would have used them by now," Loomis said. "But you might be right about that tank."

"I'm overjoyed you agree. It's made my day. What the fuck we gonna do?"

Loomis ducked his head under the muffler and inched toward the curb. "If you'll keep that gun occupied, I'll try to make it to the doorway. Then I'll keep him busy while you come in behind me."

"I don't like the odds," Johnson said.

Before Loomis could answer, a barrage of bullets splattered along the pavement at the edge of the truck, showering the underside with chips of concrete and shattered bullet fragments. One large chunk put a hole in the muffler by Loomis's head. Johnson put a hand to his face, where a flying pebble of concrete had drawn blood.

"Those odds are looking better," he said.

"We could wait," Loomis said. "With all this shooting, plenty of help's probably on the way."

"That thought may have been a great comfort to Custer in his last troubled moments," Johnson said. "It's not to me. I'm ready when you are."

"All right," Loomis said. "Go."

When he heard Johnson's Schmeisser open up, Loomis charged for the doorway, holding his own weapon in his left hand, out of the way. Bullets landed near him, apparently fired from almost straight overhead, but Loomis was moving fast, zigzagging with a sixth sense nurtured through almost three decades of war. He reached the heavy glass door unharmed, yanked it open, and plunged into the foyer of the office building, rolling to the floor as he went, bringing his weapon up to cover the stairway and interior doorways.

There was no return fire.

Loomis hurriedly checked the entry. The old elevator cage was on the first floor. The stairway leading up beyond the elevator was deserted. All the doors leading off the foyer were locked. If a lookout had been posted in the foyer, he obviously had prudently retreated. Certain he was alone, at least for the moment, Loomis returned to the front of the building. Using the butt of his gun, he knocked a chunk out of a front window. He then flattened himself against the wall as the machine pistol across the street finished the job, showering the lobby with shards of glass. When the burst ended, Loomis whipped his gun to the hole and fired at the dark shadow framed in the upstairs window. The shadow abruptly disappeared.

Loomis knew there would be no more gunfire from that source.

Johnson came running, shooting upward at the balconies overhead. Loomis held the door open, but Johnson stopped in the street, dancing, shooting, a wild man. Loomis yelled at him. Johnson raced for the door, grinning. A body fell to the pavement behind him.

Johnson charged through the foyer and knelt by the stairway, panting hard, looking up at the next landing. "There's two or three more fuckers up there," he said. "Fourth floor, I think. And some clown was shooting from the roof with a pistol."

Loomis looked at his watch. "Twelve-eleven," he said. "We've got forty-nine minutes."

"If those clowns are trapped with it, they may defuse it," Johnson pointed out.

"Maybe. But we can't count on it. We don't know what kind of fanatics we're dealing with."

"O.K. So what do we do now?"

"We wait," Loomis said. "The building will have to be taken floor by floor."

Within two minutes the foyer was full of Policía Nacional, government soldiers, and a few marines. On the suggestion of Loomis, the colonel in charge sent a detail to the rear of the building to cut off all possible escape.

Another detail was left in the lobby to guard the door and the elevator. The colonel, Loomis, and Johnson led the advance up the stairway. On each landing, the colonel delegated men to search the entire floor.

As they rounded the landing below the fifth floor, they were met by gunfire, hurried and inaccurate.

"Time is running out," Loomis told the colonel. "Why don't we toss them a grenade?"

Two fragmentation grenades were passed up the stairwell. Loomis pulled the pins, waited two beats, then tossed them. The explosions were deafening.

Johnson charged up the staircase, shooting. One was dead. The other made only a feeble gesture toward his gun before Johnson stitched him across the chest.

Cautiously, Loomis led the way on up the narrow stairway to the half-level above. The door leading onto the roof was locked. Loomis had noticed a fire ax on the fourth-floor landing. He called for it to be handed up the stairwell.

Laying his Schmeisser aside, Loomis swung the ax, shattering the door near the heavy lock. On the third blow the door swung open. Standing helplessly, his hands full of ax, Loomis saw a tall, lean man on the roof turn and raise an Israeli Uzi machine pistol, bringing the barrel up to point at Loomis's chest. Then Johnson rammed his way past, knocking Loomis aside, his gun chattering. The man went down.

Loomis picked up his gun and ran onto the roof. A short, square-built little man was running for cover behind a ventilator. Loomis yelled at him to halt. As an answer, the man stopped and brought up a Luger, aiming at Loomis.

Loomis fired a brief burst. The man toppled over backward.

Police swarmed onto the roof.

Johnson went to the tall, lanky man he had killed and rolled him over.

"Well, I'll be damned," he said. "Arnheiter. I thought I recognized him."

"Does he point to anyone?"

"Not necessarily. He's a soldier of fortune in the less inspiring senses of the term."

Loomis climbed the ladder to the water-cooling tower and pulled away the slats. A strange, awkward-looking gadget was bolted to the floor of the tower. Tools lay scattered around it.

"The bomb's in this tower!" he yelled to Johnson. "Get Coon up here!"

Johnson trotted to the door leading down. Loomis stepped over the coaming into the water tower. He leaned his Schmeisser against a corner post and picked his way through the mess of tools.

The bomb was nothing like what he had expected. No more than three and a half feet long, it was less than three feet wide. A heavy aluminum cover hid the mechanism. Loomis put an ear to the metal. There was no time-bomb tick, only a faint, soft hum, like an electric clock.

"Señor Loomis!" someone yelled from below. "This man is still alive!"

Loomis hurried down the ladder. The man he'd shot was propped up against the roof superstructure, bleeding profusely from holes in his upper abdomen and lower chest. The lungs didn't seem to be affected, but he was losing blood much too rapidly to live.

He was older than Loomis expected. The photograph apparently had been taken several years ago.

He looked up at Loomis. "Get me out of here," he begged.

"Hello, Zaloudek," Loomis said. "We've been looking all over hell for you."

"The bomb," Zaloudek said. "The bomb will go at one o'clock."

"We know that," Loomis told him. "We've got an expert from Los Alamos here. He's on his way up. You can tell him how to defuse it."

Zaloudek shook his head in irritation. "You don't understand," he said. "It can't *be* stopped. Not by *anyone*. I designed it. I built it. I *know!* Even if I had more time, I couldn't stop it. We've got to get out of here!"

Loomis knelt beside him. There was no doubt in his mind that the man was telling the truth. His fear was so strong Loomis could smell it.

"How big a bomb is it?" he asked.

"Forty-nine kilograms."

"How big a blast? Hiroshima? Nagasaki?"

"Less metal than Hiroshima. But more efficient," Zaloudek said. Despite the fear, there was a trace of pride in his voice.

Loomis looked at his watch. "Thirty-eight minutes," he said. "Before we move you, I want some answers. Who is behind this? Who or what is Hamlet? What do they want?"

"I don't know!"

"Bullshit! They hired you! They paid you!"

Zaloudek gripped Loomis by the sleeve. "I'll tell you all I know," he said. "I was contacted by a man in Lisbon. He paid me ten thousand dollars to design the bomb. He paid me twenty thousand more when I delivered the blueprints. Then he came back and promised another hundred thousand if I would build it."

"Who?"

"He used a code name. Horatio. That's all I know!"

"He's the only person you dealt with?"

"Yes."

"When did you meet Arnheiter?"

"Here, in Santo Domingo, last week. I was given the rendezvous and a code word." He struggled to see the chronometer watch on his wrist. "You've got to get me out of here!" he said, pleading. "I'll do anything!"

Loomis pulled his sleeve out of Zaloudek's grasp. Unless he missed his guess, Zaloudek had only a few minutes to live, whether the bomb went or not. "A doctor is on his way," he said. "We'll take you with us when we leave."

He went back to the bomb. He could hardly believe that the simple-looking device could devastate an entire city. Yet science and history were on Zaloudek's side.

Johnson came trotting up the ladder. Coon was behind him.

"Found him in a fucking bar, for Christ's sake," Johnson said.

"I always have a few drinks before I disarm a nuclear weapon," Coon said, grinning. "Steadies the hand."

"It's booby-trapped," Loomis told them. "Zaloudek said it can't be disarmed."

Johnson stared at him. "You shitting me?"

"No," Loomis said. "I'm just shitting."

Johnson leaned over for a closer look at the bomb. "You believe him?"

"I believe him," Loomis said. "He was plenty scared."

"Expert, do your stuff," Johnson said to Coon.

From a leather folder, Coon took out a device resembling a dental mirror. A small light was coordinated with the mirror. Coon crouched and began probing niches and holes in the bomb and its aluminum cover. He seemed in no hurry.

"Very ingenious," he said at last. "Very sophisticated. I had no idea Zaloudek was that good. I'm rather impressed."

"I'm sure they did this whole fucking thing just to impress you," Johnson said. "Can you disarm it?"

Coon probed another minute before replying. "No, I don't think so. I don't think I should try. Not until the area is evacuated. You see, the cover is rigged like a Yale lock. Tumblers have dropped into place, locking the cover tight. There is a trip wire that makes it dangerous to fish around inside. Any effort to remove the cover would be virtually certain to trip the mechanism."

"Then there's absolutely no way?" Johnson demanded.

"Not that I see. The timer is double-wired. That is, if you cut the wires, break the circuit, it will fire. I could cut through the housing here with a torch, and it might be possible then to disarm it. But that's obviously out of the question."

"Why?"

"Catch-22. By the time you cut through that aluminum, you would be too late." He stood up. "No, I advise evacuation. This device will detonate in thirty-six minutes in spite of anything we can do."

"We can't evacuate," Loomis told him. "No power, no radios, no television."

"Casualties will be high, then."

"Fifty, a hundred thousand?"

Coon slowly turned a full circle, studying the city. His answer was objective, distant, almost disinterested. "I'd say that's a good ballpark figure," he said. "But it might be more. Many more. We're dealing with a very sophisticated device. Difficult to say."

Loomis walked to the corner of the tower and knocked out two louvers for air.

Farther up the street, the celebration had resumed. Again El Conde was wall-to-wall with people. Less than a mile away the top of the *palacio* could be seen. Two miles beyond, behind the Embajador Hotel, were the Polo Grounds—and the helicopter.

Thirty-six minutes.

It might be possible.

Coon and Johnson were squatting, peering into a hole with the mirror. Coon was explaining why it couldn't be disarmed.

Loomis interrupted. "How heavy is the damned thing?" he asked.

Coon considered his answer carefully. "Frame and all, five or six hundred pounds, probably."

"Would vibration set it off?"

Again Coon considered, fondling his pipe. "Might not. The firing mechanism fortunately is electric. The system should stand a fairly severe jolt."

Johnson looked up at Loomis. "Are you thinking what I'm afraid you're thinking?"

"There's no other way. We'll have to get it out of here." He squatted beside Coon and put a hand on the bomb. "What would happen if it was kicked out of a helicopter into the ocean?"

"It'd go," Coon said without hesitation. "You see, the firing mechanism is electric, and salt water . . ."

"All right," Loomis interrupted. "It's an air burst, then. Johnson, get it loose from the tower while I get what we'll need."

Johnson turned and started hunting through the tool box.

"You going to get the chopper?" he asked.

"Not enough time," Loomis said. "And with these over-head wires I couldn't get close enough. The rescue hoist probably wouldn't take the load, anyway. We'll have to move the bomb to the chopper."

"Could we make it?" Johnson asked.

"Fifteen minutes to the Polo Grounds. Twenty minutes to get it out to sea," Loomis said.

Johnson was digging frantically in the tool box. "May take me that long to find a fucking wrench that fits," he said.

Loomis stepped down the ladder and searched for a phone. He located one on the second floor, reached the air base at San Isidro, nine miles away, and ordered the necessary gear flown by helicopter to the polo field.

When he returned to the roof, Zaloudek was dead. Loomis went to the body and made a hurried search through Zaloudek's pockets. He found nothing significant. He stripped off the chronometer watch and put it on his own wrist.

The watch now showed twenty-nine minutes until detonation.

Loomis explained to the colonel what he would need. Officers were assigned to round up the equipment and crews. A sergeant went to find technicians to restore electrical power to the building, if possible. They would need the old elevator.

Loomis climbed back into the tower. Johnson was having trouble removing the last bolt.

"The fucking threads are stripped. See?"

When Johnson spun the wrench, the nut turned on the bolt, but failed to follow the threads.

Picking up a pair of pliers, Loomis pushed Johnson aside. "Let me at it," he said. He grabbed the nut with the pliers and, pulling upward with all his strength, slowly turned the nut.

The threads still did not catch.

"Get out of my fucking way," Johnson said, advancing on the bomb with a sledge hammer.

Coon at last was jarred out of his scientific objectivity. "My God, Johnson! Don't hit it with that!"

For an answer, Johnson swung the hammer. The blow bent the bolt, canting the nut over at an odd angle. A second, harder blow moved the nut an inch up the shaft. The third knocked it clear. The bolt dropped to the roof below.

"Let's go!" Loomis called down to the colonel. Six soldiers climbed the ladder and gathered around the bomb, maneuvering for hand-holds. There weren't many. At most, only five or six could find leverage at the same time—a hundred pounds of dead weight per man.

With Loomis and Johnson helping, the soldiers struggled to move the bomb.

Slowly, inch by inch, they lifted it from the floor of the tower. Straining, grunting, stumbling over tools and each other's feet, they managed to move it to the coaming, where it was carefully lowered to a crew waiting below on the roof.

The trip across the roof seemed to take ages. Loomis climbed out of the tower and went to the front of the bomb. He found a hold and helped to guide it through the narrow door.

In descending the stairs, the full weight of the bomb rested on those below. And in the close confines of the steep half-flight down to the elevator, there wasn't much room. Loomis and Johnson took much of the framework across their shoulders. Each step down to the fifth-floor landing was agonizingly slow, the Latins ahead, those behind yelling encouragement.

When they reached the fifth floor, word came from below that electrical power had been restored. They set the bomb down and waited for the elevator. Johnson rolled his eyes at the ceiling in exasperation as the old cage creaked relentlessly up the five floors. It seemed to take forever. When it at last arrived, the doors were propped open. Loomis and Johnson retained their holds and guided the bomb into the cage. As the old elevator took the strain, Loomis could hear the overhead cables pop and groan under the unaccustomed weight.

"This fucker's going to go clean through to the basement," Johnson said.

Loomis figured hurriedly. Eight men at one-seventy-five

average plus the bomb would weigh approximately a ton. "This brass plate says the maximum is a thousand kilograms," he told Johnson. "That means it's tested for more than a ton."

"When? In nineteen-ten?"

A soldier closed the outer doors, then the accordion-mesh inner doors of the cage. Loomis flipped the lever to *abajo*. The old elevator moved downward with a heart-freezing, metallic moan. It jerked fitfully to a stop, groaned downward six more feet, then halted abruptly.

"You and your fucking ideas, Loomis," Johnson said.

Loomis frantically worked the control handle several times. The elevator wouldn't budge. The six soldiers stopped breathing.

"The cables may be binding," Johnson said. "Take it back up."

Loomis reversed the lever and the elevator rose slowly. He flipped it back to *abajo* and the cage moved downward, past the first stop, to just above the third floor before grinding to a squealing halt.

"Oh, for Christ's sake," Johnson fumed. "Doesn't anything work right anymore?"

He reached overhead to an emergency panel, secured by set-screws. Freeing the corners of the metal plate, he pushed it to one side, then lifted himself up, head disappearing through the hole. After a moment, he dropped back to the floor of the cage.

"From what I can see, it looks like a mess of spaghetti up there," he said. "The weight has twisted the cables. We've got to get this fucker out of here."

Loomis opened the cage doors and began struggling with the outer doors to the third-floor level. One of the soldiers found the emergency catch that released the doors and they swung open.

The cage was suspended more than four feet above the third level.

The colonel and the rest of the soldiers had gone downstairs to the first floor to await the elevator's arrival. From the first-floor indicator, they soon realized that the old cage was stuck in the shaft. They now came swarming onto the third-floor landing. Loomis could hear the colonel yelling, attempting to bring order out of chaos.

"Come on," Johnson said. "Let's toss the damned thing out. If they can't catch it, that's their tough luck."

But the floor of the elevator was suspended less than three feet from the top of the outer elevator door. The bomb jammed in the opening. With all of them pushing, the bomb still wouldn't go through. It lacked less than an inch of clearing the outer door.

"Only one thing to do," Johnson said. "Pull it back. We'll lay it on its side. If it goes, it goes."

With the help of the soldiers outside pushing, they managed to pull the bomb back inside the cage. They carefully turned the bomb on its side, then slid it to the edge of the cage, and through the narrow opening into waiting hands on the third floor.

Loomis and Johnson helped the soldiers squeeze out of the cage, then followed.

The colonel and his crew moved the bomb down the stairway amidst a bedlam of shouting and confusion.

"I hate to criticize people obviously doing their best," Johnson said. "But that looks like the Three Stooges hanging paper."

The flat-bed truck and police escort Loomis had ordered were waiting at the front door, and the narrow street was jammed with people. Apparently the whole town had swarmed into El Conde to celebrate the end of the war. Rumors of the bomb had spread like wildfire. Curiosity proved stronger than prudence. The crowd stood gawking at the *bomba atómica*, pressing in for a closer look. Police cleared the way as the soldiers carried the bomb to the truck. Loomis and Johnson climbed up beside it. Coon materialized out of the crowd and was helped aboard. The police escort turned on the sirens. The convoy began to move slowly through the packed street.

Johnson flopped onto his back on the bed of the truck, propped one boot up on the bomb, and studied his watch.

"Twenty-two minutes until one," he said. "Way I figure it, we're ten minutes behind your schedule."

"We'll make it," Loomis said. "Nothing can happen now."

"Maybe. But if we have a flat, don't count on me to hang around to help fix it."

The convoy reached El Conde Gate, circled the park, and began making better time out San Martín. With the way cleared by police sirens, the driver floorboarded the old truck.

"We won't be able to get this damned thing far out to sea," Loomis told Coon. "From what you know of prevailing winds aloft, what would be the best direction?"

"Straight south," Coon said. "The fallout probably will drift westward. With any luck it will miss Port-au-Prince and Kingston. By the time it reaches the Yucatán Peninsula, or is blown back by the jet streams in the upper levels, the diffusion should be sufficient to render the radiation harmless."

"Why don't we just drive this truck on out into the country and leave it?" Johnson asked.

"There's considerable population anywhere you go within twenty miles," Loomis told him.

"And the fallout would probably blow inland," Coon said. "There'd be radioactive dust. You'd have to figure on casualties from that. At sea, most of the debris will fall over open water. Just get it as far out as you can, Loomis."

"I'll do my best," Loomis said.

"What do you mean, *you'll* do your best?" Johnson asked. "I'm going too, you know."

The truck slowed and made a right turn toward the polo grounds. Loomis could see the helicopters.

He wanted to say no to Johnson. But Johnson would be needed.

"You're the one who dumped this damned thing on me," Loomis told him. "I wouldn't think of leaving you behind."

Chapter 30

MINUS 00:16 HOURS

Loomis started the engine, wound up the rotors, and pulled pitch, using the throttle mercilessly. He began moving seaward immediately after dustoff. The Hotel Embajador passed beneath the ship. And the Jaragua. To the left, Loomis could see the tanks still deployed on Avenida Bolívar. Farther to the left was the sprawling yellow *palacio* compound. The greenery and brilliant colors of the flower gardens in the Ciudad Nueva went by in a blur. The old cannon at the mouth of the Río Ozama was soon behind, and they were out over open water, climbing steadily. The sea was calm and incredibly blue beneath scattered, lazy white clouds.

The confidence Loomis had felt earlier was gone. Although his hands were steady on the controls, he felt desperation bordering on panic.

Fifteen minutes left.

Johnson plugged into the intercom system aft. "You're sure getting careless on your preflight checks," he said. "I wonder if it's safe to ride with you."

Loomis forced himself to concentrate. At 140 miles an hour, they were covering 2.3 miles per minute. In ten minutes, they would be 23 miles out.

That would have to do.

Johnson was at work securing the bomb to the frame of the ship with cargo straps. "How do we know ol' Zaloudek wasn't a few minutes off?" he asked.

"He was a perfectionist," Loomis said. "I think we can count on that."

"Maybe his watch was wrong."

"No. It was right."

"How do you know?"

Loomis held up his left arm. "I'm wearing it," he said.

Below, as the depth of the sea increased, the water gradually changed to a deeper shade of blue. Loomis pushed the throttle to the stops, risking engine heat for more speed, more altitude. A chatter swept through the ship as the helicopter's natural harmonic frequency, altered by the heavy load, suddenly was at odds with the rotor speed, setting off violent vibrations.

"Hey!" Johnson yelled. "Cut that out! This thing's walking!"

Loomis backed off on the throttle, and the vibrations eased. He looked aft. Johnson was sprawled full length, his feet propped against the bomb, holding it in place. Johnson shook his head in exasperation, rolled to his knees, and again went to work tying down the bomb. Loomis leveled off at five thousand feet. He knew now they would have to be content with their present speed.

"I hate to bring this up, in case you haven't thought about it," Johnson said. "But how in hell are we going to get rid of this thing? If we kick it out over the ocean, it'll blow our ass right out of the sky."

Loomis had thought ahead—to what he knew would be the biggest gamble of his life.

"There are a couple of parachutes back there somewhere," he said. "We'll jump. It's a calm day. The chopper may be able to take the bomb on another ten miles or so by itself before detonation."

Johnson sat up and looked at him. "Is that possible? I thought you had to stay on top of these eggbeaters every second."

Johnson was right, in a sense. Helicopters lack the natural stability of an airplane which, undisturbed by wind or air currents, theoretically could fly indefinitely once the controls were set. A helicopter's many design problems include a strong tendency to spin in the opposite direction from that of the rotor. Any surge of power, change of pitch in the rotors, or of attitude immediately requires compensation in the controls. In the early days, a helicopter pilot couldn't take his hands off the controls for a moment. Someone once described flying a helicopter as like riding a motorcycle in four dimensions. The description was apt. Now, there were a few improvements.

"This one is equipped with a Stability Augmentation System," Loomis explained.

"An autopilot?"

"Not exactly. It's just a device to allow a chopper pilot time enough away from the controls to read a map, scratch his balls, or whatever. It'll probably bounce all over the sky after a few minutes. That's why I wanted you to tie that damned thing down. But the ship should maintain altitude and attitude. With the right settings, and a little luck, it ought to be good for ten miles. That'll be enough."

Johnson came up and put a hand on his shoulder. "Loomis, I wouldn't want you to think I don't have confidence in you, or anything like that. But is this going to work?"

Loomis forced his aching hands to relax on the controls. "I don't know," he said.

"That did it," Johnson said. "Now I *am* beginning to lose confidence in you."

Ten minutes until one.

"If you've got that thing secure, move as far aft as you can," Loomis said. "I need you back there for balance."

With Johnson against the rear bulkhead, Loomis began experimenting with the Stability Augmentation System to see how long the helicopter would remain in steady, hands-off flight. The major worry was the ship's center of gravity. When they jumped, the balance probably would be altered enough to affect flight. But Loomis figured that he and Johnson were close enough to a balance on each side of the COG. If so, the point would be changed little when they jumped. The guesswork might be close enough.

Loomis found that the ship had a tendency to bank off toward the left with the SAS. The device held well for a brief time, then the flight path began to veer. Loomis became so engrossed in the problem that he let too much time pass.

Eight minutes until one.

"Get your chute on!" he called to Johnson. "We're due out of here in three minutes!"

Johnson pulled the chutes from a storage space. He tossed one toward Loomis and began wrestling into the harness of the other. He had trouble with the straps. They were adjusted for a much smaller man. "It says 'U.S. Army Air Corps' on this thing," Johnson said. "If I find 'American Expeditionary Force' stamped on it, or Eddie Rickenbacker's name tag, I'm staying with the ship."

"That one was Hap Arnold's," Loomis said. "I've got Rickenbacker's."

Loomis left the controls long enough to get into the parachute and Mae West. The chopper held steady. Three minutes had passed.

"Five minutes till doomsday!" Johnson yelled. "Let's get the fuck out of here!"

Loomis carefully set the controls, attempting to adjust for the ship's tendency to veer to the left. He wished he had more time, but he knew there was nothing else he could do but gamble that the ship wouldn't fly for a mile or two, then start spinning out of control, perhaps even circle back on them like a nuclear boomerang.

"Let's go," he said. "Sit on the deck, and push out and down. You may get lucky and miss the rear rotor."

Johnson nodded. He disconnected from the intercom and slid back the hatch. He sat on the floor, put his feet out the door, gripped the side of the frame, and leaned out, preparing to push himself out.

He pulled back in. "Oh shit," he yelled. "Look up ahead!"

Loomis stood up and looked. Dead ahead, hull down on the horizon, twenty-five to thirty miles away, was a large cruise ship. Loomis knew it was a Cunard liner, bound from St. Thomas to Kingston with more than a thousand passengers aboard.

"Go on!" Loomis shouted to Johnson. "Jump!"

Johnson shook his head and scrambled to the rear of the compartment. He knew enough about choppers to know that Loomis needed his weight to balance the ship.

Loomis climbed back into the pilot's seat and altered course. A ninety-degree turn to the east would give the cruise ship twelve miles or more of leeway. That was all he could do.

Loomis carefully steadied the chopper on the new course. He then hurried back to the hatch, motioning for Johnson to jump. Johnson scooted to the door and put his feet out. He hesitated.

"Four minutes!" he said. "How long will it take us to reach the water?"

"We'll make it!" Loomis yelled. "Just get your ass out!"

Johnson jumped. Loomis saw him clear the rotor. He didn't wait to see Johnson's chute open. He rolled out the hatch, pushing hard with his feet as he cleared the coaming.

The wind blast was terrific. Although he was worried about altitude, he waited for a moment before pulling the D-ring, hoping drag would slow him, lessening the shock of the chute's opening.

But he knew he couldn't wait long. He pulled the ring, saw the silk deploy, and then felt he was being drawn and quartered as the ill-fitting harness cut into his crotch. He fought the risers, stopping his oscillation.

Johnson's chute was a quarter of a mile away and slightly below him. Loomis pulled the risers, spilling air to move in that direction.

He turned to look at the helicopter. It was still on course, bouncing erratically, but holding fairly steady flight.

Four minutes at 2.3 miles per minute would place them 9.2 miles from ground zero, with a prevailing crosswind at the upper levels.

They might survive, if the chopper held its course.

If Zaloudek was one minute off, they might not.

Loomis concentrated on hitting the water, holding his swings to a minimum, going in feet first. He went under and waited to make certain he wasn't trapped beneath the silk before he released the CO_2 to inflate his Mae West.

The sea was calm. Gentle waves lapped at his chin. With his Mae West he bobbed easily in the deep swells. Occasion-

ally he could see Johnson a hundred yards away. Loomis
pulled out of his chute harness and paddled toward him.

He met Johnson swimming in his direction. "One minute!"
Johnson called, pointing to his wrist. "What are we supposed
to do?"

"Close your eyes," Loomis said. "Face away from it."

"I've seen a dozen training films," Johnson fumed. "I've
read the instructions a hundred times. And right now I can't
remember a fucking thing."

Loomis kept his own eyes tightly closed. "The light flash is
first," he said. "It can blind you. And keep low in the water.
Strong radiation comes with the flash."

They waited for a time in silence.

"I don't believe the son of a bitch is going to go," Johnson
said. "It's been more than a minute."

Loomis fought down an irrational impulse to turn and look,
to attempt to see what had happened to the helicopter. "No,
it hasn't been a minute," he said. "I've been counting."

Johnson started to reply, but was interrupted on the first
syllable by the detonation.

Nine point two miles from Loomis and Johnson, the mass
of Uranium-235 not much larger than a grapefruit went critical, soaring to several hundred million degrees in a hundred
millionth of a second—far surpassing the heat on the surface
of the sun. Pressures at the core went instantly to more than
a hundred million atmospheres, sending neutrons multiply-
ing, expanding faster at that moment than any other object
in the galaxy—more than five million miles an hour.

For an instant, through his closed eyelids, Loomis saw the
outline of sky, horizon, and sea and of Johnson a few feet
away. And he knew that in that instant he and Johnson were
being bombarded by a tremendous barrage of beta and
gamma rays. But at nine miles, with most of their bodies
protected by a shield of water, the dosage should not be fatal.

"Christ!" Johnson yelled. "I had my hands over my eyes.
Light came *through* my fingers! I saw the bones!"

The heat came next—wave after wave of searing air that
turned the surface of the sea into a furnace. Deep swells in

the wake of the air blast set them bobbing like corks.

Then, with an ear-splitting roar of a thousand lightning bolts, the shock wave passed. Forgetting all caution, Loomis turned to look.

A massive fireball was climbing rapidly, rolling inward, expanding as it soared toward the stratosphere, leaving a tall pillar that grew steadily into a mushroom cloud forty thousand feet high. Loomis and Johnson watched the fireball in awe.

"I'll sure say one thing for ol' Zaloudek," Johnson said. "He was one bomb-making son of a bitch."

Slowly, the mushroom cloud began to spread. The top gradually broke into a huge smoke ring. Then the residue started drifting westward.

"I think the fallout will miss us," Loomis said.

"What about that poor damned cruise ship?" Johnson asked.

Loomis watched the drift of the cloud, figuring angles. "The fallout should be behind them," he said. "They're safe."

Johnson lay back in his Mae West and studied the nuclear cloud. "And I'll say one thing for you, too, Loomis. You really know how to entertain a fellow," he said. "I haven't had so much fun in a coon's age. Now I'd like to return the favor. Why don't you come back with me to help hunt the other one?"

"What about that old contract on me?"

"Loomis, we're all heart."

The water was warm and comfortable. For the first time in weeks, Loomis felt relaxed, at peace with the world. He didn't want to commit himself. He knew he might feel different later. "I may retire from all this," he said.

"Oh hell, Loomis. You've got another year or two left in you," Johnson said. "We need you. And you may never have an opportunity like this again." He pointed to the nuclear pillar, still rising and spreading across the southern sky. "You've got to admit that these Hamlet people are a little out of the ordinary."

"There's where you're wrong," Loomis told him. "This was

just a warning for the future. There'll be other bombs, other Hamlet Groups, as long as you people are so careless with your materials."

"Maybe Washington has learned something."

"I doubt it," Loomis said. "Your power plant reactors are turning out more of the crap all of the time. What in hell are you going to do with all of it?"

Johnson shrugged in his Mae West. "How would I know?" he said. "It's not *my* problem. What's your answer on the job?"

"Tell them I'll think about it," Loomis said.

Johnson looked around at the horizon. "It just occurs to me. This is one hell of a big ocean you got out here. How long you think we'll have to wait before they find us?"

"Iberra will be here in twenty minutes or so," Loomis said. "He shouldn't have any trouble locating us. We left him a good marker."

Iberra made it in fifteen. He lowered a sling and Loomis helped Johnson into the loop.

Loomis waited in the water until the sling came back, slipped into the loop, and was lifted to the open bay of the chopper.

They hovered for several minutes, watching the huge mushroom cloud drift slowly toward the west.

Then Iberra wheeled the bird toward Santo Domingo and a long night of decontamination and celebration.